IT HAPPENED ONE FIGHT

MAUREEN LEE LENKER

sourcebooks casablanca

Cover design by Stephanie Gafron/Sourcebooks
Cover illustration by Jenifer Prince
Internal design and images by Laura Boren/Sourcebooks

Published by Sourcebooks Casablanca, an imprint of Sourcebooks
P.O. Box 4410, Naperville, Illinois 60567-4410
(630) 961-3900
sourcebooks.com

Cataloging-in-Publication data is on file with the Library of Congress.

Printed and bound in the United States of America.
VP 10 9 8 7 6 5 4 3 2 1

PRAISE FOR *IT HAPPENED ONE FIGHT*

"*It Happened One Fight* is essentially my perfect read—a funny, playful, sexy romp through Old Hollywood (and Reno!) that just delighted me at every turn. Lenker's debut is a loving homage to the classic screwball comedy, told in a fresh new voice romance readers are sure to fall for."

—Emily Henry, #1 *New York Times* bestselling author of *Book Lovers*

"An absolutely delicious historical romance set in the Golden Age of Hollywood, this one delivers. Married by accident? Forced proximity while making a movie? They don't even like each other (but oh, of course they do)? Sign me up! Dash and Joan are a fantastic couple and this book is full of banter and rivalry and the best kind of romance. Get ready for your close up—you'll be swooning like an Old Hollywood starlet after reading this one."

—Sarah MacLean, New York Times bestselling author

"Old Hollywood meets modern romance and it's a perfect pairing!"

—Abby Jimenez, *New York Times* bestselling author of *Part of Your World*

"In her lively debut, Maureen Lenker pulls back the curtain on 1930s Hollywood with this romantic tale of a smart, ambitious starlet and a farmboy-turned-playboy actor. Readers will have great fun following the twists and turns of Reno divorces, run-ins with difficult directors, and an Academy Awards show unlike any other—along with fascinating glimpses into industry powerplays. *It Happened One Fight* is aces!"

—Deborah Harkness, #1 *New York Times* bestselling author of the All Souls Trilogy

"*It Happened One Fight* is an effervescent gem of a romance: sparkling with wit, dripping with Old Hollywood glamour, and crackling with enemies-to-lovers chemistry. Dash and Davis jump right off the page with their cleverness, complexity, and deeply human choices, and their silver screen-worthy swoons will have you pining for more of Lenker's bright, verve-filled words!"

—Sierra Simone, *USA Today* bestselling author of *Priest*

"*It Happened One Fight* is a frolicking, pitch-perfect homage to the golden age of Hollywood. Dash and Joan—and their gorgeous transatlantic accents!—practically leap off the page. Maureen Lee Lenker's sparkling debut is an absolute delight for any classic film buff."

—Xio Axelrod, *USA Today* bestselling author of *The Girl with Stars in Her Eyes*

"And the Oscar goes to...Maureen Lee Lenker, for this irresistible debut that serves up Classic Hollywood with humor, heat, and lots of heart. As much fun as a night at the movies!"

—Susanna Kearsley, *New York Times* bestselling author of *The Winter Sea*

"Madcap and delightful, *It Happened One Fight* is a rip-roaring good time! Lenker skillfully twists Old Hollywood, rom-coms, and celebrity romances to a hilarious new level, giving us the historical romance we've all been waiting for."

—Joanna Shupe, *USA Today* bestselling author of *The Rogue of Fifth Avenue*

"An absolutely charming debut! *It Happened One Fight* sparkles with witty banter, classic Hollywood glamour, and a delectably swoony adversaries-to-lovers romance!"

—Priscilla Oliveras, *USA Today* bestselling author of *West Side Love Story*

"*It Happened One Fight* marries the sparkling, romping energy of Hollywood's Golden Age with a clear-eyed look at the emotional cost of success in a man's world—and the buoying effect of love. Davis and Dash call to mind the great pairings of the era, but lucky us, we get to see inside their heads in a way we never could with Bogart and Bacall."

—Jenny Holiday, *USA Today* bestselling author of *Duke, Actually*

"*It Happened One Fight* is a knockout of a debut romance! Maureen Lee Lenker pays homage to the Golden Age of Hollywood with pitch-perfect period details, snappy pacing, and a nuanced exploration of the cost of fame and the masks we wear to protect ourselves. You'll smile and swoon as the gutsy, glamorous heroine and her cocky, charismatic leading man banter and battle their way to a hard-won and heartfelt happily ever after. What a wonderful, rollicking ride!"

—Lenora Bell, *USA Today* bestselling
author of *How the Duke Was Won*

"*It Happened One Fight* is proof that no one knows 1930s Hollywood romance better than Maureen Lee Lenker. This book is how you do witty banter!"

—Nisha Sharma, critically acclaimed author
of *My So-Called Bollywood Life*

"Maureen Lee Lenker gives all the old-school feels of Fred and Ginger and Bacall and Bogart with Davis and Dash in the vintage Hollywood love affair, *It Happened One Fight*. Fast-paced, witty, and ensconced in the headlines, readers will be drawn to a bold heroine trying to make her way out of the gossip columns and onto Oscar wins, but that pesky thing called love trumps the best-made plans. Fall in love with 1930s Hollywood with a classic romance by Lenker's golden pen."

—Vanessa Riley, award-winning author of
Island Queen and *Queen of Exiles*

"*It Happened One Fight* brings all the banter and sizzle (and hijinks!) of the best Golden Age movies to the page. Lenker's perfectly matched hero and heroine are reminiscent of the most iconic cinematic pairings, and watching them spar their way to a happily ever after is pure fun from start to finish."

—Martha Waters, author of *To Have and to Hoax*

"In *It Happened One Fight,* Maureen Lee Lenker takes us on a romantic Old Hollywood romp with a totally modern twist. Reading this story feels like going back in time and getting a VIP ticket to hang out with the who's who of Hollywood's golden age. What a fun ride!"

—Kwana Jackson, *USA Today* Bestselling author of *Real Men Knit*

"Maureen Lee Lenker's adult fiction debut is a charming time machine into the glitter, glam, and drama of Old Hollywood! This delightful love story is a funny, swoony, and delightful dive into the choices we make and the choices that ultimately make us happy. Don't miss this one!"

—Denise Williams, author of *The Fastest Way to Fall*

"*It Happened One Fight* is an instant classic. A rare blend of banter, touching characters, and the kind of chemistry that lights up the silver screen. This book will win you over and steal your heart."

—Adriana Anders, award-winning author of *Whiteout*

"*It Happened One Fight* is a dazzling tribute to Old Hollywood glamor, intrigue, and passionate emotion. Lenker's debut is perfect for fans of Taylor Jenkins Reid and the classic romance pictures of the early days of cinema."

—Scarlett Peckham, author of *The Duke I Tempted*

"A fresh voice and a fresh time period and setting in historical romance. Maureen Lee Lenker's narrative voice sparkles with all the glitz and glamor of the Golden Age of Hollywood. This enemies to lovers romp, reminiscent of a 1930s screwball comedy, unfolds in a surprisingly tender tale of vulnerability, facing one's past, and ultimately living life—and falling in love—on your own terms."

—Alexis Daria, bestselling author of *You Had Me at Hola*

"Maureen Lee Lenker's *It Happened One Fight* combines sparkling dialogue, delicious humor, and swoon-worthy characters into a must-read for romance fans. Prepare to be swept off your feet... Hollywood Golden Age style."

—Janna MacGregor, author of *The Bad Luck Bride*

"A delightful and deceptively deep ode to Old Hollywood, both its love stories and the stars at the heart of them. The charm of the 1930s is deftly rendered, but so too is the contemporary resonance. Especially around the issue of owning who you really are and fighting for what you want, regardless of the fallout. Which is no longer solely the domain of studio contract-players and silver screen matinee idols, but everyday people living in the public eye of social media. Dash and Davis forever!"

—Julia Whelan, award-winning audiobook narrator

"The delicious tension crackles off the page! A delight of a debut that bubbles with Old Hollywood humor and charm. Joan is the sexy, sophisticated heroine most of us wish we could be, and Dash is just the rogue to upend her well ordered life. I couldn't get enough of watching them clash, eagerly waiting for the moment Joan will finally realize she may have misjudged the handsome devil."

—Jenny Nordbak, audiobook narrator and
author of *The Death God's Sacrifice*

"Sparks fly between two movie stars in this enemies-to-lovers romance set in the Golden Age of Hollywood. *It Happened One Fight* is a sparkling, heartfelt and glamorous romance novel you won't want to miss!"

—Maya Rodale, author of *The Wicked Wallflower*

"Maureen Lee Lenker's debut, *It Happened One Fight* deftly sweeps us into the Golden Era of Hollywood with a couple that epitomizes that delicious 'will they or won't they' dance of the classic rom-com. Her canny explorations on the crushing pressures of fame and the double-standards for women in the film industry make for a layered and emotionally charged romance. A funny, sexy debut that is as smart as it is romantic."

—Adriana Herrera, *USA Today* bestselling author of *A Caribbean Heiress in Paris*

For Mom
For being my first editor, reading countless bedtime stories, and teaching me that books are always the greatest reward.

PROLOGUE

DAVIS SLUGS DASH! IT'S KO FOR THE COSTARS

MAY 10, 1932

Sparks flew at the Cocoanut Grove last night as Joan Davis gave her costar Dash Howard the kiss-off. And we're not talking one of the romantic variety. After photographers caught the duo in an embrace in an embrace at the nightclub's back door, Davis slugged her handsome leading man before kneeing him in the family jewels. Women of America, never fear, we have it on good authority that Dash Howard is still every bit as virile as he appears.

Joan Davis seemed mighty pleased with herself too, smiling, blowing photographers a kiss, and crowing, "Eat your heart out, boys." It was a surprising end to an otherwise romantic evening. Earlier that night, this intrepid reporter spotted the duo getting very cozy in a back booth. But something spelled trouble in paradise, leading

Davis to bring Howard to his knees. The two are slated to begin production this week on their next picture together, *Love on the Rocks,* their third on-screen pairing in a year and a half. If Harry Evets plans to have his two biggest stars keep working together, he should probably consider having them insured—in case of maiming or worse! Rest assured, whatever happens on that set, I'll be here with all the juicy details as the *Examiner*'s new columnist.

—xoxo, Leda Price

Movie stars did not, as a rule, hide in the bathroom. They were far too glamorous and dignified to take refuge in a toilet stall. But when Joan Davis had seen freshly shaved Dash Howard coming toward her down the studio hallway right as she'd gotten her hands on this morning's paper, the only escape was darting into the ladies' room.

Perched on the toilet seat, she reread the story in the *Examiner* before crumpling it in her hands. "That sonofabitch," she muttered to no one in particular. Dash Howard had set her up. Just when she'd thought there was finally a man in Hollywood she could trust, he pulled the rug out from under her. He was a bottom-feeder like the rest of them.

And Leda Price. Joan had recognized her as a day player on their last picture. It was why she'd let Leda lead her to the back door to meet Dash. The two of them must've been in on it together. Parasites, the lot of them. Joan didn't balk at having to make sacrifices for her career. That was the price of success in Hollywood. But there was a difference between what she did and the way that leeches like Dash Howard and Leda Price used people.

Last night, she'd felt on the precipice of something dangerous. Sitting in that back booth, she'd felt an attraction to Dash that she'd always vowed never to let herself give in to. But he'd tempted her. Made her feel like maybe she should give romance a try after all. And then he'd proved her right all along. Well, at least she'd gotten the last laugh. She smoothed the paper out to study the photograph above the story.

They'd caught her right as her knee had connected with Dash's groin. She chuckled at the look of shock in his eyes. In a smaller picture below it, she was grinning and blowing the photographers a kiss. Dash had tried to make a fool out of her, to use her for his own publicity. Well, how'd that work out for him? At least she'd kept her wits about her when it really counted.

She supposed she would eventually have to leave this bathroom and go pretend to make love to him on set. She'd left a message for Harry's secretary last night, begging him to cast someone else or outright cancel the picture. But he hadn't deigned to offer her a response besides sending the studio car for her that morning. It was clear she was stuck making this movie. With Dash Howard. Who was she kidding? Harry was probably eating this up. He'd crow about how many tickets this headline alone would sell. Hell, he'd probably had a hand in the whole affair himself. So she'd have to grin and bear it—and beg him to make sure it was the last time she ever had to work with Dash Howard. The cad. How she'd ever found him remotely attractive she didn't know.

But this was good. It was a reminder to stick to what she'd always known. That her rules were there for a reason. Romance was for the pictures and the pictures alone. Joan Davis was a lone wolf, and her fame, her success, her status would be because she'd earned it. Taking anyone else along for that ride was a recipe for disaster and disappointment. She didn't need help, and she certainly didn't need a grinning lug of a man riding her coattails. There was one person Joan Davis could rely on, and that was Joan Davis.

CHAPTER 1

JOAN DAVIS TO WED MONTY SMYTH!

JUNE 11, 1936

Is that a new piece of platinum we spy on Joan Davis's hand? The rumors are true. Hollywood's princess is engaged to 1936's rising matinee idol Monty Smyth. It's certainly sudden! Mr. Smyth and Miss Davis have been spotted out on the town together three times in the last six weeks—and already it's wedding bells for this divine duo.

Miss Davis tells reporters the proposal was a complete surprise, and it happened over cocktails on the patio of her Beverly Hills home. "I came out with the cocktail shaker, ready to top off our glasses, and there was Monty down on one knee! Of course, my answer was immediately 'Yes,'" she told *Confidante,* a rosy glow in her cheeks—only matched by the sparkle in her eight-karat Asscher-cut diamond ring. The couple have said they are aiming for a September wedding. That's only three months away. Anyone who's somebody in Hollywood will be there.

Miss Davis's star hasn't shined quite as brightly of late—her last two films flopped at the box office. But audiences are gaga for Monty whose ten-minute scene in *Where Devils Dare* earned the tall, dark, and handsome hunk an Oscar nomination. And he can't go anywhere without a gaggle of adoring fans. It's Monty Mania everywhere you look!

Mr. Smyth's long-time roommate, Jerry Scott, was spotted celebrating at the Cocoanut Grove last night. He was blotto with a capital B, celebrating his pal's good fortune. According to our sources, Monty's already asked him to be best man.

But there's one man we haven't heard a peep from—Dash Howard, Miss Davis's costar in six pictures. He was spotted at his new favorite haunt, Café Trocadero, last night, but was otherwise engaged with a titian-haired distraction. At one time, all of America was yearning for wedding bells between Dash and Davis. And undoubtedly many were still holding out hope even after she slugged him in the kisser at the Cocoanut Grove. Has Joan Davis landed another blow? What does the King of Hollywood think about his leading lady getting hitched?

Nothing was going to spoil Joan Davis's mood today. Not the stickpin jabbing her in the side from her costume fitting. Not even the press's insistence on linking her with Dash when she was engaged to someone else. Because everything was going according to plan.

She held the skirt of her pale-blue gown nimbly between her thumb and finger as she sauntered across the lot from the wardrobe department to her trailer. She was carrying the issue of *Confidante* announcing her engagement in her left hand, her inverted art-deco manicure curled just so around the magazine so that her life-size engagement ring rested atop the photo of it on the cover. It glinted in the sunlight, and she preened as secretaries and receptionists on coffee breaks, and grips and best boys wheeling equipment down the sunny streets of the lot, called out felicitations to her.

She cheerily returned her thanks, flashing her gleaming smile and giving her best movie-star wave, which was really more of a back-and-forth glide than anything. But it did make the ring reflect the sun.

It was an absolutely perfect day, one of those miraculous early-summer Los Angeles days when everything was balmy and temperate. The type of day you'd put on a postcard. She was doing what she loved most in the world: getting ready to make a new picture, one she really believed in this time. One with potential to finally earn her the respect as an actress she yearned for. It would be her final picture with Dash Howard to boot. Harry promised.

After that night at the Cocoanut Grove when he'd tried to use her for publicity and she'd clocked him, working with Dash had been hell. She had begged Harry for four years to end this on-screen partnership. She could barely stand to look at Dash. Once, she'd wanted to move past the incident and be professionals about it. But every time it seemed they were close to a breakthrough, Dash pulled a prank and reminded her why they were like oil and water. It had taken four years of needling, but she'd finally gotten Harry to agree to let them make one last picture and go their separate ways once and for all.

But why was she thinking about Dash at a time like this? She was engaged to be married to the most desirable man in Hollywood. That pesky "box-office poison" label she'd acquired last year would be a faint memory soon.

She couldn't wait to get back to her trailer and go through the stack of announcements again, the reams of paper dedicated to her and Monty's engagement. Some were better than others. She could do very well without *The Hollywood Reporter*'s inquiry, "From Box-Office Poison to Blushing Bride?" But the cover of *Silver Screen,* bearing the caption "A Match Made in Hollywood" and featuring her and Monty in an affectionate embrace she had taken great pains to stage on her patio—that was more like it. Every paper in town, every rag, every fan magazine, anyone who cared to spare the ink to write about Tinseltown had her picture and the news splashed across it.

She stopped short to find her assistant Arlene, Evets's Studios' newest screenwriter, pacing back and forth near the steps of her trailer. "What is it?"

"Nothing, nothing, don't worry about it." Arlene waved her hands limply. "Is that the dress for the dinner scene?"

"Yes, it is." Joan struck a pose to model the diaphanous sleeve that buttoned delicately around her wrist. "It's just as you wrote it, darling. I had to show you. They let me walk across the lot in it so you could see it. But stop changing the subject. Why are you wearing a hole in the concrete? Let's go in the trailer."

"I don't think that's a good idea," Arlene said. "Why don't you go back to wardrobe and I'll take care of it?"

Joan lunged, and Arlene spread her arms across the door that had Joan's name painted on it in gold. "Joan, trust me." But

Joan was too quick for her, slipping her hand under Arlene's outstretched arm and turning the doorknob to gain entry to what had been her inner sanctum on the lot for the last four years.

She ducked under Arlene's arm and darted in, surveying the room. Nothing looked amiss. Her favorite Hurrell photograph of herself was still framed and gleaming on her dressing table; the lights surrounding the mirror were on, waiting for her to touch up her makeup; and her monogrammed robe was laid across the armchair in the corner, next to the stack of papers and magazines announcing her engagement. The only thing noticeably different was the myriad of floral arrangements congratulating her and Monty, filling the room with a cloying aroma.

Even the zebra-skin rug was perfectly placed in the center of the room, not an inch different from how she'd left it earlier that morning. Except…had it moved? That wasn't possible; it was faux, it had never been alive to begin with. But no, there it was again, a little shiver as if it were inching its way across the floor of her dressing room.

She squinted and that's when she saw it. It wasn't the rug that was moving; it was a black-and-white creature that had been camouflaged against it now snuffling its way through the center of her space. "*Skunkkkkkkk!*" she shrieked, backing up into Arlene who promptly joined in her blood-curling yelps.

"Move, Arlene, get out of my way. Evelyn will kill me if that thing sprays this dress and she has to start over."

"I told you, I told you, I told you."

The two women practically tripped over themselves, scrambling to get back out the door and slam it shut. They crouched near the door, and Joan pressed her ear against it, listening for any sign of the creature.

Arlene was above her, one hand clinging to Joan's shoulder,

the other to the railing, trying desperately not to fall over. "What are you doing?" she hissed.

"Shhhh, I'm trying to hear if it's spraying."

Arlene snorted. "You can't hear whether it's spraying through the door."

Joan grimaced. "Well then, I have to check." She turned the brass doorknob ever so slowly, inch by inch until the door creaked open, making a crack barely small enough to see through. Something scampered past the door, and she pulled it shut, yelping in terror and collapsing against it.

This time, the sound of her distress sent a harried-looking production assistant in a newsboy cap sprinting to the scene. "Miss Davis, Miss Morgan, what's wrong?"

"Joseph, thank God, there's a skunk in my dressing room," Joan hissed, pointing at the door with a deliberate motion, as if the skunk were a bomb and if they were too loud it might go off.

"Well, how on earth did a skunk get in your dressing room?"

"How should I know? I certainly didn't put it there."

"All right, all right, don't flip your wig. I'll handle it." The boy cracked the door open and slipped inside, while Joan resisted the urge to bite her nails. Everyone would want a picture of her ring finger now; she couldn't have a nail out of place.

Arlene looked as if she was going to be sick. "What if he frightens it and it sprays all over the place?"

Joan laughed. "Well, I guess it will cut the overwhelming smell of flowers. It was a bit intense, even for my taste."

Arlene shook her head, mirth and disbelief mingling on her face. "I don't understand how it could have got in there since this morning. They're nocturnal!"

Joan had a vague idea. There was one person on this studio lot who loved to have a laugh at her expense, one person who could not resist a practical joke even if it cost the studio time and money.

The sound of a scuffle came from behind the door. Joan closed her eyes and massaged the bridge of her nose. So much for her perfect day. The phone in her dressing room started to ring. Most likely someone else wishing her and Monty all their best. They could call back later.

As the shrill ring of the telephone ended, the production assistant emerged from Joan's dressing room holding the skunk aloft and away from his body, as if the creature were a live grenade. "I got him," he huffed. Somewhere along the way he'd lost his hat and a button.

Joan arched an eyebrow. "An epic struggle between man and beast, it seems."

The boy blushed. "He didn't want to come out from under your dressing table. I had to coax him out with my hat. For some reason he didn't spray, though. He lifted his tail and everything, but we got lucky."

Joan sighed in relief. At least she didn't have to face that disaster. "I'll call Harry and ask him to tell the mayor to award you a medal for your service."

Joseph chuckled. "That's not necessary. I'll just see about getting this fella relocated."

Arlene and Joan pressed themselves up against the railing of the steps leading to the dressing room, giving Joseph and the critter the widest possible berth.

"Oh, and this was tied around his neck." He handed Joan a red silk bow tie with a small piece of paper affixed to it.

She thumbed it open and read it. *Congrats to you and Monty on your engagement. Hope your marriage doesn't stink! xoxo, Dash.* Just as she'd suspected.

She crumpled the paper and stormed back into her now mercifully vermin-free dressing room. "The nerve," she snapped. "Couldn't even let me have one day."

Arlene was right behind her, tiptoeing cautiously. "Dare I even ask who?"

"You know who," Joan snarled. "Dash Howard. That loathsome, egotistical fool left that, that, that...thing in my dressing room as an engagement present."

She thrust the piece of paper at Arlene as proof and crossed to the soft pink velvet armchair in the corner, tossing her robe aside and collapsing with a heavy sigh, dramatically swinging her arm across her face. The phone rang again, and she groaned. She couldn't take any more surprise well-wishes. For all she knew, an opossum was calling with a special delivery.

"Arlene, would you answer that?"

Arlene nodded, gave one last suspicious glance at the rug to make sure it wouldn't unexpectedly spring to life, and went to answer the phone on the side table. "Whoever it is, tell them I am indisposed from celebrating my engagement."

Arlene shook her head and picked up the pale-pink phone from the receiver. "Hello, Miss Davis's dressing room. Arlene Morgan speaking. Yes... No, no, I'm afraid Miss Davis is indisposed at the moment. I beg your pardon! I am certain that whatever it is can wait."

"Who is it?" Joan mouthed, peeking out from the hand she still had theatrically flung across her eyes.

"It's Leda," Arlene hissed.

"Oh, well, she's probably steamed we didn't give her the exclusive engagement announcement. You know how she is. She thinks she owns me and Dash. Put her off."

Arlene nodded and elevated her voice to its haughtiest tones. "Why, may I ask, are you calling?"

Joan grabbed the latest copy of *Variety* lying atop the stack of press clippings on the coffee table. BOFFO AT THE BOX OFFICE AND AS A BRIDEGROOM—MONTY SMYTH VIES FOR HOLLYWOOD GREATNESS, the headline read. No wonder Dash was in top form. It must've infuriated him to see Monty atop the headlines. Because of her. She had all the press she needed. More importantly, all the press she wanted.

There was no need to speak to Hollywood's most notorious gossip columnist at a time like this. Leda had been riding Joan's coattails for years, cashing in on Dash's plot at the Cocoanut Grove. Joan didn't know how she'd done it, if it was happenstance or if Leda had been in on it the whole time. All Joan knew was the next morning the front page of every gossip rag in town had been plastered with photos of her canoodling with Dash, then slugging him. And there in the *Los Angeles Examiner* had been Leda's first byline where, ever since, she'd peddled her poison as a journalist. If you could call her that. Joan had a lot of worse names for her but she didn't use them. Because somehow, someway, Leda had discovered Joan's greatest secret. Harry had paid the reporter handsomely to keep quiet. But Joan still didn't want to get near the woman with a ten-foot pole. So no, Joan would not be answering any of her questions today. Or ever.

"Well, Miss Price, I'm sure whatever you need to tell Miss Davis, you can share with me. I'll be sure she gets the message."

Joan looked up because Arlene had gone silent—and she was startled to see her former assistant's face was ashen. Something was very, very wrong. Wordlessly, Arlene gestured for her to come to the phone, and Joan struggled to extricate herself from her seat, tripping on the as-yet-unhemmed skirt of her costume.

After what felt like an eternity but was likely only a few seconds, she pried the phone from Arlene's hands. Her assistant was gaping at her like a goldfish, her lips moving, but no sound issuing forth. The only way to deal with Leda Price was to be equally as haughty as she was.

Joan cleared her throat and put on her best movie-star voice, the one she reserved for red carpets on opening nights at Grauman's. "Leda, darling, what can I do for you?"

"Cut the crap, Joan. I'm not calling for a gushing pronouncement of your love for Monty Smyth."

"Why are you calling, then? My latest picture starts filming on Monday, but you know all about that already. So my engagement is the only news about me there is."

"Hardly," Leda scoffed. Joan could imagine her eyes glittering and her mouth turning up at the corners, like the cat that caught the canary.

"Well, spit it out, then, Leda."

"Oh, well now, I was just wondering what your fiancé, Mr. Smyth, thinks about bigamy?"

"I don't know. Shall I ask him? I hardly see what that has to do with our engagement. What's your point?" Joan knew Leda would stop at nothing to create a scandal.

"Oh, Joan," Leda purred, drawing out the final *n* like she was sucking on a candy. "It has everything to do with your engagement. Considering you are already married—to Mr. Dash Howard."

Joan laughed. "You and half the country wish!"

"I assure you this is no idle Hollywood fantasy, Miss Davis," Leda said, an iciness entering her voice. "I have a marriage certificate from City Hall signed with both of your names sitting right here."

"That's not possible," Joan spluttered.

Leda chuckled, a cold laugh devoid of mirth. "Oh, it is. And by tomorrow morning, it'll be on the front page of every paper, starting with my column in the *Los Angeles Examiner*. You shouldn't have neglected to tell me of your engagement, Joanie."

Joan heard the line go dead, but it didn't matter. The phone was slipping out of her grasp anyway. She crumpled to the floor alongside it, clutching at the satin ruffles lining her dressing table.

How was this possible? She wasn't married to Dash. She detested him. They had spent precisely zero time in each other's company off of a set since that horrible night four years ago. It wasn't as if they'd had some drunken escapade she had forgotten. That was entirely not her style.

She heard Arlene whisper beside her, "Did she tell you?"

"Do you think I'd be on the floor if she hadn't?"

"It's not true," Arlene insisted, as if saying it would make it so. Some color was starting to return to Joan's face, and she returned the phone to its receiver. "How could it be?"

"Your guess is as good as mine. But I'd bet my contract Dash Howard had something to do with it. Anyway, if Leda prints it, does it matter if it's not true? God, how could I do this to Monty? This wasn't part of the deal. He'll hate me."

Arlene knelt beside Joan and wrapped her arm around her. "No, he won't, Joan. Not if he loves you." That was just like Arlene. Believing in the knight on the white horse and happily-ever-afters. Joan knew better.

She stared up at the ceiling, searching for an answer in the crown molding she'd hand-selected. Like everything else in this room. Everything she'd come so close to losing this last year when she'd tried to make pictures without Dash. Audiences hadn't wanted to see her without that buffoon making love to her, and a string of flops had earned her the dreaded *box-office poison* moniker.

Leda had started it, part of her personal vendetta against Joan.

From the moment Joan had slugged Dash instead of making love to him, she had refused to play Leda's game, and Leda seemingly hated her for it. Joan would never be the snitch Leda wanted. She needed press but not the type Leda offered, and she did everything in her power to stay out of Leda's web. Maybe Leda's reason for hating Joan was as simple as that—Leda needed her, but she didn't need Leda. So Leda dragged her name through the mud every chance she got, trying to clear the way for a new starlet who might be more amenable to her schemes. Joan had been dismayed when the rest of the press had started tarring her with the same brush. Admittedly, the scripts for her recent films had been terrible. But she'd been so desperate to try a project without Dash, she'd agreed to them anyway.

None of that mattered now though, because this engagement was supposed to put her back on track. It was all lined up—the headline-grabbing engagement, a motion picture worth her talents finally in her grasp. Even if she did have to costar with Dash again. From the outside, her life looked like a fairy tale.

Arlene didn't know the truth. Monty most definitely did not love her. He was fond of her, to be sure. But scandal and whispers of bigamy was not what he'd signed up for when they'd agreed to this arrangement. She wouldn't blame him if he wanted to end this engagement before it had even begun. But she couldn't tell Arlene any of that.

Her mind sparked into action. "We need to get ahead of this. We have almost twenty-four hours." She stood and placed her finger in the number "one" on the rotary dial, letting the whirr of the phone spin its way to the only person who could fix this and calm her. "Harry, your office. Now."

CHAPTER 2

DASH GROANED AND ROLLED OVER. HE'D BEEN FACE-down in his bed, dreaming about a lovely blond, but that blasted ringing in his ears wouldn't stop. He must have drunk a good deal more than he'd thought. He'd lost track somewhere after the third gin martini. He pulled a pillow over his face, trying to drown out the noise. What had he done last night?

He'd gone out to the Trocadero and requested his usual booth. Some aspiring starlet—Judy or Betty or something or other—had approached him for advice, and he'd been happy to give it. And other things. The studio would pick up the tab and clean up any messes.

Harry wanted him to be a playboy. That's what everybody wanted. For him to be the embodiment of his moniker, the King of Hollywood. Lothario. Academy Award winner. A man's man who the husbands wanted to be pals with and the wives wanted to sleep with. That was his job, right? To keep selling that fantasy?

He fumbled around, making sure the other side of the bed was empty. It was. It always was. No one bothered to stick around to discover the real Dash. Whoever that was.

No one in this town was who they claimed to be. Except maybe Joan Davis. That woman was pure movie star, always had been. He snorted into his pillow. Heaven help the fool who ever thought otherwise. He rubbed his face in frustration. Why was he thinking of Joan, anyway?

He'd been having a perfectly enticing dream about a blond taking a bubble bath in an enormous champagne glass. A dream he intended to tell the studio about when he was significantly more awake and not nursing the aftereffects of a generous bartender. Maybe Harry could find a way to include a leggy girl in a champagne glass in his next picture. He rolled over and squeezed his eyes shut, striving in vain to return to the dream.

But his head was ringing. He'd really overdone it last night. Was the ringing getting louder? And now someone was knocking too. Blast! Couldn't a man have a hangover in peace?

"Go away," he bellowed to the door. But too late. Martin, his butler, was coming in with a telephone.

"I beg your pardon, sir, but they won't stop calling. They simply must speak with you."

"Damn it, Martin, this is why I hired you. To get rid of whoever 'they' is and let me nurse my headache alone. In the dark."

"If you don't mind my saying, sir, that's hardly why you hired me. At any rate, I've told them you're indisposed all morning. But now it's past noon, and they really are insisting."

Dash sat up and blinked, letting his eyes adjust to the relative darkness of the room. At least Martin had the decency to leave the curtains drawn. "It's past noon?"

"Yes, sir."

"Well, why'd you let me sleep so long?"

"But, sir, you said—"

"Never mind, just give me the phone." Martin did as he was asked, giving a meek little bow and backing out of the room. Blast it, Dash didn't mean to be rude to the man. But he was paying his butler a small fortune and he had a raging headache. He'd apologize to him later.

"Hello, hello, who is this?"

"Dash, my good fellow, this is Harry." Good God, why was the head of the studio calling him before 2:00 p.m. on a Friday? They knew he'd been out late last night. The studio made sure of it. The more times per week he was spotted at the Trocadero and written about in the gossip columns, the more money his pictures made. Thus, they had a tacit agreement that when he wasn't making a picture, they would never call him until the afternoon.

He couldn't wait to start this next film. Even if it meant enduring Joan's disdain once more. He'd get to be on set again. In his element. And it would give him an excuse to cut back on the playboy act he hated. He was increasingly losing himself in it, and he needed strict call times and an intriguing script to help him scramble back up that slippery slope. The work gave him structure, order, a purpose.

"What do you want, Harry? This better be an emergency."

"I'm afraid it is, Dash. We need you down here right away. Joan is beside herself."

Oh. He should've known. He chuckled. "Ah, so she got my engagement present?"

Harry coughed. It sounded like he was trying to cover a laugh. Dash grinned.

"Well, yes, that is part of it."

Dash rolled over and leaned on his elbow. "Well, tell her not to get her knickers in a twist. It's been neutered."

Now, that was definitely a laugh on the other end of the line. He could hear Joan chastising Harry. "I fail to see precisely what is so funny," she snapped. God, she was on a tear. He was too hungover for this.

"Joanie, he couldn't spray you! He's had his sprayer removed," Dash bellowed, trying to keep his shit-eating grin out of his voice.

Harry cleared his throat. "Be that as it may, it's not actually the skunk that's causing the stink down here."

"Of course it's not. I told you—"

"As you know," Harry barged on, "Joan is engaged to Monty Smyth."

"And? What? You want me to send a real gift?" The thought of Joan engaged to Monty, the hottest new thing on the screen, made Dash irrationally angry. And he'd rather not examine that too much. "Have publicity do it and put my name on it, I don't care. I'm going back to bed. Whatever's got her tail up, it's nothing to do with me."

"Well, Dashiell, it has everything to do with you considering you're already married to Joan."

Dash let the news roll over him. Married to Joan? This was insanity. Pure and simple. But Harry had used his full name. The studio never used his full name, not unless they meant business. It had to be a practical joke, right? Joan was pulling a fast one on him as retaliation for the skunk. And Harry was, what? In on it? Unable to see through Joan's deception?

"Screwball, thy name is woman! Joan, this isn't funny," he called through the line. "Who put you up to this, Harry? Haven't you better things to do? You've got a whole damn studio to run." All Dash wanted was to go back to bed. The last thing he needed was a prank call from the head of his studio orchestrated by a woman who couldn't get off her high horse. He moved to hang up, but he could hear Harry shouting over the line.

"Dash, are you still there? Dash, don't hang up. This is serious. This could ruin both your and Joan's careers if we don't get ahead of it. I need you down here as quick as you can."

"Harry, I don't know what kind of pills you've been taking for your stress lately, but you need to have your head examined. Joan and I aren't married. Are you forgetting she hates me?" Dash didn't mention that Joan hating him was all Harry and the studio's fault, for orchestrating that ill-fated date.

"How would this even be possible?" He was asking both Harry and the universe.

"Actually, we're all hoping you could enlighten us on that. Which is why I need you in my office within the hour."

In the background, Dash could hear Joan screeching, "Tell him to get down here at once. He's ruined my life!"

"Enlighten you? I don't even know what you're bloody talking about—"

But the line went dead, and as much as Dash Howard wanted to go back to bed, he knew there would be no peace until he did what Harry Evets—and Joan Davis—wanted. Harry Evets had given him everything: spotted him in a local production in Houston, Texas, while visiting his mother and given Dash a one-way ticket to Hollywood. So when Harry told him to jump, he asked, "How high?"

"Martin!" he yelled, but the butler was back inside his room before he'd even finished calling for him. He really was worth every cent Dash paid him.

"Yes, sir?"

"Call the car. Looks like I'm going to the studio. And then take the rest of the day off." It was the least he could do after yelling at the man for doing his job. If only his head didn't hurt so damn much. He ran his hand down his face, and a flash of memory came to him. Suddenly, his mouth went very dry. But he chalked it up to the aftereffects of his night on the town.

This particular memory was blurry—another drunken

evening about a year and a half ago. But that had been a joke. A funny little prank to torture Joan. She had ignored it. He had assumed she didn't want to give him the satisfaction. It was easy enough for her to pretend it had never happened when he wasn't there to witness her blow her top. But how the hell would that have been legal?

CHAPTER 3

JOAN DAVIS WAS FUMING. SHE LOOKED THE PICTURE OF propriety in a jade-green day dress with a wide triangular collar, but the way she was wearing a hole in the carpet of Harry Evets's office pacing back and forth was a firm indication of how panicked she was. Here she was in the epicenter of the studio, the beating heart of the most beloved Hollywood pictures—and she was itching to pick up one of the Oscars on Harry's desk and bludgeon someone with it.

Where on earth was Dash Howard? And what was taking him so long? As she turned to tread the same path in the rug for perhaps the fiftieth time, the man she loathed most in the world sauntered into the room.

She looked up and was peeved to see him sporting his usual disheveled, devil-may-care look. His tie was in a messy knot, and he'd missed a button on his shirt, but the cut of his suit was still perfect—the mark of a man who knew he looked good every time he stepped outside the house.

She'd always hated that about Dash, that he could look so irresistible without even trying when she had to grasp and claw for every shred of the audience's affection. Not just the audience. She kept to herself on set; it helped her focus. But he struck up easy friendships with everyone from extras to the boom operator.

Hell, the wardrobe department had probably given him that suit. They loved him too. It was infuriating.

His hair was sideswept, wisps of his shoe-polish-black curls springing out this way and that in a devilishly handsome fashion, not pomaded down within an inch of its life as he so often wore it on-screen. He strolled into the room as if he hadn't a care in the world, as if he hadn't possibly ruined her entire life.

But when their eyes met, she took delight in seeing the exhaustion there. They were bloodshot, and his skin had a ruddy pallor. It was evident the man was hungover. No wonder it had taken all morning to reach him. He must've been facedown in his bed half the morning. Typical.

"So nice of you to join us, Mr. Howard. I do hope we didn't interrupt your beauty sleep," she drawled, her voice dripping with false charm. She hoped he caught the sarcastic edge to her words.

He grinned at her. "Beauty sleep's not necessary for a man such as myself, Miss Davis." She bristled. He thought so highly of himself. Dash Howard believed every woman should fall prostrate at his feet, including her. Every time she thought of that charade at the Cocoanut Grove, she saw red. The false platitudes he'd tried to offer her the next morning. She'd shut those down quick. She didn't even want to hear him say "Good morning." He'd proven he was nothing but a bum—and she'd preferred the only way he communicate with her was via lines someone else had written for him. But no, he had to wheedle at her, try to get her attention with immature pranks at her expense. This time he'd gone too far.

She was determined to forge her own path in Hollywood. Not as half of a team. Much less with a man who thought he could seduce her for his own publicity.

"Not to worry, Dash, as you might find yourself taking a more permanent rest if you don't help us get to the bottom of this."

He pressed his hands to his heart in mock concern. "Why, my dear Miss Davis, I do hope I haven't upset you in some way. Your current state of mind feels a bit poisonous."

"If I was poisonous, I would have bitten you by now," she hissed. God, what this man did to her. She wasn't a violent person. But he brought out the worst in her.

"Luckily, I am well aware that your bark is far worse than your bite." Throughout this exchange, they had edged ever closer to each other, and as Joan was raising her hand to slug him, Harry cleared his throat, bringing her to her senses.

"Now, Joan, play nice. We can't have our leading man sporting a black eye."

"I wasn't—I wouldn't have—" Joan lowered her hands and clasped them behind her back.

"It wouldn't be the first time," Dash grumbled.

Joan whirled on him. "You deserved it then. And frankly, you deserve it now."

Harry coughed, calling the room to order. "Dash, I'm sure you're wondering why we've rushed you down here today."

"You're damn right I am. What is the meaning of this cryptic phone call? I'm 'married to Joan.' Why, it's absurd..."

Dash made a big show of this, but Joan watched his eyes and his dismay didn't quite reach them. He knew something.

"If you'll sit down, Harry will explain," she simpered, turning on the charm. This was his fault. Joan felt it in her gut. He was going to take the rap for it if she had anything to say about it. Leda Price wasn't going to slander her name in the papers. Not if Dash wasn't going down with her.

Dash looked at her and put his hands up in mock surrender.

"All right, all right, don't flip your wig. I'll sit down. Now, Harry, would you please tell me what the hell this is all about?"

"Somehow, I don't know how, but somehow I'm married to you." Joan started in on him, wanting him to understand what a disaster this was, but Harry gave her a look and she retreated to a leather chair on the other side of the office.

"The dame's wacky," Dash declared.

Harry sighed and leaned back against his desk, removing his glasses and rubbing the bridge of his nose. Joan felt a pang of guilt; he looked wearier than she'd ever seen him. He sat between the two Oscars the studio had won for Best Picture, the most recent for Dash's picture about a Wall Street schmuck turned hobo after the Crash of '29. Joan glared at Dash, and Dash studiously avoided her gaze by staring at the Oscar.

"Dashiell, I regret to inform you that Joan is not, as you so colorfully put it, 'wacky.' She's dead serious. You two are in fact, as the kids say, hitched."

"But how? And why did this even come up?" Dash looked as confused as Joan felt. Maybe he really wasn't responsible. But how else could this have happened?

"If Mr. Howard will allow a lady to explain—"

Dash rolled his eyes and waved his hand for her to go on.

"As I know you're aware, I'm engaged to Monty Smyth."

Dash got a wolfish grin on his face. "Yes, of course. I was sorry to hear you didn't appreciate my engagement present."

Joan scowled and resisted the urge to rise in fury. The gall of this man! "I'm not the only one who didn't appreciate it. As usual, your thoughtlessness cost the studio time and money. Your gift stunk."

"Oh-ho-ho, you'll find it's quite the opposite in this case. I made sure of it. At any rate, I don't think you invited me down here to discuss your engagement present. Have you perhaps changed your mind and opted to swap a mealymouthed sap for a more rugged type?"

Dash winked at her, and her cheeks flamed. No man knew quite how to irritate her the way he did. "I can assure you I would never. Monty's twice the man you'll ever be. He, at least, has character."

Harry cleared his throat again. Joan looked at him pleadingly. Dash was trying her patience, and they didn't have much time as it was. Leda Price was probably putting her poison pen to paper as they spoke. She needed to stop bickering and get to the point.

"As I was saying, we announced our engagement yesterday evening, and this morning I received a rather nasty phone call from Leda Price. She told me you and I are married and that by tomorrow morning, every paper in America will have a headline declaring me a bigamist."

"That vulture—you know half of what she writes isn't true."

Joan inhaled, praying for patience. "You know as well as I do that it doesn't matter. The public will lap up anything she prints. And at any rate, it seems this time she is correct."

All of the color drained out of Dash's face before he recovered himself. "How is this possible?"

Joan glared at him. She couldn't shake the sense that he was responsible.

"About a year and a half ago, the two of you were making *Wedding Crazy*," Harry began to explain. "As you may remember, there was an extensive wedding scene in that. You and Joan exchanged vows in character."

"I fail to see how that would be viewed as a legal marriage." Dash sat back, looking pleased with himself. Joan rolled her eyes.

"I know you think we're too stupid to realize that's not a

legally binding ceremony, but it's more complicated than that, Mr. Howard," she said, employing her haughtiest acting voice. Joan was from Oklahoma, but with enough elocution lessons, she could go full transatlantic socialite when it was called for. How dare he think they hadn't thought this through? Didn't he know if there were any way around this, she would've clung to it? This was *her* engagement that was ruined, after all.

"That's not what I meant and you know it, Joan. But I would like to know how a fake marriage suddenly became real. Were we even married by a real minister?"

Harry looked cowed. "I'm afraid you were, yes. Neal Dodd is on contract here, but he's also a real minister. You could say we signed him because he, er, really looks the part."

"Oh, admit it, Harry," Joan snapped, "you wanted to save money on his cleric's collar and vestments. You hired him because he could bring his own to set and the studio wouldn't have to provide them."

Dash laughed, a deep, booming, full-throated laugh. A laugh that conjured up images of the most masculine things Joan could think of—cigars and horses and wide-open spaces. It gave her a little fluttery sensation in her stomach. She hated it.

"Nothing gets by her, does it, Harry? You and I both know she's right, you old skinflint." Was Dash Howard actually agreeing with her? "But still, doesn't this have to go through the court? Joan and I never got a blood test, a license, nothing."

"That's what we're trying to work out," she replied. "Show him the certificate, Harry." Harry pulled a piece of paper off his desk and held it out to Dash. Joan couldn't stay seated any longer and came to peer over Dash's shoulder while he read it. She'd already studied it in great detail while they waited for Dash to arrive, and it looked every inch the real deal. A marriage certificate signed by Joan Davis and Dash Howard.

Dash looked truly panic-stricken now, and Joan had to admit she was relishing it the tiniest bit. If she had to endure this situation, at least Dash was feeling as tortured as she was. "But how did our names get on here?"

"It was a publicity stunt, don't you remember? Harry had us sign a gag certificate in our costumes and take pictures. 'Davis and Dash tie the knot at last!' 'Davis and Dash are *Wedding Crazy*!' Remember all the ads in the paper?"

"Doll, if I tried to remember every one of my publicity shoots, I'd have no room in my head for anything else."

Joan rolled her eyes. "Please refrain from calling me 'doll.'"

"Why? If we're married, I should be allowed to call you 'doll.'" He winked at her. "What a stupid idea, Harry. A publicity stunt of our fake wedding. Honestly. This is what Leda is using to say we're married? It won't hold up in court. These fake photos and the fact that we exchanged vows—in character, I might add—under the guidance of a real minister?"

Joan looked at Harry, urging him to go on. If she had to explain this next bit to Dash, she'd throttle him before she got through it.

"You're right, Dash. This alone won't hold up in court. But we called the Bureau of Public Records at City Hall, and they have a copy of this certificate, as well as a license fully filled out by a clerk. According to the city of Los Angeles, Davis and Dash are bound in holy matrimony."

Dash sat back in his chair. He looked as if someone had just socked him on the jaw. His entire body had gone white and his forehead had broken out in a sweat. He tugged at his collar nervously, and Joan studied him. She raised one eyebrow and looked him full in the eye. "What Harry and I would like to know is how City Hall got a copy of our 'fake' marriage certificate."

Dash swallowed and his eyes darted back and forth between them. He mumbled something unintelligible under his breath.

"What did you say? We couldn't hear you," she intoned coldly. She refused to soften her gaze. Maybe if she kept staring at him, he'd admit what she'd known deep down since the moment she'd received that phone call from Leda. That somehow this entire blasted mess was his fault.

"I said it was meant to be a joke," he muttered, barely louder than the last time.

"A joke? A joke! What did you do, you boorish, brainless, terrible man?" Joan felt herself losing control as she screeched at him. Tears were starting to course down her face, and before she could stop herself, she reached out and slapped him hard across the cheek. The crack as her hand met his face rang through the office, and everyone was silent for a moment before Dash began to laugh again. He turned his head and proffered the other side of his face to her.

"I deserved that," he said. "Would you like to take a crack at the other one?"

Joan didn't know what she wanted to do. She wanted to hit him again. She wanted to pound her fists into his chest. And bizarrely, she could not stop staring at his mouth—his full lips quivering with laughter; the muscles and sinews of his neck pulsing as his Adam's apple bobbed with mirth. So instead, she balled up her fists and stormed across the room to sit back down in the leather chair next to Harry's desk.

Dash stopped laughing and massaged the side of his cheek. It stung where Joan had hit him. He was lucky she hadn't swung at him with the hand bearing her engagement ring. That rock looked like it could do some serious damage.

He liked this side of her. Normally, she was petulant, insistent upon doing things her way. She rarely engaged with him, acting as if she was above him—ice queen deluxe. It was why he pranked her all the time, to see if he could get a rise out of her. He'd tried to apologize after that night at the Cocoanut Grove. But Joan had refused to hear it. Accused him of being in cahoots with Leda and walked straight off the set, declining to come out of her trailer until he agreed to only speak to her about their scenes and nothing else. How could anyone say they were sorry in the face of that?

She was determined to see the worst in him. So, fine then, that's what he gave her, settling for piquing her anger. He liked her ferocity. It was attractive. It was real. And damned more interesting than the cold shoulder she insisted upon. But now she was back to pouting in the corner, the mask of respectability settling back over her features. There was the Joan he knew so well. A woman so stuck on principle she'd choke on it.

Harry was still leaning against the edge of his desk, his head in his hands. "I'm afraid you need to explain to us how we ended up in this pickle, Dash."

Dash grimaced; he really didn't want to admit that he'd played such a petty prank. Or that he was drunk when he did it. Even if he still had no idea how the hell it had gone all the way to City Hall. That was never part of the plan.

"I addressed the certificate to City Hall," he confessed. "I was drunk that night, celebrating our 'nuptials' after we wrapped for the day, and I thought it'd be funny to surprise Joan with it. I snuck into her dressing room and left it on the table. She was supposed to find it and flip her wig. I've no idea how it got to City

Hall. Maybe Joan does." He gave her a pointed look. After all, she was the last one to see the damn thing.

But she didn't look guilty. She looked ready to scream, on the verge of bursting into tears. Again. He didn't want that. He wanted to evoke emotions in her, get her to do something besides turn her nose up at him. But he took no pleasure in making her cry. No real man made a woman cry.

"I never saw the damn thing," she gritted through her teeth.

"Well then, what the hell happened to it? It didn't get up and walk to City Hall," he retorted.

From her chair in the back of the room, so quiet and unobtrusive he hadn't even realized she was there, Arlene piped up, her voice barely a squeak. "I think I know what happened."

All three of their heads snapped to her at once, and she looked so cowed that Dash almost felt sorry for her. They waited with bated breath for Arlene to explain how they'd ended up in this mess.

"This would've been about a year and a half ago. I came in early that day, like always. And there was this big envelope out on the table in Joan's trailer. It had all these flourishes on it, but it was addressed to City Hall and had Joan's name on it as a return address, so I thought she'd left it out for me to mail and forgot to mention it. I put it in the studio mail that morning."

Dash didn't know if he wanted to laugh or cry. Somehow this was not entirely his fault.

Joan closed her eyes and massaged her temples. "You thought it would be funny to leave our signed marriage certificate in an envelope addressed to City Hall in my trailer, and then when I didn't mention it, you, what? Assumed I threw it away?"

"That's exactly what I assumed," he said, jumping to his feet. "Is it my fault you have the most reliable assistant in Hollywood?"

Arlene cringed and started to blurt out another apology, but

Dash stopped her. "No, Arlene, it's okay. You were just doing your job. But, look, Harry, we didn't get a license or do our blood test. Why did they even certify this? How did they get the information to fill out the license?"

Harry shook his head. "Apparently the clerk working that day was a big fan of both of yours, and she was so excited, she filed it and filled out a license for you without asking any questions. Your information is public record. Seems fame can cut through the red tape sometimes."

"So, let me get this straight. Joan and I said vows before a real minister, and then a prop marriage certificate Joan and I signed as part of a harebrained publicity stunt that Arlene accidentally mailed to City Hall was used as evidence to fill out a marriage license and declare us legally married?"

"It appears so, yes."

"Christ, if this was in a script you were pitching me, I'd say you were losing your touch. The one time City Hall doesn't get mired in bureaucracy, it has to be because a Davis and Dash fan got goo-goo eyes for our fake marriage." He slammed his hand down on Harry's desk.

With that, Joan buried her face in her hands and let loose. Dash produced a handkerchief from his breast pocket and weakly handed it to her. Surprisingly, she cautiously took it from him and began dotting her eyes with it. Boy, he'd really done it this time.

Harry leaned back in his chair and steepled his hands beneath his chin. "Well, I have an idea how to set things right, but neither of you are going to like it. I've considered the options, and I think it's the only way."

"Whatever you say, Harry, we'll do it. Just please get us out of this mess. I can't be married to D-D-Dash. I'm supposed to be marrying Monty."

Dash felt like he'd been kicked in the gut. The idea of being married to him sent Joan into prostration. His worst fears were confirmed—no one would ever want to hitch themselves to his wagon. He was good for a good time. Nothing more. And sometimes, when he was sober and not busy acting, he wondered if he was even good enough for that.

"All right, hit us with it, Harry. Like Joan says, whatever it takes. I made this mess, I'll do whatever you say to clean it up."

"You're going to have to get a divorce," Harry declared. "It's the only way. This marriage has been legally processed, and by tomorrow morning, the entire country will know it. So this is what we're going to do. We're going to call Leda Price and give her an exclusive interview, tell her it was a mix-up by someone who's no longer with the studio."

"You can blame me, it's okay," whispered Arlene.

"No, Arlene, this movie is your chance for bigger and brighter things," Joan snapped. "I'm not letting you take the fall for Dash."

Dash ignored her because, well, she was right. "Harry, why does it have to be Leda? I'd rather not give that gorgon the pleasure. Besides, she'll sense it's a lie from a million miles away. Leda has had mine and Joan's number from day one. We made her. Against our will."

Joan's eyebrows nearly shot to her hairline. "Dash, please, you said you'd do whatever it takes. You don't want to be married to me any more than I want to be married to you. Be agreeable. Please. I'm begging you."

"But why does it have to be Leda? Why can't we call up my friend Walter at the *Reporter*?"

"Because Leda got us into this mess to begin with. She's mad I didn't give her the scoop on my engagement, and she wants revenge. Besides, what do you care? You've been in cahoots with her before." Dash bit the inside of his cheek to stop himself from correcting Joan. She wouldn't listen anyway. He'd made a boneheaded mistake that night, but it hadn't been throwing his lot in with Leda Price.

"If we give her this, she'll go easy on us." Joan paused, perhaps realizing she was spewing some wishful thinking. "Maybe."

"Joan's right. It's the only way. And this way, it keeps her from finding out the real reason for the error—your drunken escapades." Harry gave Dash a pointed look.

Touché, point taken. Though Dash didn't hear Harry complaining when said escapades were bringing in a bunch of positive press to the studio. He was only following his marching orders, if Harry wanted to get technical. "Fine, we explain it to Leda. It still doesn't undo the marriage."

"Yeah, so, that's the part I don't think you're going to like." Harry looked sheepishly between the two of them. As the head of Hollywood's most glamorous studio, he had a lot of money and power. In the blink of an eye, he could end both of their careers—so if this was his plan to save them, they likely had no choice but to act on it.

"Just tell us the damage, Harry." Dash looked at Joan as if to reassure her, but she was looking up at Harry as if he were the answer to all her prayers—her brown eyes were rimmed with tears threatening to spill over again. All because he'd been a drunken fool caught up in trying to get a rise out of Joan. Well, he'd succeeded. Beyond his wildest expectations.

"A divorce in the state of California is a pain in the neck," Harry explained. "It's a lot of paperwork and could take well over a year, and even then the judge might decide not to grant it to you. So you're both going to need to move to Reno for six weeks to establish residency." Dash and Joan broke out in protest almost immediately.

"Harry, we can't do that. We're about to start another picture—"

"What will Monty say? He won't like the idea of my moving away for six weeks."

Harry held up his hand. "Quiet! Do you want to get out of this mess or don't you? Now, you're going to move to Reno for the requisite six weeks and get a divorce."

"And on what grounds, may I ask, will we be filing this divorce?" All Dash needed was for Leda Price to get ahold of some trumped-up charge against him.

"Impotency," Joan declared, a watery, devilish grin breaking out across her face.

"Absolutely not," Dash said as Harry roared with laughter. "And I don't think that's funny. If you'd like me to show you how wrong that charge would be, Miss Davis, I'd be happy to oblige." That wiped the smug little smirk right off her face. Good. Served her right. Though part of him wouldn't have minded proving his merits to her in that department.

What was he thinking? This woman had made it abundantly clear she wanted nothing to do with him. And he sure as hell didn't need a woman who didn't desire his company.

"How about extreme mental cruelty?" he retorted.

Joan glared at him, a grin curling at the corners of her mouth. "I think habitual drunkenness would be much more appropriate, don't you?"

Dash felt like she'd hit him all over again, only this time in the gut. He drank a lot. He knew he did. But didn't everyone in Hollywood? No one cared. Except apparently the portrait of respectability, Joan Davis.

"It's only habitual when women like you drive me to it," he responded. If she was going to take potshots at him, he could give as good as he got.

"Would you quit your bickering?" Harry yelled, clearly exasperated with them both. "Now, you're going to get a divorce on the grounds of extreme mental cruelty."

Joan opened her mouth to protest, but Harry held up his hand and continued on. "Because it's the easiest thing to file for, as the courts require no proof. That way we need not give any details of what that entails to the press."

"Well, you'd know all about the easiest way to a divorce, Harry, wouldn't you?" Dash couldn't resist giving his boss a hard time. The man was on his third ex-wife, and there were constant rumors that he was romancing a different starlet on a weekly basis. At least Dash would've intended to honor the institution of marriage if he'd known he'd entered into it. How was he supposed to know some starry-eyed kid would process the marriage certificate he never intended to mail in the first place?

Joan stared at him, mouth agape, but he could see the corners of her mouth twitching. She was trying not to laugh.

"I'd say that's a little uncalled for when you're the reason we're in this pickle." Harry scowled. "Now, we are all aware it's a farce. So you're going to go up there for six weeks and the studio will pay for it all."

Joan rose from her seat and wrapped her arms around the gruff, balding studio head. "Oh, Harry, how can we ever thank you enough? It's too kind." Harry patted her absentmindedly on the head and then extricated himself from her embrace.

"Don't start thinking I've gone soft, Joanie. This isn't a charity case. If the studio is sending you to Reno for six weeks, we're getting a picture out of this little 'reno-vation.' The publicity writes itself—Dash and Davis together again, only this time it's D-I-V-O-R-C-E."

Joan looked helplessly at Dash for support. "We're supposed

to be making a picture *here*! Arlene's script—I couldn't disappoint her now. It's perfect, Harry. We have to do it. You know it could be my shot at an Oscar."

Harry raised his hand to silence her. "We're not going to make a different picture. We're going to make that one. Arlene can get started on revising it right away." Arlene perked up then, clearly eager to atone for her part in the affair.

"It was already about a rancher and a woman nursing a broken heart. We'll make her a divorcée and get some location shooting out of it. Simple enough," Harry added. Arlene nodded and pulled a small notepad from her pocket, scribbling notes. "Most of the sets and costumes are already ready. We'll ship them north on the train. They'll probably even get there before you do."

Joan blinked owlishly back at Harry, seemingly at a loss for words for once. Dash wanted to laugh at her, he really did. But she looked like a tiger in a cage, and he had to admit, she'd never looked more beautiful.

"That's, well, that's okay, then. But what about the rest of it? The divorce proceedings, staying in Reno. It'll embarrass Monty. We can't make it into a public spectacle. He'll hate that."

"Joan, be honest with yourself. It's already a spectacle. Isn't it better if it's one we're controlling?" Dash retorted. She gaped at him, seemingly astonished he was capable of thinking rationally about this. He really didn't want to spend six weeks in Reno making a picture with a woman who could barely stand the sight of him. But as far as he could tell, there was no way around this.

"You're okay with this?" she sniffed.

"Do I have much choice?" The barest hint of a smile started to form at the corner of her mouth, and Dash felt like the sun was shining again.

"If we do this, Harry, we are not making it into some

dog-and-pony show, you hear?" Joan declared, looking at Dash to back her up.

"I don't know what you mean."

"You do and you know it. Okay, we move to Reno. We make Arlene's fantastic picture. But I don't want people up there photographing our every move. Every bit of this is going to be carefully monitored and controlled by the studio."

"You know we only have so much control over the press."

"Fine, but you exercise that control to the full extent of your abilities. I will not become some tabloid divorcée. Dash, are you in or out?"

"Seeing as I got us all into this disaster, I guess it wouldn't be very chivalrous of me not to agree to get us out. I'm in."

Harry grinned in delight and rubbed his hands together with glee, while Joan stood back and appraised him. Dash couldn't tell if she liked what she saw or not.

"So, Harry, when do we start production?"

"I've booked your train tickets for tomorrow. Then, we need a day to get production established. Arlene, if you start revisions tonight, can you have something ready in forty-eight hours?" Arlene nodded in assent. "So we'll start in two days, then. Right on time with the original schedule." He slapped his knee. "You know, this might just work out. Dash and Davis together again, this time on location." Harry's eyes sparkled and Dash could practically see dollar signs on his irises.

"In a true women's picture," Joan replied, a breathless wonder Dash had never heard in her voice before.

Harry waved his hand. "Sure, sure, but most importantly, it's you two crazy kids in love again. The audience will eat it up." He held out his arm as if he was seeing the marquee in his mind's eye. "Dash and Davis in *Reno Rendezvous*."

Joan spluttered. "I thought it was called *At Long Last Love*."

"It was. I gave it a new title. We have to capitalize on the moment."

Dash and Joan looked at each other and rolled their eyes simultaneously. He had to stifle a laugh because the look on her face so clearly conveyed what she thought of that ridiculous title. It was going to be a long six weeks.

CHAPTER 4

DASH TOOK A SLUG OF WHISKEY AND CLOSED HIS EYES, listening to the waves crash on the rocks beneath his friend's Malibu cottage.

"Hair of the dog?" inquired Flynn Banks, a wide shit-eating grin on his face.

"The first one was hair of the dog. This, this is to wipe the nightmare I experienced in Harry's office from my memory," Dash muttered.

"That bad, huh?"

"Worse."

Flynn laughed. Everything was hilarious to the man. He treated life as if it was a giant gag. It's why Dash liked him; he balanced out Dash's more morose tendencies and indulged his love of a good prank.

Flynn Banks was a massive star, known for his swashbuckling antics and his rapscallion persona. Which, to be fair, was less a persona and more just who he was. He was one of the only actors in Hollywood who was authentic, Dash included. One night they'd been kicked out of the backroom bar at Musso and Frank Grill after starting a pissing contest over who could drink more, and they'd been fast friends ever since.

In general, Dash preferred the company of the crew—the

best boys, grips, and tradesmen who walked the streets of the lot. He loved to banter with them on set, have them over for a weekly poker game at his obscenely big house. But Flynn Banks was the only actor whose company he actively enjoyed. So, after the revelations in Harry's office, he'd instructed his driver to take him to Malibu as quickly as humanly possible. Only Flynn would understand the self-flagellation of his mind's current state.

Flynn opened the doors to his deck and a cool ocean breeze blew in off the sea, the tang of salt and adventure in the air. Dash followed him outside and leaned against the deck, pondering the mysteries of the water. There were few things that steadied him as much as nature. This house was a sanctuary, the crash of the waves as sacred as prayer, the mist off the water as healing as holy water. He came here whenever he needed to catch his breath.

Flynn cleared his throat. "Joan give you the old ice-queen act?"

"Does she ever give me anything but? That's been her MO with me since the first morning on set after the Cocoanut Grove."

Flynn sighed. "I hate to say this, but—have you ever considered apologizing?"

Dash reached out and grabbed for Flynn's face, trying to pull up his eyelids. Flynn wrestled him off. "What in God's name do you think you're doing?"

"Checking to see if you're still in there. Flynn Banks suggesting someone apologize to a woman? Never."

Flynn chuckled. "I'll admit I don't see any use in soothing a damaged ego when one dame is as good as the next, but you have to work with this woman and you've allowed her to believe you're the biggest cad in Hollywood for four years. Which I simply will not allow. I'm the biggest cad in Hollywood. Everyone knows it."

Dash laughed for the first time in hours. This right here. This was why he loved Flynn. "I tried to apologize that next day. But she wouldn't listen. She walked away every time I opened my mouth if we weren't in a scene together. I kept hoping it would blow over, that things would go back to the way they were before that night—the easy rapport, the shared jokes, the—"

"Rampant flirtation and eye-fucking." Flynn gave him a devilish grin.

"You're incorrigible." Dash sipped his whiskey and let the smooth burn of it coat the inside of his mouth and his throat. "Once, maybe there was something there. Those first two pictures together were heaven. I've never felt that way about a woman—or a screen partner—since. We made magic together. Hell, Harry could see it. He's the one who started pairing us off together as romantic leads after that first picture with her where I only had the one scene as her chauffeur. But then I blew it. And maybe she was right anyway. Maybe any apology would be a flimsy excuse. After all, I went along with what Harry asked. I agreed to that date, to putting on a show for the press."

"But you didn't agree to Leda Price and a crew of photographers ambushing you in the alley. It was meant to be a studio-arranged date where they'd grab some shots of you dancing and having dinner. Not the farce it became."

"If you were Joan, would you believe that? She erected a fortress around herself." He sighed and turned to face his friend. "Look at the mess I've made for her. For both of us."

Flynn waved his hand. "You were drunk, you made a mistake. I do that nightly."

Dash chuckled. "You make it look a lot better than I do."

"It's all in the wrist," Flynn quipped. "No, but seriously, how could you expect some movie-crazy fan at City Hall to fill out a marriage license and file it on your behalf? It's the most ludicrous thing I've ever heard."

Dash groaned and buried his face in his hands. "It is, isn't it? Goddamn Hollywood. If I'd stuck to tending horses, I wouldn't be in this mess."

"But you wouldn't have met me," Flynn teased.

"True," Dash grunted. "And what would I do without you?"

Flynn retreated inside to pick up the whiskey bottle, calling from near the door, "Drink less and have a far inferior partner when it comes to helping you pick up women."

"Excuse me, I can pick up women just fine on my own, thank you."

Flynn returned to the doorway and leaned against it in a louche pose. If Dash had been a woman, he would've fallen for it hook, line, and sinker. There were very few objective truths in this world, but the fact that Flynn Banks was an irresistibly dashing reprobate was one of them. "Dash Howard and Flynn Banks, the two warmest beds in Hollywood."

Dash's face fell, remembering how lonely he'd felt this morning when he'd found the bed empty. Again. But he tried to brush it off with their usual shared machismo. "Not me. They always clear out after we've had our fun."

Flynn didn't notice Dash's slip. "Show me your ways, oh King of Hollywood. I seem to be a magnet for the clingy ones."

Dash laughed, short and halting. "It's the sword-fighting. They think you're the protective hero type."

"A notion of which I am only all too happy to disabuse them." He reached out to pour more whiskey in Dash's glass, but Dash waved him away. Flynn shrugged and took a swig straight from the bottle.

"Seriously, though, mate," Flynn replied. "Even as a joke, why would you stamp and address that envelope with the certificate inside? I thought we'd pledged never to fall subject to the old ball and chain."

That was the million-dollar question, wasn't it? Why had he put the certificate in the envelope in the first place? Because he was drunk was the simple answer. But had there been some part of him reaching for something he knew he could never have?

"I don't know." That was the truth. "Because I'm a cad." He reached for Flynn's bottle of whiskey and took a swig. "And a drunk."

It went down so easily that he knew he'd had enough, but he took another drink anyway. "Maybe I did it because I knew no matter how hard I tried, I would never be worth the gum on the bottom of Joan Davis's shoe."

Flynn yanked the bottle back and looked at him hard. "Dash, would I be lying if I said I didn't enjoy our nights on the town together? Sure. But the reason we've stayed friends is because you're the most decent man I know. You'd do anything to protect the people you love, and you're a damn fine actor with the only moral compass in Hollywood."

"I'm having trouble getting it to point north lately. I think I've lost sight of myself," he admitted. He looked out at the sea again, the sun edging closer to the horizon and a faint orange glow overtaking the panoply of blues that had dominated the vista only moments before.

Flynn turned, leaning against the balustrade and edging closer to Dash. His voice was barely a whisper. "Dash, if you hate Hollywood so much, why don't you quit? Go settle down on that ranch of yours in Santa Barbara and become an enigma. Hollywood loves an enigma."

"I've thought about it," he said. "But who am I if I'm not the King of Hollywood? I say I hate fame, that I could live without the spotlight. But what if I'm really a hothouse flower and I need the light and the attention to survive?"

"I didn't know you were a poet," Flynn said with a smirk.

"No, I'm serious, Flynn. I've spent so long playing the studio's version of Dash Howard, I'm not sure how to be anyone else. I've got a pretty face… What else is it good for besides pimping myself out for the studio?"

"If I've told you once, I've told you a million times, that is simply not true."

Dash started to protest and Flynn held up his hand. "We're not having this argument again. The real question is, are you happy?"

Dash thought about that for a second. Was he happy? He should be. He had a good life. He was one of the most famous men on the planet, could buy anything he could think of, and apparently was married to his highly desirable costar. But none of that was real. That wasn't happiness. There was one place he was happy. On a set.

"When I'm working," he confessed. "Being on a set is like being back in a traveling show tending the horses. It's me, my costars, and all the guys on set fine-tuning something until we get it right. When I'm acting, I'm not me, but I'm the most myself that I ever am."

"All right, old sport." Flynn clapped him on the back. "So you keep acting. But something has got to change. That much is clear."

"Well, I *am* going to Reno." He winked.

Flynn burst into laughter that echoed off the nearby cliffs as the sun slipped below the horizon. He squeezed Dash's shoulder and turned to lead him inside. "C'mon, let's get bombed and plan more pranks to piss off Joan."

CHAPTER 5

ALL ABOARD THE DIVORCÉE SPECIAL!

Before it's wedding bells for Joan Davis and Monty Smyth, Miss Davis is in need of a little renovation—one sure to break the heart of many of her fans. Davis and Dash, the golden duo of the silver screen, are married. But it's far from true love—like a plot right out of one of their pictures, the pair find themselves accidentally hitched through a clerical error on the part of a former studio employee. Perhaps someone who was equally as fearful as this publication that Miss Davis would end her days an old maid?

"It's a simple misunderstanding, and one we hope to clear up quickly, as I'm anxious to marry the man I'm actually in love with," Miss Davis told the *Examiner* in an exclusive interview.

Mr. Howard added, "Can you imagine? Me, married? I'd be breaking far too many hearts." The revolving door of socialites on Mr. Howard's arm would impress even Don Juan, and it's clear he's not slowing down anytime soon. So it's divorce for this divine duo, as Harry Evets and the studio send them north to Nevada on the Overland Limited for a much-needed cure for their troubles.

But never fear, dear readers, we have even more thrilling news—this time D-I-V-O-R-C-E spells Boffo! at the BO. The Dash and Davis picture previously titled *At Long Last Love* is going north for the summer. It was scheduled to begin production in Hollywood on Monday, but never one to let an opportunity pass him by, Mr. Evets is sending a film crew alongside Dash and Davis to film on location. *Reno Rendezvous* is a picture sure to set hearts aflutter across the globe. With a script from newcomer Arlene Morgan, Miss Davis's assistant, it's promised to be a three-hankie affair. For more from Reno, keep checking in right here at *What Price Hollywood?*

—xoxo, Leda

Joan sighed and looked out the window. Pine trees rushed by as she drew the silk scarf carefully wrapped around her head tighter and plunked her oversized sunglasses back down over her eyes.

Arlene nudged her with her elbow. "What's wrong, Joan?"

"How is it that whenever we do a joint interview, he always comes out on top?" She picked at the pilled fabric in her wool slacks, wishing she was anywhere else.

"He doesn't. He looks like a playboy. Is that what you want?

You've made it abundantly clear you love Monty and are only doing this to get back to him as soon as possible." A little sigh escaped Arlene, and Joan's heart panged. The girl was a hopeless romantic.

"Arlene, have you ever been in love?"

The color drained from her assistant's face, and Joan instantly regretted asking. "Oh, darling, I'm sorry. I didn't mean to upset you."

"No, no." Arlene waved her hand and fussed at her face, trying to adjust her already perfectly styled coif. "It's all right. I, yes, once… We grew up together. He was my best friend."

Joan turned her face back to the window, noticing the trees thinning as they seemed to be leaving the wilderness behind. She turned around and peeked above the headrest. The entire train car was filled with women. Aspiring ex-wives chugging down the tracks on the divorcée special, and now she was one of them.

She'd promised herself she'd never be here. That was why Monty was the perfect match for her. Oh, she was fond of him, yes. They enjoyed each other's company. They were great for each other's careers. But he didn't love her and she didn't love him. And that was what mattered most—because that way lay disaster. All of these women chattering around her. They'd been in love once. And look where it'd landed them—on the Overland Limited to Reno.

She looked back at Arlene, who was already recovering some of her color. "Did he… What happened? You don't have to answer if it's too painful."

"No, that's all right. Nothing happened. I never told him how I felt. He wanted to be a dancer, a Broadway star, and I wanted to make movies. And so, when we were eighteen, I went with him to the train station and waved as he pulled out on a train bound for New York City. I haven't seen him since. Last I heard, he was dating his dance partner."

"Well, maybe someday..." Joan started, but her heart wasn't in it, and Arlene gave her a wan smile as if to tell her she could see right through her but appreciated the thought all the same.

Love only led to heartbreak. She'd seen it time and again. With Arlene. With her sister. With her parents. The haunted look in her mother's eyes that Joan hadn't understood when her father had disappeared when she was only four. Love had made her mother a shell of herself. Then there was her older sister, Betty. When Hal had run off with her best friend, Joan had watched her sister fade from her always sunny self to a dark and cynical woman. Love had ruined them, so she had promised she would never be so foolish as to fall prey to it. She got all the love she needed. From her audience. Until Dash had decided that was something they should share. Tried to unsteady her with his good looks and his charm, manipulate her for a photo opp. The day they'd met she'd known he was both a temptation and a risk. One that had proved far too great to take. He'd confirmed it again with this ridiculous marriage.

She'd already learned the hard way that if she shared her spotlight with anyone, she'd end up standing in the shadows. That's why Monty was safe—the answer to everything.

"Hello, ladies," her least favorite voice in the world drawled. She turned to see the edges of Dash Howard's pencil-thin mustache plastered to the crevice between her and Arlene's seats.

"What are you doing here?" she huffed. Really, the last thing she needed right now was for a train car full of women to lose their minds over Dash Howard. He rose and Arlene squeaked something about needing the bathroom and vacated the seat beside her, leaving it for Dash.

"Don't you realize this car is full of women looking to throw themselves at the next warm body?" Joan hissed. "I'd rather not be party to a mob scene, thank you."

He chuckled, and his throaty laugh made her stomach flip. She hated him all the more for that. But God knows she'd acted enough love scenes with him. Her body simply didn't know the difference between the man and the characters he played.

"You seem to think I'm irresistible, Miss Davis? Or should I say Mrs. Howard?" She winced at that. He knew how to push her buttons.

"Don't call me that."

"But it's your name—at least for the next six weeks."

"Dash Howard, I wouldn't take your name if you were the last man alive." She slammed her hand down and found it landing on his thigh, dangerously close to other parts of his anatomy. He looked down with a mischievous grin and raised his eyebrows. The train jostled them, and she snatched her hand back, afraid it might brush against something she had no wish to touch.

"You might not take my name, but it looks like there's other things you'd be willing to take, Mrs. Howard." He waggled his eyebrows and looked pointedly at her hand, but that didn't last. He burst out laughing, leaving her utterly confused. "Oh, you should see your face. The very suggestion that you might, that we might... Even behind those sunglasses, the idea terrifies you."

She sat up very straight in her seat, wary of raising her voice. "I assure you, Mr. Howard, it doesn't terrify me. It repulses me. The showgirls at the Trocadero might not know better, but I know who you really are—a cowboy who happened to get lucky, a hack, and a two-bit drunk."

She felt very proud of her pronouncement until she looked at him. Dash Howard was a pillar of Hollywood masculinity, yet it seemed her barbs had wounded. His face had fallen at her words, and though he'd quickly covered it, the flash of hurt in his eyes was unmistakable. She'd thought his ego was so big that he was untouchable—but was she wrong? The concept that he might have a heart had long been foreign to her. She'd thought when they first met that he was the real deal. The rare kind and decent man who made her laugh. But he'd proved otherwise that night at the Cocoanut Grove. Since then, it seemed to her he was devoid of a need for anything but glory, women, and booze. The notion that he might be more than what she'd pegged him for disturbed her, and she began to find the stifling train car unbearable. She stood, unnecessarily adjusting her scarf.

"Now, if you'll excuse me, if you won't leave a lady in peace, I'm going to see myself to the dining car." Her last word was cut off by the sudden screeching halt of the train, sending her tumbling straight into his lap, her face careening into his strong chest. She flailed madly, trying to keep herself upright and instead found herself with a handful of his biceps and his thighs as a voice on a speaker crackled, "Now arriving in Reno."

Her hands were all over him, and he liked it. Shit, he liked it too much. Far too much for a woman who'd made it clear she'd only ever see him as a dumb corn-fed hick with a fondness for liquor. But his dick was having a hard time remembering that when her hand was within inches of it.

She continued to needlessly flail in his arms, making him concerned that this was likely to move from vaguely erotic to dangerous to his person within a span of seconds. He grabbed her by the arms and squeezed, trying to get her attention. "Calm down, Joan."

"I am calm," she shrieked. He moved his hands to hers, pressing his thumbs to her wrists, applying a trick he'd once learned tending horses. The motion stilled her and she took a deep breath, her eyes catching his through the lenses of her sunglasses.

Time seemed to stand still as he looked in her eyes and drew breath with her, counting the seconds and feeling her pulse slow beneath his fingers. She moved almost imperceptibly toward him, and as if drawn by a magnetic impulse, he leaned forward to meet her—but the spell between them was quickly broken as the train car full of women began to chatter and bustle around him, preparing to exit the train.

Joan recovered herself. Seeming to suddenly realize where she was, she leapt out of his lap. A strange melancholy filled him at the loss of her warm body pressed against his own, and he told himself the reason was the prospect of spending weeks cooped up in Reno on his best behavior. If Harry wanted this trip to Reno to go off without any trouble, Dash owed him that at least.

He looked up to see Joan struggling to remove her bag from the overhead compartment. It was jammed, but she was determined to yank it free with sheer force. He stood immediately and reached for it, out of instinct. "Here let me help you."

"I don't need your help, Mr. Howard. Not now, not ever." She lifted her foot to the armrest, straining for leverage to free her case. He resisted looking more closely at the flash of ankle and calf that was exposed as her trousers rode up. It was almost laughable how much she hated him. But he wasn't going to let the rest of the women on this train think he was a louse who wouldn't help his costar with her luggage.

He stood and put his hand over hers. "Let me get it." She swatted him away and resumed her ministrations, a bead of sweat breaking out on her forehead as she struggled to loosen the heavy bag from its resting place.

"What have you got in there, anyway?"

"A lady never tells." She smirked, and his mind immediately cast itself to an assortment of lingerie. He blinked, stopping himself before he began imagining her wearing it. Was he really this pathetic? Less than forty-eight hours since he'd had a woman in his bed and already he was imagining his nemesis in her underwear.

"Excuse me, Mr. Howard, excuse me," a high-pitched voice piped behind him. He switched on the megawatt "King of Hollywood" smile before facing them.

"Yes, miss, of course you can have my autograph."

The petite blond before him looked aghast. "Oh, I only wanted to get by."

"Oh, um, of course." He sheepishly slid to the side, watching Joan dissolve into peals of laughter behind the blond's head. She recovered herself as the young woman turned to face her.

"But Miss Davis, if you would be so kind, you're my favorite actress."

Joan's entire demeanor changed. The haughtiness was gone from her shoulders, and she yanked off her sunglasses, reaching for the pen the young woman suddenly produced. "Of course! Who should I make it out to?"

The blond blushed and Joan gave her the smile that had broken the hearts of men across America. "To Shirley, please."

Dash watched as Joan scrawled words across a piece of scrap paper with an eloquent flourish. "To Shirley: May your Reno rendezvous be more fun and more fruitful than mine."

Shirley practically tripped over herself thanking Joan as she made her way toward the door to the platform, and Joan was all effortless grace, assuring the woman the pleasure was all hers. But as soon as she was gone, Joan turned back to remount her efforts with the bag.

Dash couldn't resist commenting on the encounter. "That note you wrote—not exactly being discreet, are you?"

"What is there to be discreet about, Dash? We're here making a movie and for a divorce, to end a marriage entirely of your devising."

"Well, not entirely; it was part of the movie plot. And Arlene did—" He stopped at a swift glare from Joan. He was grasping now, trying to excuse the inexcusable and he knew it. But she didn't have to act like being married to him was a strange and unusual punishment.

She had both feet up on the chair now for leverage, and he couldn't help but notice that her ass looked particularly pert from that angle. And then, as if she was reading his mind, she said, "Dash Howard, you'd better not be staring at my ass."

Each word came through teeth gritted with the supreme effort she was exerting to free her case, and the last *ass* was elongated as she finally loosened the bag and tumbled headlong into the aisle, a jumble of limbs. She glared up at him, and he choked back a laugh, sensing now was not the time.

"Well, are you going to help me up or not?"

"Oh, but I thought you didn't need my help, Miss Davis?"

"I don't, but I—" Before she could finish her sentence, he'd scooped her up, luggage and all, and carried her out onto the train platform where they were met with a blinding flash of camera lights.

He resisted the urge to drop her immediately, despite her hissing in his ear, "Unhand me this instant," and instead turned to smile for the press, realizing that he'd made yet another monumental mistake.

CHAPTER 6

C-O-Z-Y IN R-E-N-O

The King and Queen of Hollywood looked more like newlyweds than divorcées disembarking from the Overland Limited train to kick off their six weeks in Reno. Dash Howard carried Joan Davis off the train in his arms as if he was a groom carrying his new bride over the threshold. And she certainly looked cozy in his arms, despite her attempts to disguise herself in a scarf and sunglasses.

Monty Smyth has not been seen on the town since his engagement to Miss Davis was announced, but we have to wonder what he must be thinking at seeing his fiancée curled up in the arms of her costar. Could the wedding be off already? Or will Davis and Dash go through with their little reno-vation?

Never fear, *What Price Hollywood?* will get to the bottom of this trackside rendezvous.

—xoxo, Leda

Joan crumpled the paper in her hands and stalked up and down the narrow passageway of her trailer, smashing it into a smaller and smaller ball in her hands. "I can't believe this."

"Don't flip your wig, Joan. It's what Leda wants," Arlene replied without even looking up from her typewriter.

"Leda! To hell with Leda. She's a conniving little snipe. No, there's no winning with her. It's him. He did this on purpose. It really gets me steamed."

"Now, Joan, you said yourself he was trying to help you with your bag and you resisted him. How could it have been purposeful?"

"I don't know, but it was. As if this whole charade isn't enough already, now he has to keep feeding the gossip rags with photo ops. I bet you he's on Leda's payroll. He's probably been taking a cut from her since that night."

Arlene looked up from her typewriter where she was drafting new pages of a scene for her reimagined script and gazed thoughtfully out the window, contemplating the pine trees and snowcapped peaks in the distance. "I sincerely doubt that," she mumbled. "But maybe he really does like you. Maybe he was trying to get closer to you, but he can't tell you because he knows you'll reject him." Arlene got a starry look in her eyes that Joan recognized as the start of a romantic flight of fancy.

"I thought you were on my and Monty's side," she groused.

"I am. I just… Is there anything better than unrequited yearning?" She sighed. Arlene bit her lip and pulled a pencil out from behind her ear, furiously scribbling on a scrap of paper. Joan had a feeling she and Dash were about to get a new love scene.

Joan didn't want to hear about Dash's unrequited yearning. The idea was laughable. He was a mercenary, out to aggrandize himself and get his picture in the paper and nothing more. She uncrumpled the piece of newspaper and began tearing it into tiny strips, capturing the edge of it beneath her carefully arched, deep-red manicure. The sound of the paper tearing sent a frisson of satisfaction down her spine. There was a delight in pulling apart Dash's face piece by painstaking piece. She imagined sinking her claws into his face herself, punishing him for making a fool out of her. Again. She dropped the pieces at her feet as she tore, grinding them into the linoleum with the heel of her pump.

The phone they'd installed for her trilled, and she ran to pick it up. Only someone she knew would have her direct line. "Hello," she answered.

"Joan, darling, I've been trying the hotel all morning."

It was Monty. *Shit.* He had to have seen the papers. She turned to Arlene and mouthed "It's Monty!" Arlene's face lit up like the sun before she turned back to her pages. That girl and her hopeless romanticism. She was going to get hurt one of these days.

Joan turned her attention back to her fiancé. He was probably phoning to call off their arrangement. She hadn't done a very good job thus far of appearing to be madly in love with him. Instead, she kept being caught in compromising positions with Dash Howard.

"Monty, sorry, I'm on set. We're about to film a scene."

"I know." There was a pause on the line as if he was deciding how much he should say. "Is everything all right up there?"

"Yes, it's…fine. Just Leda Price being Leda Price."

"I didn't think otherwise."

"Monty, what if you came up here? Then they could take pictures of us out on the town together and they'd have something better to focus on than me and my infuriating costar."

Monty chuckled. "He can't be all that bad."

"You have no idea." She sighed, the tone of a woman long suffering. "But what do you think? Could you come?"

"I don't see how. I'm only a few weeks away from starting a new picture, and I have so much preparation to do."

"But, Monty, I need you. We're supposed to be in this together." Had Arlene heard that? Joan eyed her, but her head was buried in the new pages she was writing.

"I know, but it's not good timing. And Jerry—"

Joan bit back a reply. Jerry Scott was a congenial star of Westerns at rival studio Mountain Pictures, Monty Smyth's former roommate—and the actual love of his life. When Monty had come to her with the suggestion that they get engaged to help deflect attention from his real relationship, she'd had no qualms about saying yes. They'd made this arrangement with their eyes wide open. A marriage of convenience. A union that would put her back on top of the Hollywood pyramid and ensure people stopped asking pesky questions about Monty and a series of images he'd taken with Jerry next to their shared swimming pool. But she wasn't giving up someone she loved in exchange for it. Monty, however, that was a different story. He was already doing so much for her. She couldn't expect more than that.

"No, I understand." She looked over at Arlene who was looking at her expectantly. "I miss you darling, that's all."

"Is Arlene sitting right there?"

"Yes."

A sudden knock at the door made her jump.

"Five minutes, Miss Davis."

Joan called back, "I'll be ready." She looked down, realizing she was still in nothing but her heels and her slip. She'd already spent the better part of the morning in hair and makeup, but when she'd got back to her trailer to find Arlene waiting with the paper and a cup of coffee, she'd forgotten to finish getting dressed. "Monty, I have to go. They're calling for me on set."

"I'm sorry, Joan. It's a bad time for me right now. But it'll be okay. Go out there and knock 'em dead."

Joan put the phone back on the receiver and sighed heavily, frustrated beyond measure. "God, I hate Dash Howard. Here I am supposed to be filming the first day of what could be my shot at an Oscar, and he's got me begging my fiancé for help and making a fool of myself, distracted and mixed up six ways from Sunday."

Arlene blinked back at her. "You weren't just saying that to Harry? About the Oscar? You really think so?"

Joan beamed at her. "Of course I do. I'm honored you wrote this script for me. It's the best Dash and I have ever had. Hell, you'll probably get nominated too."

Arlene blushed and started furiously typing something.

"I've never had a real women's picture before. Not like this. She's brave and she's independent and she's learning how to love, how to start over. She's a real woman. Not a facsimile of one."

"She's you," Arlene muttered.

Joan blushed. "No, she's not. She, she couldn't be... She believes in love. In the end."

Arlene bit her lip and peered at her, confusion in her eyes. "But you're in love with Monty."

Joan realized her mistake a moment too late. *Shit.* She wasn't doing a very good job keeping up appearances. And that was something she excelled at. "Yes, of course. I don't know what I was thinking. Dash and Leda have me all mixed up. I've got to get dressed, but let me see your pages."

Arlene tore them out of the typewriter and handed them to her as Joan licked her finger and paged through them. "Oh, you've given Dash's character a cabin? That will look incredible with the Sierras in the background. Your script was already flawless, but the location shooting will make this something truly special."

"Then..." Arlene began, but then she bit her lip and went to fetch Joan's skirt. "Never mind."

"Say it, Arlene, for heaven's sake. I can take it. It can't be worse than what Leda Price is peddling."

"Well, maybe in a roundabout way by causing this whole thing, Dash has done you a favor."

"Don't be ridiculous." Joan didn't like contemplating that idea. Dash Howard had caused her nothing but trouble, and he deserved a taste of his own medicine. Her eyes lit on a washboard thrown askance into the sink. It was old-looking, heavy steel. She placed her hand under it and weighed its heft. She could barely lift it. "Arlene, where did this come from?"

"It was a prop for the previous scene. Mr. Von Wild's assistant asked to leave it here, and I said you wouldn't mind."

No, she didn't mind. In fact, an idea was coming to her. A way to punish Dash for using her to get his picture in the paper. Today, they were filming a scene where his cowboy character was meant to help her city divorcée ford a stream by picking her up and carrying her over his shoulder. Arlene had only written it two nights ago, inspired by their well-publicized disembarking from the train.

Dash had rather enjoyed carrying her off that train two days ago, picking her up like she was light as a feather, but today wouldn't be so pleasant. "Quick, have you got any string or yarn on you?"

"Why, what are you—?" Joan watched Arlene's eyes go to the washboard, then back to her, then back to the sink. "Oh. No. Joan, you can't be serious."

"I am serious. How many pranks has he played on me? On our directors? It's his favorite thing. One could say I'm indulging him."

"I don't think trying to throw your leading man's back out is indulging him." Arlene crossed her arms, obviously determined not to engage in Joan's petty revenge. Well, fine, let Arlene be the bigger person. She wasn't accidentally married to the man.

Joan glared at her. "I won't seriously hurt him. He's twice my size. Just maybe embarrass him a little. Tit for tat. It's only fair."

Arlene eyed her with suspicion and muttered something that sounded an awful lot like "If I didn't know better, I'd say you were attracted to him."

Joan ignored her and her romantic fantasies. "Remember the water pistol? And the bathrobe? And the skunk!"

As Joan enumerated the pranks Dash had perpetrated against her over the last four years, Arlene broke into a smile. "As it happens, I did bring my knitting with me today."

Joan grinned broad and wide, nothing like the closemouthed smiles she fed the cameras. "Now that's more like it."

Arlene pulled a skein of heavy yarn from the bag on the small couch, while Joan heaved the washboard from the sink. "I think if we thread it through the handle, we can tie it to my waist and it will lie flat against my backside. Leda Price may call me flatter than the broad side of a barn, and stiffer too—but there's some advantage to having no ass."

Arlene quickly threaded the yarn through the handle, wrapping it around several times before fashioning a makeshift belt. Miraculously, it held. And Joan was able to squeeze her costume over it. It wasn't as smooth as she would've liked, but she hoped the director and Dash would be too self-consumed to notice until they were already rolling. That's all she needed. As she buttoned the tiny pearl at the top of her blouse, the production assistant banged on her door again. "They need you down at the water's edge, Miss Davis."

"I'll be out in a moment," she called back.

Arlene finished smoothing the back of her costume, adjusting the flounces of her jacket to conceal the bulky piece of metal hidden beneath Joan's skirt. She made a moue of disapproval and then opened the door, letting Joan pass.

Joan gingerly stepped from the trailer down to the dirt path, and her eyes caught on what was littering the walkway. Pebbles. And her skirt had pockets. She'd had enough of Dash Howard getting the best of her, catching her off guard and using it to his advantage. This time she'd be the one with the upper hand. As she picked her way down to the water's edge, she stopped here and there to pick up a stone, shoving them in her pockets until they were full.

Dash was already standing on the shoreline, his Levi's cuffed and rolled around his calves. She was struck by the fact that he had rather attractive legs. For a man. But the discomforting notion was blissfully dispelled from her mind when Fritz Von Wild, their director, barked at her, "Hurry it up!"

Von Wild was a gruff, no-nonsense Austrian with a reputation for a short temper. He was standing behind the camera in jodhpurs and a cap, looking exasperated. He sighed, putting on a good show of being the most long-suffering man in Hollywood, as she walked the last few feet down to the shore.

"Miss Davis, at last...we are ready for you," he grunted, Joan struggling to understand him between his low voice and thick Austrian accent.

Well, Von Wild and the crew might be ready for her. But there was no way Dash Howard was ready to face the wrath of Joan Davis.

Dash's toes were fucking freezing. The water here was pure snow runoff from the Sierra Nevada and he was cold. One of the grips,

Steve, was regaling him with stories about the little cabin he'd bought his family over in Truckee, and he tried to focus on that instead of the numbness in his feet. The joys of location shooting.

Joan had taken her sweet time sauntering down to the water, stopping every few moments on the path to pick up something. She was a consummate professional on set, if often cold and unyielding. So this was distinctly out of character. She was up to something.

He hoped she hadn't seen the morning papers yet. Every gossip rag from here to New York had been plastered with a photo of them descending from the train. It'd been a stupid mistake. Another in a long line of many when it came to him and Joan. But he'd genuinely been trying to help.

"Morning, Joanie," he called out. She hated his pet name for her, and he was rewarded with her peeved expression and a glint of something murderous in her eyes. Why did he enjoy bringing out the worst in her? It was perverse.

"Good morning, Mr. Howard. I trust you slept well. Or were you too busy taking calls from Leda Price?" she hissed.

"That's not fair. I would never sell you—us—out to Leda and you know it."

She squinted at him, playing at confusion. "Do I, though? Or do I actually know nothing about the man I've spent seven pictures starring opposite? The man who pulled a fast one on me on our first and only 'date.'" She gave the word aggressive air quotes. "The man who would be so foolish as to stamp and address an envelope containing a fake marriage certificate."

He inhaled and bit his tongue. She wanted a retort and he wouldn't give it to her. Because she was right. Joan didn't know him. Just not in the way she meant. She'd never cared to find out if there was more to him than a Hollywood playboy who used his fame and good looks to take a different cocktail waitress or starlet to his bed every night. He was beginning to wonder if there *was* more to him than that. He'd thought so, once. But that was before Hollywood. Before Dash and Davis. Before wild nights with Flynn. Before he'd let the only thing that truly mattered in his life walk out on him. Fine, let Joan think the worst of him. All he had to do was get through these six weeks, and then he could ask Harry for a clause in his contract to never work with her again. He doubted Joan would object.

"Are we done bickering? I would like to shoot the scene," called out Von Wild. Dash had heard the man was a tyrant, but he was thankful for someone who wouldn't indulge his and Joan's verbal warfare. They had a job to do. The script, for once, was actually pretty good, thanks to Arlene. Not to mention he was fairly certain he couldn't feel his toes anymore.

Joan turned and gave him her best megawatt smile. "Of course, Mr. Von Wild. Please excuse my costar's rudeness. I'm ready to begin whenever you are."

Dash resisted the urge to roll his eyes so far back in his head they got stuck there.

"Miss Davis, please go stand nearer Mr. Howard so we can get the dialogue. Then, he will pick you up and fling you over his shoulder—and he will cross the stream to the other side where another camera is waiting."

Joan approached him, but Dash watched warily as Von Wild whispered something to his assistant director and they laughed. It was a cold, cruel sound. He shuddered, knowing innately they'd said something unkind about Joan. It wasn't his place to protect her. Hell, he knew better than most that she probably deserved a few harsh words. But his gut roiled. Despite the fact that he would readily get into an argument with Joan, he only did so because he was provoked. Von Wild didn't know either of them from Adam.

Dash instead turned his attention to the woman in question, who was staring at him with a fiery intensity. She looked beautiful, her dark brunette hair coiffed around her, a stray curl springing up near her temple. Her pert little blouse and skirt bore a matching chevron pattern, and she wore sensible black pumps. Her backside looked rather lumpy, which was odd. Usually wardrobe did their job spotlessly. "You done primping and preening, Joanie? Because I'd rather not lose a toe today."

She looked down at his feet, and he was shocked to see a slight flicker of concern in her eyes. But then it was gone, replaced by the haughty mask he knew so well.

"Oh, I'm ready," she drawled, each word so long and pointed that cream would've curdled in her mouth. "Ready to kill two birds with one stone, in fact."

She smirked, and he was at a loss for words.

"Very well, let us begin. Rolling, sound, and action!" Von Wild bellowed.

The scene was early on in the picture. Joan's character, Carol Pearce, arrives in Reno late and attempts to hitchhike to the dude ranch where she's staying. But when she gets stranded in the mountains, she meets Joe, and he ends up bringing her back to his cabin, which requires forging the river.

Joan's entire demeanor shifted as she shook off the trappings of Joan Davis and became Carol Pearce. "Mr. Langland, how exactly do you intend on getting to your cabin?"

Dash smiled and pointed across the way. "It's over there beyond that outcropping of pine trees."

"Yes, and we are on this side of the river."

"Thought you said you were an avid swimmer, Mrs. Pearce. And I told you, call me Joe."

Joan's inner fire sparked to life and there was something new there, a devilish gleam in her eye. It wasn't what he'd imagined when he'd read the script pages that morning, but it worked. "That may be, but I'm not really dressed for the occasion."

"That's no trouble at all." With that, he leaned down to wrap his hands around her upper thighs, preparing to lift her over his shoulder. But something was wrong. Joan was heavy. Very heavy. He'd held her a few days ago on the train platform, and she'd been warm and soft. But now she was—stiff and cold? His fingers brushed against the back of her legs and he was startled to hear the rap of metal. Why, the little devil. She was playing a trick on him. She had something under her skirt. He suppressed a grin. Finally, she was trying to beat him at his own game. Doing something besides giving him the cold shoulder. He should be irritated and concerned for his health, but he was fucking delighted.

"Is something wrong?" yelled Von Wild from behind the camera.

"Mr. Howard seems to be having some trouble lifting me," Joan called out. "Perhaps he was a little too overzealous at the hotel bar last night." He glared up at her suggestion that he'd overindulge on the job, and she simpered back.

"You little minx," he hissed in her ear as he wrapped his arms more tightly around her. If he lifted from the knees instead of his back, he could avoid injury and execute the scene. So long as she didn't move too much. Who was he kidding? She was definitely going to move too much.

"No trouble, Von Wild. Just didn't expect the lady to be so heavy."

"Yes, Miss Davis has rather let herself go, I think," answered back Von Wild.

Dash stiffened. That hadn't been what he'd meant at all. "No, she's...she's lovely. I came at it from the wrong angle," he called back.

He looked up at Joan, whose devilish grin had been replaced by a look of hurt confusion. Damn it, she had just been playing a prank on him. Something he'd done a thousand times to her and to other directors. Now he'd opened her up to criticism and ridicule she didn't deserve. It was infuriating that she had him literally on his knees and somehow he was still the one who felt guilty.

"I've got it now. Let's go again."

"Back to one," yelled Von Wild.

Dash stood up and Joan had recovered herself, so they dove back into the dialogue. He tried to get a handle on her body, her weight displaced by all the extra bits and bobs she'd stuck to her person. In the struggle his palm wrapped around her ass. It didn't feel warm and inviting, like a peach in his hand, the way it had on the train platform. Instead, it clanged. Jesus, what had she put under her skirt?

"I always knew you were a hard ass, Joan, but this is a little ridiculous."

She clamped her lips together, and he was pleased to feel her body shake with laughter she refused to release. He pressed his shoulder into her thigh, trying to get leverage, and his face brushed against the pocket of her skirt. It was lumpy and hard, as if she'd stuffed it full of rocks. It suddenly hit him what she'd been stooping to pick up along her path to the river.

"I think you've put your brains in your pockets, Joanie," he muttered. His mouth was hidden from the camera by her body, and she was facing away from it, allowing them to hurl insults freely without disrupting the scene.

"What are you talking about? I haven't got—" But she stopped, realizing what he was implying. "I have not got rocks for brains," she retorted, clenching her teeth together, barely allowing each word to escape.

"Ah, but you admit you put rocks in your pockets, you little brat." He couldn't keep a hint of mirth from his voice.

"I am not a brat," she seethed.

A twang he knew she fought hard to suppress seeped into her perfect mid-Atlantic dialect. That always happened when she was angry. And he couldn't help but find it the teensiest bit adorable. "I'm giving you a taste of your own medicine. You set us up at the station."

He grimaced, all glee evaporating with the accusation. "I didn't, I swear. I know what it looked like, but you have to believe me."

"Is there a problem?" bellowed Von Wild.

"No," they both called out in unison. Not wanting to face the director's wrath, they scrambled to continue the scene. Dash bent low, using his knees to lift her with all of her added weight. But at the same time, she scrambled to jump into his arms, seeming to want to get the scene over with.

She was now successfully draped over his shoulder, her face pressing into his back. He was supposed to stand and walk across the river, a simple end to the scene and a show of Carol and Joe's immediate connection. But she was extremely heavy, and he realized a moment too late that he was falling backwards. Right into the shallow pool of ice-cold water. He heard Joan shriek before he heard the splash, followed by his own plunge into the river. Joan was splashing and screaming, thrashing in the water. He sat with his arms crossed in the foot of water, chuckling as she flailed about.

She was struggling, the weight of whatever she'd tied under her skirt keeping her down. But she wasn't in any real danger with the water so calm and so shallow. If she'd only stop her caterwauling, she'd come to the same conclusion.

Vaguely, he heard Von Wild yell "Cut" from the shore, but

it was hard to hear above Joan's yelps. He shook his head at her, unable to suppress a broad grin and a deep-throated laugh. The woman was ridiculous. At last she stopped moving, realizing she was sitting on the river bottom and in no danger whatsoever. She glared at him, spitting a spout of water from her mouth. "*That* you definitely did on purpose."

He shook his head. The audacity of this woman. "No, I could've managed if you didn't jump on me like a cat in heat. And it would've been fine if you hadn't tied, well, whatever it is you've got under that skirt."

She crossed her arms and sulked. "A washboard."

He broke out into peals of laughter, a booming laugh from deep in his gut. And soon she was joining him, carried away by the absurdity of the moment. He couldn't resist lifting his arm and sending a playful splash in her direction. He generated more force than he intended and a large wave of water crested toward her and smacked her in the face.

"Now that, *that,* I did on purpose." He grinned.

She scrunched up her nose and glared at him, but it didn't last long before the scrunch became a grin and a girlish giggle exploded from her mouth.

She looked like a drowned rat, only rats didn't have a cupid's bow mouth and an irresistible little crinkle between their eyes.

CHAPTER 7

SPLASHING AROUND

Dash and Davis can't seem to keep their hands off each other. In these exclusive photographs we've nabbed from the set of their new picture *Reno Rendezvous,* the two seem to be having quite the underwater love fest. Director Fritz Von Wild refused to comment, but we have it on good authority that this incident disrupted the entire day of shooting. It seems Dash and Davis are taking their last weeks of marriage to heart. Our source tells us that they were laughing so hard, it took a full twenty minutes to separate them. Meanwhile, Monty Smyth still cannot be found. Could their marriage be all wet before it's even begun? Never fear, *What Price Hollywood?* is ready to dive in and learn more.

—xoxo, Leda

Joan snarled as she listened to Arlene finish reading Leda Price's latest column and stared out the window of her suite at the Hotel Riverside. They'd been here filming for a week already, and she'd prayed that somehow their little incident on set would stay out of the papers. That being up here away from the studio would keep them out of the spotlight. But if anything, they were only more exposed.

It was ridiculous. There was nothing romantic about it. She'd been trying to punish Dash for creating more fodder for Leda Price, and it only resulted in them serving up more gossip on a silver platter. All because she'd had the good humor to laugh at an absurd situation. It had felt good to laugh with Dash. To enjoy his company. To do something other than bicker. Like the early days they'd spent together on set making those first two films, having a good time instead of suspecting the worst of each other. She should've known that would get twisted around into something it wasn't. What a mess.

The neon lights below blinked on and off, taunting her. She could just make out the archway in the distance that boldly proclaimed "Reno: The Biggest Little City in the World." One thing was for sure—it wasn't big enough for both her and Dash Howard. If they kept up like this, she'd murder him by the end of the week. On the bright side, maybe they'd make a picture about it.

"Call Harry now."

"Joan, it's dinnertime. He won't answer." Arlene was the most considerate person Joan had ever met, and the most loyal. "Don't let Leda get to you. You know she's still mad you didn't give her the exclusive on the engagement. And she really does seem to have it out for you."

"I don't care. Call him."

Arlene looked hurt and picked up the phone. Joan instantly regretted it. She never snapped at her assistant. Hell, Arlene really wasn't even her assistant anymore. She hadn't been in a long time. She was her best friend. Joan had let Arlene into her life because she'd recognized a part of herself when she'd discovered her friend crying in a bathroom on the lot over something unspeakably rude a director with wandering hands had said to her.

That weepy girl in the toilet stall was a girl with a dream, a girl with the talent and the grit and determination to overcome anything Hollywood would throw at her. Joan had offered her a job on the spot. But somewhere along the way, they'd become friends. Joan didn't let people in easily, but Arlene had burrowed into her heart so swiftly and so silently, she simply couldn't imagine life without her at this point. She shouldn't be snapping at her as if this was still a business arrangement.

Besides, Arlene was meant to be in Reno to be on hand to make changes to the script since the new setup and location had been put into place so last-minute. Not to do Joan's bidding. Joan knew that after this film was released, Arlene would be on her way to becoming the next Frances Marion or Dorothy Arzner.

That's when Joan realized with a sinking feeling that maybe Arlene was only her friend because she paid her to stick around. She tried to shake off the thought. It was so absurd it was laughable. Arlene wasn't like that. But it was so hard for Joan to trust anyone, especially anyone in this business, entirely. She held everybody at arm's length. It was safer that way.

This was why she needed Monty. Love and affection couldn't be trusted. But a mutually beneficial arrangement with a healthy amount of respect, that was safe. Then she'd be back on top again, loved by the only people that mattered—the moviegoing public. She wasn't going to let Dash Howard's antics and Leda Price's gossipmongering stand in the way of that.

"Hello, Norma, it's Arlene," she heard her friend tell Harry's longtime housekeeper. "Yes, we saw. Yes, that's why we're calling. Joan wants to talk to Harry. No, it can't wait."

Joan crossed the room and sat beside Arlene on the bed. "Give me the phone."

Arlene looked at her pityingly and handed it over. She wanted to ignore that look, the one that said Arlene knew what Joan was doing and didn't agree. But Harry had promised this change of venue would fix everything, and so far it was only making things worse. She needed Monty here so the press could focus on something besides Dash's blatant attempts to make them a spectacle.

"Norma, hi, it's Joanie. I know, I know. Listen, I don't care if Harry's entertaining the Queen of England. I have to talk to him. This is not what we agreed on. When this is over, I'll send you to Mexico, but I have to talk to Harry right this minute. Yes, all expenses paid. Acapulco, Cancún, whatever you want, darling. Just get Harry on the line."

She drummed her fingers on the nightstand, the edges of her perfect bloodred manicure chipping away alongside her nerves. The chenille bedspread was hot underneath her silk dress, its ridges biting into her skin through the thin fabric and the protective layer of her slip. As she waited what felt like hours for Norma to go and fetch the head of the studio, a bead of sweat dripped down her back, slick and wet against the ivory silk. The lacy flounces on her Letty Lynton–style neckline and sleeves suddenly suffocated her.

She hadn't clawed her way back to relevancy and given herself over to a man she didn't love to have it all blow up in less than two weeks. Harry had always had a soft spot for her, even after she'd been declared box-office poison. And he wouldn't want *Reno Rendezvous* to be DOA either. That was simply bad business. He would fix this. He had to. For both their sakes.

Finally, the gravelly, paternalistic voice came on the line.

"Hello? Joan, are you there? Make this snappy. I've got Louis B. Mayer in the living room."

"Screw Mr. Mayer, he's never made you a cent," Joan muttered. "We've got a problem, Harry, and it's spelled L-E-D-A. That exclusive about my divorce wasn't enough for her, it seems. She sicced photographers on me and Dash when we were getting off the train on Friday. Now she's got a source on set sharing behind-the-scenes details about us that don't have a lick of truth to them."

"I saw that. You two look very cozy without any help from gossip reporters."

A spot behind Joan's left eye throbbed. This was what she didn't need: Harry gleefully feeding these nonsensical rumors when Dash couldn't keep his hands to himself.

"You know Dash can't resist an opportunity to fake chivalry, Harry. It was a misunderstanding. I slipped on the train, and we ended up in a...compromising position."

"On the contrary, I'd say you ended up in a boffo position. With pictures like that, crowds will be lining up to see your next film."

Joan sighed and gave Arlene a look of despair. Arlene pointedly kicked her feet up onto the window seat and buried her head in the book she was reading. Fittingly, a pulp novel about Reno divorcées finding love again. Well, she couldn't blame Arlene. They couldn't fix this from a suite at the Hotel Riverside.

"No, they'll be lining up to see the next Dash and Davis picture and to speculate about whether we're making whoopee, and this entire charade has only made things worse. Since when are two costars not allowed to laugh with each other when something ridiculous happens without people assuming it means wedding bells?"

"To be fair, Joan, the bells have come and gone. You're already married."

"That's not what I meant and you know it."

"I do. But you can't blame me for finding it odd that you'd laugh with and not at Dash Howard."

Joan bit her lip and resisted the urge to scream into the phone. There was only one thing that would fix this, and she needed Harry to make it happen. "I'll still be box-office poison if this entire thing ends only with me as the first—and likely last—ex-Mrs. Howard. Announcing my engagement to Monty brought me goodwill that had nothing to do with Dash, and you're both ruining it. I need you to do something for me." Joan steeled herself. The thought soured in her mouth before she could even say it. "I need you to promise Leda she can have the exclusive for my wedding to Monty if she'll lay off."

There was a pause on the other end of the line. "You'd give that conniving witch the satisfaction?"

"I don't see any other way to get through the next few weeks in peace. She could do much worse damage if she wanted to."

There was a pause on the other end of the line. Harry knew exactly what she was referring to. Her deepest secret. He'd taken care of it. Buried it. Multiple times. But all the same, the threat always remained. He coughed. "I could sue her for that. She agreed the studio would give her money and a different scandal and she'd never breathe a word."

"Yeah, well, you'd be cleaning up in court and my career would be blown to smithereens. We have to fix this, Harry. Before she spins out of control. We need her to stay out of our hair."

"Fine. Done. I'll give her a call tomorrow."

"And then..." She paused, knowing this one would be harder, because it could interrupt production on another project. "To make sure the press stops obsessing over me and Dash, I need you to send Monty up here. I asked him myself, but he insists he can't because of his production schedule." She neglected to mention Jerry. "But if you send him with your blessing, he'll have to come."

"I can't."

"Oh, come now, Harry, I've made your studio a lot of money. I've made you very rich. I should think the least you could do is send my fiancé to visit me when the press is determined to paint me as a harlot married to another man."

"Would you give me a moment to explain?" Harry huffed. Joan could hear a booming voice calling for her studio boss on the other end of the line. "The cigars are in the bottom left desk drawer!"

"Thank you, but I don't smoke."

"Not you, Joan, damn it." Joan couldn't help but giggle. Harry was a tyrant, but she loved him. When Harry had plucked her out of obscurity and offered her a contract for $75 a week, he'd not only changed her life but also become a sort of surrogate father.

Joan had heard horror stories about other studio heads, tales of abuse and drug addiction fed by the top brass. Harry was controlling, to be sure, and he expected the best from his stars. But he was never cruel. Never laid a hand on her. And he'd helped her bury a secret that could kill her career. His kindness had saved her more times than she could count, and she needed to call on it once more.

"Harry, I am begging you to send Monty here. God knows what he's thinking after seeing that article. I've tried calling him three times already, and he won't answer."

"Joan, the reason I can't send Monty there is because he's already on his way."

The sinking feeling in the pit of her stomach reversed course, sending a flurry of butterflies to her heart. It wasn't going to be a total disaster after all.

"Thank you, Harry. I—thank you. Send Mr. Mayer my best."

"But it wasn't… I didn't—"

Joan missed whatever Harry was trying to say, hanging up

the phone as a wave of relief rushed over her. Monty was coming. Their plan could get back on track. They would work it out, take some cheesecake photos in Reno's nightclubs, and all would be well. Reporters would swarm them as Hollywood's newest item, and Dash and Davis would be all but forgotten.

She'd been cooped up in her hotel suite all day, hiding out from reporters and stewing about the last forty-eight hours. She looked past Arlene sitting in the window seat and took in the flashing lights of Reno outside her window with fresh eyes. She should be out there enjoying her first trip outside of Los Angeles in years. She ran to the closet, flouncing the ruffles around her neck and on her sleeves until they regained their shape.

"Where are you going?" Arlene called out without looking up from her book.

"Out. I can't stay in this room another minute." Arlene started to close the pages of her book, but Joan stopped her. "You don't have to come, Arlene. I'm a big girl. I can take care of myself."

"I'll believe that when I see it," Arlene muttered before returning to the book. Joan ran to the mirror and adjusted her hair, twisting her mahogany curls around her finger to restore their springiness. She affixed a cloche hat to her head and pinned it in place.

"Don't forget a wrap. We are in the mountains. It's cold at night, even if it's hot as Hades in here," Arlene called after her. Joan thanked her, grabbing a fur stole from the closet, and then slipped out her hotel door. To hell with the press. Monty was coming and that would fix everything. For now, she needed a drink.

CHAPTER 8

DASH HOWARD SAT AT THE WALNUT BAR, POLISHED TO within an inch of its life, and surveyed the smoke-filled room at Harold's Club.

He'd wanted out of the Riverside, away from the barrage of press flooding the lobby. So he'd slipped through the hotel kitchen and wandered down Virginia Street and found this cozy little casino, new to downtown Reno, and snuck inside. Here, he could hide behind the clouds of cigarette smoke and gamblers who were more interested in going on a heater than they were in a movie star. He'd walked through the doors and felt cloaked in a rare anonymity. Ignoring the siren call of the blackjack table, he'd made his way to the bar.

Dash knocked back another slug of Scotch and tried to block out the memories of his blunder on the train. The press had moved on to this new moment on set, but they'd have less fodder to spin that into something if not for those photographs at the station.

He'd been trying to help her. Joan was so damn stubborn all the time. If she'd only let him get the bag down for her, the incident never would have happened. He sighed. At the nightclubs, with legions of women on his arm, it was easy to forget what a cock-up he was. When he was being what the studio wanted, what the fans wanted, he could block out that little voice in his head that told him he'd never be good enough for anyone. So long as he stayed on track and drowned out the last of the whispers with a little booze, he could keep it together—be more mirage than man.

But Joan somehow saw right through all that. Always had. She never blinked at putting him in his place. Unlike him, she was the perfect movie star, every inch what she promised to be. He wondered what it'd be like to be the kind of man Joan Davis would marry. A guy she'd be proud to have on her arm at a premiere. Someone who wouldn't make her grimace every time their names were linked in the press. She wanted someone like Monty Smyth: suave, respectable, and deeply talented. Not a guy Harry Evets plucked out of cornfed obscurity, a clumsy hick that the studio had somehow packaged as rugged and charming in a con that was so successful, Dash half believed it himself when he squinted.

But it wasn't his ill-advised timing on the train platform he was trying to forget so much as the way Joan had felt in his arms. When he'd picked her up, like a groom carrying his new bride across the threshold, it'd felt good. Right. Like they should be doing this on the porch of a Spanish bungalow back in Los Angeles. His palm had been under her knees, but even through his sport coat he could sense the rise and fall of her legs as they rose to meet at her pert bottom that he'd got an eyeful of on the train. Leda always mocked Joan for having no ass, but he'd like to write a letter to her editor asking them to correct the record.

Joan had been wearing wide-legged trousers, which meant she'd foregone a slip, leaving only one thin layer of fabric between them. He'd held her in his arms on no less than six pictures, but this had felt different. More tantalizing because it was real and not some characters they were playing. There'd been a time when he'd thought that it could be real. That they could be something special to each other. More than costars. He was so damned tired of fighting with her.

He wanted every day to be like that one in the river—fun, easy, spirited. But would she let him ever clear the air and lay his cards on the table? What if he went to her hotel room right now, apologized for everything—the Cocoanut Grove, the marriage certificate, the train—and asked for a fresh start? He would make her listen and then maybe these six weeks could pass peaceably. They could be on the same team, instead of at each other's throats, for the first time in four years. *Yeah, right, maybe when pigs fly.*

He glanced across the casino and watched a beautiful brunette wrapped in a fur stole stride through the glass doors at the front entrance. Through the blaring lights of the slot machines and haze of the room, it was difficult to make out her face. But he liked what he saw. Not just the gentle slope of her curves in the dress she had on, but the way she carried herself. Like she owned the place. Maybe this would be the woman who could make him forget the way Joan Davis had felt in his arms, the way her laugh had awakened something in him he'd spent half a decade trying to kill. He caught the bartender's eye and waved him over, requesting a refill on his Scotch and ordering a gin stinger for the lady. Something about the dame reminded him of gin: smooth, refreshing, but with a bite.

Dash watched the bartender as he worked, studying the deft twists of his wrists as he poured ingredients in a shaker and then poured them into a chilled coupe glass. He assiduously avoided turning around to follow the brunette's journey across the casino floor. Movie star or not, he wouldn't stare at a woman like she was prey he was tracking. So he waited—ready to surprise her with a cocktail.

He accepted the drinks, nodding when the bartender offered to add them to his tab, and was about to turn to slide the stinger deftly to his right, leaving it in front of the open barstool, when the last voice on earth he wanted to hear came floating across the bar.

"Jesus, Mary, and Joseph, this has got to be a sick joke," crowed Joan, and he winced turning to face her, noticing with dismay that *she* was the attractive brunette he'd been eyeing. He didn't want to think too hard about that spark of attraction he'd felt when he didn't know who she was. "Can't I go anywhere without bumping into your ugly mug? What's a girl gotta do to get some privacy in this cowboy town?"

"I've been here for hours, so if you want to get technical, you're the one invading my privacy," Dash replied. But he didn't want to cause her any more trouble. She might never let him apologize, might never listen to him. But he could refuse to engage. So he downed his Scotch, took a wad of cash from his pocket, and threw it on the bar before turning to go.

"I bought you a drink," he muttered as he passed. He noticed with pleasure that her eyes went wide when she looked at it sweating on the bar.

"Wait."

He stilled, not wanting to turn to face her. He was a cad, yes, but he didn't want to give her the satisfaction of knowing that he was well aware of it.

"Don't you think we've given the press enough fodder?"

"Yes. I mean, no. I mean, how'd you know gin stingers are my favorite?" Her voice was tremulous, suspicious, but also hopeful? He had no idea what that meant.

Upon hearing the question, he realized with horror that perhaps the reason he'd thought this woman was a match for this cocktail was because it was Joan's drink of choice. Her strength, her don't-mess-with-me attitude had attracted rather than repelled him when he didn't know it was her. It reminded him of how things were between them before he—and Leda—had ruined everything at the Cocoanut Grove. The promise of what could've been. He could tell her he knew the drink was her favorite because it's what she'd ordered that night and he'd never forgotten. But he didn't want to bring that up. He wanted to leave her to drink in peace. He'd find another bar. One watering hole was as good as any other. And he didn't have the energy to fight with her tonight.

"I didn't. I ordered it for someone else." She didn't need to know that the someone else and she were one and the same.

"Not even in Reno seventy-two hours and already you've found yourself a date," she scoffed. "Well, I suppose I shouldn't be surprised. She stood you up, then?"

Dash turned to face her at last and gave her a weak smile that didn't reach his eyes. "Something like that. Good night, Miss Davis." He plopped his fedora on top of his head and fingered the brim as he said goodbye.

"Wait."

"Not done with me, are you?" He'd drunk enough to fell a man who wasn't used to heavy carousing on the nightly, and he preferred not to have his liquor-soaked haze punctured by truths he'd rather not face.

"No, I just… Damn you, Dash Howard, you make everything so impossible. All I wanted to say was—" She took a breath like it was a monumental effort. "You should stay. There's no reporters here. Everyone here is more concerned with cards and dice than Dash and Davis. Don't leave on my account."

It was the softest she'd been to him since the Cocoanut Grove. And so, for some inexplicable reason, he found himself removing his hat, running his hand through his black curls, and sitting back down beside her. She removed her stole and draped it across the high-backed bar chair, and a flare of want rushed through him at the sudden sight of her neck delicately draped in lacy ruffles.

"Are you certain you can deign to be seen with me, Miss Davis?" he drawled. "I do have quite the reputation." She lifted her eyebrows, in assent or annoyance he couldn't tell, and sipped from her drink. Damn it, he wasn't doing very well with his promise not to provoke her.

"I don't know anyone else here. I'd rather not drink alone."

"You should. It's good for your digestion." He winked.

"Would you like another drink?" she asked, suddenly all politeness. "It's only fair seeing as you bought me one."

"No, thank you. Maybe a tonic and lime. I've had enough."

That time her perfectly arched eyebrows lifted in what he knew was surprise. "Dash Howard exhibiting restraint. How the mighty have fallen."

She brought her glass to her mouth and sipped, staring up at him through hooded eyes as if she was trying to assess something in him. He wondered briefly if her lips would taste like the crème de menthe that gave the cocktail its distinctive flavor. But that wasn't what he asked her next.

"Why do you hate me so much?" he blurted out.

She blinked at him, owlish in her surprise. "I don't hate you." She set her glass on the bar and turned to face him. "I hate what you stand for. What you've allowed yourself to become."

"And what is that supposed to mean? I fail to see the difference."

She rolled her eyes and scoffed, whispering something that sounded suspiciously like "Men!" under her breath.

"I hate that everything in life comes easy to you because you're a man. I hate that without your name next to mine on the marquee, I'm box-office poison and you're an Oscar winner. I hate that I'm not allowed to make a bad picture without being branded with that ridiculous term, while you are granted leeway you have never once earned. And most of all, I hate that the entire world, yourself included, expected me to swoon at the sight of you. You pulled the wool over my eyes for a while. Things were good on those first two pictures. Good enough to make me believe you were different. But in the end, you were the same as the rest of them, thinking I was a pretty girl who could be a boost to your career. A pretty girl who almost fell for your act, and for you, even though I'd told myself I'd never be that stupid. It's a good act, after all, one good enough to make you a star. But we are professional partners, nothing more."

"I didn't expect you to swoon at the sight of me." Jesus, Joan was turning him sentimental. Where was Dash Howard, tall, dark, and handsome? He could use more of that guy's chutzpah right about now. He cleared his throat. "I'll admit women tend to find me easy on the eyes, but I never wanted anything from you, Joan—except a scene partner who didn't treat me like I was something nasty she found on the bottom of her shoe. You've always thought me beneath you."

"If you recall, I only started treating you that way after you ambushed me at the Cocoanut Grove. Up until then, I thought you might be a real partner, someone I could rely on. Not another man who saw me as a stepping-stone to what he really wanted. Silly me."

They'd never talked about that night. She'd made it clear it was off-limits, and he wasn't going to waste his breath apologizing to someone who wouldn't listen. He'd steered clear of it tonight once already, but he supposed when one was accidentally married and seeking a divorce, nothing was off the table anymore.

He wished he hadn't turned down her offer for another drink. This conversation would go down a lot smoother if he was corked. "You want to blame someone, blame Harry. He set the whole thing up and told me if I didn't go out with you and play it up for the cameras, I'd be washed up in this town quicker than I could say 'Jack Robinson.'"

"So why not try to work with me instead of manipulate me? You think I didn't know by then how to play the studio's little game, give them exactly what they want without ever giving up a piece of myself?"

Dash didn't know how to tell her that was a lesson he had yet to learn. And the part about Leda, how she'd pegged him for a sucker too… Joan didn't need to know that. He had walked right into a trap designed to launch Leda's career and led Joan straight into it too by accident. But it didn't matter. Joan was still talking. Faster now.

"Why'd you get cozy in the back booth instead of sticking to Harry's script? You made me believe—" She stopped and appeared to find something very interesting in the bottom of her glass.

"I made you believe what? That we could be something? That it could maybe be more than a publicity stunt? Don't tell me you didn't feel something that night too. That you hadn't felt the chemistry between us on those first two pictures and wondered what could happen if it wasn't just make-believe for a camera." He sucked in a breath and held it without realizing, needing to hear that he hadn't imagined things.

She blushed. It gave her cheeks a rosy glow that was inviting even here in the smoky haze of the casino. But she rolled her shoulders back and squinted at him, something steely in her gaze. "No. I can honestly say no. I never wondered that. I would never let myself wonder something so foolish. So we're back at our original problem, which is that you expected me and every other dame you've ever met to swoon at the sight of you. Well, not me, buster. Never me. But I was disappointed you lived down to expectations instead of laying your cards on the table. Because you made me believe you might be the one leading man in this town who'd give it to me straight."

"When have you ever given me the chance?"

"I don't give second chances. That's one thing a woman in Hollywood never gets. So why should I dole them out?"

"So, what was I supposed to do after that? Accept your ice queen demeanor? I can't work like that, Joan. I need something real from you, even if I have to draw it out of you."

"Even if you have to bamboozle me into a marriage, you mean?"

He had no response to that. But if there was ever a moment to tell her he was sorry, this was it. Only moments before she'd arrived, he'd imagined storming back to her room and making her listen. Making her see that things could be good between them. Or if not good, at least cordial. He'd dismissed it as impossible. But here she was, providing him the perfect opening and he'd had enough to drink to loosen his tongue.

To tell her he was sorry. That he'd had fun with her on set yesterday; that he liked her when she was being playful instead of holding him at arm's length. That this, being real with each other at a bar, was preferable to pretending the other did not exist. Could they let bygones be bygones and have more of that from now on?

"Joan, I'm sorry, truly." She choked a little on her drink, and he realized then what she thought of him. Sure, it was an image he'd worked hard to sell, but he couldn't bear her believing he was a womanizing drunkard who thought only of himself.

"For what?"

"All of it. The Cocoanut Grove. Trying to get a rise out of you with that marriage certificate. For the train. I didn't mean to do it. I know you think I set you up, but it was spectacularly bad timing."

She didn't say anything, but continued to sip from her drink and peer at him, seeming to search for a sign he was being disingenuous. This was impossible. Why had he even tried? He sighed and grabbed his hat. "Go back to hating me in peace. I'll leave you with your drink."

She laid a hand on his upper arm as he stood to leave, stilling him. Then she waved at the bartender, nodded in Dash's direction, and held up two fingers, the universal signal for "Make it a double."

While the bartender poured his drink, she sipped at hers and refused to meet his gaze. "You confuse coldness for hatred. I don't hate you. Hate requires passion, and I'm incapable of such an inconvenient emotion. Unless the script calls for it."

"No one's that good an actress," he sighed.

Her eyes glinted, and her lips pursed as she took a surreptitious gulp of her cocktail. She pretended it was no different from the previous sips, but he watched as she struggled to swallow, a bead of liquid resting on her pouting, bee-stung lower lip. It filled his head with the filthiest of thoughts and he wondered if he really was drunk. Maybe the altitude had affected him. There was no other explanation for his sudden desire to ravish her.

"That's easy for you to say. You fall in and out of love every other week."

He winced and debated telling her the truth. That he wined and dined women because the studio and the public expected it of him. But fall in love with these women? The idea was laughable. Having a revolving door of starlets on his arm and in his bed was better than facing the truth. That he was only a plaything for idle hands. A warm body in a cold bed.

"You know that the papers never print anything worth reading about us." There, that was a start. It wasn't much. But it was more honest than they'd been with each other in years. She looked him up and down, as if she was sizing up whether he was serious, before finally settling into the cherry-stained high-back chair.

"So all those women you parade in and out of the Tropicana are your friends, then? Or do you have a big family? Lots of sisters?" She winked at him, teasing him. Usually, he would've taken that as a cruel jab at his pride, but something was different. A strange intimacy had settled between them. So he took the chair beside her and really looked at her for perhaps the first time.

He noticed a crease between her brows he'd never seen before, one that looked more the result of worry than age. Her warm, glittering eyes held a sadness in them he had never noticed. He was seized by a sudden desire to smooth that brow, to take her and hold her and promise her everything would be all right. But that was not what she wanted. Not in a million years.

"Something like that," he finally answered. And then he remembered Monty. How could she say she wasn't able to feel strong emotion? She loved him! So much so that she needed a divorce as soon as possible to marry the man. "Besides, you're not incapable of passion, Joan. You're engaged to Monty and the papers assure me you're crazy about each other."

She gave him a weak smile and parroted his words back to him, "I thought we'd already agreed that the papers never print anything worth reading about us."

CHAPTER 9

JOAN REALIZED WHAT SHE'D SAID A MOMENT TOO LATE. Damn it, Dash Howard had made her let her guard down. Why was he so good at that? So infernally disarming? She'd admitted something she didn't want anyone to know—least of all her costar who also happened to be her husband by some ridiculous twist of fate.

Dash stared back at her in surprise, and she was stunned that he genuinely seemed concerned. She'd fully expected him to crow over her admission. But he didn't. Instead, he laid his hand on her knee, carefully glancing around the room to make sure no one was watching them.

She followed his gaze, taking in the line of roulette tables noisily clattering victory or failure to the vultures gathered around them. She and Dash were alone together. In a crowded room. Much to her dismay, the thought of it sent a thrill rushing through her and her heart began to race, matching the accelerated clacking of the ball in the roulette wheel.

He spoke, breaking this spell between them and she pulled her hand back, reaching for her refreshed drink. "You don't mean that, Joan. You're just tired. Don't let Leda, or me for that matter, get to you. You love Monty and you're going to marry him."

He was giving her an out. She should agree and gush about Monty, but she was finding it hard to keep up the charade tonight.

Focusing intently on her drink, she spoke, unable to meet his eyes. "What is love, anyway? Look at the poor, sad fools all over this town." She gestured wildly at the room, the drunken laughter and raucous gambling rather disproving her point. "They believed in love once, and where did it get them? To a two-bit ranch town waiting for a divorce."

She paused before adding, "You've called me an ice queen." He winced, as if he regretted all the times she'd overheard him muttering about her on a set. But, well, he was right, wasn't he? "Maybe I am. But being warm is dangerous. Warmth is inviting, and it leaves you vulnerable. I refuse to ever leave myself vulnerable. I don't think I could be even if I tried. I've gotten too good at being hard."

She said this all in a rush, spilling her guts as if she'd suddenly turned on a faucet only to find the water main had broken. The booze and the strange familiarity that had sprung up between them were having an intense effect on her. She tensed, waiting for Dash to laugh or, worse, mock her. But he didn't. Instead, he stared at her very solemnly.

"I understand perfectly."

"How could you?" she blurted out, then caught herself. "I didn't mean that. It's just that romance seems to come so easy for you. I've always resented that."

He grinned, the megawatt movie star smile that had been plastered across the sides of buildings around the country lighting up their corner of the room. She'd never noticed how perfect his teeth were before. No doubt the result of careful orthodontic work at the behest of the studio.

"Now we're getting somewhere. So you *do* hate me."

She almost choked on her drink. "Not hate, no, but maybe resent. Envy." That last bit had been hard to admit.

He chuckled and swizzled ice around in his glass, before sliding a piece into his mouth and letting it lazily swirl around. She found herself suddenly jealous of the piece of ice. Perhaps it was time to stop drinking. She hadn't thought that way about Dash in four years. She'd promised herself she never would again.

"What's so funny?"

"Us. Agreeing on something without even realizing it. I resent Dash Howard too."

Mere hours ago, she would've laughed at that. Thought it was ridiculous. But something in his tone suggested he was deadly serious. She peered at him. "What do you mean?"

"You promise you won't laugh? Or storm off? That you'll listen?" She thought of all the times he'd tried to talk to her and how she'd given him the cold shoulder. Determined to think the worst of him and never give him an inch to prove otherwise. But they were stuck here, together whether she liked it or not, for five more weeks. Maybe it was time she finally listened to Dash Howard.

"Scout's honor." She held up two fingers in the pledge and then for extra measure crossed her heart.

He swallowed, and she could tell he was weighing what to say. "To hell with it," she heard him mutter. "The truth is everyone wants Dash Howard, the movie star. No one wants Dashiell, the hick kid from Ohio whose first wife taught him to walk and talk and paid for a brand-new version of him only to decide the new coat of paint wasn't good enough, so she ran out on him and never looked back. Ever since, anyone who's got close enough to know the real me has realized they've been sold a bill of goods."

"And here I thought I was your first wife," she replied, striving for a drollness she did not feel. She'd been trying to cheer him up with a joke, but instead he only looked more melancholy, a sad, faraway look coming into his eyes. He laughed, but it was devoid of mirth. A short, halting huff that sent a chill down her spine. Perhaps Dash Howard wasn't the golden, untouchable King of Hollywood she thought he was.

"I hate to disillusion you, Joan, but you're hardly the first person to realize I was a chintzy proposition. Though I suppose you've known from the beginning, and it was me who's put us both in this position. For that, I am truly sorry."

Dash was admitting his faults, taking responsibility for the mess he'd made. In her experience, men in Hollywood never apologized. Never owned up to their mistakes. And here was the King of Hollywood finally letting the buck stop with him. It should be cause for celebration. She should be flagging down the bartender for a glass of champagne. But instead, there was only gnawing guilt in the pit of her stomach. She didn't like being wrong about things. And she was starting to worry she'd been wrong about him. Starting to think that the only reason they hadn't had this conversation earlier was because she had never allowed him to begin it. There was only one way to find out.

"Do you want to talk about her?" she muttered, swirling the dregs of her drink around in her glass as she followed the lazy whirlpool it created.

He winced. "Who? Josephine, you mean?"

She turned and held his gaze, her eyes darting to his mouth, the pencil-thin mustache that sat atop his infuriatingly inviting lips. "Sometimes it helps to talk about these things. Especially the things the studio would prefer the world never know," she mumbled. Lord knew she had plenty of skeletons in her closet.

Dash didn't say a word. He picked up his hat. She should've known it was too much to ask a he-man like the strapping Dash Howard to willingly discuss his feelings. She wasn't wrong after all.

He cocked the hat low on his head so it shadowed his eyes, concealing him from nosy passersby. She expected him to walk out without so much as a good night. But instead, he extended a hand to her. "Let's go for a walk."

Much to her own shock, she found herself taking it. Warm, callused hands that belied his movie-star status closed around hers, and they skipped out into the crisp evening mountain air and ambled toward the riverside.

They strolled down the walkway that lined the backside of the hotels and casinos that dotted Virginia Street, the heart of Reno's downtown. They were bathed only in the soft moonlight and the twinkling stars she could make out above the neon glare of the busy nightlife that bustled beyond their reach. They walked for a time in silence. She was startled to find it easy and companionable.

Finally, he stopped and looked out at the shadows of the snowcapped mountains in the distance. "Josephine was my acting coach," he started, as if he'd made up his mind to tell her the story. "When I was wranglin' horses in a traveling show, we passed through Texas. Sometimes I performed with the rough riders, and Josephine caught one of those shows in Houston. She saw something in me. A pliable dummy, I suppose. She was older by quite a lot, and wiser. Or so I thought. She created Dash Howard out of a lump of corn-fed clay. She shortened my name, got my hair restyled, my teeth straightened, taught me to speak in my lower register, and put me on a strict diet and exercise regime. She got me the job with the stock company in Houston where Harry discovered me.

"Along the way, we fell in love. Or so I thought. But Josephine didn't love me. She loved what she was creating. I was her Eliza Doolittle, and when she realized I was still me underneath all her primping and polishing, she left. She took my dog and boarded a train to God knows where and never looked back. Ironically, the next week I signed my contract with Evets Studios. I've become the star she always wanted. Guess I should be grateful, really. I wasn't someone she could love, so instead she created something the entire world could fall for. The only person I haven't been able to convince is myself."

He sighed and braced himself against the wooden railing separating them from the burbling river below. This was why she would never allow herself to fall in love. Because you ended up staring up at the night sky with your teeth kicked in like a chump. People always talked about getting the stars in your eyes, but they never mentioned the dark nights that came after the moonlight and magnolias had worn off. She would never have a night like that if she could help it.

A cloud shifted, casting them both in moonlight. In the dim light, she could see that a moue of regret twisted his classically handsome features, and she watched him fiddle with the bottom edge of his sport coat, twisting his fingers in knots. Dash's pain was etched in the tense, hard lines of his body, and she hated seeing his usual barrel-chested ease drawn so taut. She relished frustrating him, getting the best of him. But there had never been real cruelty, real viciousness behind their bickering. This was a deeper hurt, one she'd never recognized in him before. One she'd frankly thought he was incapable of feeling. One she'd built a life to protect her own heart against.

She reached out her hand and stilled his restless fingers with her own. She might not believe in love, but that didn't mean Dash shouldn't believe in himself. "Josephine was cruel. And she was wrong."

He shook her hand off. "Was she, though? You saw through

me pretty quickly. And why shouldn't you have? Harry might've convinced the world I'm a king, but you're too smart for that, Joanie. You always have been. It's why I've always respected you. Even when I've yearned to take you down a peg."

She swallowed her pride and was surprised to find it tasted like regret. "America loves you, Dash. They know better. You should too. That would be enough for me. It's all I've ever wanted."

His mouth creased in a sad smile. "It's like I told you. They love something that doesn't really exist. You *are* Joan Davis, but I'm not Dash Howard."

She snorted. He didn't know the half of who Joan Davis really was, of the sacrifices she'd made, the lies she'd told, the things she'd hidden to become the version of herself she'd always known she could be. And he wasn't going to. No one but she and Harry were ever going to know. And Leda—but she'd been paid a handsome sum to keep quiet.

Dash was right. She was Joan Davis. She'd fought hard to become her, to leave her past behind. Because she preferred who she was now. Joan Davis was the truest, most complete version of herself.

"That may be," she replied. "But you're real to me. And I like you. Or at least I'm beginning to."

"You'll know better soon enough." He looked back at the water.

"Why'd you tell me all that then, Dash? If you're so convinced it proves the worst about you."

"Because we're married and you know nothing about me."

She flinched as if he'd slapped her. She could cut things short here. Ask him to walk her back to the hotel. End this strange interlude and go back to sniping at each other. But she found herself wanting to linger, to draw out whatever this was. So instead she looked at him, crinkling the space between her eyebrows, trying to work something out.

He broke away from her gaze. "I'm sorry. God, that was uncalled for. Old habits die hard. I told you because I've never told anyone that before. And after all this time, it's high time you know the real me. We are married after all. 'For better or worse' is the saying, right? Well, here's the worse. The real Dash Howard. Not the version Harry and Leda insist I sell. Not the heel you've convinced yourself is who I am."

"You haven't done much to try to disabuse me of that notion."

"You've never let me."

He was right. She'd been stubborn. Unwilling to see him as anything other than what she thought he'd proved himself to be. She wanted people to see her as more than a pretty face, as an actress and a woman who should be taken seriously. Didn't she at least owe him the same courtesy and consideration? For a long time, she'd told herself no. That he didn't deserve it. But he'd been honest with her. And she wanted to know more. "I'm sorry, Dash. For not listening. For never letting you explain yourself. It's… hard for me to trust people. And you broke mine."

He paused and they stood silent in the moonlight for a minute, regrets and recriminations swirling between them and melting into the night air. "I don't think even Harry knows about Josephine," Dash continued, more quietly this time. "Just me, her, and maybe some of my old pals from Texas. I've never even told Flynn, and he's my best friend. Divorced cowboy whose older wife left him and took his dog isn't exactly the movie-star origin story the publicity department is hungry for."

"So, call Leda—" He growled at that suggestion. "Okay, fine, Walter at the *Reporter,* whoever you want. Tell them who you really are. Make Dash Howard the man you want him to be."

He huffed. "You make it sound so simple."

"And you're making it too difficult. It's not simple. It's hard as hell. I can never stop working at it, never let my guard down. Not for one second. But you said I *am* Joan Davis, and you're right." She joined him at the river's edge, wrapping her hands around the solid, soft barrel of wood creating the top bar of the railing and nudging him with her shoulder. "Maybe Dash Howard could learn something from Joan Davis."

He smiled, the first genuine smile she'd seen all night that wasn't tinged with melancholy or mischief. "And what's that?"

"There is only one person in this world who is going to get you what you want—and that's you. So you don't want to be Dash Howard, you want to be someone else. No one's forcing you to be rich and famous. Oh boo-hoo, you live in a big house and women throw themselves at your feet." He opened his mouth to protest, but she kept going. "If you want another dream, go out and get one. Tonight, I'm finally understanding something. You are not the man I thought you were. And if that means you're not Dash Howard, King of Hollywood, so be it. You don't have to be what they've made you. I refuse to be anything other than what I've made myself."

He looked defeated, a shadow of the man the cameras loved. "I don't know what I want."

"I had one dream—to become the biggest movie star in the world. To be untouchable. I was willing to sacrifice everything for it. I still am. But if you don't feel the same, if it's making you miserable, then why keep at it?"

"Acting doesn't make me miserable. It makes me feel alive. Like I'm doing something important. Like I'm part of something that gets to bring happiness and meaning to other people's lives. Knowing that there are people out there in the dark whose day is better because of me, because I got to tell a story that made them laugh or cry or forget their troubles for a while. Maybe even helped them understand some part of themselves better. How could I hate that?"

She looked at him and felt a little breathless. She'd never heard him speak so vociferously before, like he believed in what he was saying with every fiber of his being. Usually he was sarcastic, everything laced with a joke or a wry insult. But this, this was pure unbridled enthusiasm, and it made his face light up like a Christmas tree. He was handsome, of course. That was undeniable. But right now he looked positively beatific, beautiful in the courage of his convictions, preaching the very same gospel she prescribed to. "I've always felt the same," she whispered.

But just like that, the light was gone and his shoulders sank. "Acting doesn't make me miserable. But fame does."

"Okay, so then make the fame exist on your terms," she retorted, desperate to bring that effervescence back to his eyes. "My road hasn't been easy, but I didn't care if it was lonely because if I got what I wanted, I'd have the only love that ever mattered to me—the one that doesn't involve feelings and intimacy and anything complicated. The love of the audience. I resented having to share it with you, and until tonight, I'd convinced myself you'd stolen it from me." She blushed and bowed her head, too embarrassed to meet his eyes.

He spluttered, "I'd stolen it from you? And how is that?"

She looked up and made a hard-won confession. "Because I'd made the mistake of assuming you were a cigar-chomping, boys' club member who was only too happy to use me as a springboard to fame and fortune and then cut me loose from your coattails and win an Oscar."

"I won't pretend I'm unhappy about the way things have

turned out, but let's not forget you're the one who asked Harry for a break. You wanted to set yourself apart from Dash and Davis."

"As it turns out, they don't seem to like Davis so much without the other D."

"Perhaps you could do with some of the other D yourself." He winked, waggling his eyebrows suggestively.

"You can take the playboy out of Hollywood..." she quipped. She bumped her shoulder into his, ribbing him ever so softly. He chuckled on a puff of air that sounded like something between a laugh and a sigh. She joined him in leaning against the railing, looking out across the river and ever so gently laying the curve of her hand against his.

"I suppose I assumed that because Joan Davis isn't an act, Dash Howard couldn't possibly be either. She's who I am, with every ounce of my being. And I love her. I'd do anything to keep her."

Dash reached over and set his thumb beneath her chin, turning her face up and into the moonlight, making a show of studying her.

"What on earth are you doing?" She tried to ignore the thrill that had passed through her the moment his hand had grazed her skin. The sense that maybe the moonlight was actually magic. Because that was an utterly absurd thought.

"Looking for something."

"And what might that be?"

"Who you were before Joan Davis. Surely there's a secret girl-next-door lurking somewhere under all that glamour?"

She laughed, gave him a wry smile, and then adopted her most imperious tone. "If you want the girl next door, go next door."

"Trotting out that old chestnut again, are we?" He laughed, a full-throated sound that expressed a joy she hadn't seen in him all night. He removed his hand from her chin, and she felt it like the loss of a limb.

"The press eats it up."

"With good reason. The only way you'd ever be the girl next door was if your address was on Sunset Boulevard. I envy you, Joan, so content with who you are. Being enough for yourself."

She knew there was more to that sentence, the implication that he wasn't enough. For himself. For anyone. Without thinking, she reached out and cupped his cheek with her hand and he leaned into it, closing his eyes and letting her stroke his face. She gasped, the roughness of his five-o'clock stubble massaging her hand, shooting flickers of desire down each of her fingertips.

"Dash, I—"

"You what?" His voice was deep and low, like gravel wrapped in velvet. His eyes snapped open, dark as sin. Something sexual flashed in them. It shocked her. It shocked her more how badly she wanted him.

Maybe it was hearing the story of Josephine. Maybe it was realizing she'd been wrong about him. Or maybe it really was the effect of the gurgling river and the infernal moonlight. Whatever the reason, Joan was suddenly seized with the desire to kiss him.

Being a woman who always went after what she wanted, she leaned over and gently pressed her lips to his, tentatively seeking assurance that this was okay. He responded hungrily, wrapping his arms around her and tangling his hands in the loose curls at the nape of her neck. The light pressure she'd applied was met with a firm press of his lips, before he nipped at her bottom lip and slid his tongue into her mouth. She opened for him, tangling her tongue with his and reveling in how light-headed she suddenly felt. They were lips and hands and tongues and teeth, and nothing else mattered.

They had kissed hundreds of times on set, but this was nothing like any of those. Those were choreographed and perfunctory. This, this was a make-you-weak-at-the-knees, fireworks-in-the-sky kind of kiss. In fact, she could swear there really were fireworks going off. She could hear a hiss and a pop, accompanied by a brief flash of light.

She heard it again and smiled against Dash's mouth, amused that even their private moments were worthy of a Hollywood backdrop. But then a cold rush of dread shot down her spine. Because suddenly she knew. Those weren't fireworks. They were the sounds of flashbulbs.

CHAPTER 10

IS THE DIVORCE DASHED?

Is it possible Davis and Dash have changed their minds and are giving their divorce the kiss-off? The two stars certainly seem to be getting close, as they were spotted necking on the Reno riverside last night only steps from their hotel. After traveling to Reno to end their marriage, which they previously told this reporter was the result of a studio mix-up, could they be calling the whole thing off? Or on, rather?

Fans have yearned for the two stars of the silver screen to unite off-screen. But the two always firmly denied any rumors of a romantic connection. And of course there was the infamous Cocoanut Grove KO that proved there was no love lost between them. Joan Davis's engagement to matinee idol Monty Smyth should have extinguished any last hope for the kindling of the Dash and Davis flame. But could that all have been a charade? With their arms wrapped around each other, the two look more like gushing newlyweds than a couple headed for the courthouse.

And where is Monty Smyth and what does he think of all this? When we called his humble Beverly Hills abode, there was no answer. We then got ahold of his former roommate, Jerry Scott. Scott's response isn't fit for print, but let's just say he doesn't think highly of Miss Davis two-timing his best friend. *What Price Hollywood?* is hot on Monty's trail. Sources say he is on his way to confront Miss Davis in Reno today. Will he call their engagement off? Are Davis and Dash secretly in love? Check back for the latest on this Hollywood scandal.

—xoxo, Leda

"Harry, if you don't fix this, I'm going to find Leda Price and I'm going to murder her. So unless you want to be raising bail money and footing a sizable legal bill for your leading man's homicide case, I suggest you find a solution. And fast!" Dash growled into the phone, before slamming it back down on its base.

"Fuck!" he screamed to no one in particular. He looked again at the black-and-white image of him and Joan splashed across the front page of the paper. There was no denying it was them. Or that they were kissing. Rather passionately. He balled up the newsprint in fury.

He got a goofy sensation in his stomach every time he looked at the picture. It reminded him of how he'd felt last night, mesmerized by Joan, completely lost in her and their embrace. But he'd been a fool. How could they have let their guard down like that? Especially after the train platform?

Something strange had happened last night. Joan had strolled into that casino, unrecognizable to him at first, and he'd found himself under her spell. And then, Joan had tolerated him. No, she'd done more than that. She'd listened. She'd sat down at the bar, had a drink with him, and transformed into everything he'd hoped she would be with him before he cocked it all up.

For the first time in he didn't know how long, he'd felt safe. Heard. Understood. Like he could be himself. Flynn was his best friend, but he was a clown, ready and willing to turn anything into a joke.

When Joan had cupped his cheek, with the stars glimmering in her eyes and the moonlight dancing in her hair, he'd wanted her. Then when she'd leaned forward and kissed him, he'd practically levitated. It had been that good. Every spare thought about her being engaged to someone else flew out of his head. But the moment they'd heard the flashbulbs, she'd run from him, yelling something about a setup. He hadn't the heart to chase her, to make an even bigger scene. And why wouldn't she assume the worst? He didn't exactly have a sterling track record in this department.

He hadn't slept a wink, pacing in his hotel suite and ringing the front desk every few minutes to check if the morning paper had arrived. He'd contemplated calling Flynn a thousand times, but something told him that would only make things worse. Besides, the man would've been out on the town until 3:00 a.m. and then gone straight to bed. He wouldn't be in any state to offer advice until the afternoon.

The Hotel Riverside carried all the major papers for their guests, including the *Los Angeles Examiner.* In between phone calls, Dash opened his door and stared across the hall at the room he knew belonged to Joan, praying for her sake that the photo wouldn't go to print. But, of course, it had. He hadn't really heard what Harry said when he'd called, he was so apoplectic with rage. But it sounded something like "working on it" and "divorce ranch."

Besides, he didn't want to talk to Harry. He wanted to talk to her. To ask her why the hell she'd kissed him. What she meant by it. If she was toying with his insecurities. She was engaged to another man. A man she was supposedly so devoted to the idea of marrying that he'd had to hightail it up here for a divorce. Last night she'd claimed she didn't believe in love, but even so, he didn't touch another man's fiancée. He might have a reputation for being a ladies' man, but there were lines he didn't cross. So what the hell was that last night?

He couldn't take it anymore, so he stormed across the hall in his red silk dressing gown and banged on the door. "Joan, I know you're in there. Open up, we need to talk."

He expected to be out there for quite a while, if ever admitted at all, so he was surprised when the door opened almost instantly. To reveal none other than Monty Smyth.

"I think we all need to talk," Monty drawled, a sardonic smile on his face. Monty was famous for his moody, emotional approach to his roles. While Dash had risen to fame on his barrel-chested frame and leading-man good looks, Monty was a new breed of star: sensitive and quiet, a storm behind his eyes. Dash was shocked to find none of that storminess now. He expected the man to resent him for kissing his fiancée at least a little bit. But Monty merely seemed amused.

"Monty, I'm sorry. I didn't realize you'd be here already." He'd called the man at the beginning of the week. After the debacle on the train platform, he'd phoned Monty and offered to pay for his ticket, if only he'd come and draw attention away from the divorce. Monty had made noise about his production schedule but Dash had refused to take no for an answer, calling repeatedly, and finally buying the ticket and sending his private car. He'd known Joan would want Monty here to set things right. Dash had been trying to do right by them both, but last night things had got so terribly muddled.

Before he could continue making excuses, Joan pushed Monty aside and dragged Dash into the room by the lapel of his silk dressing gown.

"Did you set me up, you good for nothing, goddamn—"

"I hardly see how that's possible when *you* kissed *me*," he growled, eyeing Monty nervously. He was frustrated with her. Frustrated even more with himself and the fact that a flicker of excitement had shot through him when she'd grabbed his robe with such vigor. But he didn't want to show her up in front of the guy she was supposed to marry. He did have a shred of decency. Despite what she might think.

Monty simply smiled at him, his composure barely concealing wry amusement. Dash was suddenly seized with a compulsion to sock him. Wasn't he upset? Wasn't he jealous? His fiancée was caught kissing another man, and he looked cool as a cucumber. Joan ignored Monty's indifference and plowed ahead with her accusations.

"Because you, you, you seduced me—walking in the moonlight and—"

Her retort was interrupted by the shrill sound of the telephone, jolting them all into action as they raced to the bedside table.

"I'll get it. It must be Harry," yelped Joan.

But Monty coolly picked up the phone first and patted Joan's hand like she was a child who needed soothing.

"You have things to discuss with Dash. And you're in no state to talk to Harry. I'll handle it."

Dash locked eyes with Arlene, who was sitting in the window seat watching the entire fiasco with a bemused expression. Arlene smiled at him, obviously knowing something he did not, before abruptly picking up her hat and sauntering past. "Joan, I'm going out to grab lunch. Do you want something?"

Joan never took her eyes off Dash, throwing daggers at him as she replied, "No, thank you, I'm not hungry."

As soon as the door snicked quietly shut behind Arlene, Joan pulled him across the room to an armchair and a circular, pouf-shaped chaise longue. It was as far from Monty and the telephone as they could get.

"Tell me the truth, Dash. Are you working with Leda Price? Is this some harebrained scheme to win yourself publicity?"

Dash hated that she was back to thinking the worst of him and believing he was the womanizing cad the press made him out to be.

He wanted to tell her that the kiss had been the most magnificent moment of his wretched life, and he was sorry for making a mess of things. But instead he blurted out, "I could accuse you of the same thing, you know. You insisted we give Leda that 'exclusive'"—he waggled his fingers making air quotes—"interview about our divorce. For all I know, your entire engagement is a publicity stunt, and you decided that I make better headlines."

She raised her hand as if to slap him, and he chuckled. "I did tell you in Harry's office that you should take a crack at the other cheek."

She huffed in frustration and pulled her hand to her lap, knitting her hands together in a restless dance. Her engagement ring flashed at him, a reminder of how stupid he was being. Honestly, how ridiculous. Who was he to want her? To think last night was any different from the way things had always been?

"How dare you suggest such a thing." She was white as a sheet and chewing on her bottom lip.

"How dare I? How dare you! I remind you again: You. Kissed. Me."

Joan spluttered. "I did not." He gave her a look. "All right, fine, I did. But I don't know what I was thinking. It was the infernal moonlight. I should've known it was a setup. Just like the Cocoanut Grove. Just like the train station."

He ran a hand down his face. This was what he got for trying, for doing anything besides buying a dame a drink and showing her a good time.

"I didn't set us up at the train station," he gritted through his teeth. "If you had let me help you with your bag in the first place, that would have never happened."

"Why did you assume I needed your help at all? I'm perfectly capable of taking care of myself."

"Isn't that tiresome though, Joan? Every once in a while, don't you wish there was someone there to help you carry the load?"

She blinked at him, as if the idea had never occurred to her. "I have Arlene for that."

"Arlene can't be everything to you. She's your assistant, Joan. And she won't even be that for long. She's got a bright future ahead of her as a screenwriter. Or whatever she wants to be."

Joan smiled at that, temporarily distracted. "She does, doesn't she?"

"But then what will you do, Joan? When she moves on with her life and isn't there to handle every crisis?"

Joan looked startled, but quickly slipped on a mask of cool confusion. "I have Monty now. The perfect man," she drawled, all teeth, and he knew she was twisting the knife on purpose.

He gave her a sad smile. He might not ever be worth anything to anyone beyond the blinding gleam of his expensive smile and the pomaded hair and the slick tailored suits. But at least he hadn't convinced himself that feelings were inconvenient, something you could decide not to have. If anything, he had far too many of them.

"He hardly seems perfect when you were tempted to kiss me last night," he said.

"Temporary insanity." She waved her hands as if the memory was an annoying gnat she needed to buzz off. "And again I say, you tricked me."

"If someone being honest with you is a trick, I feel sorry for you, Joan."

"That's just it. You made me feel sorry for you, told me some sob story so I'd fall into your arms. I bet Josephine's not even real."

She might as well have gone ahead and slapped him. Or kneed him in the groin like in that infamous photograph of their illustrious beginnings. It hurt less than what she was saying now. "Oh, she's real, all right. She's the only real thing I've ever had and the only one who's ever known the real me," he said, struggling to keep the bitterness out of his voice.

"I bet you trot this story out to every woman you meet at Musso and Frank and the Trocadero."

Before he could stop himself, he grabbed her and pulled her so close he was only inches from her mouth. "I told you last night I've never told anyone that story before, and perhaps it says more about you than me if you think I need a sob story to get women to throw themselves at me. You kissed me, Joan. If you can't make peace with that, it's not my problem. But *you* kissed *me*."

He looked down, watched her swallow nervously and lick her lips. Lips he inexplicably craved more than anything. He wanted to plunder her mouth, as if she was one of the smugglers' ships he'd raided in their film *Exotic Cargo*. Her eyes followed his gaze before hungrily landing on his own mouth.

"And I'd wager you'd like to do it again right now," he growled, feeling the hot sensation of her panting breath against his neck, unable to hide the desire that she was so quick to deny.

He need only move his head down a hair and he would be kissing her. But he would never take something she didn't want to give. The men he played in the movies would ravish her here and now on this velvet-covered pouf, tear her feathery dressing gown from her shoulders and make her beg for more. But as he kept telling her, he was not the men he played in the movies. And he wouldn't touch a dame who didn't ask him to.

She whimpered and started to move closer to him, but a light cough interrupted them and they broke apart like two teenagers caught necking. Shit, he'd forgotten about Monty. What was wrong with him? He'd worked with Joan for nearly five years and he'd never lost his head like this. He was still jumbled from last night, shaken by finally telling someone about Josephine, confused by her kiss and how much he'd craved it, how he'd awoken still wanting more. That was it; it was a hangover from last night's kiss. That was all.

"As you might have guessed, that was Harry on the phone," Monty told them jovially.

Dash stared at him and was startled to find the man's eyes still full of mirth. What was wrong with him?

"He's worked out a solution to the Leda problem. He's sending you two to a more remote location, says the hotel is overrun with reporters after last night. He's secured space at the Lazy Me Ranch four miles south of town."

Joan stood and embraced Monty, making a show of it for

Dash's benefit. "Oh, darling, that's fabulous. We'll have some time to ourselves."

"Well, there's one small problem. I'm not coming with you. There's not room. Arlene and I will maintain rooms here. Harry said there's a premium on space. Apparently, quite a lot of people need a divorce right now." Monty chuckled awkwardly. "But he was able to eke out room for you both, and it's where you'll be shooting the ranch scenes for *Reno Rendezvous* anyway, so it saves the studio money on transportation."

"But how on earth will this resolve the need to show our commitment to each other, Monty?" Joan got that look on her face that Dash hated. When she was fighting for what she believed in, she was irresistible. Pure fire. But when she retreated into Miss Davis mode, she was haughty and peevish, a child throwing a tantrum. Depending on the studio to fix everything for her, when there were some things Harry Evets couldn't fix. Or didn't care to.

Monty patted her arm gently. "It will be all right, Joan. I'll stay here at the hotel and keep the reporters busy. And you can come back to town to visit me in between filming, and we'll give them plenty of the photo ops they're craving."

"*Monty and Joan hear wedding bells while awaiting Dash-Davis divorce*... I can see the headlines now. Oh darling, this is perfect."

Joan embraced Monty, and Dash's stomach plummeted. He should be relieved. This was why he'd called Monty and insisted he come. To fix the mess he'd inadvertently made. But last night, he'd felt a flicker of something different with Joan. Something he knew was dangerous to pursue. But that didn't stop him from wanting it.

He should've known better than to hope. She was still choosing Monty. And why wouldn't she? Just look at the guy. Even if the idea of Dash Howard weren't so repulsive to her, it was no contest really. Monty was charming, suave, and debonair. And most importantly, he hadn't embarrassed Joan in the newspapers on numerous occasions. Perhaps Joan had really experienced temporary insanity brought on by the moonlight and his story. She certainly looked to be very enthusiastic about Monty now, if the way she was clinging to him was any indication.

He supposed he should be grateful. Joan Davis was probably more trouble than she was worth. And this had been resolved with little incident. Harry was saving their ass. So, he'd paste on his movie-star smile and put on his chaps and play the cowboy hero they'd scripted him to be. What else could he do?

"Let's go to the ranch," he drawled, brushing past Monty and Joan, who were too busy embracing to even notice his absence.

CHAPTER 11

THE LAZY ME RANCH WAS QUAINT, IF ONE LIKED THAT SORT of thing—a rustic-looking ranch house at the foot of the Sierras, surrounded by a circle of cottages and bungalows which Joan supposed housed an assortment of divorcées and cowboys whose sole purpose was to entertain the guests.

She nervously ran her palm along the row of buttons on her high-waisted trousers and came away with a handful of dust. The memory of it made her shiver. She hated dirt and farmhouse living. She hadn't been anywhere like this since she'd hightailed it out of her family's house in Oklahoma. She hadn't been Joan Davis then; she'd been Mildred Shalk. But Mildred didn't exist anymore. She wasn't kidding when she'd told Dash that Joan Davis was who she was now through and through. She'd fought hard to become her, to kill any part of Mildred and never look back.

But after nearly a decade in Hollywood where she'd become accustomed to chauffeurs and champagne, the universe was playing a sick joke on her. Because here she was back on a godforsaken ranch, wiping grit from her eyes. At least she'd had the forethought to wear a head scarf.

She and Dash had shared a sullenly quiet car ride out to the ranch, snuck out by the driver through the Riverside kitchen into a waiting vehicle. Logically, she knew Dash probably hadn't set her up. How would he have known she'd be going out for a drink that night? And which bar she'd choose? But it was hard to shake the lessons of her past, and more than that, she hated how much Dash had unsettled her. How he'd made her mistrust her instincts and act like a fool. All because of two gin stingers and a walk in the moonlight. Romance was for the movies, not for movie stars. She'd do well to remember that.

An attractive denim-clad man turned the corner and tipped his hat at the two of them standing near the front porch with their luggage in tow like two hitchhikers dumped here by a delivery truck.

Dash took off his sunglasses, smiled that megawatt grin, and stuck out his hand. "Howdy, partner." He winked at Joan. Lord, he was insufferable.

The cowboy took it in stride. "Well, howdy, Mr. Howard." He turned to face her. "And you must be Miss Davis. We've been expecting you. I'm Travis Porter and I help run this place. Follow me and I'll show you to your room."

Joan turned to pick up her trunk and was dismayed to find how heavy it was. She struggled to lift it. The cowboy looked at Dash pointedly, as if to suggest he carry it. But Dash merely took a step back and grinned at Joan.

"Oh no. She can carry it herself. She's assured me she can. And I wouldn't want to be accused of treachery."

Joan harrumphed and started to drag the trunk through the dirt, following the cowboy who didn't seem in the least bit fazed by their hostility. She supposed he was used to dealing with relationships that had gone sour. They wound around a dirt path that traversed a wide grassy area dotted with tables and chairs full of women of all ages, sporting loungewear that ranged from long pleated skirts to palazzo pants to gingham shorts and peasant blouses. They were smoking, giggling with one another, and smiling at the young men in cowboy hats and formfitting chaps who were waiting on them. If Arlene had scripted this scenario for their film, Joan wouldn't have believed it. She found herself itching to tell her, making a note to call her back at the hotel the moment she was settled.

When they came to the end of the path, they stood between two bungalows and passed through a narrow transept until they reached a small cottage that stood alone at the back of the property, flanked by two tall pine trees. Travis Porter opened the door and led Joan inside, as she heaved the trunk over the steps. It was a single room with two twin beds side by side, across from a fireplace that was next to by a careworn easy chair. A print of a cowboy roping a steer hung above the mantel, and the windows were covered with red-and-white-checked curtains. Joan chuckled as she eyed a cross-stitch hanging over the door. It read "Marry in Haste, Repent at Leisure." This trip was anything but leisurely. The room was neat and tidy, but certainly nowhere near as full of lush creature comforts as Joan's suite at the Riverside had been. This was the price she paid for her foolishness, for letting her guard down for one second. *Vigilance, Joan, vigilance.* Feelings were dangerous; you ended up in places like this.

Dash was quick on her heels, surveying the room in a single glance before whistling in appreciation. "She's a beaut, Travis."

Stepping over her trunk, which still lay haphazardly in front of the door, Joan marched up to Travis. "Would you be so kind as to show Mr. Howard to his room now?"

Travis looked at her in confusion. "This is his room."

She grimaced and bent over to pick up her trunk. "My apologies, would you show me to mine then?"

"It's here. This is also your room." Travis looked perplexed.

She dropped the trunk to the floor, the latch flipping open and her peignoir tumbling onto the carpet. But she was too shocked to notice that her unmentionables were spilling out onto Travis Porter's feet. "I beg your pardon, what do you mean this is also my room?"

Travis took off his cowboy hat and worried it between his fingers. "I'm awful sorry, ma'am, but we did tell Mr. Evets we were short on space. This was the best we could manage without a prior reservation."

Dash burst out laughing, before climbing into the easy chair, kicking his feet up on an end table, and tipping his fedora low over his face so all she could see was his infuriating grin. She wanted to kick him, so she kicked her trunk instead.

"Ow!" she yelled, feeling her toe begin to throb through the thin leather of what she'd thought was a very sensible pump.

"I'm terribly sorry. I thought they told you before you arrived. We're not used to having movie stars come to stay, you see. The rich folk usually book into the Flying M.E. about fifteen miles farther down the road. But Mr. Evets said something about this being more private. We do have two beds in here, and Mr. Evets assured us it would be fine."

"I'll bet he did," Joan hissed. She whirled on Dash. "Did you know about this?"

He raised his hands in mock defense. "Don't look at me. I've been with you all morning. Why don't you call your fiancé and ask him if Harry neglected to mention this?"

"That sonofabitch," Joan muttered. Harry might have helped make her everything she was, but she still hated it when he toyed with her without her permission. He was supposed to be getting them privacy, not shoving them together because it was good for publicity.

"I could call the car back, Miss Davis. If this isn't satisfactory."

Joan wanted to scream yes, to run back the four miles to Reno herself if she had to. But what choice did she have? The hotel was crawling with reporters, vultures looking to pounce on her the moment she stepped into the lobby. Besides, she wouldn't give Dash the satisfaction. She was certain he was no more interested in sharing this room with her than she was with him. Even if the memory of the ferocity with which he'd kissed her made her knees wobble. If she left now, she'd be surrendering. If he wouldn't blink, then neither would she.

"No, that's all right, Mr. Porter. We were confused about the situation, that's all. We'll make do."

Dash made a show of yawning and leaning back in the chair, pushing his hat even further over his face. All she could make out was the upturned corners of his mouth and the beginnings of his afternoon shadow around his jaw. He was doing it to push her buttons, and it was infuriating. But hell, also kind of attractive. The sight of his stubble reminded her of the feel of it scraping against her jaw last night. A memory she worked to banish quickly.

Travis Porter darted his eyes between them, before apparently deciding the situation was something too complicated for him to get in the middle of. He tipped his hat and started to back out of the room. "Okay, well, you folks make yourselves comfortable. And don't forget, dinner is in the big house at 6:00 p.m."

Joan tried to slam the door after him, but her trunk was blocking it. She knelt to the floor and wrestled with it, trying to shove it closer to the bed, but she only succeeded in tearing a large hole in the silky fabric of her Chantilly lace peignoir, which had gotten caught between the carpet and the corner of the trunk. She wanted to cry. Now she'd have nothing to sleep in, at least nothing that would decently cover her in the presence of Dash.

As if she'd summoned him by thinking his name, he appeared above her. "Here, let me get that." He lifted the trunk as if it were nothing and moved it to a leather contraption designed to hold luggage, stretched open next to the hearth.

"What are we going to do?"

"What we came here to do: make a movie, eat and sleep at this ranch, and after five more weeks, get a divorce."

"I could murder Harry. Why would he think this was okay?"

Dash chuckled and resumed his place in the easy chair. "I imagine he thinks it's funny."

"Well, he's got a sick sense of humor," Joan growled. "Why would they even let us stay here together? People are usually particular about men and women lodging together."

He shrugged in that infuriatingly attractive devil-may-care fashion and replied from under his hat. "Well, technically we are married. So I guess it doesn't bother them."

She put her face in her hands and plopped to the floor, landing in the soft folds of her now-shredded nightgown. "Don't remind me. You would think you wouldn't want to keep bringing that up since it only highlights what a selfish fool you are."

He grimaced and then stood to give her a mock bow. "My apologies, my lady, but begging your pardon, how could I ever forget what a rogue and peasant slave I am?"

"Oh, don't quote Shakespeare at me. I've read *Hamlet* too, you know. You don't have to treat me like the Queen of Sheba. Just help me work out what we're going to do about this."

"First, you like it when people treat you like the Queen of Sheba. Second, what is there to work out? Do you want the bed closest to the window or the one closest to the door? I have no preference."

"I don't understand how you can be so flippant about this.

The entire point of us coming out here was to quash rumors that our marriage is more than a clerical error, and now we're sharing a bedroom." Saying the word *bedroom* sent a shiver of desire coursing through her. Or was it fear? She didn't know. She'd never felt this way. She wasn't capable of feeling this way, she kept reminding herself.

Joan thought again of how she'd felt last night wrapped in his arms: safe and secure for perhaps the first time in her life. The kind of security she hungered for, that she fought to find with her money and her fame. The sense that for once she didn't have to do it all alone. But that feeling was a lie. It was the result of years of pretending to swoon at the sight of him on-screen. Muscle memory. Nothing more.

"If Harry's plan works, no one will know we're sharing a room, so I don't see what the trouble is." Dash shrugged, shoving his hands in his pockets and pulling the curtains aside to glance out the window. "Unless you're worried that you won't be able to keep your hands off me."

"Please—I'd rather drink arsenic."

He looked back at her then and that sad, melancholy something from last night flickered in his eyes for a moment. But then his insouciant grin returned. "That can be arranged."

He threw his fedora on the easy chair, raking his fingers through his dark hair, so black it looked like shoe polish. Regrettably, it looked delectably mussed. He crossed to sit on the bed and picked up the phone on the bedside table.

"What are you doing?" she hissed. "I didn't actually mean I want to drink poison. Why must you take everything so literally?"

He held up his finger to shush her and spoke into the phone. "Yes, Mr. Porter? Could you bring me a long length of rope? Yes, like for roping a steer. Exactly. Thank you."

Joan felt her eyes get as big as saucers. "What are you going to do? Tie me up? Harry's going to hear about this."

He shook his head in a mix of annoyance and amusement. "Would you calm down, Joanie? I'm not going to tie you up." He lifted his eyebrows. "Though on second thought, don't give me any ideas."

She resented the frisson of excitement the notion shot through her, tried to tamp it down. Focusing instead on her annoyance that he'd called her Joanie. Like she was a child that needed to be soothed and petted.

"Do you remember our picture *Road to Romance?*"

"What on earth has that got to do with anything?" But then realization dawned on her. In the film, she'd played a spoiled heiress on the run from her father, and Dash had played a reporter who helps her. While hitchhiking, they end up at a roadside motel, and to offer her some privacy, his character strings a bedsheet between their two beds. "Oh, that's... Well, that's actually a good idea."

"I'm not a complete idiot, you know."

She blushed. "I don't think you're an idiot, Dash. In fact, I think you're probably too smart for your own good."

He clutched his heart, feigning shock. "Did the great Joan Davis deign to pay me a compliment?"

"Oh, shut up, I just mean that occasionally, and I do mean *very* occasionally, you have a good idea."

"Joan Davis thinks I'm a genius," he crowed. He got up from the bed and began skipping around the room in some half-cocked version of a two-step. "Call the papers, ring the president, sound the alarm: Joan Davis thinks I'm smart and that I have good ideas."

"Oh, cut it out. You act like I'm a gorgon who is hell-bent on turning you to stone."

"You're much prettier than Medusa. Far fewer snakes in your hair," he quipped, shooting her one of his famous smiles over his shoulder as he grabbed a coatrack and pretended to dance with it.

"Now who's paying who compliments." She giggled. She was giddy, the heaviness of this morning and what she'd done last night lifting from her shoulders for the first time all day. He continued to cavort with the coatrack, extending out the sleeves of his jacket he'd hung on it, making false arms for him to dance with. He was singing off-key a new popular song, "Pennies from Heaven," and she found his humor infectious.

Laughing, she reached for something near her to throw at him. Dash loved to play practical jokes on set, seemed to take pleasure in getting a rise out of her or a director. But she'd never seen him like this, smiling and silly, a gleam in his eye that made him look instantly ten years younger. She tossed her newly found projectile at him and realized in horror as it was in midair that it was her torn peignoir. He caught it gleefully, but then he stopped abruptly, dropping the coatrack to the floor.

His eyebrows lifted nearly to his hairline, and he held it up to himself. "I don't think this will fit me," he deadpanned, pressing the soft pink flounces across his broad chest.

"Well, I'm afraid I can't wear it now either," she replied, holding his gaze, gesturing to the rend in it. "I have nothing to wear to bed now that I ripped it." She gulped, finding herself suddenly parched.

"It's a good thing we'll have a sheet hanging between us, then," he said, heat coming into his eyes. Involuntarily, she wet her lips and took a step toward him. But the sudden spell between them was broken by a knock at the door.

"Mr. Howard, I have the rope you asked for," a voice called through the door. Joan sighed, though whether it was out of relief or disappointment she couldn't quite be sure. No, God, what was she thinking? Relief, it had to be relief. She was engaged to Monty Smyth. She was going to marry him, and that would fix everything. There was no room for mooning over flirtations with Dash Howard.

CHAPTER 12

DASH INHALED THE SMELL OF CHILI AND CORN BREAD and smiled. It reminded him of home. Not his palatial Beverly Hills mansion. No, the place he'd called home before he became the King of Hollywood. The farm his father had abandoned to chase oil. He shook off the memory and breathed deeply.

For the first time in years, he felt like himself, sporting Levi's and a red plaid flannel button-down shirt. He looked like another cowboy at the ranch, and he liked that. The sleeping arrangements here at Lazy Me might be less than ideal, but at least it offered some semblance of normalcy in what had been an absolutely maddening few weeks.

He lurked in the corner, trying to avoid the view of Joan hanging off Monty's arm. She'd called him and insisted he and Arlene drive out to the ranch for dinner. That was their version of "lying low" he supposed. The prospective divorcées staying at the ranch had instantly switched their attention—like a hawk locking onto prey—from the ranch's resident cowboys, Dusty and Tom, to Monty, the bright young star in their midst.

He was charming and British, so of course they loved him. They couldn't spot the bead of sweat on his brow or the way he kept pulling at the collar of his three-piece suit as if it were too tight. But Dash saw it. He knew the sight of someone uncomfortable in the skin that the studio had fashioned for them. Monty was a master at playing along all the same. Dash hadn't become the King of Hollywood by demurring to others' attention. And Monty was as good at offering the most charismatic, most irresistible version of himself to the public. The man gave good movie star, that was certain.

It was a relief, honestly, not to be the searing focal point in the room. Joan was basking in it, Dash noted with dismay, enjoying the stir her fiancé created among the women. It was true then that the only love she truly craved was that between her and an adoring public. And clearly, Monty was the man to give it to her.

If Monty's presence kept the hungry eyes of the other women in the room away from Dash, that was something at least. Some were polite, merely here to end a bad marriage. But he was trying to hide from the woman who'd cornered him the second he came in the main house for dinner. A lusty blond who'd quickly told him she was there for her second divorce. She had extended her heavily manicured hand and introduced herself as Dolores. She'd eyed Joan with suspicion from across the room and told him, with absolutely no shame whatsoever, "We could be each other's next mistake."

He didn't know who he wanted to avoid more—Dolores or Joan. That afternoon, he'd felt a brief something between him and Joan again. A flicker of attraction, a hint that beneath the images they projected to the world, there could be something real. But Joan Davis, the movie star, was back with her full mask and movie-star armor on, sporting a shimmering silver evening gown that felt out of place amidst all the flannel and riding clothes. The scoop neck and plunging back kept drawing his attention. He'd always loved Joan's back, its gentle sway, the strong set of her shoulders. But it was thoughts like these he had to avoid.

He thought back on what she'd said this afternoon before

his antics had sparked something playful in her. That she would rather drink arsenic than touch him. He shuddered and took a gulp of the glass of whiskey in his hand. What was true, then? Her repulsion at the thought of him or the electricity that had sparked between them when he'd held her nightgown? He looked across the room at her with Monty and had a sinking suspicion which it was. What had always been true with any woman who got close enough to peel back the glittering facade.

A mousy thirtysomething he'd heard call herself Anita was practically swooning. "And when you cried because you realized your love had been too proud to tell you about the accident, well, I just about died," she drawled in a broad Texas accent. "Why, it's an absolute scandal you didn't win the Oscar."

The memory of Monty's latest film sent the rest of the women in the cozy den tittering, with several of them clutching at their hearts in exaggerated shows of affection. Dash chuckled and sipped at his drink. *Better him than me,* he thought. He'd never cried on camera. Harry had always warned him it would put a chink in the air of rugged masculinity they'd worked so hard to cultivate. Well, he was the one with the Oscar. Not Monty.

Monty gave Anita a wan smile. "You're too kind, Mrs. Hodges. But I think they gave the award to the best man."

He raised his glass in Dash's direction, and Dash nodded appreciatively. Not only was the man handsome and talented, he was decent as hell. It made it a lot harder for him to hate the guy. But it also made him wonder why and how he'd become engaged to Joan. They were a picture-perfect couple, yes, but Monty didn't seem to be gaga for her. And if Dash's kiss with Joan was any indication, Monty wasn't the be-all, end-all for her either. Surely, the man could easily find a starlet who was crazy about him. And who he was crazy about.

Travis, wearing a white apron with the message COWBOYS MAKE THE BEST COOKS over his denim ensemble, interrupted their little cocktail party, banging a spoon against a pot. The noise made Joan jump, and Dash smiled. At one time, he'd believed her whole movie-star act was high-hat, but the more time they spent together, the more he saw that she really did love the glamorous life. It was adorable really, to see how out of place she was here. He liked the rugged lifestyle that reminded him of his youth, but Joan had chosen caviar and drawing-room comedies and never looked back.

"Sorry. Once a cowboy, always a cowboy," Travis said sheepishly in Joan's direction. "But y'all can come and get it. Er, I mean, dinner is served." He gave an awkward little bow in Joan's direction and then stepped aside to allow the guests to enter the dining room.

Dash lingered at the door, careful to choose a seat far from both the ravenous clutches of Dolores and from Monty and Joan. There was a chair open next to Arlene. And despite the fact that she was Joan's assistant and fiercely loyal to her boss, he'd always liked her. He smiled at the careworn tablecloth sporting a print of cacti and cowboys as he took a seat.

"Is it all right if I sit here?" he asked.

She smiled, a genuine look of warmth, and replied, "Please do."

"Thanks."

They sat quietly while Joan regaled the table with the story of how she and Monty met on a soundstage.

"I was passing by, dressed in an extravagant Orry-Kelly number, and there he was in his chaps and his hat," she said, referring to Monty's first major picture *Cattle Drive,* in which he'd played the sensitive son of a tyrannical cattle baron. "Well, I don't have to tell you all how attractive a man is in chaps."

Joan winked across the table at Dusty and Tom, and though

they were there largely to show the ladies of the ranch a good time and had probably heard jokes of such a nature countless times, they still blushed. Maybe there was something different about hearing it from a movie star. Or maybe it was the way Joan sparkled as she told it, a naughty gleam in her eye and the red swoosh of her artfully painted lips curving into a delectable smile. Dash found himself smiling too, in spite of himself.

"And then as luck would have it...he was seated at my table that night at the Brown Derby because they were short on space."

Dash snorted into his chili. *Luck.* Joan had called the restaurant ahead of time and arranged it herself. Or demanded Harry do it. He was sure of it. He'd eat his hat if luck had anything to do with it. It had studio setup written all over it. He should know.

"Is somethin' funny, Mr. Howard?" Dolores said, clipping her words in her New York accent and looking at him with malice in her eyes.

He looked up and met Joan's eyes, choking down his bite of food. Her eyes were hard and her chin was raised, as if she were challenging him to question her story. They were back to this, then. Very well, he could give as good as he got.

"I find it hard to believe that they wouldn't have been able to find a table for a man of Mr. Smyth's stature, that's all." He gave Joan a small smug smile. He didn't want to give Dolores the satisfaction of the scene she obviously desired, but he couldn't stand this game Joan was playing. And she'd been the one to accuse him of setups for the press! Something stunk of hypocrisy about the whole thing.

She glared at him, but Monty jumped in, all solicitude. "Mr. Howard has the right of it, I'm afraid. I requested to be seated at Miss Davis's table that night after seeing her looking so fetching in her evening gown earlier that day."

Dash nodded at him, a gesture so imperceptible he couldn't even be sure Monty had caught it, except for the light curl of Monty's upper lip, acknowledging the complicated dance they found themselves in. Joan smirked in his direction and laid her hand atop Monty's arm, her obnoxiously large Asscher-cut engagement ring catching the light and providing a blinding reminder to Dash of how inadequate he was.

But Dolores couldn't leave well enough alone. "Mr. Smyth, how did you react to the news that Miss Davis was married to another man?"

Joan looked like she'd swallowed a bottle of ink, but Monty was the portrait of elegance. "It's merely a speed bump on our road to happiness." He grinned.

But then Monty reached for his collar again and suddenly became very interested in his soup. Dash could see it was a lie, a well-practiced company line to make someone happy. But who was it for? Joan? The studio?

"Obviously, it threw a wrench in our plans for an early September wedding," Joan announced icily. "But Monty is worth the wait."

"Meanwhile, she can't be rid of me fast enough," Dash quipped. The room took it as he intended, laughing heartily at Dash's joke at his own expense. But he looked pointedly at Joan as he said it, and she raised one eyebrow, as if daring him to push the matter.

"Dash and Davis were only ever meant for the silver screen," she rejoined.

"It seems that's all Dash Howard is good for," he said with a grimace. The room laughed again, more uncomfortably this time, and Arlene gave him a pitying look that nearly broke him.

"But how," Dolores squeaked, "on earth can you accidentally marry someone?"

"It turns out the minister wasn't acting," Dash quipped. "The studio wanted the real McCoy. Bet they wish now they'd invested in some clerical collars for the wardrobe department. It'd certainly be cheaper than this rodeo."

"Well," Joan cut in, stabbing at her plate, "it would've been fine if somebody hadn't decided sending the marriage certificate to City Hall was a grand joke."

Dash watched as Monty squeezed Joan's leg under the table, urging her to stop. But she was right. It was his fault. Did she have to keep rubbing it in his face though?

He simpered at Dolores. "I was worried for Joanie. Thought she might die an old maid if I didn't do something about it."

Joan stood from her chair and threw her napkin down on the table. She was shaking with fury. "At least I don't have to fake a marriage to get someone interested in me."

Dash leaned back in his chair. "Oh, you don't? So, you simply adore Monty? And that kiss last night was, what? A performance for my benefit? If so, it was Oscar-worthy, I'll say that much."

The table exploded with gasps and Dash knew he'd gone too far. What sealed the deal was the wide Cheshire cat grin on Dolores's face, a sign that they'd both played right into her gossip-hungry hands.

Travis chose that moment to reenter, a dopey smile on his face, blissfully unaware of the tempest he was walking into. "Who's ready for some dancing?"

Thirty minutes later, Dash found himself crammed into the main house's living room, the collection of armchairs and couches shoved to the sides of the room while couples danced to an assortment of standards blaring over the radio. He'd tried to leave, to retreat to the bungalow. The way he'd talked to Joan was unconscionable. Even if she'd provoked him. But Travis had insisted that the ladies were excited to at last have enough men to go around instead of having to share Dusty and Tom. And the least he could do was provide some entertainment.

While Benny Goodman played his way through "Stardust" on the radio, Dash danced with Arlene. She swayed gently in his arms and looked at him thoughtfully.

"I think you're in love with her, you know," she murmured, loud enough so only Dash could hear.

"What?" He had been looking at Joan and Monty dancing on the other side of the room. "No, that's absurd."

"You were just staring at her."

"I feel bad about how I acted this evening, that's all."

Arlene clucked her tongue in frustration. "You acted that way because you're in love with her. You've been in love with her for years. It's why you addressed the envelope with the marriage certificate."

"Oh God, I hope that's not why you mailed it in."

Arlene blushed. "No, I swear I didn't know what was in the envelope. I thought Joan had left it for me to mail."

Thank God for small miracles. He knew Arlene was a hopeless romantic, but he thought she had more sense than to scheme up something like this.

"You've seen too many of our films, that's all. We're good at faking it for the cameras." Here they went again, someone buying into the Dash Howard image and not being able to parse the difference between fact and fiction. It was exhausting.

"Maybe." Arlene shrugged. "But I know Joan, and I've never met anyone who drives her crazier than you do. And you'll do anything to get her attention. It's why you're constantly pranking her. You two are crazy about each other, but you're too proud to admit it, so you drive each other nuts instead."

Dash stared at her open-mouthed. Was this truly what Arlene thought of them? That like schoolchildren they couldn't confess their feelings so he did the on-set equivalent of pulling Joan's pigtails to get her attention? It was absurd.

"You've read too many novels. Joan and I can't stand each other." Or at least Joan couldn't stand him. And he was...working on it.

She looked up at him, that expression of pity in her gaze again. "I just hope you're both not making a mistake you'll always regret."

She was silent then, swaying as the song wound to its conclusion. As it ended, Travis rose from his spot in the corner and made a pronouncement. "Now comes my favorite time of the evening! I get to choose your partners for the next dance. It's a long-standing tradition here at Lazy Me because, well, usually there aren't enough fellas to go around. Tonight, we've hit the mother lode when it comes to male guests—but round here, we honor our traditions. Especially when we have the opportunity for a beloved pairing in our own midst."

Dash groaned. He knew what was coming before Travis said it. "So without further ado, Dash Howard and Joan Davis, will you please lead us into the next dance?"

Joan crossed her arms from the other side of the room and refused to budge, until Monty gave her a slight shove in Dash's direction. It looked like this was happening, no matter how much they both hated the idea.

CHAPTER 13

JOAN WOULD NOT DANCE WITH DASH. NOT AFTER WHAT he'd pulled at dinner. The nerve. It was his fault they were here, sharing a bungalow and dancing with divorcées at a ranch. His fault she'd ended up at the one place she'd vowed she never would be: back on a plot of dusty land, trying to secure a divorce and licking her wounds.

But Monty nudged her and whispered in her ear: "People talk, Joan. Go make nice with him. It'll help smooth over the scene at dinner. Any one of these people could call up Leda when they get back to their room tonight. Dolores looks like she's begging you to give her a reason to gossip to anyone who will listen."

She huffed, realizing he was right, and went to join Dash, picking her way through the small crowd and the mass of gingham and paisley prints dotting homespun cotton dresses. She held her arms out to him and gave him a smile she knew he'd see through. He wrapped his arms around her, placing one hand at the small of her back. She shivered as his bare hands met her exposed flesh. The sensation sent the memory of their kiss ghosting through her mind, and she tried to shake it off. She made a show of kissing him on the cheek, the chastened movie star dancing with her leading man, and she was dismayed to find a spark of electricity zinged across her lips as she met the coarse stubble coating his jaw. She knew he'd shaved before they'd come to dinner, but Dash couldn't keep a smooth face for long.

The strains of Fred Astaire singing "Cheek to Cheek" started to wind through the speaker at the corner of the room, and Joan obliged with the lyrics, pressing her cheek to Dash's. She might as well make a good show.

"Don't get any ideas," she hissed in his ear, hoping this was enough to quiet any gossip hounds among them looking to tell the press about their spat.

"On the contrary, I wanted to apologize," he whispered back at her.

"For which of your sins? There are so many."

He stiffened against her; the question clearly aggravated him. Well, good, she could get under his skin just as well as he could get under hers. How dare he flaunt their kiss at the dinner table, tell the world her engagement to Monty was for show. So what if he didn't know that was the truth? She resented how he seemed to see through her, understand her. It was dangerous in more ways than one. Hadn't he done enough damage already?

But he did answer her. "For what I said at dinner. It seems I can't be around you without starting something. I'm sorry."

"Why would you say those things in front of strangers? Any one of them could report back to Leda."

"I know. I couldn't help myself. You kicked me where it hurt, and I lashed out."

"When are you going to start dealing with your feelings like a grown-up?"

He turned her around on the dance floor, so no one could see his mouth and muttered into her ear, "When you start taking responsibility for your actions. You're not blameless in this. You kissed me. You provoked me tonight at the table. Your little victim act is all wet, Joan. We both know it."

"I am not playing the victim. And I didn't provoke you. I was merely responding to your jabs at my relationship with Monty. If I didn't know better, I'd say you were jealous." She expected Dash to rail against her, to become immediately defensive at the suggestion. But he didn't. Instead, he went quiet, the grip of his hand on her back loosening and his fingers intertwined with hers going limp. It was as if the fight went out of him. Like he wanted to prove his disinterest in her then and there. A flicker of disappointment coursed through her at the sudden loss of close contact, but she tucked the confusing feeling away to pull out and examine later.

They danced in silence as the song wound to a close, Astaire's voice warbling through the radio. "I bet Fred and Ginger don't have these kinds of problems," she muttered under her breath.

As soon as the song was over, Dash dropped his hands and Joan turned to return to Monty, who had been dancing with the box-blond Dolores. Monty was currently trying to loosen the death grip of the woman's hand wound tightly around his neck and was giving her a wan smile. Joan rushed to rescue him, but as she turned to go, Dash grabbed her hand and pulled her back to him. He searched her eyes, and she didn't know what he was looking for. He looked sad and a bit wounded. But then he said, "I'm not jealous, Joan. I just don't think you should be making such a song and dance of marrying a man who doesn't love you. He should've slugged me after last night. Why didn't he? You convinced yourself you're cold, hard as nails, but you still deserve to be loved. Everyone does."

For once, Joan didn't have a haughty retort. She was stunned. She'd never considered marrying Monty a sacrifice. She never intended on falling in love, so what did it matter if she married for convenience? For protection? To secure her place at the studio? Women, and men for that matter, had been doing it for centuries. Love complicated things unnecessarily. But Dash was making her feel guilty about it. Like she was doing something terrible. And he didn't even know the entire truth of it. Who was he to make her feel that way and to tell her everyone deserved love when he'd admitted how spectacularly his own brushes with it had misfired?

She wandered back to Monty in a daze, and he leapt at the chance to take her back, almost pushing Dolores out of the way.

"If you'll excuse me, my fiancée requires my attention," he said, wrapping his arms around her. "There you are, darling," he announced before kissing her. Joan should revel in this public display of affection. She and Monty had agreed to put on a good show for the sake of keeping up appearances with their marriage, but he'd never gone this far. Even with cameras around. But it felt sterile. Worse than the heavily choreographed screen kisses she'd enacted time and again, which more often than not were a chaste pressing together of lips. This was flesh against flesh, but there was no warmth in it, no passion. Nothing like the embrace she'd shared with Dash last night.

When Monty broke apart from her, a new song had started up, but she was so muddled she couldn't even register what was playing. "I'm sorry, I had to do something to get that Dolores woman off my back," Monty murmured.

"Don't apologize, darling. We're supposed to be getting married. A little kiss here and there is to be expected." She was distracted, her thoughts a hash over what Dash had said to her, what he meant by it, and why this kiss with the man she was going to marry couldn't hold a candle to a stolen moment on a riverbank.

"You look upset," Monty replied. "Is it because of me? We've never talked about kissing before. I wasn't sure if it was all right."

She looked at Monty, and that haunted, brooding look that had won him fame and fortune stared back at her. He looked sad. Like she'd let him down. Because she had. By kissing Dash last night, getting caught and photographed, she'd not only hurt herself, thrown a wrench into her attempt to secure her place in the Hollywood firmament, but she'd risked something that Monty needed too.

She laid her head against his shoulder, craving the comfort she had hoped he could provide when she first agreed to this scheme. "It's not you, Monty dear. It's Dash. He's so infuriating. And confusing. If I didn't know better, I'd say he didn't want me to marry you."

Monty rested his head against hers, and she closed her eyes as they danced, swaying to the lilting strains of Ruth Etting singing about losing a man. "You're letting Leda get under your skin. If he didn't want us to get married, why would he have sent for me to come here?"

"What?" She jolted, narrowly avoiding banging her head into Monty's jaw. It was soft, fresh, and smooth, nothing like the rough, chiseled angles of Dash Howard.

Monty blinked at her. "I thought you knew."

"Knew what? I called Harry up after that little exposé ran on our fun and games while filming at the river. I'd been playing a prank. Ridiculous! So Harry promised to send you to me. That he would fix everything."

Monty looked confused. "I never heard from Harry. I was already on my way here by the time that story ran. Dash called me up the day you got here, told me that he'd made a terrible mistake, and I had to come set things right for us both. I resisted at first. You know I wasn't keen on coming up here. And I thought it was best to lay low. But he booked the ticket himself. Wouldn't take no for an answer. Hell, he even sent his car to take me to the station."

"But Harry said—"

No, wait, Harry hadn't said. Joan remembered her distraught conversation with the head of the studio. When she'd thanked him for doing what she asked, he'd tried to tell her something. In her relief, she'd hung up the phone without letting him finish. She'd assumed that Harry Evets had fixed things. Because that's what the studio did. For better or worse.

But it hadn't been Harry at all. It had been Dash, the man she assumed was constantly undermining her for his own benefit. He'd done something to help her. To put her more at ease. To counteract the stories and photographs she'd accused him of planting for publicity. He'd done something purely for her. To make her happy. That wasn't at all like the man she believed Dash Howard to be. But it was like the Dash Howard she'd seen last night. The man who bared his secrets to her in the moonlight. The man *she'd* kissed. Of her own volition. And he'd kissed her back, made her weak at the knees. It had been unlike any kiss she'd ever experienced. But she'd stuffed that feeling down, locked it away—because she had a fiancé, for God's sake. She wasn't supposed to be thinking about another man's kisses.

The room suddenly felt claustrophobic, as though the walls covered with wallpaper sporting a pattern of horses and mountains were closing in on her. There were too many people in here. And despite the fact that her entire back was exposed in her low-slung Adrian gown, she suddenly found the room oppressive, overwhelmed by everything.

"I need some air," she told Monty, pushing her way through the dancing crowd and running for the front door of the main house. There was no sign of Dash. He must've left and gone to bed. She could dimly hear the gasps and mutterings of the other ranch guests as she moved through them. Monty was calling her name and following close behind, but she couldn't stop until she was outside. Away from this noise and this music and this stifling heat.

She burst onto the front step, sucking in the cold night air of the mountains. It was bracing and it burned in her lungs, but it was better than the sticky, cloying scent of overperfumed divorcées and earthy cowboys. She leaned against the doorframe, looking up at the blanket of stars twinkling above her. She hadn't seen stars like this in years. She hadn't wanted to. Hollywood had all the stars she needed, and she had once been the brightest among them. She soon would be again. Alongside Dash Howard. Who she hated. Didn't she?

Monty caught up to her, slightly out of breath. He closed the door behind him and the din of partygoers flattened from a roar to a whisper. "What's wrong, Joan?"

What could she say to him? To her fiancé? *I think my longtime costar who I've been locked in a battle of wills with for five years might not be the man I thought he was. He might be someone decent and kind, and I've been horrible to him because I didn't want to believe that was true.* She didn't hold any illusions about what her engagement was, and they both knew Monty was in love with another man. But she couldn't bring herself to say it. Not the least because she was still trying to wrap her head around all of this—the kiss, the fight at the table, the revelation that Dash had brought Monty here. So instead she said, "I got overheated. Perhaps I drank too much champagne."

Monty wrapped his arm around her shoulders, which were now dotted with gooseflesh from the chill of the mountain air. He looked at her, and there was understanding in his eyes. A sad look of familiarity that seemed to say *I know what you're going through because I've been there myself.* But he was too decent to say it. Instead, he rubbed her shoulder, trying to warm her up, and merely said, "You're shivering now."

She giggled, a bubble of hysteria mounting in her throat. What was happening to her? It was as if the earth had tilted on its axis when she'd stepped off the train to Reno and now nothing would ever be the same.

"I really thought he would've told you," Monty whispered. "After I saw the kiss, I assumed you knew."

She pressed her hands into her eyes, the ghosts of the stars flickering against her eyelids with the pressure. "No, I thought it was Harry. I called and asked him to send you. I misunderstood. I've been terrible to Dash. Accused him of awful things. And all this time, he brought you here, he was trying to fix things. He's done nothing but be honest with me and try to help me. Last night, he told me things. Things he said he's never told anyone else. And how did I repay him? By accusing him of setting me up. By refusing to admit that *I* kissed *him*. That some part of me wanted him." She cast Monty an apologetic glance. "Sorry."

Monty waved his hand as if to say "It's nothing" and leaned back thoughtfully against the door, pulled a pack of cigarettes from his breast pocket, and struck a match against his shoe. He inhaled deeply before issuing a thin line of smoke from his mouth. There was only the sound of the wind whispering through the pines for a moment before he spoke. "I think he might understand. Or at the very least, be willing to hear an apology."

What had Dash said? That she needed to take responsibility for her actions. That she wasn't blameless. She hadn't wanted to hear it. Take responsibility? That's what she'd been doing since the day she stepped off the train in Los Angeles. Joan Davis was nothing if not responsible for herself. It had been that drive, that independence, that *responsibility* that had got her all the things she'd dreamed of. She didn't need anyone. She'd erased her past and built this present—and love had been a luxury she couldn't afford. Frankly, it was one she'd never wanted. Not from anyone but her audiences. It wasn't that she didn't think she was worthy of it; she didn't want it, couldn't allow herself to.

"This doesn't change anything between us, Monty. I still need you." He didn't answer her, but exhaled, threw his cigarette to the porch steps, and ground it out with his mahogany wing-tipped shoe.

"You know I didn't want to come to Reno."

She nodded. "But you did. Because I needed you. Because Dash convinced you to. And all I've done is complicate matters. I'm a liability now." She choked back tears, fearing that she might have ruined everything.

Monty was silent for a minute. He didn't look at her, but then—"You know Jerry won't speak to me. Ever since we announced the engagement. He won't even take my calls. I didn't want to come here because I thought parading through a series of photo ops would only make things worse."

"But Dash convinced you? How?"

Monty smiled a closed-lip grin as if he had a secret. "He's very persuasive when he wants to be. And he cares more about you than you think."

Joan opened her mouth to protest, but what was the use? Monty was probably right. She didn't want to hear it. Hadn't wanted to for five years. "Maybe Jerry will talk to you again now that I kissed Dash."

Monty laughed. "I don't think it's your feelings—or lack thereof—for me that he's worried about."

"But surely he understands that this is what you must do to protect your careers."

"He doesn't care about that. He would've been willing to throw it all away for us. But he comes from a wealthy family. He didn't spend his whole life dreaming of a way out, of being somebody else."

Joan winced at hearing her own reasons for needing to marry Monty parroted back to her. "You and I are cut from the same cloth, Monty dear. We never had anything, and we've worked too hard for our little scrap of something to let them take it away from us now. I've been a fool. But I promise, we are still a team. We'll fix this together. Dash means nothing to me." She tried to ignore the pang of guilt and regret blooming in her chest as she made this pledge.

Monty smiled at her wanly, the haunted, hungry look in his eyes hitting her in a new way. He chucked her on the chin and kissed her weakly on the cheek. "I never understood why you agreed to this scheme, Joan, but if it's what you want, I won't desert you. You're shooting all day tomorrow, and I'll scout around Reno for some prime areas for us to be photographed. Go get some shut-eye. You'll feel better in the morning."

Somehow, she doubted that she'd ever feel better again, her mind was such a jumble and her nerves so frayed. But she patted Monty's hand and whispered, "Thank you."

Arlene pushed her way through the screen and joined them on the porch. Her face was pink, and she was breathless. "What'd I miss?" she huffed.

Monty and Joan exchanged a knowing look. "Nothing," they replied in unison. "Seems like you were having a good time."

Arlene's eyes sparkled with excitement and exhaustion. "Travis taught me the two-step." Joan gave her a look. "It's nothing like that! He's just friendly, that's all."

"You'd better take her home, Monty, before Hollywood loses its next great screenwriter to a cowhand."

Monty chuckled and pushed off from the side of the house that he'd been leaning on. He offered his arm and walked Arlene down to the flashy car he'd driven them both over in, opening the door for her and giving Joan a little wave. She watched him get in the car and peel away, the cloud of dust he kicked up obscuring his car from view as it headed back down the dirt road. Her options now were to go back inside to the crowd of cowboys and would-be divorcées or go to bed, so she set off back to the tiny bungalow she was sharing with Dash, holding her gown gingerly between her fingertips to avoid it dragging on the dirt path.

Monty was decent; particularly after the spectacle she'd been making of herself. But she could do this for five more weeks. She could apologize to Dash, grin and bear it through making this picture together, and win the divorce that would secure her the safety of a perfect Hollywood match. She'd still be alone. Spiritually if not literally. But wasn't that how she preferred it? The only way it had ever worked?

She'd have her audience back, and maybe the respect of the industry—if they found the script as good as she and Arlene believed it to be. That was what she wanted, wasn't it? That's how she liked things. How she'd always known it had to be. All she had to do was keep her temper and avoid any sudden urges to kiss her costar in the moonlight.

Before she knew it, she was back at the cottage. Dash had left the door open for her. That was foolish; there were bears and God knew what else lurking in the woods at the base of the Sierras. But it still warmed her to know that in spite of everything that had happened tonight, he'd made this gesture of goodwill.

She toed off her silver-heeled sandals and took them in hand, creeping into the room as quietly as she could and turning the lock of the door behind her. She could hear the rise and fall of

Dash's breathing opposite the side of the sheet he'd strung up between their beds. The sight of the sheet reminded her of this afternoon, the tension between them when she'd accidentally pitched her ripped peignoir at his head. Oh God, her nightie! What would she wear to bed now? She'd forgotten about it in the mess of the evening. Suddenly that sheet looked threadbare, and she could see Dash's silhouette clearly through it, outlined by the crack of moonlight streaming through the red-checked curtains.

She plopped on the bed and buried her face in her hands. She couldn't sleep in this Adrian gown. It would be ruined. She whimpered and lay back on the pillow, too tired to work out a plan. She expected to hit the cool cotton of the crisp white pillowcase and was baffled to find her head connecting with soft folds of flannel. Joan sat up and picked up the strange piece of material sitting on her pillow.

It was pajamas. To be precise, it was a man's pajama top, complete with buttons down the front and a piped collar. There was a note tacked to it. *Joanie, I'm sorry for the way I acted at dinner. No matter what, I was unconscionably rude and you deserve better. Truce?*

Joan pressed the note to her chest. It was more than she deserved. Especially knowing that he had been the one to bring Monty here. She wiggled out of her dress and stood only in her silk underwear, as the backless gown had required her to go braless. Hurriedly, she slipped on the flannel shirt. It was made for Dash, who towered over her on set. She wasn't a tiny woman by any means, but he was broad-shouldered and barrel-chested and as tall and strong as an oak. It fell to her midthigh, stopping just above her knee. Enough to cover up the important bits.

She snuggled into it and laughed quietly. It was another page from the *Road to Romance* playbook. In the film, her character had not packed pajamas and Dash's character had given her his matching set to preserve her virtue. Dash hadn't worn an undershirt in the scene, and the men of America had followed suit, sending undershirt sales plummeting. The studio had received angry letters from clothing manufacturers for months.

Joan climbed under the covers and pressed her nose against the soft fabric of the shirt. It smelled like Dash, clean and masculine, like Ivory soap and fresh air. This gesture had been clever. And decent and kind. All things she was starting to realize were true of Dash too. She held the sleeve up to her nose and inhaled deeply, getting lost in the scent of this man she was discovering anew. He had told her last night that once people realized who he really was, that he wasn't Dash Howard the movie star, they cast him aside. Disappointed with what they found.

But she was having the opposite experience. Dashiell Howard the farm boy from Ohio was much better than Dash Howard the movie star. Considerate, thoughtful, and even a little bit shy. She found herself suddenly angry. At Josephine. At anyone who'd ever made Dash believe he didn't deserve someone who saw him and loved him for who he really was. She was even upset with herself, for unwittingly adding to his pain. She stared at the ceiling, the cracks in the plaster matching the ones in her resolve.

"Dash, are you awake?" she whispered. He didn't reply, but all the same, she whispered, "Thank you. For the shirt, for the sheet...and for Monty. For bringing him here."

She paused and she thought she heard him roll over, but when she held her breath and craned her neck to listen through the sheet, she simply heard the gentle rise and fall of his breathing, as when she'd first entered the room. "Good night."

She curled up into a ball, tucking her knees beneath the hem of the flannel top. She closed her eyes and whispered on a single exhale, as if it were a prayer, "You deserve to be loved too."

CHAPTER 14

DASH BLINKED, THE GLARING MIDDAY SUN MAKING IT A challenge to keep his eyes open. His head bobbed forward in a bid for sleep, and he forced himself upright, wary of falling off the chestnut horse he was currently sitting astride. They were supposed to be filming a key scene in *Reno Rendezvous,* one where his character, Joe, takes Joan's out for a horseback ride in the Sierras. Arlene had rewritten it last week.

But Dash was struggling to stay awake. He'd tossed and turned all night. He'd been awake when Joan had returned to the bungalow, but had stayed still. The sight of her body silhouetted in moonlight through the sheet he'd hung between them would've been enough to prompt a sleepless night. He'd seen nothing but the shadow of her nakedness, but the gentle curve of her backside, the round suggestion of her breasts, the arch of her long neck, and the slope of her spine had been tantalizing.

But it wasn't the whisper of her body that had robbed him of sleep. It was the soft words he'd heard her utter, like an invocation: "You deserve to be loved too." She thought he was asleep or she would never have said that aloud. But what did it mean? What did he want it to mean?

"Mister Howard, have you heard a word I am saying?"

He shook himself from his exhaustion-fueled reverie. He

hadn't realized Von Wild had been talking to him. The short-tempered man gave a huff of exasperation. "I said that we need a shot of you riding toward the camera. We will get this single shot before we bring Miss Davis into the scene."

Dash tipped his hat in acknowledgment and nudged the horse with his heels until he got far enough away to pick up decent speed while riding toward the camera. This was easy as pie. He'd learned to ride a horse before he could walk, helping Pa run the farm in his mother's absence. If he couldn't focus enough to do this, he might as well give up now. But they got the shot in one.

Dash patted his horse, soothing the beast who responded to his slightest nudge. He relaxed into his saddle. This was his domain. The chance to flash a bit of the real Dash to the cameras. He loved it when he got to ride a horse or use his hands on camera. Audiences seemed to lap up the rugged masculinity, but he liked feeling useful. The love scenes, the heroic speeches, those always felt like they belonged to movie star Dash Howard, the carefully constructed, falsest version of himself. But when he could just *be* on-screen, ride or rope a steer or split rails, he got to bring something true and real, something practical, to his work. He got to be the man they all thought he was for a moment.

He nodded at the cameraman, Phil. Phil had been with Dash on almost all of his pictures and was part of his weekly poker nights, had been for almost three years. Dash had been at both of his kids' christenings. He'd specifically asked Harry to send Phil along to Reno so he'd have at least one friendly face on the set. Normally, the studio assigned out cameramen like factory workers on a conveyor belt. But Dash liked being surrounded by people he knew, so he could come to work feeling like he was part of a family. "How's the wife?"

The guy smiled. "She's good, expecting again." Phil loved

being a dad, and it made Dash's heart fit to burst seeing how much he loved his family.

"Send her my best. Tell her I owe her a Philippe's pickle and French dip."

Phil laughed. "The cravings haven't started yet, but when they do, I'll be sure to give you a call."

He loved the way he could just be Dash with Phil, another one of the guys. It made him a better actor, and it gave him solid ground to stand on when he was making a picture—touchstones beyond the whirl of the movie-star trappings. Talking to Phil helped get him out of his head, shake some of the fog of the exhaustion from his brain.

But his relaxation was short-lived, as he watched Joan tromp onto set in a cowgirl hat, ill-fitting boots, riding pants, and a gingham blouse. She looked like the women at dinner last night, Reno divorcées ready to play at ranching. Only more beautiful, more untouchable. Arlene was a few steps behind her, muttering something in her ear. Behind them both was a handler who was escorting a whinnying horse, which Joan looked at with a mixture of naked fear and disdain.

He was supposed to be teaching her character to ride in this scene and slowly falling for her beneath the dappled sunlight of the pines. By and large, he and Joan made glamorous movies, set in drawing rooms and society settings. If the script called for some adventure or something rugged, he obliged, but Joan was best with dialogue, with using the verbal alacrity of her tongue and her striking beauty to coax the audience into her confidence. He could not remember ever seeing her anywhere near a horse. Now he could see why.

He'd seen her storm down a hallway in three-inch heels, never missing a step, but she walked uneasily in the boots, and she eyed the horse like it was a foreign agent come to kill her. Joan Davis was not built for ranching.

Von Wild looked at Arlene first. "Why are you here?"

"We only rewrote the scene last week. I need to be here in case we need to make any changes," Arlene replied, refusing to wither under the man's gaze.

Von Wild harrumphed. "You are a writer. I am a director. This picture is mine now." Arlene sighed, gave Joan a supportive look, and went to sit in the chair with her name on it, positioned amidst with the cameras.

"Miss Davis, why are you not already on the horse?" asked Fritz. Joan gave him a death glare, a look usually reserved for Dash. In response, the horse bucked and blew air out of its nostrils. It seemed no more interested in having Joan ride it than she did in mounting it.

"I think it's pretty clear why not."

"We do not have time for these shenanigans," Fritz muttered.

Dash rolled his eyes. What they didn't have time for was a director on such an extended ego trip that he couldn't plainly see that Joan was terrified. But if he knew anything about Joan, he knew she was too proud to admit it. "They can sense your fear, you know," he murmured, trying to make it clear he wasn't mocking her.

Joan scoffed, but he could detect the uncertainty in her voice. "I'm not afraid. I just hate horses. Ranches, dirt, horses, I detest all of it."

He'd never known Joan had such strong feelings about the outdoors. But then again, they spent most of their time together comfortably nestled on a soundstage. "Well, there's your problem. He knows you don't like him. Don't worry, I've got plenty of experience in that department. I'll teach him how to get by." He winked at her, hoping she would take it as the good-natured joke he intended. Then he jumped down off his horse in one swift motion and passed the reins off to the trainer.

He patted Joan's horse's nose and neck, whispering soft assurances as the horse transformed from a bucking, irritated creature into the picture of docility. "There, see, he just needed a little confidence boost. Now put your foot in the stirrup."

Joan stared at him, the haughty irritation vanishing from her gaze, leaving only fear. "I can't do it, Dash."

"Nonsense. I've never known you to shy away from a challenge, Joanie. Of course you can."

She glanced up at the horse, its haunches towering far above her head, and swallowed. He'd never seen her look so cowed by anything. Normally, she charmed everyone from the director to the grip, insuring they photographed her good side and favored her close-ups in the edit.

"Look, I've read this script. It could be your Oscar. The Academy laps this stuff up, Joan. Scorned woman finds new love in Reno while seeking her divorce, only to lose him in a tragic accident. Then she goes on to fulfill his dream of opening a ranch to rehabilitate rodeo horses. It's the role you've been begging for, and it's Arlene's chance too. This script is good enough to launch her career. I know how badly you want it, Joan—for yourself and for her. You can prove them all wrong: the gossip columnists crowing over our marriage, the headlines that named you box-office poison, the fools who think women have no place in production… Hell, even Harry, who can't seem to give you an interesting script no matter how much you plead. All you have to do is put your foot in the stirrup. I'll help you."

She closed her eyes, took a deep breath, and mouthed counting to ten before placing her hands on Dash's shoulders, pressing down, and heaving her body upward to get a foot in the stirrup. But as soon as Joan pushed herself up, the horse edged away from her, sending her plummeting forward as she grabbed desperately at Dash's cowboy hat, which brushed off his head and fell to the ground.

She was finally able to get purchase on the back of his flannel shirt, but by that time it was too late. Try as he might to avoid it, to leave her some shred of dignity, her crotch was pressed against his face. She was practically straddling his neck as she scrambled to get her balance. Dash would've laughed if he didn't find a wave of lust crashing over him; it was so strong he was practically drowning in it.

Joan was wearing a charming riding costume, thick to protect her from the leather saddle and the horse's coarse hair. He wished there was entirely less fabric between them. He resisted the urge to press his face farther into her, to inhale her scent. Pain pierced through his cloud of want as she kneed him square in the solar plexus, still flailing in her attempt to gain her balance.

"Stop moving. Joan, stop and I'll put you down. Ouch, stop it, Joan, stop it." She wasn't listening or perhaps she couldn't hear him over her shrieks of terror. There was nothing for it then. He lifted his free arm, the one not currently preventing her from slipping off his shoulders, and gave her ass a slight pat. It wasn't a slap, but enough of a bite to get her attention. A sharp pulse of desire shot through him at the contact, and he fought the urge to return his hand there, to cup and knead and explore.

At the contact with her backside, she went quiet. But only for a moment.

"Why on earth would you—"

"If you'd listen for a second and stop your hollering, I'll explain. Stop moving, you're making it worse." Her writhing fear was replaced by a taut stillness. At least she was listening. "Can you put your hands back on my shoulders?"

Joan did as she was told, and he placed his hands around her waist, holding her above him. Her dark-brown hair cascaded in waves around her face, and her fear had been replaced with sultry annoyance. Their eyes met, and she licked her full, bee-stung lips. He was certain she hadn't even realized she did it. But then she sucked in her breath, a short intake that was nearly imperceptible, and he knew she felt the same strange thing crackling between them. Electricity arced through his hands, and he tightened his grip on her hips for fear he would drop her.

She looked down at him hungrily now, her eyes hooded, accentuated by the angle, as he held her above him. He yearned to lower her gently until their lips met. To ease her into another kiss like the one they'd shared only a few nights ago. To press and slide her against him until he felt the heat of her grinding on him.

She looked at him with such longing. It would be so simple to slide her down his body, wrap one hand around the back of her head, and gently press his lips to hers. So easy to tease at those lush, full lips painted in a brilliant shade of red until she granted his tongue entry. Her hands would tangle in his hair, palming his head, their scene forgotten as they lost themselves in each other.

The breathless spell between them was broken by the harsh cough of Fritz. "We are not filming the love scene today."

The words seemed to bring Joan back to reality. She blushed and leaned back, restoring a respectful distance between them. The hooded, hungry look was gone, replaced by her most amenable demeanor. One that was all business. "No, Mr. Von Wild, of course not. Dash was just trying to help me with the horse."

He remembered himself and his task a moment too late. She swatted at him, urging him to action, and he cleared his throat.

"Right, yes. As I was saying, put *one* foot in the stirrup." Keeping her hands firmly on his shoulders, Joan gingerly stuck her foot out and did as she was told.

"Now, can you grab hold of the saddle, up there where the horn is above the pommel?"

She stared at him blankly, the confusion and terror seeping back into her gaze. Of course. She didn't know horses. Or saddles.

"The handle up there, jutting up above the seat." He was suddenly aware of how provocative and phallic a saddle looked. He swallowed down his urge to tease her about it as she reached for it. His eyes practically bulged out of his head, and he stiffened in his jeans watching her delicate hand and long fingers wrap itself around the horn. He closed his eyes, dismissing visions of her hand encircling other things on his person. From off camera, Arlene coughed pointedly, calling him back to himself.

"All right, now that you've got a good grip, use it to pull yourself up and over. I'll help push you." She did as she was told, gingerly removing her other hand from him and gripping the saddle like a life preserver. He couldn't look away as she lifted her other leg and began to slide it over the horse. His brain conjured images of her doing the same to him, and he'd never wished to be a real cowboy so fervently in his life. As she mounted the horse, his hands slid lower to her backside, helping push her into the saddle. Her ass was small and perfectly shaped, filling his hands like the ripest, lushest peach he'd ever beheld.

In a matter of moments, she was astride the horse and looking far more confident than she had minutes ago. But he was struck by the loss of her. His hands ached to touch her again, and he yearned for the gentle return of the warm press of her body against his own. With a breathless whisper in the dark, she had him turned upside down. He cursed himself for wanting something he knew he could never have. Another thing to add to what was seemingly an ever-expanding list.

"Mister Howard, if you would kindly return to your horse, we could film this scene now," Fritz drawled. Dash nodded in acknowledgment, leaning to pick up his hat from the ground and knocking it against his thigh to brush the dust from it as he strode back to his own mount.

As he went, he kept looking over his shoulder at Joan, making sure she was still safely astride the saddle. One would never have known she wasn't a born horsewoman; she looked every bit her movie-star self, tall and luscious and proud, ready to do what she did best. In turn, the horse had relaxed, lazily chewing a piece of grass he'd found.

As Dash climbed back atop his horse, he returned his gaze to his own saddle. Only to look up and see Joan looking once again perturbed, the skittish look returned to her eyes, and her shoulders slumped. Her hands wrapped around the reins were white at the knuckles. Fritz was muttering something to her he could not hear.

He nudged his heels against his horse and rode over to them both, as Arlene rose from her chair to join the fray. "Fritzy, what seems to be the problem?"

"I was telling Miss Davis that her costume is not sexy enough. We want to believe that a rugged cowboy like you would fall for her. She looks too uncomfortable on the horse."

"And I was explaining that I need a moment to find my footing because I haven't been near a horse in years." She shuddered. Dash admired the thread of steel that ran through her, her refusal to let this situation or Fritz Von Wild cow her.

"If Miss Davis would only unbutton the top buttons of her blouse, I feel it would greatly improve the scene," Fritz explained in a tone that implied Dash and Joan were idiots that he could hardly believe he had to endure. Dash and Arlene exchanged a look. He couldn't be serious.

"And I have explained to Mr. Von Wild that I don't believe Carol would do that. She's nursing a betrayal from her husband of fifteen years. She's wounded and closed off in every sense of the word. The beauty of this story is that she's not in Reno looking for love. She wants a fresh start. Carol is not the type of divorcée to display her bosom to every man she meets."

Dash smiled. He'd never known a director to outsmart Joan Davis yet. She'd studied this business inside and out, and she knew every script like the back of her hand. What's more, she knew the lighting setups and the costumes, and she worked it all to her advantage every chance she got. He'd been the beneficiary of it more times than he could count, something he hadn't even realized until he'd started doing more films without her. Fritz von Wild's predilection for cleavage wasn't going to fly with her.

Arlene chimed in, "She's right, Mr. Von Wild. I wrote this scene to be subtle. Joe falls for Carol because she's not like the other divorcées looking for a cowboy to have some fun with. She's closed off, but capable."

Fritz got red in the face and turned on Arlene. "Who do you think you are?"

Arlene blushed but answered, "The screenwriter."

"Yes, that is right, the screenwriter. But I, I am the director and this is my set. There is one person in charge here and that is me."

"But you don't understand the scene the way I've written it. This is a women's picture, it needs a light touch."

"Are you implying I do not have the light touch?" Von Wild spluttered.

"I 'zink' it's very clear you do not," Arlene retorted.

Fritz turned bright red and started stomping his foot and pointing his finger in the direction of the trailers. "Out, out! Do you hear me? Get off this set at once. I'm going to tell Mr. Evets you are not allowed back here. I am the director here. Not some, some, some mealymouthed girl."

Joan opened her mouth to intercede, but Arlene simply looked at her and shook her head. "Save your fight for the scene," Arlene said. "You, no, *we've* worked too hard to get here. Save the scene, that's all that matters." She patted Joan's leg in reassurance and walked off in the direction of the trailers.

Fritz smirked at all of them, clearly pleased he'd got his way. "Now, your blouse, Miss Davis."

"Absolutely not," she replied, steel in her voice.

Von Wild seemed to realize there was no winning this argument and stomped off back to the camera, muttering something about Miss Davis not having anything worth showing off anyway. Dash opened his mouth to explain that Joan Davis was the most gorgeous woman he'd ever met and anyone who didn't agree was a fool. But before he could get the words out, Joan shook her head at him, a silent plea to ignore it.

She nudged her heels against her gray horse, who miraculously moved at her suggestion. As she rode past Dash toward the clearing where they were to shoot the scene, she muttered, "Arlene's right. He's not worth the oxygen."

Dash was furious, but Joan seemed unaffected. The only thing that seemed to upset her was the way the man treated Arlene. But not the abuse she'd suffered. Was this what she faced on sets regularly? Had he been too caught up in himself to notice?

A mix of shame and fury roiled in his stomach. He was angry on her behalf, but ashamed of what a fool he'd been. He'd told her she needed to take responsibility, but he hadn't realized that this was what she was up against every day. It dawned on him that most of the time it was probably even more of an uphill battle. Because she didn't usually have a script like the one Arlene had written them. A script Von Wild clearly did not understand the nuances of.

But Dash wouldn't start a scene. He'd only enact the one that was scripted for them, if that's what she wanted. So he followed her out into the meadow, the stark outline of the Sierras behind them creating an eye-catching natural backdrop.

They began filming, and Joan gave a beautiful performance. Dash could tell the role really meant something to her, that she was connecting with it in a way that she never had with some of the damsels in distress or haughty society women she'd played opposite him in the past. It was subtle and nuanced and wonderful.

He couldn't have asked for a better acting partner. She made it so simple to play a cowboy jaded by his experiences with the flock of Reno divorcées, but falling in love with her in spite of himself. They'd played dozens of love scenes, but this felt different—more real, more natural, more inevitable. He chalked it up to Joan's acting because anything else felt too dangerous.

But it seemed Fritz Von Wild didn't find Joan's performance as rapturous as Dash did. They'd filmed the entire scene in a wide shot and he'd held his tongue, mostly. Muttering things under his breath out of Dash's earshot, but within range of Joan. Dash resisted the urge to throttle the man every time a blush of pink rose to Joan's cheeks or she narrowed her eyes in obvious anger. Fritz had sent in the hair and makeup team for touch-ups, ever so subtly arranging Joan's hair in a more blatant come-hither style.

They were switching to close-ups now, where they'd hold on Joan's face throughout her monologue about her heartache and the betrayal she'd suffered. Joan looked nervous, more out of sorts than he'd ever seen her on a set. While Fritz was off chatting with the cameraman, Dash rode over to her so their horses were practically touching.

"You'll be the tops, Joanie, don't worry."

She humored him with a smile. "Thanks, Dash. If Von Wild would let me be, I'd be fine. But he's getting in my head. And this is *the* scene, Dash. This movie could change everything for me. Arlene wrote it to be that way. She knew what I needed and she delivered. Combined with marrying Monty, it could put me back on top. But not if this scene isn't perfect."

He swallowed down the pang of jealousy that flared when she mentioned her marriage to Monty. He had one job right now: to support her, to make her feel like she could deliver the performance he knew she was capable of.

"Places!" called out Fritz, and Dash clucked his tongue and nudged his horse back to his mark, making sure he was out of frame and not pulling focus from Joan's big moment. "And action!"

Joan closed her eyes for a moment, her rigid posture transforming into something softer and more vulnerable. Then she looked at Dash. He gave her the cue. "Excuse my asking, Mrs. Pearce, but what brought you to Reno? You hardly seem like the usual type we get on the ranch."

"Believe me, Mr. Langland, I'm as surprised as you to find myself here." She paused, a catch of emotion in her throat. Dash swallowed the urge to reach out and touch her, reminding himself none of this was real. She gave him a sad little smile. "I'm sure it's a story you've heard a hundred times before. I was a fool, you see. A fool who thought the man I loved and worshipped meant it when he said that he would love and cherish me until death do us part. It was our anniversary. Fifteen years! I went early to his office to surprise him before we went to dinner—and that's when I discovered him with his secretary in his arms."

Joan straightened her spine, took a deep breath and prepared to continue her lines—a grim determination etched across her features. It was perfect. Unexpected.

"Cut," bellowed Fritz from off camera. Joan closed her eyes, visibly dreading what might come next. "Miss Davis, what exactly was that?"

She gritted her teeth. "I was under the impression it was my monologue, Mr. Von Wild."

"It's all wrong," he declared. "Your husband has abandoned you, you need to feel desirable again. You crave pity from this man. There should be tears."

She lifted her chin, the signature Davis temperament flaring behind her eyes. "I disagree, Mr. Von Wild. Carol is strong. She is nursing her wounded heart after a betrayal, but she is not about to have an emotional breakdown in front of a man she's only just met."

Fritz rolled his eyes. "I appreciate your ideals, Miss Davis, but we are talking about the character here."

Something steely glinted in her eyes and she tossed her hair back, reminding Dash of the spirited horse she was currently astride. "Yes, Mr. Von Wild, I know that. And I am telling you I do not believe she would cry in this moment."

Dash tried to help, interjecting, "I agree, Fritz. Joe's met hundreds of tearful divorcées on the ranch. They're a dime a dozen. He wouldn't fall for a lady like that. It's her strength he finds attractive."

Fritz looked at Dash like he'd sprouted three heads. Clearly, he wasn't helping matters. Joan gave him a look of silent gratitude, but Fritz couldn't let it go. "As she will not unbutton her blouse, I fail to see what audiences or any man would find attractive about Miss Davis at all. But we shall go again."

Dash expected Joan to lash out, to stand up for herself. But she ignored Von Wild altogether, staring pointedly at the ground. He was startled to see her eyes were clouded with tears. It dawned on him then what Fritz was doing. Joan wasn't interpreting the role the way he wanted, so he was bullying her into the emotions he demanded. Von Wild ran back to the camera and before Dash could even be sure his hat was cocked at the right angle, he yelled out, "Action."

Joan looked up at Dash, her eyes swimming. She clenched her jaw, trying to deliver the lines. But they came out watery, completely the opposite of the steely grace she'd possessed only moments before. To hell with this. It wasn't the performance Joan wanted to give. Nor was it the one the scene called for.

"Cut!" Dash yelled out. He could swear he saw steam come out of Von Wild's ears at the word. The diminutive director took off his cap and trampled it under his feet.

"Just what do you think you are doing, Mr. Howard?" he bellowed.

"The scene's not right. You bullied Joan into crying, and I believe Miss Davis is owed a moment to recover so she can deliver the performance as she sees fit."

"Why, you puffed-up, untalented, corn-fed louse," sputtered Von Wild.

"Go ahead, Fritzy, I can take it, but you need to treat Miss Davis with the respect she deserves."

"Respect? What respect does she deserve? She is box-office poison," he hissed. "The public turned their backs on her because she's so unappealing… I am trying to save her career, but it is no wonder moviegoers won't touch her with a ten-foot pole if this is the way she behaves. She looks ridiculous!" He went toward her, jumping to grab at her shoulders. "These shoulder pads, they are absurd."

Joan closed her eyes and flushed bright red. "I am not wearing any shoulder pads, Mr. Von Wild. Those are simply my shoulders. They're broad, you see, because I have to carry so many of my directors on them. But I don't need *you* to remind me of my shortcomings. Leda Price and every other columnist in Hollywood has that handled."

Von Wild got a wild look in his eye and swatted at the horse with the riding crop he was notorious for carrying on set. The gray, nervous creature spooked immediately and reared onto its hind legs. Joan reacted quickly, grabbing at its mane and holding on for dear life, narrowly avoiding being thrown.

Dash's stomach plunged at the look of pure terror in her eyes. He sprang into action, leaping from his own horse. While others on set cowered and cringed at the bucking creature, he held out his hands, urging steadiness with his gestures and his soothing words. Once the horse had stilled, he reached for Joan and she wrapped her arms around his neck, clinging to him desperately as he helped her dismount. She was shaking under his touch, and even once her feet connected with solid ground, she did not let go of him. Instead, she buried her face in his neck and curled herself into him.

He threaded his hands through her hair and massaged the base of her neck, murmuring assurances in her ear. "Joanie, it's all right, I've got you, you're safe. I won't let anything happen to you." He kneaded her back with his other hand. He could feel her pulse racing at her hairline, and he stroked at her pressure points, feeling her heart slow to its normal rhythm.

He wanted to tear Von Wild to pieces. It was one thing to speak to her the way he had. That alone was unacceptable, beyond the pale of the pointed barbs of his and Joan's spats. But to endanger her life? To deliberately humiliate and terrify her because he didn't like her acting choices? He could throttle the man. Except that his hands were full with Joan, and suddenly, letting her go was unthinkable. Keeping her securely pressed against him, he confronted Von Wild.

"If it wouldn't scare the horses, I'd sock you on the jaw," he growled. "Joan was prepared to give the performance of her life, if only you'd support her. But all you care about is if she's showing enough cleavage for you. You're not a director, you're a lech. I'm taking Joan and we're walking off this set right now. As soon as I can get to a phone, I'm calling Harry Evets to have you replaced. And if I have anything to say about it, this will be the last set you ever step foot on, you sniveling shrimp. You're not fit to wipe Joan's boots, much less witness her give the performance of her life."

With that, Dash picked Joan up, as he'd done in jest on the train. This time she didn't wrestle or object. She merely laid her head against his shoulder and laced her arms around his neck. She nuzzled at his throat, and as he carried her away, he chuckled as she raised her head to yell after Von Wild, "Fuck you, Fritzy, and the horse you made me ride in on."

There was the Joan Davis he knew. The woman that he'd known from their first day on set had the potential to turn his entire life upside down. He just hadn't expected it to happen now, after all this time.

CHAPTER 15

JOAN WAS EXHAUSTED. SHE'D SLEPT WELL, CURLED UP IN Dash's pajamas. But the combination of preparing to give an emotional performance, defending herself and Arlene against Von Wild, and the shock of adrenaline that had come as she fought to stay on a bucking horse had drained her.

She buried her face in Dash's neck, inhaling his masculine scent of pine and clean, fresh soap. His arms felt so different now than they had last week when he'd carried her off the train. Then, they'd been unwelcome. But now they were a comfort, solid and reassuring, a sense that she'd always be safe so long as she clung to him. Everything about him, from his scent to the way he held her, was solid. She wanted to sink into the feeling and never climb out. And that scared her—because Joan didn't want to trust him, didn't want to consider that she might have feelings for anyone. Least of all Dash Howard.

She looked up at him, and she was bowled over by the gleam of fierce protectiveness in his eyes. He looked ready to face down an invading army. This was not the Dash Howard she'd known, the insouciant man unable to take anything seriously, especially his leading lady. She'd blamed him for a lot of things that weren't his fault, but there was still one thing she couldn't explain—the Cocoanut Grove, the photographers out back. Had she misunderstood? Everything was muddled now.

His eyes met hers and she swallowed, remembering how it had felt when she'd been pressed against him trying to mount her horse. The protectiveness in his gaze shifted to something hungry, and she licked her lips in anticipation. No, this would not do. She was engaged to Monty. She had to stop before she did something she regretted. Again.

He inclined his head ever so slightly toward hers, and she resisted the pull of rising to meet him, instead finding her voice. "Thank you," she trilled. She coughed, clearing her throat. "For what you did with Von Wild. You've never stood up for me like that before. No one has."

His brow furrowed and storm clouds crowded his face. "I'm sorry I haven't done it sooner. Joan, is that how things always are?" he asked, barely suppressing the rage in his voice.

How to tell him that what Von Wild did was tame by comparison? That most of the men in Hollywood treated her like she was either a prize to be won or a piece of meat to be carved up between them. Hell, forget Hollywood. The world. Dash didn't know the things she'd done to change her life, to become a star. She wasn't ashamed of what she'd done. It'd been worth it. A woman had one thing to sell that the world was willing to buy, and she'd exploited that to her own ends. But she knew if Dash knew, if the world knew, being branded box-office poison would be the least of her concerns. But he'd asked, and he looked at her with such righteous anger, she had to tell him. At least part of it.

"They're not all like Von Wild. Purposefully cruel, I mean. Usually, it's wandering hands or a leering look before we shoot a love scene." She shrugged. "It's the way things are."

Something dark and angry flashed in his gaze, and he set her down at last, her cowboy boots kicking up a cloud of dust around them. She immediately mourned the loss of his arms around her.

"That's…that's not acceptable. How have I never noticed?" He looked stricken.

"Because I never wanted you to. I've told you before—the love of the audience is all I've ever desired." That had been true once. But she was starting to wonder if she'd been wrong. "I'd have done anything to get that love, the public acclaim, the security of my face on a fan magazine and the bank account that comes with it. And I damn near have done anything—so if a director or a producer wants to get handsy, I let him. And I've learned creative ways to evade them over the years. There's no point in making a scene. It'd only make it worse for me."

She was so determined to do everything on her own, so convinced it had to be a solo effort or it wasn't worth a damn. Dash made her wonder if there might be something to the idea of a partnership after all.

He looked chastened. "I'm sorry I didn't see it. I've been so caught up in myself. I thought you hated me, distrusted me."

She nodded. "I did. And you know why. We've been over this. Dash, don't play dumb, you set me up that night. Why would I have trusted you after that?"

He bowed his head, dipping his cowboy hat low over his face. "You're right. Of course, you're right."

She paused to take him in, and there was a reticence in his manner, something she wasn't accustomed to. "There's something you're not telling me."

"No." He waved her off.

"C'mon, Dash, I know your tells after five years. It's obvious you're lying."

He stopped, put his hands on his hips, and turned to look up at the mountains, arching and stretching his back. He looked so…masculine. It was irresistible. And infuriating. "It was obvious you didn't want to hear my apology. I tried, but you wouldn't listen."

"You didn't try very hard," she scoffed.

"Joan, you wanted nothing to do with me. You turned your back and walked away every time I even tried to tell you 'Good morning.' So then I swore to myself I wouldn't waste my breath trying to apologize to a pigheaded woman who was so certain she'd been wronged that she'd stuff cotton in her ears before she'd hear me out."

"Yeah, well, I swore I'd never marry a man like you, and look how that went."

He chuckled and looked at her, an expression of wonder in his eyes. "You really are something, Joan Davis." He cleared his throat and continued. "Fine. If you're actually ready to listen, then fine, I'll tell you all of it. That night… It wasn't what you thought."

"In what way?"

"I did take you there because the studio thought it'd be good publicity for us to go out together. I was trying to do what I was told. I didn't want to screw up yet another good thing in my life. But when I picked you up, I don't know, it all changed. We'd made two pictures together, and I knew how I felt about you. That I liked you. That you were fun and easy to work with. I figured we'd have a night on the town, a couple of laughs, and go back to work the next day. And then there you were, coming out of your house looking like something out of a movie."

"Well, I mean, that's because I am…something out of a movie." She smirked.

He laughed and put his hand to the back of his head, scratching it in thought. "That you are. But, no, I mean, I swear to you, I didn't intend to be like Von Wild, like those other men, and assume that because you were my costar you'd fall into bed with me. I only took you out because Harry insisted."

She nodded. "But that wasn't a typical studio setup. You didn't even take us to the table they'd reserved by the bandstand."

He swallowed, clearly nervous. "Because I didn't want that night to be something tawdry the studio cooked up. When you came out of your house to the car, I knew then that I wanted a chance with you. A real chance. So I took us to a back booth where we could have more privacy. I thought things were going well."

Her heart started racing in her chest. She had felt something; she just had been scared. Frightened of what it could cost her, of being thrown off the path she knew was the only one for her—no entanglements, no romance, no love. Instead, all she said was, "They were."

"So why'd you run off like that then, Joan? I was desperate. I searched the entire nightclub for you. Then this girl came up to me and said she knew where to find you. That I needed to wait for you outside the kitchen door and you'd meet me there. That you wanted to go somewhere quiet where we could talk. She seemed vaguely familiar, but I didn't know her from Adam."

"Leda," Joan hissed. Suddenly, it was all making sense. Dash hadn't set her up. Leda had. She'd hoodwinked them both, maneuvering them out the backdoor of the Cocoanut Grove for a photo opp she'd orchestrated. Joan had always wondered how a bit player had turned one juicy set of tabloid photos into a daily column and an entire career. This was how—she'd been the brains behind the whole thing. She'd used Joan and Dash to establish herself, and all this time Joan had assumed it had been a purposeful scheme concocted by Dash with Leda's assistance. "You should've told me it wasn't you. You should've made me listen. Instead of trying to get my attention with childish pranks."

He kicked at a clod of dirt with his foot, dust settling over the tips of his boots. He shoved his hands into his pockets and looked pointedly at the ground. "What was the use? It *was* my fault. I was stupid enough to believe Leda, stupid enough to lead us both into that. Josephine once told me I was as dumb as a fence post, and in that moment I knew she was right. What was the point in making excuses?"

She wanted to take him in her arms then, to tell him that he wasn't stupid. That she'd been wrong. Jealous of how easy fame and accolades came to him, she'd made assumptions about him. But he might be the best man she'd ever known. Besides Monty. The thought of her fiancé was enough to remind her to restrain herself, to not give in to the urge to fling her arms back around Dash. Sure, they'd agreed that discreet intimacies with other people were acceptable, but when it came to her and Dash, discreet had never been part of their vocabulary. She'd already made a big enough mess, so she stuffed down the urge to beg Dash to take her back to their bungalow and ravish her. Instead, she crossed her arms over her chest in a protective stance. "It wasn't your fault."

"If I'd made you listen, though God only knows how I would've done that, would you have believed me if I'd told you the truth?"

Joan wanted to say yes. But she knew she wouldn't have. After that night, she'd been determined to only see the worst in him. And he'd been only too happy to live down to those assumptions. "I might not have," she admitted. "But I was wrong, Dash. I saw what you, what Harry, what Leda, wanted us to see. And I never bothered to look any further, satisfied with my assessment that you were as bad as most of the other men in Hollywood."

He got a pained look on his face. "How do you put up with it?"

"If it makes you feel better, they're usually not as critical of my acting as Von Wild. That, I cannot abide."

Dash chuckled. "Leave it to you to draw the line at someone questioning how you do your job. A wiser man wouldn't dare."

Joan preened. It killed her that people thought she was just a pretty face. Being the most beautiful woman in the world was a short-lived triumph. There was a new "It" girl every week. But acting ability, real undeniable talent—that was forever. And she was finally getting the chance to prove it. Von Wild would not screw this up for her. She didn't care how many Oscars he had lining his shelf.

"Protecting my image is the only thing I have," she admitted. "I'm not going to let it go without a fight."

"A fight that includes marrying a man who doesn't love you." Dash had the decency to look chagrined. "I'm sorry, I shouldn't have said it. But it's obvious he's not crazy about you. Do you love him?"

"Of course I do, it's—"

"Stop kidding yourself, Joan. No woman kisses me the way you did that night on the riverbank if she's in love with her fiancé."

She blushed. They'd found some odd sort of détente here in the woods. She stopped and admired the afternoon light in the trees, the river where last week she'd put rocks in her pockets and given Dash a taste of his own medicine twinkling in the distance. It was calming. Or maybe it was Dash. She didn't know anymore. She was all mixed up, and she found herself wanting to open up to him the way he had to her before she'd kissed him. "I can't love any man. I promised myself a long time ago I'd never fall in love, and now I don't think I could if I tried."

"Why? You're so sure of yourself in every way, so unafraid to take charge. Why should this be any different?"

Dash had been honest with her, hadn't he? He'd brought

Monty here. He'd stood up for her on set today. Could she tell him? "It's a long story."

"What else do we have to do today? Besides call Harry and get Von Wild off this picture."

"Which I'd appreciate if you'd let me do." Dash had been there for her today. In a way that no one ever had before. But there were still some things she had to do on her own terms.

"But—"

"No, Dash, it needs to come from me. I'm grateful for what you did back there. Standing up for me. You're the tops, really. But Harry needs to understand that I won't continue to accept this on set. If I'm forging a new path for myself, it's time I demand better." She did deserve better. She had always swallowed the abuse, let it pass, telling herself it was worth it. But God damn it, she was Joan Fucking Davis. It was time she believed that too. "If not for me, then at least for Arlene. I fought for this script to get made because I believed in it, but she deserves the world. I won't have her kicked off her first set because she was defending me."

She expected Dash to protest, to insist that Harry was more likely to listen to him because he was a man. But he simply said, "You're right. Of course it should come from you."

That simple assent took her breath away. Was this what it was to have a true partner? To not keep the wolves at your door at bay all by yourself?

He gestured helplessly at her, reaching for her hand, then retreating. But she couldn't help herself, so she reached back, taking his hand in hers. The rough calluses of his palm pressed into hers. They weren't the hands of a movie star but of a rancher, of a man who knew his way around a horse and a day's hard work. The type of hands she'd spent a lifetime running from. Dash had a butler, for God's sake. He was a movie star who lived in a mansion.

But his hands told a different story; they held the key to the real Dash Howard.

She absentmindedly stroked at his palm with her thumb, and they walked in a comfortable silence. They entered the shadow of a copse of pine trees, the shade chilling her as they escaped the midday sun. The clearing was cool and dark, and Joan took a deep breath, inhaling the woodsy scent that reminded her of the man currently holding her hand. She was starting to know him and maybe, just maybe, he wanted to know her too.

"Love is for the birds," she murmured. He stared at her, but he didn't interrupt, giving her the courage to go on. "What I mean to say is I don't believe in love because I've only ever seen it end in disaster. My father ran out when I was four and left my mother a shell of herself. Then my sister fell prey to the same sickness as my mother. The two people I loved most in this world—and love ruined them both."

"Tell me more about them." He nodded. "About the brave little girl you must've been."

"I don't talk about my past. It's not befitting a movie star like Joan Davis. The press would have a field day."

Dash frowned. "Do you really think I would tell Leda? Or any of them?"

"No! No, I didn't mean to imply you would. I know that now. I was wrong to suggest you'd had a hand in that stunt at the train station." She swallowed. "And the kiss, for suggesting you had set me up. I was angry with myself and flustered. It was badly done."

Dash smiled as if he was enjoying a private joke. "When I told you to start taking responsibility last night, I didn't dare hope you'd have a change of heart so soon."

Joan paused, grinding a hole in the dirt and the undergrowth of the trees with the toe of her boot. "I'm bad at apologizing. It means looking back, and I can't bear that. I can only look forward. I have to fight every day for every inch of what I have, and sometimes I forget not everyone is out to get me. I told myself you're my enemy for so long, I started to believe it."

Dash nodded, a warm understanding in his gaze. "I'm not though. I suppose I've done a good job of convincing you otherwise, but I've never been. I made a stupid mistake, and you saw what Leda wanted you to see. I only ever wanted a fair shot at being your partner. I wanted someone who had my back onscreen, the way I knew I had yours. But the only way I could ever break through all your walls was by acting out, kicking at the base of that pedestal you're perched on. It wasn't exactly the mature way to handle things. And for that I'm sorry."

"It seems we both owe each other apologies. What would you say to starting over? A clean slate and all that."

"I'd like nothing more." He grinned, a quick flash of those expensive teeth, and tipped his cowboy hat in a gesture she would've previously interpreted as mocking. She knew now it was merely awkwardness, a man fumbling around for an authentic piece of himself.

A fresh start meant he deserved to know who she was. It meant telling him the things she could've told him in that back booth at the Cocoanut Grove if the idea hadn't terrified her. It still did. But somehow, she knew it would be okay this time. She took a breath and dove in.

"My father left when I could scarcely remember him. My mother... It was like my father took her with him that day and left an empty body in her place. She couldn't see the two girls in her house who loved her and needed her so desperately because she was too busy chasing a ghost." Suddenly, it was all spilling out. The story of the girl she'd once been. "We had a busy farm, horses, cows, and pigs that needed tending. But my mother could scarcely get out of bed. Avoiding ruin fell to me and my sister. Every day I woke before dawn to do my chores: muck out the barn, milk the cows, pile the hay. My hands were rubbed raw from the work, red and blistered. And I could never get the grit from my eyes and my mouth no matter how hard I tried.

"Then one day my sister took me to see a traveling show and there was a girl dancing. Typical fare, feathers and fans and the like. She looked so happy, so carefree. The audience loved her. They fell silent at the sight of her and erupted in thunderous applause when she had finished. It was the most beautiful sound I'd ever heard. And she had the most stunning hands I'd ever seen—white as porcelain and they looked soft as down. I vowed that day that someday my hands would look like that, that someday the world would love and admire me as that tent full of people admired her."

She stopped, suddenly out of breath. She hadn't intended to tell him all that. It was too much. But Dash squeezed her hand. He raised it to his mouth and kissed it gently, like a knight greeting his lady fair. Then he turned it over and kissed her palm with the reverence of a saint, the lightest touch of his lips sending a shock of want through her.

"You have exquisite hands now, Joanie," he murmured into her palm, the rush of air against her skin leaving her breathless with excitement. She folded her fingers together and closed her hand, frightened by what the brush of his lips against her skin could make her feel. He wrapped his hand around hers and dropped their arms back between them so they could resume their walk. The forest observed them, but it stood silent, in judgment or approval she wasn't certain.

"Seeing that girl dance, that's the day I first became Joan Davis. You know that's not my real name?"

Dash smiled. At last. "Does anyone in Hollywood use their real name?"

"Well, it's at least one I chose for myself. I wasn't leaving it up to some team of studio stuffed shirts. I could've been named Lucille Crawford or something truly anodyne like June."

"Joan Davis fits you. It's strong and proud. It tells the world who you are before you ever open your mouth."

Joan gasped, the slightest puff of air escaping from her lips before she could stop it. Because he'd spoken aloud something she'd dreamed of at thirteen, when she'd first imagined her new name. He'd understood what was in a name. That it was the first step to becoming who she most wanted to be.

"It's much better than Mildred Shalk, anyway." She shuddered.

He wrinkled his nose in mutual disgust. "That really is terrible. Mildred doesn't suit you at all."

She laughed then, full-throated. It felt good to laugh with Dash, to be herself around him. For so long, it'd been biting words and a mask of indifference between them. This was freeing, exhilarating, to let go of all those walls, to shed the haughtiness and the disdain and see him with clear eyes. At last. And to allow him to do the same.

"So that's why you hate the ranch, the horses, all of it."

"You've noticed." She laughed, but it was cold and devoid of mirth. "I spent the first eighteen years of my life living in dust in Oklahoma. It coated everything. My hair, my eyes, my clothes. I would scrub and scrub and scrub, and still it'd be there. Under my fingernails or in my ears. I could never escape it. When I saw that dancer, I knew that was the answer. That I could finally be free of the filth and the thankless, excruciating hard work if I could only be like her. I vowed to do anything it would take." She hoped he wouldn't ask what "anything" entailed.

"And you have. You were a farm girl with nothing, and now you're Joan Davis, movie star, a woman capable of bringing every man she meets to his knees."

She smirked. "Except Fritz Von Wild, apparently."

"He'll be scrounging for forgiveness soon enough. Don't forget. I've heard you with Harry when you really want something. You're like a dog with a bone. A particularly vicious dog who happens to have a stunning back and warm brown eyes."

She giggled. God, who was she becoming? Giggling at a man's compliments. She once thought women like that foolish. But strangely, now she liked it. There had always been tension between them, but this was new. The electricity that sparked in the air when he said such things. "Well, there's one man I could never bring to his knees. Even if I wanted to."

"Who?" Dash asked, completely without guile.

"You," she replied. "Maybe that's why I can't seem to avoid bickering with you. Because Joan Davis doesn't impress you."

"She does," he whispered. "She always has. Even when I was trying to knock you off that pedestal, I was always in awe of you. You seemed untouchable in a way I could never be. I envied that, how everything seemed to roll off your back. How you never compromised who you are. It always seemed like a magic trick to me. And let's be honest, you couldn't avoid bickering with me because I gave you every reason to think the worst of me."

She laughed. "You're nothing if not self-aware, Dash Howard." She smiled at him, looking up at his deep-brown eyes. "You're not at all the man I thought you were. You're decent and kind." Dash laughed. "What's so funny?"

"Flynn has tried to tell me the same thing. I've never believed him."

"Ha, well, normally I wouldn't advise listening to anything Flynn Banks has to say, but in this case he's right."

Dash looked at her and grinned, a twinkle in his eye and that crooked smile that drove women around America wild reappearing. "So I'm not a Hollywood playboy hell-bent on bending women to his whims?"

Joan was ashamed to think she'd ever lobbed such a charge at him. Worse that she'd said it to him so often, dismissive of his fame and his popularity when she'd fought so hard for hers. But there was no malice in his words and his eyes sparkled with mischief.

"It never occurred to me that fame might cost you as much as it has me," she answered. "I've had to fight to stay on top, but at least I'm unapologetically myself. You have to wear a mask every day. Why do you hide behind that macho persona, Dash, the dissolute drunk who takes a new girl home from the Trocadero every night? Why be the guy with the rotating bevy of starlets in the corner booth at Chasen's if that's not who you really are or even want to be?"

He grimaced and knelt to the ground to pick up a leaf that had fallen from a nearby oak. He twisted it between his hands, shredding little holes in its green tendrils. "It's easier, isn't it? Giving them what they want. Besides, I've gotten so good at playing the version of Dash Howard they expect that I don't know if I can be anyone else."

Joan put her hands to his and stilled them. She stroked at his fingers and he dropped the leaf into her hand. She picked it up and examined it, cracks of sunlight coming through the pinholes of light he'd made in its waxy surface. It reminded her of Dash, the glimmers of himself he'd shown her. "You can be. I know you can be. You're a brilliant actor, Dash."

"Why, Joan Davis, did you just compliment my acting?"

"If you tell anyone, I'll deny it." She stuck her tongue out at him and he laughed. But then it was quiet again, that expectant stillness that came in the moments before one's entire life changed.

She looked up and met his eyes, clutching the leaf in her palm. The sun moved between the trees and his face was dappled in light. It caught the glints of pain and tenderness in his soulful brown eyes. It warmed the growing stubble on his chin. Joan realized she'd never seen a man look so beautiful. His hair was mussed, his usually pomaded mane topsy-turvy. He looked wild and rugged and real, not at all the veneer of Dash Howard the movie star.

She longed to palm the broad planes of his chest, to take the weight of who he really was into her arms and dot it with kisses. She was envious of the sun as it danced across his body, licking him with its beams. He was both sacred and profane, a study in shadow and light, and she wanted to worship and defile him at the same time.

A hunger passed between them, a mutual longing, and for one breathless moment it seemed that Dash would seize her in his arms again. She imagined taking everything she wanted from him, but then he smiled, shy and sad, and the spell was broken.

Without noticing, they'd made it back to the bungalow. But she wanted to linger in the woods a moment longer. Once they were back there, they'd be Dash and Davis again, entertainment for the divorcées and the staff. With obligations to the studio, their public, and Monty.

Here, it was simpler. They stood, quiet and reflective, looking at their shared bungalow that had only yesterday seemed a gross insult. Now, Joan was happy to be sharing it. To not be in this alone. It was an odd feeling. She'd always assumed that anyone else muddied the waters, cheapened the experience, or risked ruining it altogether. But was it possible they made it richer?

Dash broke the silence. "I do have one question. I grew up

on a farm too, and if I do say so myself, I have a way with horses. I would think someone with your upbringing would be more comfortable around them."

"Why, you," she proclaimed, swatting at him and grabbing for his hat to batter him with it. He easily held her off, laughing so hard that his eyes watered.

"I was only joking." His eyes glinted with mischief. "Besides, your ineptitude gave me a chance to get more familiar with some of your better assets."

Her cheeks colored. She hadn't imagined it, then. That pulse of attraction between them when he'd held her as he helped her onto the horse. A live wire of unadulterated want had sparked to life inside her, but she'd tried to douse it. It was too complicated, too confusing.

But if Dash had felt it too, what did that mean? It was getting harder to insist that the kiss between them on the riverbank hadn't meant anything. She'd been so angry, convinced herself that he'd ruined everything on purpose, seduced her. Now, she feared she'd been the one to ignite a fire she didn't know how to control.

"I've never liked horses," she muttered. "One of them kicked me when I was a child. He was wild, hadn't been broken. My sister had bought him from a huckster in town, not knowing any better, and he'd promised her a docile mare. I had the bruise for weeks. Mother never even noticed. Just sent me out there every day to tend the brutal thing. I was terrified."

He pulled her to him, wrapping his arms around her and welcoming her into the crook of his arm. She pressed her face into his bicep, reveling in the softness of the plaid flannel contrasting with the hardness underneath. The sense of safety that had ebbed when he'd set her down rushed back to her at once, and she sank into him as he cooed and stroked her hair.

There was genuine anger in his gaze, but his touch was pure tenderness. "Of course you were, you poor thing. Your mother had no business sending a child out to care for an unbroken horse." He held her more tightly and the bubble of dread in her chest that had arisen at the memory popped. "Horses can sense your fear. I can imagine it was hard to tend to them after that experience. Every single one must have been skittish around you."

"Yes," she admitted. "I hated it. I felt like such a fool today. Joan Davis isn't afraid of a challenge, and here I was felled by a silly horse."

"I could never think you a fool." He pressed a kiss to the top of her head and she fought back tears. She had never told anyone about her life as Mildred Shalk because it would ruin her image. But also because she didn't want pity. Millions of people around this country had hard lives. She'd merely fought for a better one and earned it with sacrifice and luck. No one cared or wanted to know about her childhood. They wanted the glamour. So did she, if she was being honest. She hated remembering, hated thinking about the bone-deep exhaustion and constant fear she'd left behind. Mildred Shalk had always been afraid. Joan Davis was fearless.

But it felt surprisingly good to tell Dash about Mildred, to let him see why she loved being Joan Davis with every fiber of her being. Why marrying a man she didn't love was simple if it meant she would still be Joan Davis and never again have to face life as Mildred Shalk. Only now she was starting to wonder if it really was that simple. If it had ever been.

CHAPTER 16

DASH CUPPED A HAND TO HIS EYES AND STARED OUT across Lake Tahoe. It was good fishing weather, the perfect day for a trout competition. He closed his eyes and let the afternoon sunlight kiss his face. He missed this. Quiet days on the lake, nothing but sky and water and fresh air.

He thought about Flynn's suggestion that he leave it all behind, sell the mansion in Hollywood and go live on his ranch. He was so very tired of playing this game.

But he realized with a pang what that would really mean—no more nights with Flynn in the Malibu cottage staying up until the sun rose; no more poker games with Phil and the cadre of production crew he'd befriended these last few years; no more laughing until his stomach hurt after he'd pulled a practical joke on set; no more discovering a character, getting to know him inside and out until the work lived in his bones; and worst of all, no more Joan.

A few weeks ago, he would've said that was the dream. But now all he wanted was more time with her. More minutes to absorb her wicked sense of humor, revel in her courage, and admire her beauty.

Joan strode up beside him and passed him a cup of coffee. "Afternoon, partner," she drawled and winked. He turned and took her in. She was wearing high-waisted navy shorts with a line of five large brass buttons on either side and a cream-colored blouse with a deep V-neck and a sailor collar. He dismissed the desire to painstakingly undo each of those buttons and cast his eyes to the ground.

It didn't work; instead, he was mesmerized by her bright-red toe nails winking out of her white shoes. Her creamy, perfect legs were exposed, and she wore a tantalizing gold anklet with a whistle charm hanging off the band, lying against the ridge of her ankle bone. He was suddenly possessed with a desire to lick the soft indentation below it. To follow her flesh to her sculpted calves and up her long legs to what he imagined were lush thighs and a thatch of brunette curls that matched the ones on her head.

He had to stop this madness. So he averted his eyes to her face. It was unadorned with makeup, the constellation of her freckles shadowed by the brim of a large white sun hat and the warmth of her eyes obscured behind round sunglasses in whimsical cherry-red frames. It was the most casual he'd ever seen her, and it made his stomach do somersaults. Because it meant she trusted him with this version of herself. He resisted the urge to double over, the realization like a sock in the gut.

"You look nice," he managed to choke out.

She blushed. "Truly, it's nothing."

"The simplicity suits you. Not that the glamour doesn't, but it's nice."

She didn't say anything, just smiled and turned her head to look across the lake while taking a sip of her coffee. He didn't know what to say to her. That day with Von Wild had fundamentally changed their relationship for the better; she'd been kinder, warmer.

Part of it was the atmosphere on set. They'd been working with a second-unit director all week while they waited for Von

Wild's replacement, Bob Kucor, to come up from Hollywood. But it was becoming increasingly difficult for Dash to resist the urge to take her in his arms and kiss her senseless. Yet he couldn't. For all the tension between them, she was still engaged to Monty Smyth, the man currently strolling toward them. "Afternoon, Dash, ready to fish?"

Monty looked tanned and handsome in short shorts and a tight white polo shirt with a low-cut V-neck that exposed his buff and hairless chest. Dash's own jeans, long-sleeved flannel shirt, and boots suddenly felt stifling, the collar choking him. He nodded in assent and started unbuttoning his sleeves, rolling the cuffs up to his elbows and freeing his forearms. He thought he saw Joan glance down at his suddenly exposed skin, but he had to be imagining things.

Once he'd finished, he realized he was being insufferably laconic. "It's a good day for fishing," he offered, searching for conversation. He felt awkward, caught between this woman he was falling for and the man she was set on marrying.

Monty laughed. "I wouldn't know. I've never touched a fishing pole in my life."

"Awful long way to drive for it, then," Dash huffed. What was the matter with him? He had no right to be jealous.

"Oh, it was no trouble. The studio sent a car. And besides, I've barely seen Joan all week. You've been monopolizing her time."

A pang of guilt bloomed in Dash's chest. Did Monty know how he felt? Did he see his attraction to Joan? How could he? He wasn't on set with them, wasn't in that bungalow where Dash had to sit on his hands to avoid tearing down the sheet he'd hung for privacy. And that was a damn good thing. "Well, we *are* making a picture."

Joan smiled wanly, clearly uneasy at this strange tension that had sprung up like a fish leaping from the lake. “I’m sorry, Monty. I know I called you up here for photo ops in town, and I’ve been leaving you on your own in the hotel. The picture is very demanding, and I’m so tired at the end of the day.”

Dash needed this conversation to end. It was excruciating. Apparently somebody up there liked him because his prayers were answered by the sound of Travis shooting a blank into the air. The ranch guests milling about the shoreline jumped at the sound, but it had the desired effect, bringing all attention to the owner of the Lazy Me Ranch.

“All right, folks! We didn’t drive you all up here from the ranch to socialize. It’s time to get started on the 15th Annual Lazy Me Trout Competition. There’s two prizes—whoever catches the biggest trout today will get the Lazy Me Big Kahuna trophy, and the lucky miss or fellow with the most trout to their name will get a blue ribbon. And of course both champions will be going home with bragging rights.”

“I’d rather go home with Dash Howard,” called out Dolores from the crowd. They all tittered with nervous laughter, while Dash struggled to maintain his composure.

“Well now, that’s up to Mr. Howard,” Travis rejoined, and Dash sent him a look of silent thanks. The moment was soon forgotten as Travis passed out fishing poles and tackle boxes, making sure anyone who wanted to participate was outfitted for the task.

Soon, Dash was standing at the end of the dock examining his fishing line and selecting bait. Monty was to his left with Joan a buffer between them. To his right was Arlene. She had already been at the dock when he’d arrived, ready for the day in galoshes, jean capris, and a flannel shirt. He supposed it was better than Dolores, but he didn’t need to hear more of her nonsense about how he and Joan were secretly pining for each other. Mostly because he was starting to think she was right. At least in his case.

"Hello, Miss Morgan, you look like you know what you're doing." She looked askance at Joan and Monty struggling to get a worm on a hook and then back at him.

"My father was a fisherman, and I could stand on his boat before I could walk on solid ground. So I hope you're not intending to win today."

He chuckled; he liked her in spite of her meddling. "I wouldn't dream of it."

But then suddenly Joan was at his side. "You do know, Arlene, that Dash grew up on a farm in Ohio. I bet he could catch a fish with his bare hands." She winked at him.

"I didn't know that. The fan magazines failed to mention that." That's because according to the fan magazines, Dash Howard was born in New York City before his love of horses took him to Texas.

"Oh, Arlene, tell him about the new scene you're writing!"

Arlene blushed. "It's nothing. I thought you needed a big dramatic moment. Can't let Joan have all the fun."

"She's being modest. I know I keep saying this picture is going to win lots of awards, but if this scene turns out the way I think it will, with your acting chops, it'll get you your second nomination in a row. Wouldn't that be wonderful?"

Arlene got a dreamy look in her eye, and Dash knew exactly what she was thinking. Because he couldn't help thinking it himself. For the first time in his life, Joan was praising him to others instead of insulting him.

"Well, we'll see," he replied, a ball of emotion tightening in his throat and making it hard to speak. He coughed, trying to recover himself. "I can't hope to best a fisherman's daughter, but I do aim to give you some stiff competition."

"I hope that's not the only stiff thing you're offering!" Dash turned to see that Dolores had wedged herself into the corner, putting herself between his station and Joan and Monty. The nerve of this woman. He struggled to come up with a rejoinder, something that would shut her down but that wouldn't be rude. But what did you say to a person who behaved this way? Joan glared daggers at her.

"He's not a piece of meat, Dolores," she growled.

Dolores laughed, a tinkling weak thing that sounded like a toddler ham-fistedly playing a xylophone, and tossed her peroxided hair over her shoulder. "I was talking about a drink," she simpered. "What did you think I meant, Miss Davis?" Her mouth widened into a fake, perfect O, the exact size for a ping-pong ball, all mock innocence.

"You know perfectly well what I *know* you meant. Just because he's on the cover of a magazine doesn't mean you have the right to harass him, to treat him like he's yours for the taking."

"All I wanted to know was if the great Dash Howard would deign to have a drink with me later," Dolores snarled. "But maybe he's too busy with you in your bungalow."

Monty's head snapped up at that, looking back and forth between the both of them, and Joan looked stricken. It was absurd. Nothing had happened since that one kiss in the papers—and Monty already knew about that. Hell, the whole world did. So why did Joan look so guilty?

Dash should intervene. Tell Dolores of course he'd have a drink with her and suffer through another round of cocktails with yet another person who only wanted him for what they thought he had to offer—a ticket to a screen test or bragging rights. But he was weary of all of it, of continuing this charade where he was photographed on the arm of whatever blowsy dame the studio threw in his path. Of sitting through another minute of listening to someone prattle on about themselves while never stopping to ask about him. Because of course they already knew everything there was to know about Dash Howard. They'd read it in a magazine. In a paper. Seen it in the movies. Something had changed since he'd come to Reno, since he'd told Joan the truth. He couldn't be that man anymore.

"I don't appreciate what you're insinuating about my costar," Dash finally replied, fighting to keep even a hint of anger out of his voice, to give her only cold steel.

Dolores smirked. "Please, we've hardly seen the two of you since you arrived. And you're sharing a room. This is Reno after all. Anyone staying at Lazy Me isn't some bright-eyed innocent. We know what happens behind closed doors, and you're married. You couldn't resist trying to melt Hollywood's Ice Queen, could you?"

Joan lunged at her, but Monty was too quick, capturing her wrist in his palm and pulling her back. She huffed and Dash almost laughed. He could swear he could see steam coming out of her ears. He couldn't hear what was being said, but Monty was muttering fiercely in Joan's ear. Dash clenched his jaw so tightly, he was surprised he didn't crack a molar.

"Joan Davis is not an ice queen," he gritted out. "She's a talented actress and a consummate professional."

Joan looked at him, meeting his eyes for the first time in several minutes. There was gratitude in her eyes, but something else too. Something he couldn't place. Monty was observing the scene with concern, his fishing pole forgotten. But he didn't look miffed at Joan's interference. Instead, he was staring at her with a queer look of understanding. Dash didn't know what to make of it. He watched as something tugged at Monty's line, the force pulling it into the water. But before he could tell Monty to mind the pole, Arlene piped in.

"Perhaps you need to read those fan magazines more closely, Dolores. I can tell you firsthand that making movies is long, exhausting work. And that would be why Dash and Joan haven't been socializing with you. We've all been working ourselves to the bone. They're in Reno to do a job, not to rub elbows with you. Monty, dear, you might want to tend to your fishing rod." Monty jumped and turned around in time to catch the pole before it slid all the way off the dock into the depths of Lake Tahoe. But the fish that had the line was strong, and Monty Smyth was not.

The next few moments seemed to pass in both slow motion and extreme rapidity. Joan watched Monty in open-mouthed horror as he clung to the pole, his feet edging off the dock, while Dash took two big steps toward him and caught him by the collar of his shirt. The taut fabric was no match for Dash, and it tore under his hands, leaving Monty safe and dry with his fishing pole in hand, but his shirt in tatters. Dash rushed to apologize. "Monty, I'm so sorry. I never meant to—"

But the man grinned, slow and easy, and patted him on the shoulder. "It's quite all right, Dash, quite all right. Lucky for me I brought a change of clothes. I never had a sporting chance at this fishing competition anyway."

He turned to go, and Joan moved to follow him, eyeing Dolores nervously. Monty peered at her, seeming to mull something over. "It's all right, darling. Stay and see who wins." She opened her mouth to protest, but Monty simply raised his hand and walked away. Joan didn't follow.

Dash turned back to his fishing pole, noticing the line was jiggling, and reeled in a 27-pound rainbow trout with ease. Arlene beamed at him. "Well done, Dash!"

Right, then, there was one thing he could do today that didn't involve fending off sexually voracious divorcées or trying to work out what Joan Davis and Monty Smyth were thinking. So he turned back to the rod, placed a new piece of bait on the line, and threw himself into the competition.

He passed the next hour largely uneventfully, managing to catch three more fish, including a 40-pound trout. Dolores was busy flirting with a ranch hand who'd come to help her with her pole. Dash had had to resist rolling his eyes at the cutesy voice she'd put on, playing dumb and holding the rod upside down when only minutes before she'd seemed entirely capable. He felt sorry for her really. Clearly, someone had taught her this was how women were supposed to catch a man. Dolores knew how to fish, all right; she just didn't want trout.

Joan sat next to him on the dock, having removed her shoes to drag her feet lazily in the water. They exchanged few words but instead sat in companionable silence, with her murmuring words of encouragement or praise each time he caught a fish but dutifully avoiding calling attention to him. He appreciated it and wanted to tell her, but somehow he couldn't find the words.

It was worrying enough being wedged between Arlene and Dolores. One woman who was convinced they were soul mates and another who could probably give Leda Price a run for her gossip-hounding. So instead, he simply enjoyed Joan's company—the warmth of her hand around his wrist when she helped him bring in the 40-pounder, the tinkling sound of her laugh that reminded him of silverbells on Christmas morning, and the divine sight of her body languid and comfortable in the late afternoon sun.

It hit him then that technically she was his wife. That this was the way it could be between them if things were different. If he'd never agreed to that stupid studio date; if he hadn't fallen for Leda Price's schemes. But Joan was going to divorce him and become Mrs. Monty Smyth. It was what she wanted. And who was he to stand in her way? He wanted her, but more than that, he wanted her to be happy. To get everything she had spent her entire life fighting for. He'd already done plenty to mess it up.

Travis rang a bell, calling an end to the competition. "I'll be coming round to count and weigh the fish and then we'll declare our winners," he called from the end of the dock. He came to Arlene first, and she proudly counted out ten trout. Dash beamed at her; she'd said she would win and she had. He only had four. But he did have the 40-pounder, making him the winner of the Lazy Me Big Kahuna prize. Travis patted him on the back and thrust a trophy into his arms. It was ridiculous, a plastic gold fish affixed to the top of it.

"You should put that next to your Oscar," Joan quipped, sending everyone around them but Dolores into peals of laughter.

Dolores scowled. "At least he actually deserved this one," she muttered.

Travis, who had been completely oblivious to the afternoon's bickering on their end of the dock, stared at the woman open-mouthed, bearing a striking resemblance to Dash's winning fish.

Joan looked at Dash with concern, asking him with her eyes if he was okay. It touched him more than she'd ever know, and he gave her a curt nod, urging her to let it go. Ignoring Dolores seemed the most effective tactic.

But to his surprise, Arlene interjected. Her blue ribbon affixed to her chest, she marched up to Dolores and looked her dead in the eye. She'd clearly had enough of her antics. "You know, Dolores, there are words for women like you. But I wouldn't like to use them outside of a kennel." *Note to self: Do not get on Arlene Morgan's bad side.*

Dolores huffed, blowing a lock of her hair up into the air and back across her eye. He suspected she thought it made her look like Barbara Stanwyck, rather than the actual effect of resembling a Pekingese. "Puh-lease, everyone knows that the only real skill Dash Howard has is in the bedroom. He sleeps with anything that walks, and that's how he got where he is today. He's a corn-fed hick who's good at grimacing for the camera in a wooden-headed approximation of—"

Dash had started walking away, not wanting to listen to the words she was saying. She didn't deserve his breath. But he turned when he heard the sound of Dolores's voice interrupted by a loud splash that echoed across the lake.

Joan had hauled off and shoved Dolores in the lake. Fuck, he didn't condone violence, but if that wasn't the most attractive thing he'd ever seen, he'd eat his hat. She was standing on the edge of the dock, her dark curls blowing back in the wind, and she looked absolutely gorgeous as she bristled with fury. Joan was defending him. Him. Dash Howard.

Dolores was flailing and sputtering as two ranch hands sprinted down the dock to fish her out. But Joan was spoiling for a fight, and by the sound of it not running out of steam anytime soon. "You horrible woman, you don't know what you're talking about. You disgust me. You're not fit to kiss Dash Howard's boots. He's the finest man I've ever known. I'm…I'm proud to call him my husband, you hear me? Proud!"

"Joan." The single word split the pine fresh air and stopped Joan midbreath, a puff of air that might've been a gasp escaping from her lips. Dash turned to see Monty behind him. He'd changed out of his fishing togs into linen slacks and a sweater, back to the brooding gentleman audiences loved. "Time to go."

CHAPTER 17

JOAN WAS THE ONE WHO'D PUSHED ANOTHER WOMAN into the lake. So why then did she feel as if she'd been doused with cold water? When she'd come to her senses, realized what she was saying, and noticed that Monty had borne witness to it all, the air had whooshed out of her lungs.

It hadn't been enough to be photographed kissing another man in the papers. No, now she was causing a scene on that man's behalf. A man who was, through no fault of her own, technically her husband.

Monty gestured to her, and she followed him onto the shore, sand seeping in through her peep-toe wedges. But she ignored the tiny rocks grinding into her heels. Far more concerning was the grim look on Monty's face. As if he'd swallowed a rotten egg. Only she was the rotten egg.

"Monty, I can explain," she began, trudging behind him up the beach.

He held up a hand. "Not here, Joan." She swallowed hard and nodded. The least she could do was as he asked. What had she been thinking? She hadn't been. She'd simply allowed herself to get carried away by the late afternoon sun and Dash's striking figure on the end of the dock. He'd rolled up his shirtsleeves, exposing his forearms, and goodness, did men not realize the effect that had on women?

It drove her wild. Every time he tugged on his fishing rod, the muscles in his forearms flexed and rippled, leaving her breathless and a little parched. And then that terrible Dolores woman wouldn't let Dash be. It was as if she knew exactly what to say that would hurt Dash most. Joan couldn't stand for it, not when he'd stood up for her on set. She'd discovered what it meant to have someone in her corner. And she was finding she not only liked having someone there, but also liked being that person for someone else. Joan had always been a lone wolf, but she was starting to hunger for a pack.

They came upon the car Monty was borrowing while in town, a cream-colored Lincoln with the top down. It was long and slick and lush, not as fine as the Rolls-Royce Monty was well known for driving about town. But still far from inconspicuous, with its long, thin nose and undulating sides, accentuated by whitewall tires.

Ever the gentleman, Monty opened Joan's door first, gesturing for her to climb inside. She swallowed, her throat giving the impression it was more choked with sand and dust than she had on her feet. But she climbed in, hoping that Monty would end this silence. Yell, castigate her, anything was better than this quiet.

Monty wordlessly walked around the car and climbed behind the wheel, peeling out of their lakeside picnic area. Joan resisted the urge to look over her shoulder to catch the expression on Dash's face, instead clamping her wide white hat to her head as Monty put the car in drive and it picked up speed. The wind whipped through her hair, and she soon abandoned her hat, pulling it into her lap. Her cheeks burned, and she wished that it was from the sun but she knew it was the white-hot glow of shame.

They drove in silence for a time, a charged quiet so unlike the companionable one she'd shared with Dash on the dock. Monty climbed higher into the mountains, heading back in the direction of Reno and the Lazy Me Ranch.

After an interminable length of time, Monty at last pulled off into a lookout point above the lake. Nestled amid a stand of pines, he and Joan looked out across the northern end of the lake. It glistened and sparkled in the afternoon sun, and Joan longed for what this moment could have been—a romantic moment between a couple engaged to be married. Or at least that's what the papers would've seen. That's what mattered still. That's what Joan had to salvage.

"You have to understand, Monty. That Dolores woman was awful. The things she was saying to Dash. I couldn't countenance it."

He smiled, a sad little smile with a wisp of hopelessness to it. "You're in love with him."

"No, I'm not."

He reached for her hands and stilled them in her lap. "I'm not asking you, Joan. I'm telling you. You're in love with him."

She opened her mouth to protest again, but Monty shook his head no. In love with Dash Howard? Why, the notion was ludicrous. Just a few weeks ago, she'd hated him. Detested the sight of him. There had been nothing so ignominious as discovering she was married to him. And yet, since they'd come to Reno, something had changed. Dash had changed. Revealing himself to be a softer, kinder man beneath the grinning lothario facade that kept him in the lap of luxury. But love? That was absurd. Joan Davis didn't fall in love.

"Monty, I'm not, really I'm not. I got carried away by the heat of the day and, and—" She couldn't very well tell her fiancé about the attractiveness of another man's forearms, could she?

He grinned that sad little smile again. "There's no use denying it. I saw the way you looked at him. It's the same way I look at Jerry. Besides, I know you. You'd only raise hell like that for someone you truly care about."

Joan tried again to deny it. "No, it's just that Dash defended me on set with Von Wild, and I can't describe to you what that was like, Monty. It felt like for the first time in my life, I wasn't alone. I wanted him to feel the same. That's all."

Monty sighed, slightly exasperated now, and dropped her hands. He tucked his fedora low over his brow and leaned back in his seat, gazing out at the lake. "You can lie to yourself, Joan, but you can't lie to me."

The heat returned to her face again. She hated it. She'd vowed when she came to Hollywood never to be ashamed of anything again in her life. Not after being ashamed of her raw farmer's daughter's hands, her threadbare clothes, and her paltry bank account for so long. Shame was for Mildred Shalk, not Joan Davis.

There was no room for shame when she was chasing the thing she wanted most in this world, the only thing that could give her the safety and surety she craved. She had to remember that. Stay the course. But she could at least apologize. "I'm sorry if I embarrassed you. It won't happen again. I'm committed to this, Monty, to us. I won't mess it up for us, I promise."

He chuckled, low and devoid of mirth. She raised her sunglasses and was stunned to see he looked as if someone had placed an impossible weight on his shoulders. "There is no 'us' to mess up, Joan. There never has been."

"That's not true! I'm wearing your ring, aren't I?"

"It might as well be made of aluminum for all it means. It's a farce. It's always been a farce, and I should've known better."

Joan closed her eyes and inhaled. She couldn't believe what she was hearing. This couldn't be the end. "Don't be mad, Monty, darling, please. I made a mistake, but we can fix this. I know we can."

"You don't understand, Joan. I'm setting you free. One of us deserves to be happy, at least. I've ruined things with Jerry, probably for good. But you still have a chance with Dash. It was one thing when you were unattached. When I knew that any affairs you might have had were purely physical. I was willing to live a lie for both our sakes, but can you really say that's what you still want?"

She opened her mouth to tell him yes, of course it was, but he added, "Think about it, and I mean really think about it before you answer me."

She looked out across the lake, the sun glinting off its royal-blue depths, stretching out to its darker middle, so deep and unknowable it looked black as pitch. What did she want? She had been so sure it was Monty, this mutual marriage of convenience, a lie that would protect and elevate both of them.

She inhaled, the heady smell of pine flooding her senses. A series of memories came to her unbidden: the look of hunger on Dash's face when he'd held her around the waist helping her mount her horse; the understanding in his eyes when she'd told him about her childhood; the feel of his mouth pressed against hers, rough and demanding; the funny feeling she had in the pit of her stomach the night he'd left her his pajamas; the sense this last week that for the first time in her life, she wasn't alone. That wasn't love. It felt safe, secure, not at all the untethered, wild thing she'd always known it to be. But was that another thing she was wrong about? Tears of frustration sprang to her eyes.

"I can't love him," she gasped.

"Oh, but you can." Monty smiled. "And what's more, you do." He fished his handkerchief from his pocket and handed it to her. She caressed the interlocking M and S embroidered in the corner, finely stitched into the silk, before dabbing at her eyes.

"I didn't mean for this to happen. I never... He's not... I don't know how it did. I promised myself I'd never f-f-fall in l-l-love." As she struggled to get these last words out, she was overcome and began to cry in earnest, a river of tears running down her face. This was not the glamorous crying of the movies. It was real and ugly—scrunched-up face, red eyes, and burbling snot. If Leda Price could see her now.

Monty chuckled, a genuine laugh this time. "We never mean for these things to happen." He wrapped his arm around her shoulders affectionately and bid her press her head to his shoulder, and she quickly obliged.

She cried some more, weeping into Monty's shoulder until she found herself able to continue. She sniffed and raised her head to meet his eyes. "I'm so sorry, Monty. Can you ever forgive me?" The sun was dipping lower in the sky now, its lazy pace abandoned for a swifter race to the horizon.

He leaned down and kissed her temple, the brush of his lips an affectionate reassurance. "Joan, there's nothing to forgive you for."

"But..." She sniffed, struggling to regain control of her emotions. "I've ruined everything." She toyed with the handkerchief in her hands, twisting it into knots.

He patted her head now, as if she were a small child. "On the contrary, my dear, you might have saved us both."

She burrowed further into his shoulder, unable to stem the flood of emotions overtaking her. But Monty simply held her and let her come to terms with the truth of what he'd said. That she was falling in love with Dash Howard. That the last man on earth she'd expected had broken through her defenses. No, not even that. He'd shown her there was another way than what she'd always believed love to be. That love could be quiet and mysterious, that a person could be her port in a storm rather than the hurricane itself. How strange.

They sat there for some time, watching the sun go down over the lake. When the first twinkling of starlight flickered in the dusky evening, he turned the key in the ignition and pulled back onto the road.

"What happens now?" she asked.

"Well, much of that is up to you. But I don't belong here. I'll go back to Hollywood. I won't be a cad and be the one to end our engagement. But you should at least give yourself a chance, Joan. Why throw away happiness before you've even really tried to grab at it with both hands? I'll always be here for you. In whatever way you need me to be."

She nodded, overwhelmed by what a good man Monty was. How kind, how understanding. Her instincts hadn't been wrong; he *would* have made a good husband. If they weren't both in love with other people.

"Time to take you back to the ranch."

She swallowed. The ranch. Where Dash was. Where he was waiting in a cramped bungalow they were sharing, thinking God knows what about what she'd done this afternoon and where she'd been since. "What should I tell Dash?"

Monty smiled warmly, taking a hairpin curve on the mountain road with ease. "The truth, of course."

A bubble of emotion rose in the back of her throat. Dash didn't believe anyone could love him. Would he believe her? Or would he think she was mocking him? Playing a trick? "I don't know if I can. I don't even know if I know what that is."

"You can. I believe in you." Monty reached over and squeezed her hand. "If Dash is the kind of man I suspect he is, and I daresay he must be to make the mighty Joan Davis sick with love for him, he'll welcome what you have to say and make it easy for you."

She swatted at him playfully. "I am *not* sick with love for him."

But she couldn't keep herself from grinning as she said it, dizzy with the thought of it. At the prospect that maybe she could have this tender, fragile thing she'd always believed she had to deny herself. Monty returned the grin, swatting right back, until she surrendered, and they broke out into warm laughter that followed them down the mountain toward the blinking lights of Reno and the dark safety of the ranch.

CHAPTER 18

DASH SAT ON THE BACK PORCH OF THE BUNGALOW, LEAN-ing back on his hands and marveling at the stars. He hadn't seen this many stars since he was a boy on the farm, a blanket of them as far as the eye could see. He picked out his favorite summer constellations: Hercules, the strong man; Andromeda, the doomed princess; and good old Ursa Major and Minor. They were centuries, if not millennia old, and still they kept watch over them all, silent and unmoving in the sky. Hollywood liked to boast that they had more stars than there were in heaven, but the idea was laughable. The very notion that anyone would know his name or care that'd he lived centuries from now was absurd. No, these were real stars—bright, twinkling, and unchangeable.

He'd forgotten what it was to feel small in the world, an infinitesimally tiny speck in the universe. Everyone from Harry Evets to Fritz Von Wild to the hat check girl at the Trocadero was dedicated to reminding him how important he was. To hell with that. They were all propping up a fantasy.

He had no idea how long he'd been sitting there. Long enough to watch the dusky lavender of the early evening sky fade to a deeper purple before resolving itself into an inky black dotted with the brilliant diamond patchwork nature was offering up. After Joan had left, the afternoon had passed in a blur. He hadn't even bothered to apologize to Dolores. She'd deserved it. He'd simply watched Joan and Monty trek across the sand to the car before disappearing between the pines. Arlene had given him a knowing look before suggesting they both catch a ride back to the ranch with Travis. He didn't need to be asked twice, and he'd followed, sitting silent in the back seat while Travis waxed on about the history of the lake and the surrounding environs.

As soon as he'd got back, he'd headed straight for the bungalow, leaving Travis to call a cab to take Arlene back to the Hotel Riverside. But sitting inside with only a sheet between him and all of Joan's things made him antsy; her scent was everywhere, the clean floral hint of gardenias with a note of citrus. He'd come out to the porch to clear his head.

The still of the night was interrupted by the sound of a screen door swinging on its hinges, and the sight of Joan's red lacquered toenails peeping through her open-toed shoes strode into view. She smoothed her shorts and sat on the porch step next to him.

She nudged him with her shoulder, unbearably close. "Penny for your thoughts?"

"I was thinking how nice it is to feel small for once," he replied.

She sighed. "You could never be small. Not to me."

"I'd like to say there's no need to flatter me, but I like it." He scratched his chin thoughtfully. "But what I'm trying to say is I like being small. I *want* to be small. Being the King of Hollywood, pretending to be something I'm not, is exhausting. Leda Price thinks we're the center of the universe, but look up. These stars have been there for billions of years, keeping silent watch over generations of foolish people—warlords and star-crossed lovers and, yes, even movie stars. And when we're gone, they'll still be there. Makes me feel like my problems don't amount to a hill of beans, and I like that."

She murmured her approval, and the deep-throated hum

coming from her mouth shot straight down his spine, filling him with want. He didn't know how much more of this he could take. But her next words were like being doused in cold water. "You must know that what Dolores said today… It's not true."

The ache in his chest he'd been fighting against all evening bloomed afresh. "Which part?" he managed to choke out.

"All of it," she replied, setting her hand atop his knee. He should stop her; a better man would. But it was all he'd ever wanted. "You're not a corn-fed hick who grimaces for the camera. You're a fine actor and an even better man. One who deserves to be seen and cherished for who he really is."

Her hand slid farther up his leg, resting on the top of his thigh, and he turned to meet her gaze. Her brunette curls were windblown, a tendril of hair lying against her cheek, and without thinking he reached to brush it back and tuck it behind her ear. She looked down and blushed. Even in the twilight, he could see the high color in her cheeks. But then she looked up to meet his gaze, something remarkably like defiance and a hint of fear swirling there. The starlight sparkled in her eyes, crystalline and bright. It was a good thing he was already sitting down because the very sight of her made him weak with want.

Before he could say anything, she leaned over and kissed him. It was light as air, a puff of desire against his lips. He could feel the brush of her eyelashes against his cheeks. Butterfly kisses, his mother had called them when he was practically too small to remember. The sensation was as fragile and as sweet as spun sugar, and he wanted a deeper taste of Joan. But something within him broke when she kissed him, knowing that a stolen moment like this would never be enough.

He pulled back from her and managed to grunt out a single word: "Monty."

She pressed her forehead to his and caressed his cheek. "What about Monty?"

He gripped her shoulders and nudged her back, bringing his hand to hers and removing it from his cheek. He stroked her fingers absentmindedly, and then he realized she wasn't wearing her engagement ring.

He stood up in a frenzy. He wouldn't be the cause of more disappointment, more wrong turns in Joan's life. "Where is he? He can't throw you over. Nothing's happened. I'll tell him so myself." He spun his head about wildly, hoping to catch a glimpse of headlights or something, some sign that it wasn't too late to set things right.

She stood and reached for his hand. "Dash, it's all right."

"Where's your ring, then?"

"I took it off. It's inside."

She swallowed, doubt entering her eyes, and panic began to course through him. This couldn't be happening. "Because of me? Joan, I… Please, we'll go to him tomorrow. I'll explain everything. I won't ruin this for you."

She chuckled and stroked his knuckles. "It *is* because of you, but it's not what you think."

Oh God, he'd been such a fool. She had been determined to marry Monty. Her career depended on it. And he'd somehow marred things. "You've fought too hard. I won't be another man who derails your dreams. You know I think you deserve better than marrying a man who doesn't love you, but I will not stand in the way of what you want, what you've been fighting for. If you don't believe in love, that's your business, not mine."

"Monty didn't call off the engagement."

"Thank God." His heart rate slowed. He hadn't ruined things after all, then. "But why did you take off—"

She kissed him again. Harder, with a bruising passion that rattled him. Her teeth nipped at his bottom lip, and she buried her hands in his hair before wrenching apart from him and pressing her forehead to his, gasping for air and clutching at his collar. "Monty didn't call off the engagement, but he asked *me* to think about doing so."

"Why? Why would you want that?"

"Because you're who I want, you fool."

"You want *me*?" he spluttered. It was laughable. He couldn't believe the words he was hearing. Joan Davis wanted him. Joan, who only a few weeks ago had acted as if being married to him was a fate worse than death. Joan, who'd defied his expectations at every turn since they'd come to Reno. Who made him dizzy, half with frustration, half with need. Wanted. Him. It wasn't possible. "I don't understand."

"I don't understand it myself." Joan half shrugged, looking remarkably like the lost little girl she'd worked so hard to leave behind her. "I don't believe in love. But I want you. Against all odds, I want you, Dashiell Howard. I think maybe I've always felt this way. I had been so convinced you were a scheming louse that I could convince myself the intense emotions that flared in me every time I saw you were disdain and annoyance instead of naked want. And since I've learned otherwise, I've been too stubborn to admit it. Luckily, Monty has enough sense for the three of us."

Dash reached for her, wrapping his arms around her and palming her ass. It was as delectable in his hands as it had been that day on the train weeks ago. Only now, it seemed, it was his for the taking. No longer a forbidden fruit. He crushed her to his chest in a fierce embrace and set his chin atop her head. "No, I don't think Monty has much sense at all."

She twisted her head to peer up at him. "How can you say that? When he's sent me here, to your arms?"

"That's precisely why. Any man in his right mind wouldn't give you up so easily. I have half a mind to call him up and tell him so."

"Let's make a deal," she said. He raised his eyebrows and peered at her. "Let's not talk about Monty or the engagement or any of it again until the morning."

"I don't know if I'll be done with you by the morning."

Joan giggled, a thrum of desire ringing beneath her laughter. He'd meant it as a joke, as a come-on. But also as a promise. Once he had Joan, he would never be done with her. He knew that now.

But her laughter was a heady sound, and he hardened further as it echoed through the trees. It was the best sound in the world, better than silver bells on Christmas morning or the tinkling of rain on a tin roof. He wished to hear it for all the days of his life. It quieted the doubts in his mind, the ones that said this would only be one night and she'd forget him. Go back to Monty. To the life she'd built that didn't leave room for things like desire or romance or Dash Howard. She'd leave him behind. Just like every other woman he'd ever made love to. Right at this moment, he almost didn't care. He wanted her too much.

He bowed his head to meet hers, finally initiating their kiss. He tangled his hands in the soft curls at the nape of her neck and tasted her as if he were a hungry man wandering in the desert and she was his salvation. He teased at the corners of her mouth, and she opened for him, their tongues meeting in a dance as old as the stars themselves. She was delectable, that hint of citrus that followed her wherever she went rising up to meet him, only mixed with something darker and headier. He cocked his head to the right, seeking to find the proper angle from which to devour her.

She moaned, a deep-throated hum that vibrated across his tongue and shot straight to his cock.

He fisted her blouse, pulling her closer to him, and ground into her. He was rewarded with a breathy gasp as he rubbed against her most sensitive spot through her shorts. It struck him suddenly that they were both wearing entirely too many clothes. He broke apart from her and showered her face with kisses. He moved from the edges of her mouth to the elegant tip of her nose to those downy, soft eyelashes to her forehead and back again to her mouth, writing an essay of his desire with his lips.

"I love your freckles," he murmured, lavishing each of them with a kiss. She closed her eyes and smiled a beatific smile, absent-mindedly mussing his hair with her fingers.

"I've always hated them," she admitted on a breathless puff of air. "Movie stars don't have freckles."

"They're perfectly imperfect," he said as he found a spot behind her ear that made her gasp and arch into him. "Like you. I will require hours to devote proper attention to them. To kiss them all."

He swirled his tongue around the whorl of her ear, finding a freckle dotting the edge of her earlobe. He nipped at it. "Like this one here," he whispered, before moving lower to a constellation of them on her neck. "And these here."

He reached for the silk tie at the top of her blouse, fumbling with it until it fell open in a wide vee, exposing the round curves of the tops of her breasts. They were gloriously freckled too, and he huffed, something between a chuckle and a groan of desire. He moved to kiss them. "And these."

As he pressed his mouth to her chest, she tangled one hand in his hair, holding him there. His thigh was between her legs now, and she rubbed against him, mewling as her breaths grew shorter. He reached down with his other hand and palmed her through her shorts. Even with the fabric, he could feel how warm she was, how much she wanted him. As she writhed in his arms, he pulled her blouse from her shorts and lifted it, lowering himself to his knees to kiss her belly. It required an effort not to spill in his jeans as he knelt. He throbbed even harder as he lifted the shirt to find a litany of freckles dotting her stomach. He'd never seen her like this, exposed, no makeup or Hollywood lights to obscure her imperfections.

He grabbed her ass with his hands, pushing her into his face, and he inhaled, recognizing her gardenia perfume along the edge of her high-waisted shorts. He dipped his tongue beneath the waistband, and she flinched with desire, pushing herself forward until she was nearly straddling his face. "Tell me, Joan," he growled into her belly. "If I keep going, will I find more?"

She didn't answer, merely panted, pressing her hands into the deck and arching backwards. He reached for the brass buttons on the sides of her shorts. He nimbly undid the top two, and practically came as he spied the edge of her pink lacy underthings. But he wanted to drag this out, to make it good for them both. They'd had this date with destiny for six years, and he was going to revel in it for all it was worth. Particularly because he couldn't shake the feeling that this was temporary. And it might break him when it ended, but rational thought had ceased to dictate his decision-making several kisses ago.

So he sat back on his haunches, the leather soles of his boots digging into his own ass and helping him focus on something besides the blood rushing to his cock.

"Why did you stop?" she whined, reaching for him.

"Because I need you to answer me. If I keep going, will I find more?" It had started as a flirtatious game, but now he had to know, had to see for himself if the freckles on her face were accompanied by more between her legs, on her thighs. Was her entire body a map for him to chart and circumnavigate at his leisure?

In answer, she undid another set of buttons and pushed at the shorts until they fell from her waist, leaving her sitting in her blouse and dainty silk pink underwear that mirrored the shape of her shorts and were dotted with roses.

The fabric was so delicate it was practically see-through, and he could see the telltale shadow of more freckles and a thatch of dark curls. He groaned, and she leaned forward to kiss him, hard and fast, practically knocking him flat. If he wasn't already on his knees, this would've sent him there. "Take me inside and I'll show you," she murmured against his mouth.

He'd practically forgotten they were outside, exposed to the world. This was what her revelation had done to him. But he didn't need to be asked twice. In one swift movement, he stood and picked her up, one arm curled protectively around her back, the other slung under her thighs. Her shorts lay on the ground forgotten, and he kicked at the screen door with his boot, struggling to open the door. As he hooked it with his foot and maneuvered them between the door and the threshold, she reached to caress his cheek and he rubbed his face against her hand, mesmerized by the sensation of her touch against his stubble. He leaned down to kiss her, her lips now almost bee-stung from his ministrations, and stumbled backwards into the room, nearly colliding with the makeshift sheet barrier he'd strung up.

She clung to him and giggled as he fought to keep them both upright. She dissolved into peals of hysterical laughter, and he couldn't suppress the matching grin on his face. "What's so funny?"

She buried her face in his neck, trying to regain composure. "It's just like our picture."

He laughed then, deep-throated and full. She was right. It was a ridiculous moment of life imitating art. But he might as well see it through to its natural conclusion. He threw his head back and imitated the clarion call of a trumpet.

She shrieked with laughter, and for the first time in years, he felt solid and strong, as if his insides matched his outsides.

"Blow down the walls of Jericho," she cried out, and she snatched at the sheet, tearing it from the rope it was hanging on. He moved to bring her to the bed and pulsed with need as he watched the mirth in her eyes darken to pools of desire again. He laid her down gently, her mahogany curls fanning around her face. She looked downright sinful in only her underwear and her blouse, her face flushed with need. He turned to toe off his boots and began to unbutton his flannel shirt. But he whirled around at the breathy sound of his name.

Joan had stood up again, and she'd made quick work of her blouse. She stood now only in her pink bra edged with lace and her pink tap pants. They hadn't bothered to close the curtains, and her entire body was suffused with moonlight. She practically glowed, and his throat went dry at the sight of her. He'd never seen anything so beautiful in his entire life. It was if a goddess or a wood nymph had wandered in the back door.

"Look at me," she whispered.

"I can't look anywhere else," he intoned. Their eyes met and she didn't blush or avert her eyes. Instead, she held his gaze as she reached behind her and undid the clasp of her bra. It sprang loose and she reached her fingers to the straps, languidly pulling them from her arms and touching herself as she went.

He couldn't suppress a groan as she dropped the bra to the floor and stood tall, her small, perfectly round breasts exposed to him. Her nipples were the same rosy color as the flowers on her underwear. He took a step toward her, desperate to get his mouth on her. But she held up a hand, stilling him, and nodded. "Now you."

He reached for the buttons on his shirt, fumbling in his need to get it off. "To hell with it," he muttered, watching the buttons pop off and scatter about the room as he discarded the material on the floor.

"Still not wearing an undershirt, I see," she drawled. He couldn't suppress a grin at the memory of it.

"All the angry letters from the undershirt manufacturers of the world weren't enough to reform me." He chuckled.

"I'm glad." She took a step toward him, reached out, and pressed her hand to his chest. His skin pebbled under her touch, and he inhaled sharply as she plucked at his nipple with her fingers.

But the moment was over all too soon, as she stepped back. He didn't have time to mourn the loss of her touch though, because she was reaching for the silk band of her underwear, and soon the filmy material was on the floor, pooling around her ankles. She stepped out of it and kicked off her low-slung wedges as well, now completely bare before him.

It was as he'd imagined—her entire body was dotted with the same freckles everywhere. As if the sun had kissed her and marked her for its own. On her right hip, there was a small constellation of them that looked remarkably like the Andromeda cluster he'd been admiring earlier this evening. He knelt before her and gently pressed his lips to it. "Forget the night sky," he whispered. "These are the only constellations I have use for from now on. I could spend the rest of my days mapping them with my tongue, cataloguing them with my lips, and charting them with my hands."

Joan wasn't sure if she was shivering from fear or desire. Maybe both. She'd never felt so vulnerable. She shuddered under his touch and he raised a hand to her curls, finding the small knot of her desire. He licked his thumb and swiped it across her most sensitive spot. He lowered his head and kissed the inside of her thigh, sucking and swirling his way from one freckle to another.

She couldn't hold back a series of breathy pants, and so he reached for her, slipping his fingers through her slick folds and pressing his palm against her until she groaned.

"You're soaking wet," he marveled. He slid one finger inside her, and she bit her lip, trying not to cry out.

"Oh fuck," she huffed.

He added a second finger and began pumping her with his hand. He placed his other hand behind her, and she shivered at the feeling of his callused hand gripping her bare ass, no fabric between them any longer. He allowed her to brace herself against his shoulder as she rode his hand with abandon.

She looked down, barely able to perceive him through the haze of her desire. He gave her a look of pure hunger. "I want to taste you, Joan. May I?"

The question made her tighten around his fingers. She couldn't answer. He curled his finger inside her and she moaned, short and quick. "Can I taste you, Joan?"

She brought her hands to her breasts and pinched her nipples, which were already standing taut and erect with need. "P-p-p-l-l-l-ease," she panted.

He didn't wait for a second invitation and buried his face in her, inhaling deeply as he licked from the hard nub at her center down her seam to her opening. He licked and swirled before replacing his fingers with his tongue, dipping into her and lapping at her. Joan had had her fair share of lovers over the years, but it had never felt this good. She was delirious with pleasure. A wild and dangerous thought sprang to life. What if she could have this forever?

She tensed at the notion, and Dash must've noticed

immediately because he raised his head briefly and whispered, "Let go, Joan. Come undone. I want to see you lose control."

Maybe, just this once, she could. Give in. Surrender to pleasure, desire, all of it. Give up a modicum of that control. It wasn't as if she needed encouragement. Her body had a mind of its own and she arched her pelvis further into his face, more brazen than she'd ever been, as if seized by some wild and unknowable part of herself. He slipped his fingers inside her once more and pressed a kiss to her clit. He grazed the sensitive spot with his teeth and rubbed the stubble of his jaw over her. It was heavenly, rough and tender and raw and everything she'd ever wanted.

She was pleading now, panting harder and harder until she broke forth into a keening cry, clenching around his hands and becoming a taut wire of pure desire. She melted in his arms, a pool of jelly, held upright only by the force of his hand against her ass and her knees pressing into his shoulders.

He leaned forward and kissed her opening, her clit, and her thighs before he stood and carried her to the bed. She placed her hand behind his neck and drew him to her, tasting herself on his lips. It was intoxicating, a heady blend of Dash's clean, masculine scent and something musky and darker. She took his bottom lip between hers and sucked. He broke away from her and pressed his forehead to hers, their heavy breathing the only sound in the room.

She looked down and could see the hard length of him straining against his jeans, so she undid his belt buckle and button until his jeans were open and she could see him inside of his underwear. She hissed as he shivered at the touch of her hand to the fabric, drunk on her own power. He whimpered, and she pressed a kiss to his cheek before reaching her hand inside his waistband and taking him in her grip.

He was hard as steel, a velvety rod that she could barely wrap her fingers around. She drew him out and gasped at the sight of her lacquered nails and dainty fingers encircling his impressive girth. A bead of liquid seeped from the head, and she rubbed at it with her thumb, slicking her fingers. She let go for a moment, bringing her fingers to her mouth. He kneeled on the edge of the bed exposed, watching her intently. So she took each finger one by one, placing it in her swollen mouth and making a show of sucking each one.

"Christ, Joan, you're going to kill me." He groaned and a lock of his hair fell over his eye, making him look like a disheveled rogue. She reached for him again, but he was too fast for her, shucking off his jeans and his underwear in one swift motion.

He stood above her now completely naked, his cock jutting toward her, erect and needy. He was a beautiful man; a light, nearly invisible coat of hair dusted his chest until it became darker around his navel. He seemed to be flexing every muscle in his body, which she knew to be impossible, as he held himself still for her. She drank in the sight of him, relishing this opportunity to see Dash Howard exposed in a way he never had been.

"You're beautiful," she whispered.

He grinned, the corner of his mouth tugging upward in a cockeyed fashion. "Not ruggedly handsome?"

He was nervous before her; she knew because she used humor in the same way to cover her anxiety. She shook her head. "Dash Howard the movie star is ruggedly handsome. But you, Dash the man, you're beautiful."

He shivered involuntarily and looked down at her with hooded eyes. He could smolder like nobody's business, able to bring women to their knees with a single glance. Or so the posters touted. But holy hell, this was something else, a dark and hungry look only for her.

She came to her knees and crawled to the edge of the bed,

pressing her hands to his chest, exploring the hard lines and ridges of his body. She palmed the sides of his rib cage, wandering around to his back, exploring the dips and valleys there before arriving at his ass. It was firm beneath her hands and she gripped it, using him to pull herself up so she could kiss him. She gave him a long and punishing kiss, and he wrapped his arms around her, clutching her to him.

But she broke away and dipped her head to his chest, taking his nipple gently between her teeth. He inhaled sharply, and she smiled against him. She kissed him, swirling her tongue around his nipple until he grunted, gripped her bare ass, and rolled them both down onto the bed. He sucked at her neck and held himself aloft above her before palming her breasts.

Her already taut nipples hardened further at his touch, and he grinned at her. "Two can play at this game," he murmured, before lowering his head to suck and kiss her. He laved one nipple with his tongue, kneading the other with his fingers.

She'd always been self-conscious about her breasts. They were small by Hollywood standards, and she'd had plenty of directors humiliate her by asking for extra padding, but Dash didn't seem to have any complaints. He buried his head in her chest, and she writhed beneath him until she reached lower and took him in hand. He was hot and heavy in her palm. He shuddered as she worked him, fisting his hands in the sheets.

"This is all I've ever wanted," he ground out. He reached for her and stilled her, making her stop. "But what do you want, Joan?"

No man had ever asked her what she wanted. She'd had to take it for herself. She grinned, a sultry, lazy smile that lit up her whole being. "I want you inside me," she answered.

"Then take me," he replied. "I'm yours, always have been."

She pressed one last kiss to his mouth and then gently pushed at his shoulder until he flipped over, pulling her on top so she was straddling him. Slowly, she sank onto him, feeling him stretch her as he filled her inch by inch. The further she went, the harder he bit his lip, looking at her like he was ready to explode.

Soon she was seated on top of him, and she stilled for a moment, relishing the feeling of fullness. It was pain and pleasure and the most wonderful thing she'd ever felt. He filled her up, and she tightened instinctually around him.

He leaned forward and kissed her, and she lifted herself up, raising her hips until only the tip of him was still inside her and then slowly lowering herself back down. He swore again as she reseated herself, tilting slightly so that he hit a spot inside of her that made her gasp.

She began to move up and down, thrusting onto him. He reached for her and she met his lips with a kiss. The sensitive tips of her breasts grazed his chest, and she reveled in the sensation of feeling his skin everywhere. She swiveled her hips and her body, tracing a circular teasing pattern atop his chest with her breasts, and he groaned, pulling her down into a feverish kiss. She rode him hard, her pace quickening as ecstasy mounted once again.

He wrapped his arms around her and suddenly rolled them over so that he was on top of her. She dug her fingers into his back, urging him to go deeper and harder, until they were fused body and soul. His pace grew frantic as he neared completion, and he locked eyes with her, lust and something else, something deeper and dark, mingling in his gaze.

No one had ever looked at her like this, not a lover or even a scene partner playacting. This was something you couldn't fake. Not if you gave the greatest performance in the world. She was giddy at the thought, and she wrapped her ankles around his haunches, urging him on.

It was animalistic now, her hips taking on a mind of their own, rising to meet his as he thrust into her again and again. She took his mouth, kissing him as fiercely as she could, trying to convey the depth of her passion for him. When he reached down and placed his hand between them to stroke her, all rational thought left her; she was merely arms and teeth and tongue and sensation. Pressure mounted in her, and every inch of her pulled taut and crackled with electricity. Finally, stars exploded behind her eyes as she bit into his shoulder to avoid screaming his name. Moments after, bursts of light still flashing before her eyes and a tingling sensation giving way to a weightless warmth, he found his release, spilling into her and whispering her name like it was a prayer before he collapsed onto her.

They lay like that for a moment, their breathlessness in sync as they slowed their breathing and came back to themselves. Then he rolled off of her and curled onto his side, pulling her to him and tenderly kissing the tips of her breasts, before moving to her lips and ending on the tip of her nose and her eyelids.

"I love you," he whispered. "I think I always have. You're extraordinary, Joan."

The words should've terrified her. But they didn't. She sighed and snuggled closer to him. All this time she'd been searching for security, certain that money and fame were the only means to it. But she'd never felt as safe as she did at this moment, lying here naked next to Dash, tangled in sheets soaked in the sweat from their lovemaking. He was wrapped protectively around her, one hand cupping her ass, another around her shoulders. No audience, no applause had ever made her feel like this.

She pressed her hand to his heart and found comfort in its steady beat. His arms were a haven. She raised her hand to caress his jaw and he burrowed into it, kissing her palm. His eyes, only moments before smoldering with desire, were now heavy with sleep.

"You make me feel safe," she whispered, dotting the words in between kisses as she showered his face with them. "You're my sanctuary, my port in the storm of life, Dash Howard."

He sighed and pulled her closer, tucking her beneath his chin. She raised her fingers to the hollow under his collarbone and above his heart, lightly dancing in the indentation. Then she raised her mouth to kiss him there.

His heartbeat under her palm had slowed, and his eyelids fluttered with sleep as she nestled closer to him, tangling her toes with his and nudging her knee between his thighs so that they were twined together from head to toe. She rested her head on his arm and looked out the window. Stars that matched the ones he'd sent exploding behind her eyes spread out above them in an inky blanket. She suddenly understood what he meant earlier about feeling small, the comfort of it, of knowing you weren't alone out on a pedestal somewhere.

Sleep was beckoning, but she watched out the window as the stars twinkled and danced, more real and more beautiful than anything she'd ever known. She pressed her face into his chest, snuggling against him, as she drew the sheet over them both. The sound of his heart was lulling her to sleep, beating in time to the words she'd never thought she'd want to hear. "I love you, I love you," it thumped over and over.

She wanted to say it back. To make the song of their hearts one and the same. To write it in the stars quietly flickering in their silent glory out the window.

I love you too, Dash Howard. That's all you have to say. Instead, she clung more tightly to him, burrowing into his chest and willing the words she could not say straight from her heart into his.

CHAPTER 19

DASH'S HEART WAS GOING TO BURST OUT OF HIS CHEST. He couldn't do this. What was Arlene thinking? The scene she'd promised him had arrived yesterday, and they were to film it shortly. And he couldn't even ask her about it because she'd gone back to Hollywood with Monty. Apparently, Harry wanted to talk through some of her revisions in person.

Arlene called the scene his character's "dark night of the soul." The scene after Carol tells him she's leaving Reno because she can't trust her heart with anyone, no matter how she cares for him. Alone in his cabin, Joe gets drunk and breaks down sobbing, before running out into the storm that will take his life. It was a masterpiece of screenwriting, designed to make the audience weep. But it called for him to cry on-screen. And he simply couldn't do it. He was shocked Harry had even allowed Arlene to write it.

No one would respect Dash Howard if he cried on-screen. Over a woman, to boot. All the sacrifices he'd made to craft himself into a paragon of masculinity would be for nothing. With one scene, he'd risk his whole career. And then what would it have all been for?

He paced back and forth in the small log cabin they were using for a set, ignoring the chatter of the crew while they prepared for the shot. He tried to calm his nerves by thinking about Joan, the stolen moments they'd shared this past week. But that didn't help; it just reminded him of the things left unsaid. Namely, that she loved him. That her engagement to Monty was officially off. She hadn't put the ring back on, true. But she'd done nothing to officially end the relationship publicly either. And if he blew up his career with this scene, what would he have then? The answer terrified him.

Their new director, Bob Kucor, was reviewing the script pages in his director's chair to the right of the camera, making hurried notes on the pages. He was a departure from Von Wild, quiet, kind, and understanding. Dash had never worked with him before; he was known for directing women's pictures. He realized now that was because Kucor was good at directing women; he spoke their language and treated them with respect. Something that seemed to be in shockingly short supply in Hollywood.

Before he knew it, it was time to start rolling. This was it. Now or never. "Pull yourself together, Dash," he muttered. This was what he loved about his job, wasn't it? Acting. So act, God damn it. He shook the nervous energy from his hands, took his place on his mark, and shoved down the feeling he was going to vomit while he waited for Kucor to call "Action."

The word came, and he palmed his face, going through the motions of a man distraught. He stumbled across the room and grasped for the whiskey bottle on his character's bed. Sitting on the bed in a defeated slump, he tore the stopper from the bottle with his teeth and took a swig of the cold tea the crew had filled it with. This was it. The moment he was supposed to break down and mournfully repeat Carol's name until tears were streaming down his face.

He looked up—and there, next to the camera, was Joan. His

heart caught in his throat. Now he really couldn't do this. She was counting on him to get this right. To make this picture as good as they both knew it could be. But how could he do this when it was the one thing Harry had always insisted would be the surest way to send his career down the toilet? "No one wants the King of Hollywood to be a sissy." How many times had he heard that?

He met Joan's eyes and she gave him an encouraging smile. He closed his eyes, trying to summon some emotions from the depths of his soul. But nothing was there but sheer terror.

He opened his eyes and gave Kucor a blank look before launching into his lines, repeating Carol's name in a fashion he knew was entirely unconvincing. "Cut," yelled Kucor.

The man gave him an understanding look. "Shall I give you a minute?"

Dash nodded and watched as Joan pulled Kucor aside and whispered something in his ear. Quietly and without much fuss, Kucor cleared everyone from the set, leaving only Joan in the room with Dash.

He leaned back against the wall and pressed his hands to his eyes. "Christ, I can't do this."

She came to kneel next to him on the bed and pulled his hands from his face. "Yes, you can."

He let his hands drop and turned his head to look at her. "I can't, Joan. I'm not as good as you are. I've always known that."

"That's bullshit and you know it," she intoned. "You're the one with an Oscar."

"Because Hollywood is sexist and hasn't given you enough good roles."

She laughed, short and halting. "Well, I won't argue with that. But, Dash, you're a good actor. A great one when you let yourself be. It's why Arlene wrote this scene for you. For us."

An ugly thought flickered in his mind: the notion that perhaps Joan was doing all of this, making love to him, because it was good for the picture. But he tried to silence it and focus on what she was saying.

"Arlene wanted to give you the chance to show a new side of yourself."

He shook her off and stood, pacing the room again. "That's the trouble. Hollywood doesn't want a different side of me. It's why I'm trapped in this role the studio and I have built: the golden boy, the rugged playboy. That's what audiences want from me."

Joan stood, grabbed him by the upper arms, and gave him a searching look. "If I didn't know better, I'd say you were afraid."

He swallowed down the urge to lash out at her, to question her support as possessing an ulterior motive. Joan always could see right through him, even before she'd known the most intimate parts of him. "I'm not...afraid. I just don't want to do something monumentally stupid, that's all. I've given up a lot to get here. I don't want to lose more than I already have."

She took his hands in hers, pressing his thumbs to her wrists in the gesture he'd used to calm her only a few weeks ago with the horses. "Dash, let me ask you a question. Why did you become an actor?"

"Because Josephine wanted me to be one," he rattled off.

"No." She squeezed his wrists with a hint of too much force. "I don't believe that. Maybe that's why you started. But if that was true, you would've quit after she left. Before you ever got to Hollywood. So, okay, maybe the question isn't why did you become an actor, but why are you still one? You've told me you hate what Hollywood has made you, so why keep at it?"

Her question hit him like a ton of bricks. It was an answer he'd been searching for himself lately, ever since Flynn had suggested he give it all up. Why keep at it indeed? "Because," he started, emotion catching in his throat as he forced himself to admit the truth. "Because before you, us, it was the only thing that made me happy."

She nodded, urging him to go on. He did, the realization pouring out of him in a wave that was picking up speed. "Because there's nothing that I love more than being on a set, getting to know my crew, helping bring a story to life. Because people think we do it for the fame or because some part of us is broken, and maybe that's true, but acting, just acting without all the fan magazines and the studio politics and the phony posturing, is a noble profession. Because it's my, our, job to inhabit the best and worst of humanity, to bring empathy to the basest and the most remarkable among us for the sake of bringing some nugget of truth to the screen. We get to make people's lives better, bring them hope, joy, sorrow, any emotion you can name. We get to make their lives brighter, more vibrant, even if the people they think we are aren't real."

Joan nodded. "I wanted fame because I wanted what it could grant me—wealth, safety, security. I love acting too. And I hate being underestimated. But you, you've always loved it for the purest reasons. You've made me realize that's why I love it too. I've always known there was no other path for me, but if I told you that you had to give up acting tomorrow, that it was all over, what would you do?"

He crossed over to the small window on the edge of the cabin, looking out the warped glass to the shadows of the mountains beyond. "I have a ranch. I could make a life there."

He wanted to say that he'd be wherever she was, but he didn't know if that was something she was ready to hear. Now. Or Ever. Maybe this thing between them was temporary, a magic spell cast by Reno and this production. She still hadn't told him she loved him.

She came to stand next to him and placed her hand on his back, stroking it up and down in a lazy, calming pattern. "But would that make you happy?"

On his worst days, he'd thought it would. But the reality was that would be a half-life, an existence that would always feel a little bit dimmer, emptier, without the rush of performing, the promise of being a storyteller. He shook his head.

If he was being honest, the fear of losing that was why he was so afraid of this scene. Joan had tried something different, and now she was having to claw her way back into the audience's favor. What if they came for him next?

Joan wrapped her arm around his waist, barely reaching the other side of him, and leaned her head against his bicep. "Take a chance, Dash. You said you wanted to change things, to shake off your persona, to be an actor instead of the invention of your fame. Arlene has given it to you in this scene."

"What if they hate it?"

"I was branded box-office poison, and I'm still here fighting." God, this woman could read his mind. It comforted and terrified him at the same time. "You'll bounce back. But for what it's worth, I don't think they'll hate it. I think they'll eat up the idea of strapping Dash Howard brought to his knees by love. And you never know, you could teach somebody a thing or two. That some things in this world are worth crying over." She looked at him pointedly, stood on her tiptoes, and strained to kiss his cheek.

Was that what he thought it was? An admission that love was worth the risk with the right person? Or was it her knowing exactly what he needed to hear? Joan pulling the strings to make sure this picture was what she needed it to be? Did it even matter which? Because she was right. He could do it. Because this was the type of actor, the kind of man he wanted to be. The reason he'd started this whole crazy thing in the first place. If he wasn't willing to go there, to bare his soul, what was he even doing? If he couldn't deliver, then he was the thing he hated most—a hollow man, a piece of cardboard, designed, cut out, and propped up by the studio. Didn't he want to be more than that?

He reached for her and stole a quick kiss, hoping he'd find some proof of the sincerity of her words in her lips. She leaned in to him, making the kiss last longer than intended. But when she broke away, his heart sank as he watched her look at the door to make sure no one had seen.

He could use that disappointment, hold onto it and channel it into the scene. She gave him a questioning look, and he simply nodded at her, a brisk, sharp jut of his head, trying to contain this roiling morass of emotions until the moment it would be helpful to unleash them.

She ran to the door, picking her way between the heavy lights, the camera, and the myriad wires for the sound equipment. She flung it open and called out to the crew, who were smoking and teaching horseshoes to Bob Kucor. "Mr. Howard is ready now."

They filed in, taking their posts behind the equipment and waiting for Kucor to settle back into his chair. The man steepled his hands beneath his chin, waited for the notification that sound was speeding, and calmly told Dash, "Whenever you're ready, Mr. Howard."

Dash gave Joan one last look. She was perched behind the camera, her body bristling with nervous energy, but when their eyes met, she gave him a wink. It invigorated and irritated him. He nailed the scene in one take.

CHAPTER 20

"READY FOR SOME ACTION?" DRAWLED PHIL, WINKING AT Dash.

The cameraman was teasing him. It was time to film the big love scene with Joan, and this was a familiar dance between them. Phil teased him, he joked back about preferring to kiss a fish or some such creature, and they laughed, knowing they'd dissect the scene later that week over beers and a round of poker. Well, the joke was on him now. There wasn't anything—or anyone, for that matter—he'd rather kiss than Joan. He still didn't know if she felt the same way.

Somehow five weeks had passed in a flash, and it was their final week of shooting. The last week before things were officially over between him and Joan. On Monday, they'd go to the courthouse and secure their divorce. He was trying not to think about it, trying to ignore the expiration date this relationship had been stamped with before it had even begun.

He needed to focus. He and Joan were standing on the porch of his character's cabin, and he was meant to grab her by the wrist and draw her to him in a passionate embrace. But every time he looked at her, he thought of their shared nights together, the tantalizing glimpses of Joan standing in the moonlight in her underwear—or better yet, completely naked. He needed to get ahold of himself.

"Mr. Howard, do you have any questions? Are you ready?" Kucor asked him, heading to his position behind the camera.

"No." His voice cracked, caught on the provocative memory in his mind, and he cleared his throat. "No, Mr. Kucor, I'm all set. I grab her wrist and pull her up to me on the porch and kiss her until you yell 'Cut,' right?"

"Right." Kucor gave him a queer look and smiled. "But don't forget, you've been falling for this woman since the moment you met her. You are crazy about her, and now finally you're acting on that pent-up desire. Let's see that in the mere curl of your hand about her wrist, the lust in your gaze."

Joan cracked him a smile and whispered so only he could hear, "So, no acting required, then." He suppressed a nervous laugh and nodded at Kucor, taking his place inside the door.

"Places! And rolling, sound speeds, action!" Kucor bellowed from behind the camera, his more genteel approach evident in the tone of his voice. Dash steeled himself and opened the door, following Joan out.

"Carol, don't go. You can't deny you feel this. There's something between us."

Joan whirled on him, and he was gutted to see tears in her eyes. "No, Joe, there can't be. I'm barely out of a bad marriage, one I was so certain would last forever. I can't fall in love again."

"Frankly, darling, you can." He grabbed her then and pulled her to him. Pushing his body against hers, he could feel Joan's soft curves. She was wearing the same wool suit she'd been sporting the day they'd filmed the scene in the river where she'd tried to play a trick on him. That had only been five weeks ago. Everything had changed. Or nothing. He wished he knew which.

He brought his lips to hers and reminded himself to stick to the chaste kisses increasingly demanded by the censors. But as he pressed into her, inhaling her scent and tangling his fingers in her artfully mussed curls, he couldn't help letting his other hand wander from the small of her back to her ass. He palmed it, and Joan moaned under his mouth.

"Cut!" yelled Kucor.

He came over from behind the camera to speak to Dash and Joan so only they could hear. "That was lovely, wonderful, but Mr. Howard, could you keep your hands a little, er, higher on Miss Davis's body?"

Joan blushed deeply and Dash fought the desire to preen. He coughed, choking down a laugh, and nodded at Kucor. "Yes, of course."

Joan bit her lip and bowed her head, giving him a look that was half chastisement, half encouragement. "Be careful," she hissed. It was infuriating that he found her so sexy when she looked chagrined.

She turned and found her mark, ready to start again. Well, if she could be purely professional about it, he could too. At least this was an improvement on the way filming love scenes with her used to be—awkward and mechanical.

He steeled himself, forcing himself to remember that right now he was Joe and not Dash. He got it on the second take, exhibiting more self-restraint than he'd ever believed himself capable of.

"Wonderful, wonderful," chimed Kucor. "We need to reset for a close-up now, so feel free to take a break but don't go far."

"Shall we go for a walk?" Joan asked. He gestured for her to lead the way, as she headed into a crop of trees that took them back to the river. As soon as they were safely in the shadows, he reached for her hand and tugged her to him, delivering the deep kiss he'd been longing to give her in the scene. He half expected her to push him off or swat him away.

But instead, she wrapped her arms around him, holding him to her as he lapped at her mouth, nipping at her bottom lip. Their tongues tangled together and Dash stiffened at the sound of Joan's breathy pants. This time it was him who needed to remind her where they were. If he didn't, he feared she'd regret it.

"Joan, I can't, we shouldn't." He broke apart from her, breathless with desire.

She closed her eyes. "You're right, of course, you're right." She sighed. "What is it about you that makes me throw common sense and professionalism out the window?"

From anyone else, Dash would've known that was a compliment. With Joan, he wasn't so sure. She valued common sense and professionalism above all else. Maybe she thought he was a bad influence. Hell, maybe he was.

He'd awakened last night to find her tangled in his arms, and his heart had nearly burst. He'd brushed a kiss to the top of her head and snuggled against her, looking forward to waking up with her. In the bungalow, it was just the two of them. Uncomplicated. Out here, he didn't know what they were to each other, besides the best acting partner either of them would ever have. And what if that's all they were? What if this was temporary, a stolen season for her before returning to her Hollywood life? He wanted to believe that they meant more to each other than that, that the way she kissed him and touched him held words she hadn't been able to say.

She tangled her hand with his and raised it to her mouth, pressing a quick kiss to the top of it, before setting off deeper into the undergrowth. Eventually, they came to the river, and she invited him to take a seat next to her on a rock. He did and wrapped his arm around her shoulders, scooting her to him. She sighed in contentment and rested her head to his. He tried to quiet the voices in his head Josephine had put there, the ones saying that he wasn't enough and never would be. He brushed a kiss to Joan's temple and held her close as they listened to the burbles of the river licking over the rocks.

He wished he could freeze this moment in time and live in it forever. Holding her on the banks of the river, having filmed the best love scene of their career. For all intents and purposes, she was still engaged to Monty. And he didn't understand why, if this thing between them was more than an on-set affair, she didn't call it off once and for all.

Suddenly, he couldn't take it anymore. He had to know. "What is this, Joan? What do you want?"

What did she want? To be wrong about love. Its costs. To be brave enough to try. Her heart caught in her throat. "I don't… know." She knew what Monty would want her to do. End it. Grab happiness, the version of it that was sitting on this riverbank, with both hands and never look back. But she couldn't do that, could she? Because love meant nothing but heartache. Sooner or later.

Dash sprang from the rock and started pacing along the river, running his fingers through his hair in a gesture she'd come to know meant he was stressed. "How? How can you not know? How can you lie there in my arms night after night, share what we've shared, and still be uncertain?"

"I told you about my mother, but I didn't explain about my sister." Joan took a deep breath. She hated thinking about Betty and Hal. But Dash needed to know all of it if he was going to understand her uncertainty. "She was felled by the same affliction. Love. When we were kids, she was incredible. The mother neither of us had. But it was hard. There was so much to do. Always another thing in the barn to repair, a bill to pay. She had to keep track of it and keep us fed. I did my chores the best I could, so she'd have one less thing to worry about. But then she met Hal."

Dash stopped and stared at her. "I take it I'm not gonna like Hal by the end of this story."

God, this was what made him magic. Here she was telling him one of the worst bits of her life, and he could still make her laugh. She nodded. "I didn't like him from the moment he answered Betty's ad looking for a boarder. He was smug and slick and a little too friendly, with a wandering eye. But Betty was nuts for him the second she saw him standing under the creaky eaves on our porch, promising to fix the leak in the roof. She wouldn't hear a word against him. Not even when the rumors started. And when Hal left—he ran off with some town floozy—so did the Betty I'd known and loved. All that remained was a bitter woman and a bucket in the living room in place of the leak he'd never fixed. I took one look at that bucket and vowed never to fall in love."

Dash bit his lip and looked away from her, out across the water.

"That's why I chose Monty. A loveless marriage would mean no disappointments. But you've made me question that vow I made. You've made me wonder if maybe I was wrong."

He turned back to face her and she could see the hope in his eyes. "Does Betty know about Monty? What does she think about her kid sister shacking up with a guy she doesn't love?"

"She doesn't know. Or if she does, it's only because she read it in the paper." Joan shrugged, trying not to let Dash see how much this was still an open wound. How much Betty was yet another reason she had hardened herself. Because wanting someone's attention, someone's affection, hurt too much. Whether it was a man. Or your sister. "After Hal, she turned to the church for comfort and became someone I didn't recognize. She's never approved of Joan Davis. I've invited her to premieres, to come stay with me. But she says we're little better than prostitutes. I haven't seen her since I left when I was eighteen."

Dash scoffed. "She should have more respect for all you've accomplished. What you've done, the woman you've become. It's nothing short of incredible."

Joan eyed him warily. "I don't want your pity, Dash. That is one thing I could never abide."

"I don't pity you, Joan. I'm in awe of you." A puff of air escaped her mouth. Whatever she'd been expecting him to say, it wasn't that. "But I'm not Hal. And I'm not your father."

"I know that." She did. But old habits died hard.

"Do you? Because you accused me of using you for publicity. Not once. Repeatedly."

Joan's heart sank. She scrambled to stand up in her costume pumps.

"But that's different," she sputtered. She had no leg to stand on and she knew it. She was grasping at straws, fighting for something she hadn't even realized she was afraid to lose until this very moment.

"How?" He looked at her stonily. There wasn't judgment in his eyes, just a genuine question.

"Because everything is different now." She gestured weakly at the idyllic setting surrounding them. As if that could explain things.

"No, it's not. You're still engaged to Monty."

She swallowed. "I'm still engaged to Monty." She nodded.

"Why?" He gripped at her shoulders and searched her eyes for an answer she was afraid she couldn't give him, no matter how much she might want to. "He let you go. He told you to choose me."

"And I want to, Dash, I want to choose you so badly. But next week, we'll be divorced. A clean slate. As if none of this ever happened." It all rushed out of her mouth, and she regretted it before she'd barely put voice to air.

He couldn't have looked more wounded if she'd slugged him. But to his credit, he didn't yell. He didn't do anything except square his shoulders, stick his hands in his pockets, and look across the water. "Then nothing's changed. So be it, if that's what you want." He knelt and searched around the ground before choosing a smooth-looking rock, picking it up, and turning it over in his palm. "You shouldn't have toyed with me, Joan. You of all people should know better." He coughed, and she recognized the sound of him clearing emotion from his voice. "Or maybe I'm not enough for you. Maybe I never was and never could be."

Oh God, this wasn't what she wanted at all. She didn't want to lose him and she didn't want to hurt him, and she didn't know how to keep either from happening. Because she was terrified. More afraid than she'd ever been. More than when that horse had kicked her. More than when her sister had stopped being someone she recognized. More than when Leda learned her greatest secret. More than when she'd been branded box-office poison. More even than when she'd learned her carefully constructed plans had been dismantled by the man standing in front of her.

"You are enough, Dash, you *are*. Just because Josephine left, just because the public fell for one version of you, that doesn't mean you're not worthy of love. You deserve to be cherished for who you really are."

"Just not by you." There was no bitterness in his voice. Only sad resignation.

She had to do something. She couldn't let him think this meant nothing. A wild idea seized her. But what if it wasn't that wild? What if it was crazy enough to work? What if all she had to do was be brave? Dash had been brave, hadn't he? He'd filmed that magnificent scene Arlene had written for him and delivered a performance she'd known he was reluctant to unleash. Joan Davis was not a coward. So she'd better damn well stop acting like one.

She swallowed. "I've been thinking about our divorce."

He turned away from her and threw the rock, skipping it out across the water. The plonking sound it made as it skimmed over the river matched the pounding of her heart in her chest. "So you've mentioned." His voice was peculiarly devoid of emotion and that chilled her. "Look, Joan, I made you a promise and I'm a man of my word."

She let out a breath she didn't realize she was holding. "What if I didn't want you to be?" God, in the movies, no one ever mentioned the abject fear that was involved in loving someone.

He stared at her as if she were a difficult math problem he had to work out. "Six weeks ago, being married to me was a fate worse than death."

The memory of that day in Harry's office, his embarrassment and her fury, still burned. She grimaced.

"You let me have your body, Joan, but not your heart. And a body can't live without a heart, not for long. You said it yourself. You're still engaged to Monty. Regardless of his thoughts on the matter."

She fought back tears and turned away from him, staring out at the water, her eyes locking on the spot where his rock had sunk. She nervously smoothed her skirts. "Hell, I'm making a hash of this."

She precariously fell to one knee, wincing as she felt the sticks and pebbles under her knee pull at her stockings. "Dash…"

Dash turned around. She suppressed a laugh as his eyes practically bulged out of his head.

"I don't want you to be a man of your word. I don't want anything but to try to make this work. Dash Howard, what I'm trying to say is, will you stay married to me?"

He blinked at her, the portrait of a peevish owl. For a moment, the only thing she could hear was the ebb and flow of the river and the beating of her own heart.

"Say something," she breathed, her voice quavering, on the verge of breaking. This was unbearable.

"You're going to ruin your costume," he mumbled.

She huffed and stood, her heel catching on a rock, sending her careening toward the water. He reached for her and caught her, her hands meeting his chest as she steadied herself. There was plenty of fresh air out here, but as their eyes locked, she couldn't seem to swallow any of it. She pressed her hands into his chest more firmly, as if drawing strength from him and then moved them to grip his arms.

He was quiet still, and their eyes met, his gaze oddly far more stabilizing than his embrace. The warmth of his brown eyes had deepened into a dark mahogany, swimming with something that looked suspiciously like hope. He didn't say anything, but instead he brought his mouth to hers, fitting the hard line of his lips perfectly to the lush curves of hers. He kissed her with as much passion as he could muster, as if he were willing to give her the words she could not find. He slid both his hands up the sides of her cheeks and into her hair, tugging her more tightly to him so he could get purchase on the corner of her mouth.

He broke apart from her and cradled her face in his palms, and for the first time, she felt her own fragility. She'd done everything in her power to project an image as a pillar of strength, a woman who'd clawed her way to the top of Hollywood and was willing to do anything to stay there. But with Dash, maybe she could be vulnerable and shed some of that armor. It was a freeing thought. She nestled her face into the side of his palm, as finally he spoke.

"I told you the first night we made love that I love you," he murmured, crushing her to his chest and pressing his chin to the top of her head. "I think some part of me has always loved you. If I'm being really honest with myself, it's why I addressed the certificate in the first place—not because I was drunk or playing a stupid joke on you, but because I wanted it to be true so badly."

She threw her arms around his waist and hugged him fiercely, squeezing him as though her life depended on it. Maybe it did. "You saw something I didn't, something I was too blind and stubborn to admit. That I don't have to do this alone. That it's better with you. That I feel safer with you than I ever have looking at all the zeros in my bank account or seeing the stacks of my fan mail. You make me want to risk it all, Dash."

She still couldn't say the words. Couldn't tell him she loved him. But she hoped he knew, that he understood. That this was enough. For now. Her hands wandered to the front of his chest once more, stopping briefly over his heart before continuing upward to cup his face between them as she struggled to tell him how she felt. "I have told myself for years that I couldn't fall in love, that love was for fools. But with you, Dash, I feel anything but foolish."

"That's lucky then, because I'm a fool for you." She pressed her lips to his in answer, and he moaned.

She broke it off and rested her head against his chest. "You still didn't answer my question."

He cupped her chin, bidding her to meet his gaze. "Yes, Joan Davis, I will *stay* married to you."

She couldn't suppress a wide smile, toothy and radiant, one

she would've considered undignified in front of a camera, and giggled. "It's mad, isn't it?"

He grinned like a kid on Christmas morning, giddy and half-drunk on excitement. "No, it's everything I've ever wanted but never thought I'd have. Hell, ten minutes ago, I was convinced you would never truly be mine."

"I didn't believe it myself until this moment."

He leaned down and kissed her, long and sweet, a languid kiss that promised years more like it. When he came up for air, she whimpered, mourning the loss of him.

"We have to go back to the set. They'll be wondering where we are," he murmured, clutching her to him and grazing her jaw with his own, making her shiver when his stubble made contact with her face.

"You're right, of course," she groaned. "Somehow it seems you've always known what's good for us."

He laughed, so loud and genuine it sent a flock of birds twittering out of the nearest tree. "Or at least drunk me did."

She giggled and wrapped an arm around his waist, nestling under his shoulder and turning to head back into the trees. "I'll have to remember to thank him sometime, next time you're soused."

There was still one thing though. She bit her lip, thinking.

"I know that look. What is it?"

"Please don't be angry, but can we keep this to ourselves for a little while longer?" She waited for his response. He had every right to be hurt. Dash deserved to be loved by someone who would loudly and proudly claim him as her own, but she wasn't quite ready to be that woman. The second they went public with their relationship, they'd be Dash and Davis, not this quieter, truer version of themselves. She wanted to be certain that this new fragile thing they had could withstand that scrutiny. To get the words *I love you* to finally unstick from the roof of her mouth. "I want it to be us and only us. Until it has to be otherwise."

He looked like he wanted to refuse, to question her. But instead, he smiled and asked, "What about Monty?"

She laughed, relieved that this was his biggest concern. Dash was so damnably decent. Of course his first worry was for the other man in this bizarre Hollywood love triangle. "Hell, Monty knew before I did." Dash chuckled.

"I have an idea," she added, stopping herself before gnawing on her carefully manicured fingernails. She hadn't done that since she was a child.

"I don't know whether that should excite or scare me," Dash retorted, pressing a kiss to the top of her head.

"Both."

He laughed and she felt impossibly young in that moment. As if his laughter was the stream over the rocks, eroding her fears and her doubts. "Let's go to the courthouse like we planned next week. Only when we get there, we'll tear up the divorce papers and surprise everyone. What better way to rub their noses in how wrong they are about us than to ruin their juicy divorce photo opp."

She was getting excited thinking about it. This was what she did best. Spun things to her advantage, pulled out all the movie-star stops. What better way to make a mockery of this entire accidental marriage and divorce vacation than to upend it in a way no one expected. "They're expecting me to drop my ring in the river, an old Reno tradition. Arlene sent me a whole schedule for the day from the Evets publicity department, timed to the minute. Let's pull the rug out from under them."

"By making a publicity stunt out of their publicity stunt, you mean?"

She winced. He still didn't fully trust her. Why should he? "You're right. I'm sorry, I didn't mean… I know you wouldn't want that. I don't want to use you like that, Dash. And I'm sorry I ever accused you of the same. I just… I don't want to share you. Let's keep this sacred. Between us. Until the moment we can't anymore."

He was quiet as they wandered nearer their filming area, and she wondered if maybe she was wrong about all of it. They were on the edge of the other side of the trees now, close enough they couldn't guarantee there wouldn't be a crew member on a smoke break wandering around. But that didn't stop him from taking her hand.

"This would help you, wouldn't it?"

"Yes, but that's not why I—"

He took her chin between his thumb and his forefinger, holding her face still. "Hush, no explanations, no excuses. It would help you, yes? It would accomplish the same thing you wanted with your marriage to Monty. Put you back atop the Hollywood ladder. Make you the talk of the town. Remind everyone why they fell in love with Dash and Davis to begin with. And all that goodwill, combined with the performance you're giving, will get you that Oscar."

Everything Dash was saying was true. And she'd be lying if she said the thought hadn't crossed her mind. She just didn't want him to think this was all it was about. She wanted both. Him and the love of her audience. Was that really so terrible? But instead of all that, she nodded.

He gritted his teeth and huffed out a breath. "Then, we should do it."

She forgot how close they were to the rest of the crew and threw her arms about him, showering him with kisses. "It'll be worth it to see the look on Leda's face. Her and all those other vultures who hang around us like we're carrion. Imagine how betrayed, how irritated they'll be that we've turned the tables on them."

At first, he was stiff in her arms, and she worried that she'd made a mistake bringing Leda into it. But then he crushed his mouth to hers in a punishing kiss, and her knees buckled at the force of it, falling into him. He broke the kiss at last, and she gasped for air. "Don't forget one thing," he growled. "Joan Davis, the real Joan Davis, is mine."

If her knees hadn't already gone weak from his kiss, that would've turned them to jelly. She nodded, a bit stunned by the force of his kiss and his declaration. "I'm Mrs. Dash Howard," she said, a bit dazed, tangling her hands in his hair and dotting a line of kisses along his jaw. "And that's how it's going to stay."

A growl of assent rumbled in his throat as he leaned in to kiss her again, but a production assistant burst through the trees, and she quickly sprang apart from him. Dash looked a little bit sad as she rushed to put distance between them, but the look was gone as quickly as it had appeared.

The production assistant seemed oblivious to the love scene that had been occurring, instead appearing extremely relieved to have found his quarry at last. "There you two are. Mr. Kucor is ready for you now."

Dash looked at Joan and tilted his head, as if he was asking her *What now?* Her heart was beating out of her chest, but on the outside, she managed to look cool as a cucumber. "Lead the way, Davey." The production assistant nodded and turned to take them back to the set.

Dash moved to follow and caught Joan's eye. She winked and moved her hand across her lips in a sealing motion. Then she twisted her wrist as if she was turning a key and pantomimed throwing it over her shoulder. It was meant to be a cute nod to their temporary secret, but a pocket of dread burrowed into her chest at the stray notion that she'd just thrown away the key to her heart.

CHAPTER 21

JOAN PUT HER HEEL ON THE STEP OF HER TRAILER AND made sure they were alone before blowing Dash a kiss. "I'm going to change and then I'll meet you for lunch," she promised.

She strode into the trailer and, after closing the door behind her, spun around in a circle like a schoolgirl. "Wheeeeeee," she trilled, unable to suppress her glee, her fear temporarily forgotten in the face of her happiness.

"I wouldn't get too excited," drawled a voice that had the cold precision of an ice pick. Joan snapped her head to the armchair at the front of her trailer, and a wave of dread trickled down her spine as she spotted the sickening silhouette of the curve of a rooster feather. Only Leda Price would wear a hat like that.

Joan whirled on her. "Who let you in here? You have no right to be here. This is my private space. I'll call for Mr. Kucor, and he'll have you thrown out quicker than you can say 'Jack Robinson.'"

Leda simpered at her. "I don't think you will. Because I think you'll want to hear what I have to say."

Joan was already headed for the door, ready to holler for whoever was near, but something in the tone of Leda's voice stopped her. It was cold and cruel and sadistically self-satisfied. Even when Leda had called Joan with the news of her marriage to Dash, she hadn't sounded this pleased with herself. Joan squared her shoulders and turned to face her.

"All right then, spit it out."

"I'm astonished at you, Miss Davis. You cling so fiercely to your reputation as a star and consummate hostess, but you haven't even offered me a glass of water."

"Seeing as you're in my trailer uninvited, the only glass of water I'm offering you would be one thrown in your face, so why don't you cut the bullshit, Leda."

She simply smiled and hugged her handbag with its mother-of-pearl clasp more tightly to her. "*Tsk, tsk,* such language. I'm sure my readers would love to know Joan Davis has a foul mouth."

Joan ran her hand down her face and tried to get control of herself. She was playing right into Leda's hands. She took a breath and counted to ten before sitting on the sofa across from her. "Very well, Miss Price, what can I do you for?"

"You've been keeping secrets from me, Miss Davis. And I would have thought by now you'd know that I cannot abide being the last to know something."

Joan shrugged, trying to play it off. There was no way Leda could know about her and Dash.

"I understand Mr. Smyth checked out of his room at the Hotel Riverside two weeks ago."

Joan bit back a reply. Give Leda a hint of the truth and nothing more. That was the only way to deal with her. "Yes, he had to get back to work at the studio."

"No, I don't think he did. I think he took the first train back to Los Angeles because you ended your engagement."

Joan laughed haughtily, making an effort to dish out as good as Leda was giving. Technically speaking, they hadn't ended their engagement. Not yet anyway. "What a ridiculous supposition."

Leda smirked. "It's not, at all. What's ridiculous is that after coming to Reno to seek a divorce from Dash Howard, you've fallen in love with him and are planning to stay married to him."

Joan gasped. How could she know? They'd only decided on it. And they'd been completely alone.

"You're wondering how I know this, but surely you must realize that I have eyes and ears on every set, Miss Davis. Particularly when the stars of a picture are as interesting to my readers as you and Mr. Howard. Based on what I hear from one Dolores Reacher, you've been making fools of yourselves for weeks now. I'm surprised Mr. Smyth didn't jilt you more publicly. It's enough to make my hair curl."

She smirked again, and fluffed her already heavily coiffed and curled titian-red hair. "Not that it needs it," she added.

"If you're fishing for compliments, you won't catch any here," Joan replied. "You have nothing. You can't prove it."

"On the contrary, I have quite a large something. Something that shows a rather lot of you. I think my readers would be very interested to learn the naked truth of how Joan Davis broke into Hollywood."

Joan rolled her eyes. "This again? Harry already paid you a handsome sum to keep that quiet. What'd you do, spend it all on hats already?" Joan eyed the monstrosity perched on Leda's head and pursed her lips in disgust. "Besides, Harry destroyed every copy."

"I find that I require a different kind of payment than a financial one. And I'm certain for the right price there must be someone out there who still has the footage."

"If you expect me to turn into a blushing schoolgirl, I won't. I did what I had to do to secure the life I wanted. I would do it again."

"Can I quote you on the record?"

Joan growled, "You must be off your nut." She got up and started pacing the tiny length of the trailer from the bedroom in the back to the armchair Leda sat poised upon like a feline overseeing her domain.

She wasn't ashamed of what she'd done. She'd needed the money and the work, and it'd got her noticed by Harry Evets. She had the career she'd dreamed of because of it. What's more, she'd enjoyed it. She was proud of her body, and she enjoyed sex, and it was high time the rest of society stopped acting like they were in a Nathaniel Hawthorne book in public and a torrid pulp novel in private. It was the height of hypocrisy.

But Joan and Harry knew that didn't matter. It's why they'd paid Leda off once already. The thought of everything it could cost her if it came out now made her nauseated—the Oscar nomination she knew she was on the verge of securing, the fight to shed that dreadful label of box-office poison that Leda had bestowed on her, and most of all, Dash.

If they stayed together, the secret would taint him too. With all he'd given up for his career, how could she ask that of him? He was already taking a gamble with the scenes in this film. For her. For both of them. A risk she had pressured him into.

The prickling sensation of déjà vu crept up the back of Joan's neck. Here it was—the bill for love coming due. She'd avoided it for so long, thought maybe she'd get lucky and never have to pay if she kept her head on straight. And then Dash, just now, had made her believe that maybe she'd been wrong. Maybe she could love someone and it wouldn't end up costing her everything. But she'd scarcely had an hour or two to relish it before Leda showed up with Cupid's IOU.

Leda had said nothing while she paced, watching Joan like

a predator sizing up its prey. Joan was too nervous to sit down again, but she finally came to a stop in front of her. "So if you don't want money, what do you want? You wouldn't bring this up if you weren't trying to blackmail me."

"You've finally caught on, then. Perhaps you're smarter than I thought, Joanie." She sneered Joan's name, as if the very word disgusted her. "What I want is for you to throw Dash over. Go through with the divorce."

Joan reeled as if Leda had socked her on the jaw. "What? Why? Surely our romance is good business for you. It made your career, after all. You cut your teeth humiliating me and Dash, made us hate each other because I was too blind to see that you'd set us both up. If I didn't already hate you, Leda, I would now—for all the time you've cost us." Joan didn't mention that her own stubbornness and scorn for love had played its part too. Leda didn't need to know that. And knowing her, she probably had gotten a tip and already did.

A flicker of something that looked an awful lot like regret passed through Leda's eyes, but it was gone in an instant, replaced by a malicious gleam. "You and Dash might have made my career, but that's only because I made you too. We're nothing without each other. Without all the ink I've spilled over you, you wouldn't be half the stars you are today. But somehow that's never registered with you. I made you and I can break you."

"So this is, what? A power grab? Revenge? Labeling me box-office poison wasn't enough for you?"

Leda's mouth twisted into a moue of disapproval. "It didn't stick. The public still loves you. Still eats up every inch of newsprint you occupy. So, fine, I'll use that adoration and attention for my own purposes, then."

"What will my throwing Dash over accomplish for you?"

Leda looked like the cat that caught the canary. "I'd call it a life lesson. I'm tired of teaching you, teaching anyone who underestimates me, the same thing. That nobody does anything in this town without my hearing about it. And if they do, they'll regret it. How does it feel to have regrets, Joan?"

Joan swallowed down her fury. "I've made a career of trying to avoid regrets, to banish them to the past. I won't give you the satisfaction. Fine, publish the pictures. Harry will sue you for violating the terms of your agreement."

"And Mr. Howard, what will he think?" Leda smirked.

"Go to hell, Leda. Dash is a big boy. He can decide if he wants to stick by me or not. Odds are, he'll recover from it. I probably will too after a year or so. The audience has a short memory." Joan wished she could be as confident as she was trying to sound. The truth was she knew Dash already had his doubts. What would this do to them? To him?

Leda preened and dug into her handbag, fishing out an envelope. "I thought you might say that, so I brought some insurance."

Leda handed it to her, and the bottom fell out of Joan's stomach when she saw the name scrawled across the return address: Josephine Howard. Dash's ex-wife. It had to be. And the woman was still using his name. "What is this?"

"The look on your face suggests you know who Josephine is." Leda smiled. "It's a letter laying out all the ways Dash Howard has failed to meet his responsibilities to his first wife. How he used her to become a star, then deserted her and left her in desperate straits. How everything about him, from his smile to his style to his reputation as a lifelong bachelor, is phony. How Dash would be nothing without his first wife. And the ingratitude he showed her for his success."

"But that's not true," Joan gasped. "It's the opposite. She

deserted him. Before Harry even discovered him. Broke his heart. Made him think he's unlovable."

Leda laughed, a short, halting, cruel sound. "Does it matter? Who will my readers believe? Hollywood's most notorious womanizer, regularly photographed with a different girl on his arm, or a jilted wife with a sob story?"

Joan moved to tear the letter to shreds. And Leda smirked. "Don't bother. As if I wouldn't make copies."

"What are you going to do with it?"

"Josephine has offered to share everything with me and the *Examiner*. A true exclusive. For a pretty sum, of course."

"You wouldn't," Joan hissed. "This would…this would break him. And you know what it will look like to his fans."

Leda blinked, making a mockery of the moment, as if Joan had told her something she didn't know. "Hmmm, you're right, I think. The public may love a bachelor unwilling to settle down, but a man who deserted his wife for fame… Well, I don't think they'll take so kindly to him, do you?"

Joan pressed her fists to her eyes, bidding herself to stop tears from spilling over. The things Josephine was accusing Dash of… It would destroy him to have the worst moments of his life thrown back in his face and twisted around to make him the bad guy. Joan felt as if all the blood were draining from her body, the color leaching from her face, turning her into an image more devoid of color than the silver screen. She knew Dash had been so careful with her, with his heart, because he thought she would pull the rug out from under him. But Josephine would do it for her.

And the worst of it was that if Joan's secret got out too, he might not even have acting to fall back on. He'd be tainted by association. If it was her secret alone, they could weather the storm and figure it out together. But Josephine could break him, make him believe the worst of himself all over again, and Joan couldn't allow that. Not when he was finally starting to see what a good, kind, wonderful man he was.

How could she have let this happen? Made them both so vulnerable. What a fool she was! She'd broken her only rule, and now look what it would cost them. If she did what Leda asked, she'd break Dash's heart. Either way, she'd hurt him. But at least if she played Leda's game, he'd never know about Josephine's scheming and he'd still have his career. He wouldn't have sacrificed for nothing. He'd get over her because he'd still have the one thing that brought him joy—his work. He'd said it himself. Before Joan, acting was the only thing that made him happy.

It was better this way, wasn't it? End it now before either of them got hurt more than was already inevitable. She'd given love a try and discovered she'd been right all along. That it only ended in heartbreak. Better to just accept it now. She could fall on her sword to keep him safe from Josephine. And from herself, if she was being honest. Joan Davis wasn't a girl meant for romance and stars in her eyes. She knew that now. Better not to drag him into it more than she already had.

He'd be hurt; she knew he would. But this way he wouldn't know the depths of Josephine's treachery and he could keep the job he loved. She knew in her bones that his work in this film would catapult him to new heights, proving to the world he was a truly gifted actor. And she'd be damned if she'd let Josephine Howard take another thing from him.

"So I tell him we'll go through with the divorce. Tell him he was right about me all along. It was all just a game to make the picture better. What then?"

Leda licked her lips and peered at her, pursing her lips as if what she was about to say next left a bad taste in her mouth. "No."

"No, what?" Joan huffed, fisting her hands in her skirt so as to resist the urge to shake Leda silly.

"No, you're not going to tell him. You're going to let him walk in there thinking your plan to stay married is still in place and blindside him. Every picture of him walking out of that courtroom should be of a guy who just had his heart broken."

Joan gasped. "But that's so cruel."

Leda put her fingers to her chin mockingly. "Hmm, what was that headline I'd devised—'The true story of Dash Howard, wife-deserting louse'? Maybe below the centerfold, another headline: 'Joan Davis, the naked truth: sex fiend and stag-film star.'"

Joan's stomach seemed to plunge from her body. Leda had her. And she knew it. "Why? Why are you doing this?" But Joan knew why. Because she'd been like Icarus and flown too close to the sun. She'd become no better than all the women she'd always disdained, blinded by love. And now, the worst of it was she wouldn't be the only one suffering the damage.

"Do you remember when we were making *Dancing Dames* and Adela Luce came to the set?" Leda interrupted her spiraling thoughts.

"What has that got to do with anything?" Joan could feel her nerves fraying the longer this went on.

"You all were tripping over yourselves to impress her. I'd spent days on that set as a day player hoping someone would notice me. You, Dash, the director, anybody. And here you were kowtowing to a gossip hound. It made me realize something. That being an actress would only make me miserable. I used to want to be like you so badly, beloved by everyone. But it costs a lot to be loved."

Leda couldn't have hurt Joan worse if she'd stabbed her in the chest and twisted the knife. Yes, it cost a lot. Too damn much, apparently. Leda plowed on. "Adela made me realize there was something more powerful than love—fear. I needed to become the only woman in town who knows everyone's secrets. Secrets are worth a whole lot more than fame. I figured that out early. You should've too."

"Adela is twice the woman you'll ever be," Joan spat out. "People respect her because she respects us."

"And I suppose her husband owning half of publishing has nothing to do with it." Leda snapped. Joan wanted to protest that Adela was funny and warm, nothing like Leda's conniving ways. But would that have mattered half as much if her husband didn't own some of the biggest papers in the country and have a seat on the studio board? Joan hated to admit the answer was probably not.

Leda looked at her fingernails, painted a color Joan once had heard dubbed "Jungle Red." Looking rather like a bird of prey with painted talons, Leda carefully examined her perfect manicure, picking a speck of dust out from under one nail.

"You think you're smarter than me and better than me. You always have," she drawled, something wild coming into her eyes. "I saw the way you looked at me that night in the bathroom at the Cocoanut Grove. You thought I was someone who could be shrugged off with platitudes of advice. I'd been trying to get a meeting with you for weeks. I thought we could be a team. I wanted to get you to agree to an exclusive interview. Thought maybe we could help each other. Outsmart the men. But you ignored me, brushed me off. I sent you a letter even, gave it to a script boy to pass along to you."

"I never got any letter," Joan protested. She suspected the script boy had given it to Harry for disposal, if he hadn't chucked it himself.

Leda waved her hand, dismissing the excuse. "It hardly matters now. Can you honestly say you would've listened to me?

Made time for a nobody who wanted access instead of an acting career, but who didn't have anything to offer but her chutzpah and her grit?"

Joan had nothing to say to that. Leda was right. She wasn't rude. She didn't step on people. And she always had time for her fans. But in the early days, she had ignored people she didn't think were useful. It was part and parcel of her plan to never let herself become vulnerable. If someone couldn't help her career, why risk letting them in?

Until she'd found Arlene, she'd never even had a confidante or a friend. She'd built her walls as high as she possibly could. She'd always believed it was better that way. That this was a road she had to go alone, for better or worse. Dash was the only one who'd ever made her wish for something different. And Leda was here to destroy that, to prove to Joan that she'd been right all along.

"You could've helped me," Leda continued, a pleading note in her voice Joan had never heard before. "I was naive enough to believe you might want to work together, to help us both. If you'd only once recognized that I was fighting the same battle as you—fighting tooth and nail to earn a modicum of the respect the men in that godforsaken town get with a simple smile. I still am. I'm doing the same as you, Joan. Whatever it takes to stay on top. It's what I've done for the last six years. From the moment you and Dash played right into my hands. Did you know I was only supposed to get pictures of you dancing near the bandstand? It was meant to be pin money, enough to pay my rent. But you and Dash were such easy marks that night. It was like taking candy from a baby. And once I'd had a taste of the power that came with my pen, I was never going to give it up. Would you?"

Joan turned her back on Leda and braced herself against the edge of the small table. She didn't want to hear it. She hated that she empathized with Leda, understood how hard it was to be a woman in Hollywood. But they weren't the same. "You can justify your actions all you want, Leda," Joan gritted out. "But you can't excuse what you've done. What you're still doing. You want power. You want to stay on top. Okay, I understand. But you've ruined people's lives. You still are. I sacrificed a lot to get where I am. You know how much and are willing to sell that secret to the highest bidder. But I've never hurt anyone. At least not knowingly."

"You will now," Leda sneered, her voice as sharp and piercing as needles.

"Why? Why insist on something so cruel?"

"The cruelty is the point," spat out Leda. "Everyone thinks you're so perfect, the consummate movie star. But I've longed to put a chink in that armor for years. To make you feel what you made me feel—the ignominy of being ignored, of being looked down upon by the people who could help you most, and knowing that everyone around you is certain they're better than you. Labeling you box-office poison didn't do the job, but this ought to. Now at least one person will see you the way I do—as a callous huckster who only cares about herself. The only person that seemingly matters to you. And it means I get to make you miserable while still capitalizing on your fame. I get to kill two birds with one stone. Maybe you'll finally understand who really holds the cards here."

Joan whirled and turned to face Leda, drawing herself up to her full height but still falling short of the top of the ludicrous feathers on Leda's hat. "You think I think I'm better than you?" Joan said. "I am. But it's not because I'm rich or famous, it's because I'd never do this. I'd never ruin someone else's life to make a point, to cling to some twisted idea of power. You want to be my sister in Hollywood, want me to empathize with trying to run in the boys' club. Well then, you can't be worse than they are. You have to have some decency, some shred of care for the havoc your words wreak."

Leda flinched, and for a moment Joan thought she might be getting through to her. But then she stepped forward, coming disturbingly close to Joan's face with a maniacal grin. "You've always seen me as your enemy. And maybe I am. What else could I be when you've never given me room to be anything else? It's convenient to sit on your high horse when you've had Harry Evets in your pocket, making sure you don't have to ever sink to my level. Well, I don't have a protector," she scoffed. "So I've done what I had to do to make sure I don't need one. I am my own protector. I pull the strings in Hollywood as much as Harry Evets or Louis B. Mayer. You've always treated me with disdain, like I'm a bug to squash beneath your heel or at best a spider to leave unattended in the eaves. Well, Joan, spiders can bite—and sometimes we're deadly."

Joan swirled about madly, looking for something in the trailer to stab, to hit, anything to take out her frustrations. "Dash will hate me," she pleaded. "He'll hate himself, buy into the lie that he's unlovable. It'll confirm every terrible thing he's ever thought about me."

"That's the general idea."

"Why drag him into this? Doesn't *he* at least deserve better?"

Leda shrugged. "Sometimes collateral damage is necessary. And I want him to know the truth about you. To hate you like I do. So if you breathe even a word of this to him, I'll know. I want him to loathe you with every fiber of his being, to think you've sold him out. Because you are going to. And if you choose him, if you do the slightest thing to even soften the blow, your reunion won't be the next day's headlines, I promise you that. Your choice is simple—the careers of Dash and Davis, or the man you love."

Joan huffed a small mirthless laugh, running her fingers through her hair in absentminded anxiety. "Simple, yes. Everything I ever wanted, or everything I never thought I could have."

Leda straightened, adjusting the fox stole she had wrapped around her neck. "The choice is yours, Joanie, but you have a week to make up your mind—and mark my words, I'll be watching." Leda took mincing steps to the door and turned to deliver her final blow. "And just so we're clear, if you don't choose wisely, I *will* find another way to teach you this lesson. I've waited a long time for this. Oh, and I'm still owed those exclusive wedding pictures of you and Monty."

Joan watched Leda clamber her way down the trailer steps. She wanted to run after her and do something terrible—push her down the stairs, pound her fists into her. But she was frozen. Paralyzed by the choice, which was really no choice at all, Leda had left her with. Because she'd promised herself that she would never fall in love. She'd seen what it had cost the people she cared for most in this world and known it was much, much too expensive to ever give herself over to it. But she had. Against her better judgment and every vow she'd ever sworn. And now, one way or another, she'd pay the price.

CHAPTER 22

DASH STOOD AT THE BOTTOM OF THE WASHOE COUNTY courthouse steps and watched Joan pose with the imposing pillars at its entrance. She smiled wanly, unease written on her brow. But the cameras didn't care. She was dressed smartly in a cream-colored plaid dress with a wide collar that formed a delectable, starched frame for her face. It featured big brass buttons down the front, and as he'd watched her dress that morning, he'd longed to undo them. To muss her perfectly coiffed hair, tucked and pinned to within an inch of its life under a chic matching cap. He had yearned to pull her back into bed and forget this circus awaiting them. But soon it would all be over, and Joan would be his for good.

"Miss Davis, give the courthouse a kiss!" yelled a photographer in the mob. She grimaced and did as she was asked, daintily pressing her lips to the pillar.

"Bet you're glad you're almost a free woman," cried a reporter from the crowd.

"Better luck next time," crowed another.

Dash fingered the small gold wedding band in his pocket and its matching brother. He'd asked Travis at the ranch to pick them up for him, telling him they were needed as a prop for the film. The blissfully accommodating cowboy hadn't questioned the ludicrous excuse, merely delivered the next day. The cries of the press brought him back to the moment at hand. "Pucker up," one called.

It was tradition for divorcées to kiss the courthouse pillars on their way in and out of the Reno institution, a winking nod to their newfound freedom. But watching Joan enact this charade left a sinking feeling in the pit of his stomach. He knew it was part of the act she had planned, that they'd discussed together. It would make the surprise all the sweeter when they walked into that courthouse side by side and asked to have their marriage license certified for real this time, instead of requesting a divorce.

But he'd waited so long for someone to love him as he was. He still wasn't quite convinced it had happened, that this wasn't some elaborate joke. But one couldn't feign the kind of passion they'd shared in their bungalow. These last few days Joan had come undone in his arms every night, allowing a level of abandon he'd never seen in her before. She'd clung to him tightly afterward, as if she was trying to capture their stolen, secret moments and press them on the pages of her memory.

It made him feel like a teenager necking in his father's barn again. But his desire for Joan wasn't the immature fumblings of a teenage boy. No, for the first time in his life, he felt like a man—not Hollywood's version of masculinity, but the one he had kept long hidden for fear someone would extinguish the sensitive soul at his core. Josephine had crushed it once, and he'd never risked exposing that part of himself again. Until Joan. With her, he was both protector and protected. He'd never felt safer than these nights tangled up in her, peering out the window at the blanket of mountain stars as they fell into blissful, dreamless sleep.

They'd wrapped his part on the picture yesterday. His character died in a tragic accident in a storm, and Joan's character returned to Reno to take over his ranch in his memory, triumphing in her grief. She still had a few days of shooting left, and he'd planned to stay on in Reno on his own dime so they could have a proper honeymoon.

He smirked as he watched her strike yet another pose for the battalion of photographers, cheekily holding her cream-colored gloves in her right hand and coyly tucking her hair behind her ear with the other. They thought they knew her, that they had some stake in her, but they'd never have what the two of them shared. The secret intimate moments, the feel of her hot and wet, pulsing with want. He stiffened at the memory of her tightening around him. They'd barely slept last night, as she'd wanted him over and over and he'd been only too eager to appease. They'd pushed each other to the bounds of ecstasy until they were practically limp.

But there had been something desperate in Joan's lovemaking last night. And when finally she was spent and curled into him, letting him wrap his arms around her, the wetness of her tears had pressed against his bare chest. He hadn't asked what was wrong, simply held her until her breathing slowed and she drifted off to sleep.

He'd lain awake, wondering if she was regretting their decision. This morning she'd hardly spoken, apparently overcome with nerves. But Dash hadn't said anything about any of it. He'd put on his best double-breasted suit and shined his shoes, wanting to give her space. After all, they might already be married but she'd had no say in the matter. Today she would be choosing him. Till death do them part. And that was another matter entirely. One that would twist the stomach of the sturdiest constitution in knots. She still looked nervous, grimacing for the cameras. But it would all be over soon.

She eyed him, and he followed her cue, pushing through the

crush of photographers and reporters. "All right, that's enough, let me through, let me through."

He placed a few well-timed elbows as he worked his way to the front of the crowd. "I think it's about time I take my wife inside and give her what you're all clamoring for—her freedom."

The crowd roared with laughter, and the only way he could grin and bear it through the lie was the thought of relishing the looks on their faces when he and Joan came back out of that courthouse with rings on their fingers, legitimizing their marriage for all to see.

He wrapped his hand around Joan's arm and moved to pull her to the courthouse, but he was startled to find her trembling. He leaned down so only she could hear. "What's wrong?"

She looked up at him and he'd never seen her look sadder, as if all the life had gone out of her in that moment. But she shook her head and led him under the shadow of the pillars and the courthouse dome until they reached its heavy double doors. Joan looked up at the Greek keys carved into the stone entryway and squared her shoulders, as if girding her loins for what was to come. He strengthened his grip on her arm, seeking to reassure her. "It's almost over. And then it'll just be us again."

She made a strangled noise and cast a glance back over her shoulder at the crush of reporters following them up the stairs. "It'll never be 'just us' again," she muttered, before reaching for the heavy brass door.

She was right. He knew it. But he hoped that since they'd already been married, the press would lose interest quickly. That they could control it. Together. So he simply tipped the brim of his fedora at her and escorted her inside.

They sat quietly in the back of the courtroom with the lawyer Harry had assigned to them. It seemed an eternity before the judge, a diminutive balding man with a kindly face, called out their names. "Joan Davis v. Dashiell Howard," he called out.

The lawyer motioned for him to follow them to the front of the courtroom so their case could be heard. The judge tsked. "Been reading a lot about this one in the papers." He chuckled. "I suppose you'll be wanting that divorce at last."

This was it. The moment where they changed everything. Where Joan claimed him as hers before all the world. His heart nearly burst at the idea that anyone would be proud to do so. He truly had never believed it possible. He unbuttoned his jacket and reached for the rings inside his interior breast pocket. "Actually, Your Honor..." he began.

But Joan cut him off, looking straight ahead, refusing to meet his gaze. "That's correct, Judge Littlefield."

It would've hurt less if she'd kicked him in the teeth. "No, it's... We're... Joan, look at me." She kept her head firmly turned to the judge. He reached for her arm, and she was like stone.

The lawyer Harry had assigned cleared his throat and plastered his few remaining strands of hair to his pate. "In the case of Joan Davis and Dashiell Howard, we'd like to petition the court for a dissolution of their marriage."

He willed Joan to explain what was happening. They'd agreed to continue the charade. But not like this. Why keep it going now? "Joan, tell him what we agreed." He turned to face the judge, daring to take his eyes off Joan. "Your Honor, I'm sorry, please, there must be some mistake. This isn't... We didn't—"

"There is no mistake," Joan intoned. He reached for her, and she flinched but refused to turn to face him. She was like a sphinx. Cold and unmoving. Had she changed her mind? Surely, she would've told him; they could've talked about it. Why were they here? If she needed more time, she could have it. They didn't have to do this today.

"Joan, please, talk to me. What is this about? Do you need more time?" He was going to be sick. His stomach had plunged to somewhere around his knees. This whole situation was spiraling out of control, and he gripped the table in front of him to steady himself. The ceiling spun above him. The bright lights of a flash blinked in the corner of the room, and he threw a hand across his face to cover his eyes.

"There will never be enough time," she answered. The sound was harsh and cold, so unlike the Joan he'd come to know and love these last six weeks. Oh God, had it all been an act? A plot to cajole a performance out of him for her own ends? Had it all been a lie? A terrifying thought emerged. What if, after years of practical jokes, this was a ruse to humiliate him and have her final revenge? If it was, she'd gone farther to carry it off than he'd ever dreamed possible.

"On what grounds do you request the divorce?" the judge inquired, seemingly ignorant to the fact that Dash's heart was currently shattering into a million pieces and his guts were threatening to spill themselves all over the floor of the courtroom. The question called forth a memory of him and Joan only six weeks ago, circling each other like two predators in Harry Evets's office. He remembered with a pang the grounds on which Harry had said they should file. What a first-class chump he was. They were certainly fitting now.

Joan had seemed not to hear the question. Finally, she was looking at him, and he couldn't read her face. She appeared stricken. But if he'd ever believed her to have a conscience, he doubted it now. No one with a heart could do this, could lead him to believe they were going to stay married and then rip his heart out of his chest and hold it up for the judge to see. Dash looked at her, searching for an answer she seemed incapable of giving, before turning to face the judge. "On the grounds of extreme mental cruelty, Your Honor," he spat out.

The judge continued on. "Whose?" He was so rote, so matter-of-fact about witnessing Dash's life and everything he'd believed fall to pieces in a matter of moments. Perhaps the man saw thousands of men and women getting their guts stomped out on a daily basis. He was, after all, here to give a rubber stamp to the inevitable consequence of heartbreak.

Dash wanted to hiss, "Hers," in answer to the judge's question, wanted to grab Joan by the shoulders and shake her until she told him why she'd done this, how she could be so cruel, if the nights they'd spent together had really meant nothing to her. But before he could do anything, Joan sighed, her breath sounding like it held the weight of the world.

"Mine, your honor." At last, he heard a quaver in her voice. As if the immensity of what she'd done had finally hit her.

The judge looked down at his paperwork, shuffling it through his hands. He might as well have held Dash there in a vise. He looked slightly perplexed, reading the form. "It seems the names were mixed up on your form. Your witness, Mr. Evets, wrote that it was the other way around."

"No, it's..." She paused and took a breath. "It's not a mistake. I'm no good. I'm impossible to live with. And he's better off without me." Joan's voice broke for a moment, but she quickly recovered herself. "I hope that won't delay things."

Dash stared at her open-mouthed. What a fool he'd been. Or perhaps she really was that good an actress. There was a dim roaring in his ears, his confusion and anger overtaking him, muffling the sounds of the judge telling Joan that "No, it's no trouble, I'll simply reverse the names. The lawyer only has to sign off on it."

Dash needed to get to her, to figure out what was going on. The flash went off again as he reached for her, and he stumbled, the edge of his wing tips catching on the leg of the table. He grabbed for the table, stopping himself from hitting the floor. He stayed there bent over, trying to recover himself and swallow down the bile and misery building in his throat. He didn't know how long he'd stood there, but he heard the judge stamp the paperwork and bang his gavel, moving on to the next case.

Just like that, it was done. He and Joan were divorced; the stupid, drunken joke erased as if he'd written it in pencil. Dash and Davis belonged only to the movies once more. And he'd been stupid enough to believe that more was possible. That this time, things were different. That Joan saw him for the man he truly was and she loved him. But it was happening all over again. Because no matter what he did, Dash Howard was not a man anyone could love. He should've known better.

Joan had already seized the paperwork and was turning to scurry out of the courtroom. She didn't even have the courage, to tell him to his face that she'd lied to him and used him. He felt drunk, as if he was stumbling through a fog. He reached into his breast pocket for his cigarette case; a smoke would calm his nerves. His fingers closed around the wedding bands he'd stowed there. It was like a sock in the kisser. What would he do with them now?

Joan was a few steps ahead of him, and she opened the courthouse doors, the blinding flash of cameras and crowing of reporters hitting them in a wall of sound. Joan hesitated for a moment before stepping out into the sun and waving her divorce papers at the crush of the press in a gesture of triumph. Dash squeezed the wedding bands in his palm. Fine, she wanted to turn this into a publicity melee? She could. He'd have no part in it.

He held a hand to his face, trying to obscure it from photographers, while he grabbed her hand and pressed the ring he'd intended to give her into her palm.

"Finish the job then," he hissed, before pushing his way

through the reporters and collapsing into the waiting car the studio had left for them. He didn't care what happened to Joan now. He needed to get back to the Lazy Me, clean his stuff out of that godforsaken bungalow, and get the hell out of Reno.

CHAPTER 23

THE NOISE WAS DEAFENING AND JOAN COULD BARELY SEE a foot in front of her as the frenzy of flashbulbs went off when she stepped back out onto the courthouse steps. She wanted to reach for Dash, to push through the mob together and escape, laughing all the way as they'd planned. But instead, she had to stand there like a prize idiot, preening for them while he walked away with a heart she knew she'd broken. She closed her eyes for a moment and could still see the unrelenting glow of the camera lights popping behind them. She wanted to throw up, to scream, anything but continue putting on this farce. But she knew if she gave Leda the tiniest opening, it would all be over.

So she opened her eyes and pasted on a smile, blinking back tears that she hoped the photographers would assume were her reaction to the cameras. Honestly, she usually relished this. Being the center of attention, soaking in the adulation, knowing that she'd won the love she'd fought so hard for—the only love she'd ever believed mattered. Dash had pressed something small and hard into her hand before escaping down the steps. She'd watched him go, her heart sinking lower with every step he took away from her. He'd locked himself safely in a waiting car and sped away from the mess she'd made.

The catcalls of the press continued all around her as she opened her hand and gasped. It was a small gold wedding band, gleaming and glinting as the flashes of the cameras hit it. He'd whispered something to her as he'd given it to her, but she'd been too crushed by the vitriol in his voice to process what he meant. "Finish the job," he'd said.

She'd been standing there staring at it so long that she'd missed her window to shove it in her pocket. One member of the press pool practically knocked her off her feet as he was jostled toward her. "Is that a ring?" he crowed and the news spread like wildfire down the courthouse steps.

"Ha, can't believe they bothered."

"It must be made of chintz and not gold!"

"Some circle of eternal love that is!"

Every word was a knife in her gut. Dash had bought her a ring. He'd intended to make it official in every way today, and she'd blindsided him. But how could she have done anything else? Leda had left her no options. And some part of her had always known this was how it had to be. She'd just forgotten for a little while. Dash had made her forget. She was better off without him then, wasn't she? He was a distraction, a liability—and now she was free of him. So what if it felt like someone had scraped her insides clean with a rusty spoon; it would pass. It had to.

"Are you headed to the Truckee then, Miss Davis?"

"Gonna throw it in, Joanie?"

That's when it hit her. What Dash had meant. Kissing the courthouse pillars was a Reno tradition, yes, but there was another rite of passage even more ridiculous in nature. Newly divorced women walked a block from the courthouse to the Virginia Street Bridge to throw their wedding rings into the Truckee River, a final shedding of the shackles of their marriage. Joan had heard about it when she arrived in Reno six weeks ago, but she'd laughed it off. She hadn't had a ring from her sham marriage to Dash at the time, and even if she had, it seemed wasteful in the extreme. Now Dash, and all of these vultures hounding her, wanted her to do it.

The idea of it brought a lump to her throat. She wanted to pocket the ring, keep it as a memento of what she'd never had, a reminder of all the reasons she should never fall in love. But if she did, there'd be questions. The second they'd cottoned on to what she was holding, she'd been left with no choice but to go through with the last indignity of this cockamamie tradition. Leda would be thrilled. The sight of Joan throwing her ring into the river would move papers off the stands like hotcakes.

She pasted on her best movie-star smile and cleared her throat. "Ladies and gentlemen," she called out to the crowd on the steps. "If you would let me through, I'd be only too happy to oblige and cast this symbol of my accidental marriage into the Reno tide!" This was it—the way forward. *Remember to be Joan Davis, Movie Star. No one else.*

They cheered and parted down the center, clearing a path for her. Each step was leaden, and she struggled to hold herself upright. When she reached the bottom of the steps, she squared her shoulders and turned to stride the block from the courthouse. It might as well have been a walk to the gallows.

They formed a mob around her, walking alongside her. "Miss Davis, what will you do now? Is your wedding to Monty Smyth still on? Why did he leave Reno?"

Oh God, Monty. He would be so disappointed in her. But he knew as well as she did that in Hollywood this was the way it had to be. Movie stars didn't have the luxury of marrying the people they loved. And why should they? They had wealth, fame, luxury… Wasn't that enough? The universe didn't owe them love too.

She smiled and shook her head. "I think I should close this chapter before I answer any questions, boys."

They laughed and kept pelting her with inquiries, but she kept her head down, focused on putting one foot in front of the other. After what seemed an eternity, she was there. She heaved a heavy sigh and looked out across the water, glinting in the sunlight.

"Living up to the bridge's namesake, are you?" a reporter called out and the crowd laughed. Locals had dubbed this spot the "Bridge of Sighs," an appropriate nickname considering that was the name of a bridge in Renaissance Venice prisoners crossed over before facing their deaths. She felt as grim and hopeless as if she faced an executioner instead of a mob of gleeful photographers, reporters. But she gave another heavy sigh for their benefit. Never mind that the sighs were real, that she could swoon right at that moment from the weight of it all. They didn't know that—and if she did her job right, they never would.

"Throw it in, throw it in," the crowd began to softly chant. She struck a pose for the cameras, her hand outstretched over the edge of the bridge, the ring dangling from her fingers.

"Smile," someone called, and she did, hating herself for it. To them, she was getting her kicks enacting a silly tradition after ending a meaningless marriage, the result of what they'd been told was a clerical error. They didn't know, and likely didn't care, that on the inside her stomach was twisted in knots, her knees were threatening to give out, and her heart had splintered into millions of tiny pieces. She hated herself so thoroughly right now. For what she'd done to Dash. But for doing this to herself, for letting this happen when she'd known better since she was a small child.

She imagined shoving the ring in her handbag and fighting her way through the crowd, ignoring their confusion and their questions as she hailed a cab and chased down Dash. She'd find him packing in the bungalow, she had no doubt. She'd throw herself into his arms and confess the whole thing, and then they'd make love in the small bed that had been the source of her greatest happiness.

"Aw, c'mon, toots, drop it in the river!" cried a man from the middle of the mob, bringing her back to herself. The glare of the sun on the river hurt her eyes. It was harsh and unforgiving. Pinned there on the bridge between the hungry press and the roiling river, she remembered why that dream could never be. Why she'd been a fool to even entertain the notion that she could love someone and it would end well.

She gave the ring one last look. It was lovely. Truly. Dainty and simple. Nothing like the ostentatious jewels the studio borrowed for her to wear to premieres and various events around town. It was so much like Dash, the unvarnished, true version of himself. She wished she could've worn it. Unthinkingly, she lifted it to her lips and kissed it gently, pressing all her yearning for the foolish fantasy of what might have been into the gesture.

"What's she doing?" she heard a woman in a pillbox hat whisper to the man beside her. Swallowing down her wistful dreams, Joan turned on a dime, giving the crowd a wink, transforming her earnest kiss into nothing more than a joke for the cameras. "Now that's what I call a kiss-off," she crowed, struggling to keep her voice from breaking.

Dash would see the photo, read what she said, and it would reaffirm the worst about her. That this was all a gag to her. A publicity stunt. But it was better this way, that he think her so cheap and low. Because if he tried to come after her, if he tried to get the truth from her, she wouldn't be strong enough to resist him. And for the sake of them both, she must.

Relishing the tang of the hard metal against her lips and the whiff of the scent of Dash that still lingered on the ring like a ghost, she balled up the ring in her fist, pulled her arm back, and threw it into the river. It arced, spiraling in the light, as it raced toward its watery destination. The press crowded around her, pushing and shoving, to watch it go. But the sound of them had become a dim roar in her ears. All she heard was the gentle lapping of the river and the nearly inaudible plunk of the ring as it hit the surface. She didn't so much as blink and it had disappeared, sinking into the dark water, no doubt to join a pile of countless other wedding bands beneath the waves.

Because Joan wasn't special. Heartbreak didn't make her unique. It made her one of the million hopeless saps she'd swore she'd never become. Even if she was struggling to remember why she'd ever bothered with such a vow.

She knew what she had to do now. What she'd always done. Work. She'd call Harry and ask him to get her in a new picture as soon as she got back. To hell with the week off written into her contract. She didn't even care if it was a good picture. She needed to be on a set, playing somebody else in order to remind herself who she really was—Joan Davis, the girl who would never fall in love.

CHAPTER 24

SIGH-O-NARA OVER THE TRUCKEE

Joan Davis looked gleeful as she ceremoniously hurled her wedding ring into the Truckee River on Tuesday. She kissed the ring, gave reporters a wink, and quipped, "Now that's what I call a kiss-off." Those hoping for even an ounce of regret from Miss Davis would've been sorely disappointed; if the studio had asked her to act the part of merry divorcée, she couldn't have given a more convincing performance. Miss Davis was game for all the Reno traditions, striking a pose and kissing the pillar at the entrance to the Washoe County Courthouse before finalizing her divorce. After, she led reporters to the so-called Bridge of Sighs to hurl her ring into the river as a symbol of her renewed freedom. But Mr. Howard was nowhere to be seen, leaving the scene before the ink was dry on the divorce papers. Perhaps he was eager to return to a willing starlet now that he is free of the yoke of matrimony?

And what of Miss Davis's erstwhile fiancé, Monty Smyth? Is the wedding still on? Well, we have been promised something picture perfect, and we don't like to renege on our promises. *What Price Hollywood?* will remain your steadfast correspondent when it comes to Davis and Smyth's nuptial bliss.

—XOXO, LEDA

Dash awoke to the sharp slap of cold water hitting his face. "Blarghhhhh," he cried, swiping madly at his eyes and sitting up, heaving as he spluttered out the drops that had landed in his mouth.

He cleared his eyes and looked up to find Flynn Banks standing over him, an infuriating smirk on his face.

"What the hell did you do that for?"

"Do you really need to ask me that question?"

Dash looked around him. His head was throbbing and the sunlight streaming in the window was worse than an interrogation lamp. He slowly made sense of his surroundings. He was at his ranch. He'd never made it to his bedroom, but was curled in a stack of towels and blankets in the corner of his kitchen, still wearing his suit from the courthouse. Snatches of memory returned to him. Joan's betrayal. His mad dash to the bungalow to pack his stuff. His decision to take the Greyhound bus to Santa Barbara and hitch a ride to his ranch. After that it got blurry. He just remembered tequila. A lot of tequila.

"How'd you know I was here?" he grumbled, starting to extricate himself from the morass of towels he'd slept on.

Flynn set down the bucket and extended a hand to help him

up. "You called me. Last night. I could barely understand you. Said something about Joan Davis breaking your heart. That you were moving permanently to your ranch. Which last we discussed was not something you wanted to do. You sounded like you were in trouble so I tore myself away from Eileen—or no, wait, was it Ella? Doesn't matter. At any rate, I hopped in the Jaguar and drove here quick as I could. Found you passed out. That's all I know."

Dash swayed on his feet. He was both hungover and still the teensiest bit drunk. He wasn't even aware that was possible. *Shit.* Flynn hurriedly pulled out the chair by the window and ushered him into it, then moved to the stove to make a pot of coffee.

"Now what's all this about Joan? I thought you hated her."

"I did. I do." Dash groaned and buried his face in his hands. He wanted to throw up. And he didn't think it was only on account of the booze. "I'm an idiot."

"Oh, well, I've always known that, mate, but that's beside the point." Flynn plunked a cup of coffee down in front of Dash and pulled up the chair across from him, looking exactly like a child ready to hear a good bedtime story.

"It's a long story, but suffice it to say, Joan and I fell in love in Reno. Or so I thought. But she was using me. For publicity. Which brings me back to being an idiot for thinking otherwise."

Flynn laughed, and it made the ringing in Dash's ears worse. This was not what he needed. What he needed was to get blitzed again and stay that way for the next year at least.

"I fail to see exactly what is so funny about any of this."

"You. Spending five years pretending to hate Joan Davis when you were in love with her the whole time."

"Was not."

"Fine. Keep lying to yourself." Flynn leaned back, took a sip from his coffee cup, and rubbed his chin while looking thoughtfully out the window. "You know, I've always known Joan Davis to have a stick up her arse, but she never struck me as the type to do someone that dirty."

"Are you supposed to be my friend or hers?" growled Dash.

"Yours. Which is why I'm trying to get you to think critically about this. She may be the haughtiest dame I've ever met, but she's not a scheming gorgon."

"She's not haughty," Dash replied automatically.

Flynn gave him a look. "You're really doing a fine job convincing me you hate her."

Dash groaned. "I don't hate her. I hate what she did to me, what a fool she made of me."

"So don't let her win, then. The car is out front. Get yourself cleaned up and I'll drive you back to LA. We'll have you out with a new dame tonight, no problem. Dash and Flynn, painting the town red again. I was getting bored without you anyway. I need the competition to keep me on my toes."

Dash looked out the window at the ranch he'd bought three years ago. It was bathed in the morning light, hills and valleys spread before him like a field of gold. He owned the piece of land but never bothered to visit. He'd been too busy, too caught up in making movies and selling the world a lie. "I don't want that."

Flynn got up and set himself to cleaning up the kitchen. For a scoundrel, he was really the tidiest man Dash had ever met. "Okay, you're right, take a night off, nurse that headache, we'll get you back on the horse tomorrow."

There was only one horse Dash wanted to get back on right now. And that was a real one. "I'm not going back."

"*Pfffft,* that's ridiculous. Of course you are." Flynn didn't even turn around, just kept rinsing the mug in the sink.

"Not right now." Dash thought about everything that had

happened. Not just Joan, but the movie. The work he'd put in. How renewed he'd felt, how fulfilling it had been getting to do something different, going farther with his emotions in a scene than he ever had before. He'd fought it, sure. Hell, he still wasn't convinced Joan hadn't pushed him into it for her own ends. But did that mean she'd been wrong? Could he give acting up? He didn't know. He didn't want to. But he didn't want to go back to the way things were, either. And he couldn't face Joan or the press right now. The thought of it was unbearable. "I need some time to clear my head."

Flynn turned and stared at him, a look of horror on his face. "That is the worst idea I've ever heard."

"What?"

"I haven't had a clear head since 1925. Clear heads only lead to overthinking things."

Dash laughed then, and instantly regretted it for the way it made his head throb. "I think maybe you could do with some overthinking once in a while."

"I'm not the one who woke up in a pile of kitchen towels."

Dash shrugged. Flynn had a point.

"Look, okay, so you fell in love with Joan Davis. And she turned out to be a stinker. Fine. In my opinion, you dodged a bullet. Marriage is for the birds. She's an attractive dame with too much dough. They're a dime a dozen in Hollywood. We'll find you another one. Here, I'll have you a date lined up before you even get back to town."

Flynn reached in the breast pocket of his wrinkled jacket and pulled out a little black book, which he promptly started paging through. "Harriet… No, went out with her last week and forgot to call her back. Dorothy, moved back in with her mother. Edith, Dorothy's mother." Flynn dog-eared the page he was looking at and winked at Dash. "Sometimes the older vintage is better."

Dash groaned. "I don't know why I thought you could help me."

"Because I'm all you've got." Flynn threw the book at him and went to pour Dash a fresh cup of coffee. "Look through it and tell me if you find something you like. If they've got a red line through their name though, forget it."

"What does that mean?"

"That they're screwy."

Dash gave his friend a hard stare. He suspected it more likely meant Flynn had led them on and then failed to deliver. His friend had a penchant for clingy women, and he never learned. Too bad Dash didn't have the same tendency.

"I don't want to date one of your castoffs."

Flynn gave him a look of mock outrage, pressing his hand to his chest. "You should be honored to date one of my castoffs. Besides, they'll think you're a perfect gentleman after they've been out with me. C'mon, Dash, come back to Hollywood. It's no fun doing this without you. To hell with what anyone thinks of you. We're all gonna kick the bucket. Might as well have some fun along the way. Joan Davis is the same as any woman. Something you'll regret the next morning. Forget her."

Flynn had finished doing the dishes and was putting them back on the shelf, while Dash mulled what his friend had said. The man was a cad. But sometimes he had an idiotic way of getting at the right thing while saying the absolutely wrong one. Joan Davis *was* a woman he regretted the next morning. But not for the reasons Flynn thought. It was because he thought she'd seen him and loved him and that he'd done the same for her. Well, at least he'd kept up his half of that. He had no reason to have a guilty conscience. Even if he did have a pocketful of regrets.

What had Flynn said? *To hell with what anyone thinks of you.* He'd never done very well with that, had he? Even now he was sitting here nursing a royal hangover because he'd spent so much time worrying what someone else thought of him. "You know what, you're right."

"'Course I'm right. I'm always right. Right about what?"

"Doesn't matter. I'm not going back. I need some time to think. Figure out what I want."

"When you figure it out, I'll help you get over her. Or under her. Whatever you like, I won't judge."

"From a man who has been arrested for public indecency for having sex out of doors no less than six times, that means so much," drawled Dash.

"Fresh air is good for my performance." Flynn shrugged.

"You ever think maybe laying off the booze might be good for your performance?"

Flynn snorted. "Absurd." He threw the dish towel he was holding, and Dash caught it in midair. He looked down at it meaningfully. Was this a metaphor for something? Was the universe telling him to throw in the towel? Or was he just drunk? "Besides, without you around, there's more to drink for me."

"And more to flirt with. I'm sure it's good for your ego and your libido when I'm not around."

"Much as I miss your ugly mug, I haven't heard the ladies complaining." That should've cut Dash to the quick. It was a sore subject for him. But he took it in the playful way Flynn intended. Because to be honest, right now he didn't much care if any of Flynn's usual carousel of starlets and cigarette girls missed him. He sure as hell didn't miss them. And it was freeing to admit that.

But he knew Flynn was trying to draw him out of himself, so he stood and shadowboxed, miming like he was irritated with his friend, before grabbing Flynn and wrapping his arm around his neck.

He'd barely had him in a hold for a few seconds before Flynn was crying "uncle." But that suited Dash fine. The sudden intense movement had once again sent a ribbon of pain coursing through his head.

"Drunk," Flynn muttered.

"Heel," Dash retorted.

"Playboy degenerate."

"Takes one to know one," Dash replied. "Besides, not anymore."

Flynn clasped his hands to his chest and stumbled backwards. "Oh, you're breaking my heart."

Dash chuckled. "You'll survive, I'm sure. Besides, I'm not convinced you have a heart to break." He sat down and rested his head against the table. He was confused and mixed up six ways from Sunday. But there was one thing he knew how to do. To work the land, water the horses, use his hands. So he'd stay here. Because right now, that was the only thing in this mixed-up world that made a lick of sense.

CHAPTER 25

HOLLYWOOD DREAMS ARE DASH-ED AT 'RENDEZVOUS' PREMIERE

Hollywood Boulevard was awash with fans on Tuesday night hoping for a glimpse of their favorite on-screen duo, Joan Davis and Dash Howard. But the crowds were destined to be disappointed, despite having braved the November chill. Dash Howard was nowhere to be seen. Joan Davis arrived on the arm of her fiancé, Monty Smyth, looking ravishing in a satin gown of seafoam green. The two were all smiles, despite rumors of their relationship being on the rocks. And *What Price Hollywood?* has heard directly from Miss Davis that their love is for keeps.

But Davis's on-screen lover Dash Howard was a no-show. No one in Hollywood has seen hide nor hair of the erstwhile playboy and movie star since the day of his divorce in Reno. Perhaps he'd become a bit too accustomed to the joys of matrimony? Harry Evets assures this eagle-eyed reporter that Howard is simply taking a much-needed vacation. But whoever heard of a three-month getaway? Rumors abound that he's holed up on a ranch in Santa Barbara and is perhaps looking to retire from pictures. Say it ain't so! To think of all the sacrifices so many in this business, including Mr. Howard himself, have made, and that his would come to naught. It breaks one's heart! Never fear, whether Howard is simply getting some well-earned R&R as the studio claims or is planning to dash our dreams, *What Price Hollywood?* will be the first to know.

—xoxo, Leda

Joan kicked the newspaper into the rosebushes bordering the front of her Beverly Hills home. She didn't need to read it. She'd seen it already. Someone had seen fit to leave three copies of it in her trailer this morning. The production assistant who'd brought her a morning cup of coffee had been startled to find her starting a small fire in her dressing room wastebasket. But she didn't want to look at it, read it, even think about it. All she wanted to do was work.

She'd called Harry before she even got to the train station in Reno, and he hadn't asked any questions when she'd demanded he put her in something, anything, right away. Instead, he'd drudged up a forgettable screwball comedy and paired her off with a leading man who was not Dash. That was all that mattered. From there, she'd gone on to an ensemble piece set in a hotel where she played an heiress. And now she was making a melodrama about a woman whose lover had abandoned her when she became pregnant with his child. She'd scarcely had a day off in three months. And that was the way she wanted it. She woke up, she went to the studio and worked for fourteen hours, then she came home and went to bed. And on the weekends she went out with Monty, long enough to get their picture taken and keep up appearances.

Her exhaustion was bone-deep and that was bliss. Because if she was tired, she wasn't sad or heartbroken or thinking about Dash and all the ways she'd been a fool. The only thing she dreamed of now was her queen-size bed and its black-velvet art deco headboard. She couldn't wait to crawl into it now.

She stuck her key in the lock of her Beverly Hills home and called out as she entered, "Arlene? Are you here? I'm home."

"We're in the living room."

We? Most nights she came home to an empty house. Arlene wasn't technically still her assistant. But she still came over a couple of nights per week to check on Joan. She insisted it was because she was bored and missed her, but Joan knew better. Still, she appreciated it.

She walked into her living room, her eyes glancing at the beautiful Hurrell portrait hanging over the mantle Harry had gifted her on her first anniversary at the studio. The woman in that photograph was confident, self-assured, and most definitely not dumb enough to lose everything over a man.

But then she realized who "we" was. It was Arlene, of course, but also Harry Evets and Monty Smyth.

"I didn't know I was having a dinner party," she drawled.

"You're not," Arlene declared, a tad too cheerfully. "You're having a 'You're miserable and what the hell are you going to do about it?' party."

"Oh no, I'm not." Joan started backing out of the room. There was nothing to talk about. She'd made a mistake and now she had to forget about it, move on, throw herself into her work. Like she'd always done.

But Arlene came and gently grabbed her by the shoulders, frog-marching her to the ornate art deco mirror that hung on the wall next to the entryway. "Look at yourself."

"I can't believe you would ambush me like this."

"Joan, listen to Arlene. Look at yourself," Monty said from his place in the armchair next to the coffee table. Joan looked at him, watching him swirl his drink, looking for answers in the whisky, before knocking back a hefty slug.

Then she did as she was told. She was surprised at what she saw. It certainly wasn't the woman in the portrait hanging on the other side of the room. There were dark circles under her eyes. Her lips were tight and drawn. And was that? Jesus, she had a few gray hairs right at the top of her hairline. She'd call her beauty operator in the morning. She touched her face and peered deeper into the glass before shrugging Arlene off. "So I'm a little tired. I'm on my fourth picture in nearly four months. I'll take a break for Christmas."

She turned around to see that Arlene had crossed her arms over her chest and was tapping her foot.

"What?"

"Joan, you're not tired. Well, you are. You've been working yourself half to death. But that's because you're sad. Dare I even say heartbroken. And you're trying to convince yourself you aren't."

Joan laughed, a hollow, empty thing that had no heart behind it. "That's preposterous. You read too many novels, Arlene."

She looked around the room for support. From his perch on the couch, Harry Evets patted his tie hanging over his rounded belly and leaned forward to stub out his cigarette in the green glass ashtray on her black glass coffee table. He gave her a disbelieving look. She turned to Monty, lazing in the grass-green wingback chair. Pity was etched across his face.

"It won't work, Joan. I've tried it. Believe me, it doesn't work."

She wanted to play dumb and act like she had no idea what he was talking about. That she hadn't been trying to distract herself, to do the one thing she knew she could. The one thing she'd thought actually mattered. Until Dash.

She nodded and slumped onto the couch next to Harry. He was chuckling. The ass. "I'm sorry, I still can't get over what Arlene told me. I don't believe it. You and Howard? Dash and Davis?"

Arlene sighed from her perch in the corner. "It's so romantic, isn't it?"

Joan glared at her. "Really not helping."

Arlene bit her lip and gave Joan a sheepish look in return before turning to Monty. "Sorry, Monty."

He waved his hand as if to say it was nothing. Ah, so Arlene still didn't know Monty's secret. Thank God for small miracles.

"All these years I've been angling to get you and Dash together for publicity, and the second you actually fall for each other, somebody cocks it up," Harry continued. "Who was it, Joanie? Dash? Leda Price? Or are you too damn proud to get out of your own way?"

Joan shot from her seat, quivering with outrage. "I don't have to sit here and listen to this." But Arlene came up and took her hand, rubbing her thumb over her hand in a soothing gesture. It reminded Joan of the way Dash had squeezed her wrists when she'd been so afraid of the horse. She hated being reminded of him.

"I take it the answer is all of the above," chortled Harry.

"No." Joan whirled to him. "It wasn't. It was silly, a bout of insanity. It would never work. And who told you, anyway?"

Joan hadn't told anyone, not even Arlene, about what had passed between her and Dash in Reno. She knew Arlene would consider it destiny and obsess over getting them back together. And that simply wasn't possible. Only one person had an inkling of the truth. But of course he was sitting right there. "Monty. How could you?"

He had the decency to look sheepish and reach for his glass, which was nearly empty. He swigged the last of it and sat up straighter. "How could I not? You're miserable, Joan. We can all see it. And we decided it's high time we do something about it."

"I've got it under control. I will forget about it and we're going to get married, Monty. Everything will be fine. You'll see. This is how it has to be."

"But why does it have to be that way?" Arlene asked, the innocence and hope in her voice so pure it nearly brought Joan to tears. "If you love Dash and he loves you, what happened? Why has he disappeared to Santa Barbara and won't answer the phone?"

Joan sighed. She realized she would never escape their meddling and their needling if she didn't tell them all the truth. Maybe then they would see how hopeless it was. "Leda Price is what happened."

Arlene gasped. "I knew it!"

Harry merely reached for his drink and patted his stomach thoughtfully. "Let's hear it, Joanie. What'd she threaten you with? It's nothing old Harry can't fix."

Harry's words hit her like a sudden and massive tidal wave. That's exactly what Leda had said, wasn't it? That Joan had Harry as a protector. She'd relied on him, of course, and been grateful to him for the career he'd help her build and maintain. But she'd never truly appreciated the immensity of that. What it really meant to have someone in her corner at all times.

Joan began to pace in front of the fireplace, the heels of her pumps flattening the rug in a familiar pattern. If she wasn't careful, she'd wear it thin. She watched as Arlene fluttered nervously around the room, sweeping ashes out of trays and freshening Harry and Monty's drinks.

Maybe Harry wasn't the only one in her corner. She'd been too frightened and proud to see it before. Because here were three people who cared about her. Who had come here tonight to try to fix something she had broken. But did she really want to drag them all into this mess? Monty had problems enough of his own. And Arlene was just getting started in this business.

Harry knew, though. "Harry, she's trying to lord you-know-what over me again," Joan said.

The studio boss spluttered with rage and reached for his topped-off vodka soda. "How dare she! I paid that harpy a pretty penny to keep her mouth shut. I could sue her for this."

Joan gave him a look. She was pretty sure someone violating the terms of their blackmail payoff would not hold up in court.

"Fine, fine, you're right," Harry groused. "But that little shrew is getting too big for her britches. Besides, she has no proof. We destroyed everything. I had a team working day and night to track down every last copy. The negatives too."

"Would someone mind informing me exactly what we're talking about?" Monty drawled, sitting forward on the edge of his chair. Arlene had leaned against the back of Monty's chair and Joan almost laughed at how strongly she resembled a cocker spaniel waiting for a treat.

Joan glanced back and forth between Monty and Harry, and then looked to Arlene, who was failing miserably at trying not to look too eager to hear Joan's story.

"Perhaps you and Arlene should go, Monty," she whispered.

She couldn't risk involving them in this mess. God knew Monty was already keeping enough secrets. And Arlene may have been only four years younger than Joan, but she was still a girl really. "To protect yourselves."

Monty rolled his eyes. "After everything we've been through, Joan. I have the biggest skeleton of all in my closet." He snorted. "Literally. What's a few more bones in the mix."

Arlene looked at him, dawning comprehension on her face. It hadn't been Joan's secret to tell, but if the girl worked it out for herself, well, okay then. Monty was right. She should be ashamed to have even contemplated excluding him. He was a part of this, after all. Through no fault of his own.

"Arlene, just you then..."

"If you think I'm going to walk out on my best friend when she needs me most, you've got another think coming, Joan Davis. Go ahead, do your worst, shock me."

Joan had to bow her head for a moment to choke back tears. No one had ever called her their friend before. She'd feared that Arlene would forget about her once her career took off. What had Dash said? That her only friend was someone she paid to be there. But Arlene had organized all of this. Brought these people together. To help her. One didn't do that for someone one didn't care about.

But could she really tell them? For so long, in the upper echelons of Hollywood, only she and Harry had known about this. She hadn't used her current stage name. Only a fool would have. Harry had seen the film in an adult theater on Santa Monica Blvd. that he liked to frequent. He claimed he was "scouting for new talent," but he wasn't fooling anyone. And he *had* discovered Joan there, after all. He'd phoned the underground production company to track her down, and signed Joan to a contract. Then he'd called the company back, had the film removed from the seedy little theater's rotation, and tracked down every last negative.

But Leda had found out about it somehow, likely from one of the people who'd made the film. But the more people who knew, the more likely it was to get out. And while she wasn't ashamed of what she'd done, she knew that would mean nothing to the puritanical mobs devoted to decrying Hollywood as a place of vice and iniquity.

She swallowed and cast her eyes to the portrait once again. Hurrell had photographed her on a couch, her hair hanging over her left eye, her best side to the camera. She looked arrogant and open, not a come-hither pose so much as a dare. Or better yet, a promise. That those who tussled with Joan Davis would regret it. That's who she needed to be. Right here. Right now.

"When I first got to Hollywood, I was looking for work, something to get me noticed. But more important, something to make sure I had food on the table and could pay my rent. I was willing to do anything to avoid crawling back to Oklahoma. So when an offer came for a stag film, I took it."

She watched Monty and Arlene carefully. Waiting for the inevitable shift to come, for their bodies to tense or for one, or both of them, to turn away from her. For the slightest hint of disgust to enter into their voices. But Monty blinked owlishly and then he erupted into laughter. "That's it? You were naked in a film?"

"And more," she replied. If they were going to know, they should know all of it.

"Oh, so you had sex while someone filmed it," Arlene interjected. "Who cares? You've never exactly built your image on the notion of being chaste. You're not Mary bloody Pickford. People like you because you're sensual, Joan."

Joan's jaw dropped. Arlene. Hopeless romantic Arlene was

saying this. As if her greatest secret were nothing. No, not nothing; as if it were an asset. Something she admired or found impressive. Joan gripped the mantel to hold herself upright and held back a hysterical wave of giggles.

Monty reached for his glass and continued to laugh into it. "Jesus, I thought you were going to tell me the studio covered up the fact you killed someone in an automobile accident or something."

"God, no, nothing like that." Joan exhaled a puff of relief. She couldn't help smiling.

"Be that as it may," Harry interjected, "this will still be a bridge too far for the pearl-clutchers who keep the movie houses bustling and our coffers full. And Leda Price knows that."

The clock chimed midnight. Joan hadn't realized it was so late. They'd been filming a difficult scene today, the one in which Joan's character's lover walks out on her. It'd hit a bit too close to home and required her far more takes than usual.

Monty took his gold-plated cigarette case out of his breast pocket and offered one to Harry before lighting one himself. He took one long drag and looked thoughtfully at Joan. "Why didn't you tell Dash what you told us? Work it out together. Why'd you let Leda get her way?"

Joan closed her eyes. She was hoping to skip this part. To go to the grave with the secret if it meant Dash would never know, if she could protect him from getting hurt again. Worse than she'd hurt him.

She eyed Monty nervously. "Dash's first wife is trying to blackmail him."

Monty choked on his drink. "He was married? Before you, I mean."

"Yes, but she was awful, and she broke his heart and deserted him, and if he knew about any of this, it would kill him."

Harry said, "So, I'll find out her address and pay off the old bag. Easy fix."

"No, I–I appreciate that, Harry, but then Dash would find out. Leda would catch wind of our meddling and tell him, I'm sure of it." She looked around the room, locking eyes with everyone there. "And he can't know. It was part of my deal with Leda. I took care of it. Please."

She pleaded with her eyes and they all looked soberly back at her. They had to know how important it was that the truth never reach Dash. "Leda threatened to ruin both our careers if I tried to circumvent her and so much as breathed a word of the truth to him. She hates me, and she's out for blood. But I won't let her get to him too. At least not more than she has already. This way, we both have our work. I broke his heart to keep him safe. There was no other way."

Monty looked at her sadly and shook his head. He didn't need to say anything. Joan knew he was thinking about how he'd tried to make the same choice, become engaged to her rather than going public with his relationship with Jerry. He'd chosen his work too. And he'd regretted it.

Well, Joan wasn't Monty. "It would've happened eventually. I know that now." Monty and Arlene looked at her like she'd sprouted a third head.

Harry had more to say, interrupting the thick and pregnant silence in the room. "Don't you know I have the power to make anything Leda says an empty threat?" he sputtered.

Joan looked at him sadly. "Don't you know that your power only extends so far when it comes to the court of public opinion?" she replied. "If she published Josephine's story, it would not only crush Dash, but also tarnish the image of him you both worked so hard to build. Not to mention the taint of my secret if he'd stuck by me. We could both be out of jobs if Leda ever prints what she knows."

"I could block her from the studio, bar her from every premiere for the next decade."

Joan wandered over to the other side of the couch and plopped down onto it, feeling weighed down by the futility of Harry's offer. "What good would that do? She'd just retaliate, slander you next. We all know you're not squeaky clean either, Harry. And I won't be the reason every one of your contract stars has their dirty laundry plastered across the pages of the paper."

Harry crossed his arms, but he didn't say anything. He knew she was right.

"I've known my whole life that love was dangerous. I forgot my own rules. But I remember them now. I've learned my lesson." She leaned her head back against the sofa and closed her eyes in defeat.

"You can't really believe that." Joan cracked her eyes open to see Arlene looking at her with the saddest expression she had ever seen.

Then Monty piled on. "You're being ridiculous. You know that, right?" She had never seen Monty so frustrated before. Not even the day at Lake Tahoe when she'd made of fool of them and Dash.

She wanted to rage and scream. Why didn't they understand? This was the way things were. She'd accepted it. Why couldn't they?

"Joan, do you really think no one in this room loves you?" She turned her head without lifting it. She didn't know what she'd expected Harry to say. But it wasn't that.

"Harry Evets, are you getting sentimental on me?"

His cheeks reddened, but he reached out and grasped her

hand with his fingers, the iron strength of his grip a grounding sensation. "I'm an old man. I've earned the privilege."

"So what are you saying?"

"I'm saying I love you, Joan. Every infuriating, entitled, demanding, talented, complicated inch of you."

"We all do," piped up Arlene.

She gave Monty a sad look. "Even you?"

"Would I have agreed to marry you if I didn't?"

She couldn't sit still any longer, standing to sweep more stray ashes off the glass countertop of the coffee table into the green glass ashtray. She'd bought it on Catalina Island on one of her first vacations as an actress—a symbol of all the nice things she wanted to surround herself with. It was cheap sea glass, but it sparkled in the sunlight and she'd always loved the pale-green cast it gave off. She examined it in her hand and noticed it had a chip in one corner. She could see her reflection in the glass, obscured slightly by the mound of ashes. She huffed a humorless laugh. That was her—imperfect, a little chipped around the edges, and if Leda Price had her way, smeared with soot.

She cradled the ashtray in the crook of her arm and turned to face the room, surveying her friends here. Yes, her friends. Not her business associates. Not her colleagues. Her friends. Something she'd never believed she'd have; something she hadn't realized she needed until tonight if she was being honest.

Harry, who'd ironically discovered her by watching the film that was threatening to bring her entire life crashing down around her like a house of cards. The dirty old man might have his peccadilloes, but she loved him. For his loyalty. For believing in her, then and now. For never giving up on her.

Arlene, who'd once been a script girl and was now on her way to being one of Hollywood's premier screenwriters.

Then there was Monty. Dear, sweet Monty, who she'd admired from afar and then realized they could be the answer to each other's mutual problems.

There were those who were cynical. Hell, she was too. That would say Hollywood was a dog-eat-dog town where everyone was out for themselves. But she'd found her people here, her family. The realization crashed into her like a locomotive. She wasn't alone. Dash had made her see it, had made her understand that she didn't have to be a martyr on some lonely mission, holding everyone at arm's length.

Somehow in spite of clinging tightly to that belief for years, she'd found a family. A ragtag bunch, but she loved them. And against all odds, they loved her. In spite of all her protestations that there was no room in her life for love, they adored one another. Making movies, making money, might have been the thing that brought them together at first, but it wasn't what had brought them here tonight. That was something deeper, something far more real if infinitely more intangible. The only thing that mattered in the end.

She cast her eyes to the empty armchair on the other side of the couch, the twin to the one Monty was sitting in. Dash should've been there. In that chair. But now he never would be. Feeling this love, this ferocious outpouring of support, made it all the more bittersweet to know he'd slipped through her fingers. That Leda Price and Josephine Howard had snatched her happiness from her grasp, that she had let them. Because she was afraid.

"You know who else loves you?" Monty interjected. "Dash Howard."

"No, he doesn't. Not anymore. I made sure of that."

Harry and Monty gave her a confused look, but Arlene simply

crossed to the side table next to the couch and opened the drawer, pulling out the issue of the *Examiner* bearing the photograph of Joan dropping her ring into the Truckee River. Joan had no idea how Arlene had known it was in there. "See for yourselves."

Arlene held out the paper and Monty snatched it from her grasp. "Jesus, Joan, did you really have to go this far?"

"Leda said I had to sell it or she'd squeal. So…I sold it." She gave a sad little shrug. "She said she wanted him to loathe me as entirely as she does. To never want anything to do with me again. That if he didn't come away hating me, she'd publish all of this. If Dash knew any of it, he would've tried to fight for me and she would've ruined us." Her voice broke, realizing that she'd let go of the only person who ever believed in her as much as she believed in herself. But she squared her shoulders and pushed on. "It needed to be this way. To protect him, he needed to hate me. I broke his heart, but I kept him safe. Even if it meant giving the performance of my life. He believes that I'm heartless, and it's gonna stay that away."

Monty whistled in amazement at the image plastered across the paper still lying in his lap. "You weren't kidding when you called it the performance of your life. It's a shame they don't give Oscars for newspaper photographs."

"She's going to win for *Reno Rendezvous* anyway," Harry retorted, unthinking.

Joan darted her gaze to him and glared at him out of the corner of her eyes.

"What? I've seen the rushes. It's the best work you've ever done, Joanie."

She turned to face the mantel, the empty spot she'd left there since the day she moved in. It had always been reserved for her Oscar. That tiny gold statuette had seemed like everything to her. Vindication for the way she'd gotten her start, proof that she was an actress who deserved respect, and a vote of confidence from her peers. But suddenly, it seemed like little more than a gold-plated piece of tin, a victory as hollow as the metal itself.

Because her performance wouldn't have been half as good without Dash. Without the very real turmoil and love she'd felt for him on that set. But even more so, without his support—the way he'd stood up for her against Von Wild and nurtured her as she blossomed under Kucor's direction. The performance he'd given to match hers, to make the picture stand out even more by going toe-to-toe. They'd both done the best work of their lives on this film. Joan had always had this performance in her, but Dash had allowed his talent to bloom to its full potential.

Would that little gold man mean anything without the man she truly wanted? She'd once believed that winning an Oscar would be the pinnacle of her life, the crest of an illustrious career. But now everything was a muddle. Suddenly, that place on the mantel wasn't the only thing that felt empty.

She turned back to face her friends. "What if the work and the recognition for it isn't enough anymore?"

Harry got a twinkle in his eye, Monty grinned, and Arlene burst into tears. "You do still love him. I knew it, I knew it!"

Joan didn't know if she wanted to roll her eyes or cry. Because damn it, she did. She'd been lying to herself for three months. Convincing herself it was for the best. But she loved Dash Howard and she wanted him back. "I've got an idea. But we need a plan. If you'll help me?"

"We thought you'd never ask," Monty said with a grin.

CHAPTER 26

DASH LOOKED OUT THE WINDOW AND WATCHED THE PINKS and purples of the February sky slowly become eclipsed by a bloom of orange as the sun rose over the hill in the distance. He flipped the switch on the radio sitting on the small card table he'd set up near the window. A new tune by Tommy Dorsey swelled to fill his kitchen, and he looked around at the shabby state of things—the pile of dishes in the sink, the coffee stains on the card table, and the threadbare curtains doing little to conceal the increasing beams of light striking every surface as if determined to highlight the grubby conditions in which Dash was living.

He scratched at the beard that had gone from mild scruff to full mountain man in the nearly six months since he'd come here. He wore his pajamas slung low on his hips and was shirtless, as he leaned against the window frame and bathed in the glow of the rising sun, turning his back on all the things he still needed to fix. He wished he could say he was at peace. But he was feeling restless, itching for a new part, the exhilaration of reading a script for the first time and discovering the secrets of the man he would bring to life.

Hell, he missed other people. The crew. His poker buddies. Phil's wife had the baby back in December. They'd sent him a photo in a Christmas card—the kid was the spitting image of his dad—showing them surrounded by their large Asian family, the proud grandparents beaming in the back. It made Dash's heart ache. He wanted that.

He even missed Flynn, despite the fact he was a bad influence. He'd come up to visit several times, even bringing some girls with him once in a bid to coax Dash back to LA. He couldn't blame the guy for doing the only thing he knew how. But seven months later, Dash still didn't have any answers. He just knew he was lonely. And he was so goddamn tired of being lonely.

He'd wanted to get away from the trappings of Hollywood—the press, the publicity shoots, the hangers-on. Needed to clear his head. Only he'd spent the last seven months in a fog of work and fatigue, rising with the sun, working all day, and collapsing in exhaustion at night. He hadn't cleared his head so much as built a schedule with no room for anything in it but the grueling work of fixing the house and surveying the land, turning it into something his younger self would've been proud of.

The sun was fully above the hill now, and he was already behind. He was planning to build a pen for cattle today, and then he was going to see about actually buying a herd. He popped the lid off a tin of coffee grounds and spooned some into the metal coffeepot on his ancient stove before screwing the two pieces together and pouring water in the top. He opened the kitchen drawer, slightly off-kilter, making a mental note that it was another thing that needed fixing, and pulled out a small book of matches, lighting the stove.

The song wound to a close, the last few melancholy notes of Dorsey's trombone warbling their way across the kitchen and straight into Dash's soul. He waited to see what would play next, but an announcer cut in. "We interrupt our morning music hour with a special bulletin from Hollywood. This morning the nominations for the Ninth Academy Awards were announced."

Dash stopped dead in his tracks. Somehow he'd forgotten the nominations were being announced today. Every year, he'd listened eagerly. Hell, last year the studio had even helped him throw an all-night party that carried into the early hours of the morning while they awaited the news of his first nomination. Maybe he'd cleared his mind of that world more than he'd thought. He just hadn't been able to shake the one person he was most desperate to forget.

"Joan Davis." Yes, that was the one. Wait, no, the announcer was saying Joan's name. *The announcer was saying Joan's name.* Dash couldn't help himself; he let out a loud whoop. There was no one around to hear him for miles.

"She did it," he crowed. He'd known the work that Joan was doing on *Reno Rendezvouz* was award-worthy, the type of performance that would make the rest of Hollywood sit up and take notice. But he'd skipped the premiere back in November, ignoring every one of Harry's phone calls about it. He hadn't been able to bear the idea of seeing her again, especially in their romantic scenes—scenes he'd filmed believing she was really in love with him. It was far too painful. But he'd hoped that the studio hadn't ruined the picture, that it was as good as what he'd remembered.

He was happy for her. But it was a bittersweet happiness, tinged with the reminder that she'd been willing to make him a pawn in her game to get it. A game he still couldn't understand, except for grasping that he'd lost. And that he'd never truly had a shot at winning, or even been allowed to play with a full deck.

He'd been the one stupid enough to believe that she loved him, that she wanted to be his wife. But Joan Davis had always loved one thing and one thing only: being a movie star. So whatever her antics at the courthouse had been about, it was to that end—promoting the cachet of her name. Why he'd needed to be a casualty of that, whether it was convenience or cruelty, he supposed he'd never know.

The sound of his own name pulled him from this morass of thoughts. Wait, but that meant… The announcer recapped the list of nominees for Best Actor and sure enough, he was included. A dopey, uncontrollable grin spread across his face. He'd done something no one ever had before. He had been nominated for Best Actor two years in a row. He, the rugged he-man beefcake, had proved himself. Had made Oscar history. He nearly collapsed into the rickety blue chair he had positioned at the card table.

He'd followed some of the reviews. His performance had gone over the way Joan had predicted. Critics had hailed this new emotional side of him, proclaiming they wanted to see more of this sensitive Dash Howard. It had fueled his sense that if he went back, it would need to be on his terms. But this nomination was proof. He didn't have to be the playboy King of Hollywood anymore. He could be something more complicated. Joan had broken his heart, but she had at least given him this.

The phone on the wall echoed shrilly across the kitchen, and he reached for it without thinking.

"Hello," he mumbled, still a bit dazed.

"Dash Howard, is that you? I was beginning to think I'd never hear your voice again."

"Harry." Dash couldn't suppress a huge grin. It was strangely good to hear Harry's voice. To have this piece of his life back. "I'm sorry I've been ignoring your calls. I needed some time."

"Well, I'm calling 'time's up.'" Harry chuckled. "You've been nominated for your second consecutive Oscar, you big idiot."

"I heard," Dash muttered, absentmindedly scratching at his bare chest. He smelled smoke and looked over at his coffee pot, which was currently bubbling over. Hell, he'd forgotten. He stretched out the phone cord as far as it would reach and leaned to flip the stove off.

"... Joan... "

"Listen, Harry, I was trying to stop the kitchen from catching on fire. I didn't hear what you said. Could you repeat it?"

"The long and short of it is, it's time for you to come back, Dash."

Dash crushed the phone against his neck, holding it there between his head and shoulder while he found a dish towel to mop up the coffee that had spilled onto the stove. It didn't really deserve to be called coffee; it was more like burnt brown water.

"You're right, Harry. I'm ready now. I've been hiding out for too long."

There was a beat of silence on the other end of the line. Dash wondered if his connection was bad. "Harry, are you still there?"

"Yes, I just didn't expect you to agree without a fight."

Dash laughed. "Believe or not, you old codger, I miss you. I miss the studio, all the fellas. And I miss my work."

"Well, that's great news, Dash, great news. Makes the next part a bit easier."

Dash's stomach fell. He imagined the "next part" had something to do with Joan Davis.

"Well, you heard Joanie got nominated as well?"

"Let me stop you right there, Harry. I'll do anything you want. Except ever make a picture with Joan Davis again." He had to have some sense of self-preservation.

"No, no, nothing like that. At least, not yet." Harry chortled. "But Dash, you know how much this nomination means to Joan."

He did. The firm reminder of how much it meant to her was glinting in the window. He didn't know why, but he hadn't been able to get rid of the ring he'd bought—the wedding band he'd hoped she'd put on his finger that day. He didn't answer Harry, but instead choked back the lump of rising sadness and anger in his throat.

"Your nomination is already one for the history books, but think how much better it'd be if you won two years running. I want to give you both the best shot at success here."

"So, what are you saying?" Dash knew with more certainty than he'd ever possessed in his life that he wasn't going to like the answer.

"I've arranged a series of press events for you in the week before voting ends."

"Events? Plural? No."

"Dash, I've been very patient with you. More patient than any other studio boss in this town would have been."

"And for that I am grateful, believe me. But I can't be around her, preening for the cameras for whatever dog-and-pony show you've concocted. I'll do solo interviews, as many as you like, but not with Joan, please."

The line was quiet. Dash turned and leaned his back against the kitchen sink, keeping the phone cradled between his neck and shoulder and leaning his arm against the counter, while running his fingers through his hair with the other hand. He waited for an answer and for a brief moment wondered if Harry had simply hung up on him.

"Fine. But you have to do one—"

Dash groaned, massaging the space between his eyes with the tip of his forefinger and thumb. "You don't know what you're asking."

"No, *you* don't know what you're asking. I made you, Dash Howard. And I can break you. Sid Grauman has very graciously offered to let you and Joan do the handprint ceremony at the

Chinese as part of your campaigning. But only if it's the two of you. Together."

Dash glanced over at the wedding band on the windowsill. He knew what that would mean to Joan. All she'd ever wanted was to be loved by the masses. To join the likes of the immortal greats, with her hands and feet forever enshrined in cement, would mean practically as much as the nomination itself.

It was the type of thing he hated—flashy publicity stunts with no real meaning behind them. And while his feelings for Joan were still a muddle, he had to admit he resented the idea of doing anything for her. Not when she'd already used him so completely and discarded him like a filthy tissue.

But Harry wasn't asking him, he was telling him. So it looked like Dash Howard would finally be returning to Hollywood. But maybe this time he could hold on to a piece of himself a little better. The piece of himself that Joan had helped him recover, that he'd found more and more of every day he'd spent out here on the ranch. He'd told Joan that acting was one of the few things that made him happy and that a life without it would be an empty one. Now, he'd proven to himself unequivocally that was true. He didn't want to stop acting. He just wanted to stop pretending. Well, there was no time like the present.

CHAPTER 27

THE DAIMLER THE STUDIO HAD SENT PULLED UP TO THE curb on Hollywood Boulevard. Joan looked out at the flashing lights and the crowd of reporters gathered around the matching slabs of wet cement waiting for her and Dash. There was a pair of spotlights, flanking the courtyard. They made a lazy arc across the sky as they tilted back and forth, as if they were telling the city: "Here is where the action is! Something important is happening!"

Something important *was* happening—something she'd dreamed of since she'd read about the new tradition of the stars dipping their hands and feet in cement at a Hollywood movie palace.

Her stomach did somersaults as she took a breath and prepared to step out of the car onto the red carpet. Once, it would've been all excitement. Delight in the knowledge that the legions of fans pressing at the metal barricade lining the sidewalk were there for her. That with her hard work and her grit and her gumption, she had earned their adulation. No, more than that: their love.

But tonight, she was all nerves. Because tonight she was putting into motion a plot she'd spent months putting together. Tonight, she was going to get Dash Howard back. Or make a fool of herself trying.

Joan looked at Arlene, sitting beside her in the car, who gave her a reassuring pat on the knee. Arlene had been nominated for an Oscar too, for her spectacular script. Joan knew a victory for her would mean big things. That was her pretense for bringing Arlene along tonight, hoping to drum up more support for her as a bystander. The real reason was that Joan needed Arlene for emotional support and to ensure everything went according to plan.

Joan had worn a black-and-white crepe dress with a flouncy skirt that ended midcalf to keep the hem from dipping into cement. It had a twist around the waist, accentuating her hips, before rising to its sleeveless top with a kerchief tied around the neckline, matching the knot at her midriff.

It was simple and elegant. Joan had chosen it knowing it was the first time Dash would see her in nearly seven months. He'd had a thing for her shoulders. The smattering of freckles across them had driven him wild during those precious stolen nights in their bungalow. She'd spent seven months missing him, seven months simpering for Leda Price, keeping up a fake engagement that was draining the life from both her and Monty. Seven months cowering under the weight of one decision and the constant threat of Leda's wrath. Seven months wondering if Dash was okay, if he would be coming back, if he even still wanted the career she'd forsaken him to protect. He'd told her life on his ranch wouldn't make him happy, but what if he'd changed his mind?

Tonight, she would get an answer to this question and so many more. Harry had done his part. He'd made up a convincing story and demanded Dash be here. Dash had done the last thing she'd expected: He'd agreed. So maybe Dash wasn't done with Hollywood after all. Because he was here fulfilling the requirements of his contract, doing one of the things he hated most—putting on a show for publicity. No matter what happened tonight, at least her sacrifice had not been in vain. Or worse, an act of pure self-preservation.

She took a breath, leaned over and gave Arlene a squeeze for luck, and then nodded at the valet to open her door. The din of the crowd was deafening, as if she'd suddenly turned the volume up as high as it would go. She let the sound fill her to the brim. The "box-office poison" brand was a distant memory now. In the end, her plot had worked. Her engagement and the success of *Reno Rendezvous* had put her back atop the heap. She had her pick of plum roles now. And the final feather in her cap, an Oscar nomination.

But the noise was tinny, her success bittersweet. She wrapped her mink stole more tightly around her arms and stepped out into the brisk air so typical of Hollywood in late February. But it wasn't the sudden chill that left her breathless, it was the sight of Dash standing across the courtyard. He was wearing a perfectly tailored pin-striped suit and his dark curls were pomaded back on his head. She stifled a giggle as one rascally stray curl sprang from his forehead and laid itself artfully across his brow. Dash didn't notice; he stood with his hands clasped behind his back, surveying the crowd.

Joan paused, grasping at Arlene's hand behind her for reassurance. She wanted one more moment to look at him before being thrown into his orbit and the cacophony of the crowd. He'd shaved recently and the hard lines of his jaw glistened in the flashes of the spotlights and flashbulbs, his pencil mustache teasing her above his full upper lip. He was perfection.

She'd always hated his ability to make any woman weak at the knees, resented the ease of it. But she knew better now, that he believed that quality to be a curse preventing anyone from ever knowing the real Dash. Yet she'd become another woman who'd disappointed him. She hated that she'd perpetuated the lie that he'd been taught to believe about himself, if only to keep him from an even bigger hurt.

Tonight, the crowd was expecting Davis and Dash—the Queen of Hollywood who'd only recently reclaimed her crown, and her King. If nothing else went according to plan, she'd have that at least. She took a deep breath, squared her shoulders, and finally moved from the place she'd been rooted on the foot of the red carpet.

She turned her smile to the line of women at the edge of the sidewalk, one of them holding up a little girl, her arms reaching out over the barricade. Joan cast a glance over her shoulder at the crowd and looked back at Arlene, who nudged her in the direction of her adoring fans. She reached for the pen a gloved hand from somewhere in the mob extended to her and made her way down the line, signing autographs, until she came to the child.

Joan knelt down so her eyes were level with the girl's. "Hello there, what might your name be?"

"Mary," answered the child, the *r* coming out more like a *w* in the distinct patter of childlike innocence and unformed consonants.

Joan smiled. "That's a lovely name. My mother was named Mary." The child returned the compliment with a wide grin, exposing the missing tooth in the front of her mouth.

"I want to be just like you when I grow up, Miss Davis," the child proclaimed, looking up at her mother for approval.

Joan lifted her eyes to meet the woman's gaze. Her face was careworn but bright and earnest in a way that had nothing to do with the Hollywood floodlights. "It's true," the woman confessed. "She's too young to see your pictures, but she cuts every one of your photographs out of the newspaper. And we buy her all the fan magazines."

Joan lifted a hand to the sudden pang in her chest. She'd been this girl. Mesmerized by the glamorous photographs of movie stars she'd seen on drugstore shelves, dreaming of a life like the one she saw in black-and-white. Only she'd been ambitious instead of starry-eyed, cold and mercenary instead of innocent and open. She would never apologize for it, but she wished she'd known that she could be softer. That she needn't always close herself off from the world.

"You don't want to be like me, Mary," she said. "You want to be better than me, bigger than me." She winked at her and the girl let out an infectious giggle, one that sent a titter of laughter down the line of bustling autograph seekers.

Joan reached out her hand to the girl and took her dainty fingers in her own. "Promise me something, Mary," Joan asked, never more serious in her life. "Promise me that you'll never choose fame over love."

The girl nodded, a solemn look on her face, and used her other hand to draw an X over her chest. "Cross my heart."

Joan looked back at the girl's mother, who had something eerily like understanding in her eyes. She watched as the woman's gaze drifted to Dash, then back to Joan, a question in her eyes. Joan simply gave her a curt nod, and the woman nodded in return as Joan turned back toward the carpet. Arlene grabbed her arm and whispered in her ear, "Now who's the hopeless romantic?"

Joan laughed, a sad little acknowledgment of the truth of Arlene's words. Arlene let her go, walking over to join the various security and studio brass observing the event. Joan braced her shoulders as she headed to the carpet. The crowds of reporters and ushers parted for her like the Red Sea.

She knew the moment he saw her. The easy, languid stance he'd taken was replaced by something stiffer and more aloof. The devil-may-care smile he was flashing for the cameras tightened ever so slightly, imperceptible unless you truly knew him. His eyes met hers, but then darted away as he turned to pose for another camera.

Harry had worked hard to get this moment for them tonight, had pulled strings with Sid Grauman personally to get this. So it was time for her to put on a show. Time for her to be the damn good actress she knew she was. And maybe more, if Dash would allow it. This first part was the easy bit.

She strode into the pack of cameramen surrounding Dash, laid her hand on his arm, felt him tense under her, and turned to give them a megawatt smile. "Darlings! Now the party can really begin. Joan Davis is here!"

They erupted into a cacophony of laughter, calls for her to look their way, and general attempts to get her attention. She pasted a smile to her face and turned slowly back and forth making sure they all got their shots. Dash muttered out of the corner of his mouth, "Laying it on a bit thick, aren't you?"

Joan cracked back, "If cheesecake's what they want, cheesecake's what they'll get."

Dash smirked at her. "Yes, of course, I forgot. There's no part you're better at playing than Joan Davis the movie star."

She faltered. "And what is that supposed to mean?"

"I thought you'd take it as a compliment."

"From anyone else I would," she confessed. She looked up at him, the hurt in his eyes evident for only a moment before the wall came down, leaving only a stony gaze. "But I know what you think about pretending to be something you're not."

"I wish you'd forget what I think," he muttered, looking down at a piece of lint on his suit jacket and flicking it away.

"I can't," she whispered. "Not now, not ever." The only indication he heard her was the muscle in his jaw that pulsed as he clenched it.

At last the flashbulbs stilled for a moment, and an emcee rushed out to the microphone that had been placed in front of the wet cement, waiting for her and Dash to make their marks. This was the only calm in the storm she'd see tonight. The short man in a tuxedo, his hair seemingly slicked to his head with axle grease, yammered on about the traditions of Grauman's Chinese Theater and the history that was about to be made tonight. She turned to face Dash, trying to keep a smile in her eyes, while the fissure in her heart was widening.

"I'm so sorry for Reno, Dash, so sorry," she whispered.

He blinked at her, seemingly stunned and confused by her words. "Why?"

"Because you deserve better."

He laughed; it was cold and shrill. But if someone had photographed them at the moment, it would simply have looked like Joan had told her costar a funny joke. Only the ice in his voice gave him away. "We both know that's not true. If you believed that, you never would've done what you did."

Joan closed her eyes, summoning some inner reserves of strength she wasn't convinced she had. "I don't know how to explain—"

"Then don't. You got your revenge, Joan. You were mad at me for ruining your precious engagement to a man you don't love, furious that I'd dared to sully your plans. That anyone would shake the foundation of the pedestal you'd built for yourself." He was practically snarling now. But the reporters seemed to be hanging on the emcee's every overdramatized word. "I should've seen it coming. But instead, I let you carve me up. Hell, I handed you the dagger on a silver platter. But baby, I came out of it alive—and I'm not gonna stand here and let you twist the knife further to assuage your conscience."

Joan wanted to scream, to tell him it wasn't true, to pound her fists into his chest. She raised her hand to do it, but caught herself in time. There were cameras everywhere. And the last thing her newly reinstated goodwill with the public needed was for her to cause a scene with their golden boy. So she balled up her hand and swung it to her side. But not before Dash caught a glimpse of the massive Asscher-cut engagement ring from Monty.

"Where is good old Mr. Smyth, anyway?" Dash asked. "I want to give him my condolences."

Joan bit the inside of her cheek. She deserved this. And worse. But that didn't mean it still didn't hurt. That she didn't want to shrivel up into nothingness rather than endure Dash's contempt for one more moment. But Monty was an essential part of tonight's plan, so she replied with the lie she'd prepared in advance. "Harry thought it best he not be here tonight. That for the sake of our chances with the Academy, it should be Dash and Davis alone this evening. Especially since you weren't at the premiere."

Dash grinned sarcastically and shook his head. "I was a little busy...recuperating," he drawled. "You might not have heard, but I was stabbed. In the back, as it happens."

God, this wasn't going to work, was it?

But Dash kept going, sighing, something sad and resigned in his eyes. "If it makes you feel better, I should really be thanking you. You encouraged me to stop buying into this whole charade, to stop selling a version of myself I think people want. You told me what I saw was what I got with you. I should've believed you, not the lovesick schoolgirl performance you gave me. But at least it made me realize that pretending to be something you're not only leads to heartbreak. You taught me that. So thank you."

Her throat was choked with tears, knowing what that admission cost him. A strange mixture of pride in his newfound self-confidence and guilt at the evident hurt in his words roiled in her stomach. But she was saved from responding by the man at the microphone finally ending his little speech and waving his arm in a sweeping motion in Joan and Dash's direction.

Usherettes, in black satin dresses that resembled the uniforms of cigarette girls with their short tutus, came to either side of them and proffered their hands. It probably would've helped if she or Dash had listened to a word the man was saying. He nodded at them, and without thinking, she looked at Dash, silently asking, "What do we do now?" She was touched to find him looking back, a moment of shared connection still possible in spite of everything.

She smiled and took the hand of the usherette, who whispered under her breath, "You're supposed to step in the cement now."

Joan smiled again, beaming for the crowd with a more earnest look. She stepped forward and her heels squelched into the wet cement. She looked over as Dash did the same, digging his dress shoes into the slab. They looked at each other, and she grinned in disbelief. It was wild that this was happening. What a concept, enshrining your footprints in wet cement. It was ludicrous when you stopped to think about it. He answered with a laugh, the first genuine one she'd heard all evening, and she couldn't suppress the flicker of hope that sprang to life in her chest.

The next few moments were a blur as the cameras flashed and the crowd cheered. The usherettes helped them off the slab, making sure they stepped out and away so as not to disturb their freshly made prints. They offered them towels and clean shoes before gesturing them to their knees and handing them both pens to sign their names in the cement.

"Ladies first," Dash drawled and the crowd ate it up, women all aflutter while the men cheered.

Joan had wondered for years what she would write if this moment ever came. The first time she'd ever gone to the beach in California she'd practiced writing her name in the sand, imagining it was this hallowed courtyard. Should she go for something funny? *Dear Sid, you owe me a new pair of shoes.*

She looked at the man next to her. Dash was watching her with curiosity, the hostility in his gaze softened. He lifted his shoulders a little as if to say "What are you waiting for?"

"You'll have to excuse me." She smiled at the emcee, a nervous laugh escaping her. "I'm used to someone else writing the words for me to say." That earned a chuckle from the crowd. But Dash simply continued to study her, and if she didn't know better, she'd almost say he was concerned.

"I'll go first," he murmured, extending his hand to the usherette and gripping the pen she set there without tearing his gaze from Joan. It was kind and considerate, everything she knew to be true of the man he was. She smiled, blinking back tears.

"Why not?" she crowed, trying to hide the sudden paralysis and emotion that had gripped her. "You like to do everything first anyway. You won your Oscar first, after all." But she cast him a look of pure gratitude.

"I have no doubt Miss Davis will be joining that club shortly," he replied, looking directly at the reporters. He could've mugged for the cameras then, given them that phony Hollywood playboy patina they all expected. But that version of Dash was nowhere to be found. Instead, there was something heartfelt in his voice that fanned a flicker of hope, letting it grow to a more constant flame. Some part of him still cared for her. Or at least respected her.

He leaned over and dashed something off. "Dear Sid, May this cement our friendship," it read. She couldn't suppress a genuine giggle. It was funny and playful, even a bit corny, but it was Dash

Howard through and through. He added the date, "February 26, 1937" and then signed his name with a flourish.

Now it was her turn, and she knew at last what to write. The only thing she could. It wasn't funny nor clever. It was just what she felt.

She leaned over, feeling the tip of the special pen drag in the cement. "May happiness always find you and your heart guide you in all things," she inscribed, feeling Dash watch her as she carved out every word. She looked at him, willing him to understand that these words weren't for her. They were for him. They were all she wished for.

With that done, all that was left was for them to place their handprints in the remaining space. Joan leaned forward and pressed her hands into the cement. It was cold under her fingertips, like mud squelching between her toes. She leaned her weight into it, really trying to make a lasting impression. A hysterical laugh bubbled up from her, but she turned it into a movie-star smile before it exploded from her lips. That's what she'd always been trying to do, wasn't it? Make a lasting impression. Well, she'd gotten her wish. In more ways than one. Because she'd made a lasting impression on Dash as well. She just prayed it wasn't as permanent as something written in cement. She glanced over at him as he laughed at the cement rising between his fingers.

He looked at her, nodded at the message she'd written, and the ridiculous position they were both in. "At least you can say it was worth it," he told her, a sad smile ghosting across his face. "You got what you wanted."

Cement underneath her fingernails, the man she loved next to her, smiling but hating her? No, that wasn't at all what she wanted. And she was dying to tell him that. But it had to wait. They were surrounded by cameras and fans. She needed to stick to the plan.

At the prompting of the usherettes, they leaned back onto their heels and held their cement-coated hands up to the cameras. Joan smiled until her face hurt, and her arms were sore. Then all at once it was over. The emcee waved more ushers out, who started to move the press toward the barriers, where the crowds were already beginning to thin. A prerecorded announcement reminded everyone that the event was over but to be sure and check out *Reno Rendezvous,* now in its fourth month in theaters.

Someone handed Joan and Dash each a towel dipped in warm water, and she got to work cleaning the cement from between her carefully manicured fingers. She'd opted for clear polish, so they wouldn't get marred in the process.

Dash pawed at his hands with the towel, obviously in a hurry to go. He made his way across the courtyard, looking for his driver. She watched him walk away as he ambled to the street corner, keeping his head down, trying to go unnoticed, shifting back into the uneven posture that was his true stance.

She stumbled, her heel getting caught in the hem of her dress as she tried to stand. But she needed to go before he realized what was happening. She looked back and saw Arlene waiting patiently, bathed in the streetlights, her and Dash's new symbols of immortality still wet and glistening in the spotlights.

This was it. She hoped it worked.

CHAPTER 28

DASH WAITED ON THE CURB, HOPING HIS DRIVER WAS nearby, and glanced up at the night sky. The blanket of stars he'd come to love so well on his ranch were invisible, obscured by the neon gleam of storefronts and nightclubs up and down Hollywood Boulevard and the overpowering glow of the spotlights signaling the absurd ritual he and Joan had just enacted. All he could see were lights and goddamn palm trees.

A black Cadillac pulled up to the curb, and he reached for the sleek handle, hopping into the back. He didn't pay any attention to the driver; they knew where they were going.

He tugged at the tie around his neck, pulling it until it was completely loose and hanging around his collar. Still, he couldn't breathe. The lights and the cameras had him practically crawling out of his skin. He'd forgotten how much the whole thing grated on him. Or maybe it wasn't that. Maybe it was that it was the first time he'd seen Joan since she'd emotionally sucker punched him at a Reno courthouse.

He felt a bit dazed. By Joan, yes, but also by what had just happened. He'd wanted to hate tonight. It was the antithesis of what he loved about his job—a dog-and-pony show of the highest order. But the sight of his handwriting and his hand and footprints enshrined in cement had made him surprisingly emotional.

It was a reminder that the work mattered. When he and Joan and Harry Evets were turned to dust, that little piece of concrete would still be there. Someone would see his name and know that he'd lived and been worth remembering.

Maybe, he realized, that was why these things meant so much to Joan. They weren't about fame; they were about making a mark on the world nobody could erase. He could understand the appeal of that. Joan had looked magnificent tonight, her shoulders bare and tantalizing in the spotlights. But her usual movie star mega-watt smile had scarcely concealed a sense of unease. There'd been that flicker of self-doubt when she'd tried to apologize to him. This should've been a victory for her, the prelude to the Oscar she deserved—and she had looked sad. Strangely, that made him sad too.

They drove north on Hollywood Boulevard, and Dash waited for the driver to make the right turn that would take him back to his home in the hills. But instead, the driver turned left back toward Sunset. "Have you gone screwy or something, Bill? The house is the other way."

"Sorry, old chap, slight change of plans." Dash was startled to see the man in his chauffeur's uniform and cap was not his driver of the last five years, but instead none other than Monty Smyth.

"Monty?"

"Guilty as charged."

"What the hell are you doing here? Where's Bill?"

"Bill is...indisposed."

"What does that mean?" At that, Monty shot him a backwards glance and grimaced.

"Dreadfully sorry, but it means I gave him $100 and told him to bugger off because I needed the car for the night."

What was happening? Why was Monty buying off his driver?

Had he entered some strange alternate universe where he was living in one of those screwball pictures he'd made with Joan? He reached down and pinched himself. Hard. He yelped.

"You're not dreaming," crowed Monty. "Sorry to disappoint." Monty nearly veered into a parked car and the person behind him honked at them.

"Watch where you're going," Dash growled.

"Sorry!"

Of all the bizarre situations he'd found himself in over the years, this might take the cake. Dash looked out the window and watched bright lights give way to quieter neighborhoods as Monty barreled down La Brea. He had a sinking feeling he knew where they were heading, and when Monty turned left on Wilshire, it confirmed his fears. "No."

"No, what?"

"No, you're not taking me there."

"Where?"

"Oh, come off it. You know where—the Cocoanut Grove."

Monty didn't answer.

Dash was about five seconds from jumping over the bench seats and throttling the man. But he took a deep breath and asked, "What is this, anyway? Isn't it enough that you won the girl? You gotta kidnap me too?"

Monty laughed, but it was clear he didn't find the situation remotely funny. "You're a bigger fool than I thought."

"Don't have to tell me twice," Dash grumbled. "But you're not being very chivalrous about this. When the knight wins his lady fair, he's supposed to ride off into the sunset and leave his competition to nurse his broken heart in silence."

Monty chuckled and slammed on the brakes as someone changed lanes in front of them. Jesus, he was going to die while the man who was marrying the woman he'd loved was driving. How was that for dramatic irony.

Acting as if nothing had happened, Monty peeled away when the light changed green. "Let me ask you something. Did you ever believe Joan was marrying me because we were madly in love?"

Dash winced. He didn't want to be rude, but he wasn't a liar. "Well, no, but—"

"And when you were in Reno, did you believe she was in love with you?"

"Like a lunkhead, yeah, I did."

"So why wouldn't you trust your instincts then?"

"I think it's pretty obvious why. They were wrong. I still don't believe she's in love with you, but heck, what do I know? Maybe you two have got something a sap like me can never understand."

Monty darted in and out of three lanes, trying to veer around traffic and nearly hitting four separate vehicles in the process. A cacophony of horns and colorful language followed them down the block.

"You could slow down, you know. I'm not in a hurry."

"But I am. She won't like it if I'm late."

Dash didn't know who *she* was. But he had an idea. And he was pretty sure he wasn't going to like it. "Fine. Ram us into a traffic light for all I care. But answer one question: Are you in love with Joan?"

"No, I'm in love with Jerry Scott," Monty stated matter-of-factly. "I thought you would've cottoned on to that by now, but I guess people see what they want to see."

Dash's mouth fell open. Did Monty Smyth just admit he was gay? And in love with his former roommate? Dash had seen those pictures of the two of them swanning around their pool. He sure as hell wouldn't have ever taken a photo like that with Flynn Banks. But he knew better than anyone the weird shit the studio would make you do for publicity. He'd chalked it up to that. God, maybe he really was an idiot.

"Does Joan know?"

"Of course, what do you take me for?"

Everything was suddenly making sense. Joan's determination to marry Monty and their sudden engagement. Monty's lack of jealousy. His insistence Joan explore a relationship with Dash. But it didn't matter, did it? Because Joan still had thrown him over. Chosen her career, her independence, and a loveless marriage over a life together. Hadn't she?

"Tell me something, Dash. Don't you think that Joan has always had something of a touch of the martyr about her?"

Dash thought about it. The stories she'd told about being unable to love. About her mother. Her sister. Sacrificing everything for the career she loved. "Yes, but only when it comes to what she loves more than anything. She'd do anything to keep that safe."

"Precisely. You are that thing. She broke your heart to protect you."

"That makes no sense."

"Don't worry, it will."

Monty bypassed the glamorous entrance to the Ambassador Hotel, complete with red-carpeted stairs, and peeled off into an alley. Dash knew before Monty screeched to a halt that he'd guessed correctly where they'd been headed. He hadn't been here in five years—and the last time he had, Joan had kneed him in the crotch. What a metaphor.

"I take it this is our final destination," he growled.

Monty grinned at him sheepishly. Dash had no doubt Joan had told him the whole story. Hell, he'd probably read about it in the papers. "Go through the kitchen and into the Cocoanut Grove through the back entrance. Joan is waiting for you at your booth."

Their booth. The words made Dash's insides twist into knots. She'd remembered. Five years and he hadn't come near this place. He'd haunted every other nighttime hot spot in Hollywood—the Troc, the Cinegrill at the Roosevelt, Chasen's, the Chateau, the list went on. But he'd never set foot inside this ridiculous chintz tropical paradise since the night Joan—no, not Joan, Leda Price—had ruined everything. He didn't have to now either. He could hop out of the car, sprint down the alley, and hail a cab. But something in him was propelling him to go inside. To find out what all this was about.

Dash muttered, "God damn it," and reached for the door handle, the crisp California spring air hitting him in the face. He was halfway out of the car when Monty called after him.

"Dash, wait. Can I ask you something?"

Dash paused, gripping the shiny silver door handle for strength and taking a deep breath. "Sure."

"Are you still in love with Joan Davis?"

Dash snorted. It was preposterous. Still in love with Joan Davis? After what she'd done? But then he closed his eyes, wrinkled his nose, and pinched his brow. He'd said when he came back to Hollywood he was going to stop pretending. So far, he'd done nothing to make good on that. Maybe it started with admitting to himself that he still loved Joan. That he hated what she'd done to him, but that he could never ever hate *her*.

He shrugged, defeated. What was the use in lying to himself? To Monty? "I am...but don't hold it against me."

Dash emerged from the busy kitchen into the dimly lit cavern of the Cocoanut Grove. Everything looked the way it had that night.

The papier-mâché palm trees flanked the dance floor, the stuffed fake monkeys perched in their boughs. The room was choked with cigarette smoke, a boozy haze, and the weight of a hundred Hollywood secrets. He had to laugh. Here he was, resolving to be himself, something rare and real, and he was in a room that epitomized this town—all surface illusion and hucksterism for the sake of glamour. And more goddamn palm trees.

He didn't have to look for Joan. He knew where she was. The back corner, tucked away from the stage in a booth for two. He'd chosen it that night, bypassed the very public table Harry had reserved for him at the front of the stage and taken Joan to the little alcove where they might have some privacy. Where he could have a date that was more than a publicity stunt, show her who he truly was, and get to know something of her real self too. It might've worked, too, if not for Leda Price and her schemes. The memory still left a bitter taste in his mouth. Maybe that was the moment everything broke. Maybe they never really had a chance in Reno after that.

He was about to head in the direction of their booth when something froze him in his tracks. The voice emanating from the stage that was currently blocked from view by a row of palm trees. It was Bing Crosby. He'd know that velvet croon anywhere. Bing had been singing that night. A fresh new face in Hollywood then. He listened harder and groaned at the crackle of the lyrics through the microphone. "They're writing songs of love, but not for me," Crosby opined. A little on the nose, wasn't it? He'd eat his hat if Crosby had been the original singer on the bill for tonight. No, this was purposeful.

He ran a hand down his face as Crosby intoned, "Although I can't forget the memory of her kiss, I guess she's not for me." The memory of that searing first kiss Joan had laid on him the night on the Truckee riverbank came to Dash unbidden. She'd accused him of setting her up for publicity. But she'd been the one stringing him along the whole time. Hadn't she?

Christ, he needed a drink. And here there was only one way to get one. He had to take a seat at a table. He walked the perimeter of the dance floor until he came to a row of booths lining the back wall. He couldn't see her yet, but he knew she was in the one on the end, farthest from everything.

He took a few more steps and she came into view, wearing the same black-and-white number she'd had on at Grauman's. She couldn't have beat him here by more than a few minutes. Not the way Monty had been driving. She couldn't see him yet; he was hidden by a palm tree. So he took a minute to really take her in. She was still gorgeous. That was hardly surprising. From her perfectly coiffed hair to that gown that embraced her shoulders and her neck like a lover, Joan was every inch the movie star she'd dedicated herself to being. But there was something else there too—a hard line to her mouth, a tense set to her shoulders, the ghost of exhaustion under her eyes, and the telltale nervous drum of her manicure on the table. She was afraid. The most uncertain he'd ever seen her. And in that moment he decided he'd hear her out, whatever she had to say.

He slid into the booth. "Funny seeing you here."

She smiled, but her lip quivered and curled. God, she was so jittery. It should reassure him, make him feel like he had the upper hand. But instead it made him nervous too.

Before she could reply, the waiter was there, ready to take Dash's order. "Scotch, neat," he gritted out, not taking his eyes off Joan. While working on his ranch, he hadn't taken a single drink after that first night. He'd used the work, the exhaustion of a hard day's labor, to numb the loss of Joan and the reminder of her betrayal. But tonight, he needed some liquid courage.

Joan twisted a napkin in her hands. He was certain if it were paper and not cloth she would've torn it to shreds by now. "Thank you for meeting me here."

"You didn't leave me much choice in the matter."

Joan winced. "Sorry, but I didn't think you'd speak to me unless I took matters into my own hands."

Dash sighed and ran a hand down his face. "What is this then?"

"An apology."

Dash smirked, his face twisting into something he barely even recognized. "You already apologized at the ceremony. If that's all this is, I'll go." He moved to get up and was intercepted by the waiter who already had his drink. Dash looked back and forth between the server, who looked utterly confused, and Joan, who had a pleading look on her face. He'd ordered it, hadn't he? He might as well drink it.

"Fine. You've got as long as it takes me to finish this Scotch." He sat back down and reached for the drink, wincing at his first taste of alcohol in months.

Joan eyed his glass longingly, and even though he was still angry with her, Dash couldn't stand the look in her eyes. She looked like a lost little girl. She looked, in fact, like Mildred Shalk. "Hell, you need this more than I do." He slid his glass across the table, savoring the few sips he'd taken.

"No, don't—"

"Take it. I insist." Joan shot him a grateful look, picked up the glass, and knocked the whole thing back in one go. Damn, she was one hell of a woman.

"You're right," she began, smoothing the edges of the tablecloth and then gripping the table as if she were holding onto it for dear life. "This isn't just an apology. I brought you here tonight because I have to tell you something. Something I should've told you in Reno. But first, I need to explain what happened. Will you let me? I promise if you still hate me afterward, I'll never bother you again."

"I don't hate you," he replied before he'd even had a chance to think. So much for the upper hand. Crosby finished his song and launched into a rendition of "When Your Lover Has Gone." Hell, didn't this guy know any happy songs? Or at least songs that weren't about your lover walking out on you? Were these the songs Joan had asked for? If so, her choices weren't doing her any favors. They evoked bad memories.

Joan had perked up at his retort. "I'm glad."

Dash was getting frustrated. Couldn't she get on with it? He was half afraid some photographer was gonna pop out from behind the palm trees and snag yet another picture of them doing something that could be misinterpreted. "Look, Joan, if you're on a public apology tour because you think it'll help you win your Oscar, it's not necessary. If you don't win, the Academy is a pack of idiots."

"I don't care about the Oscar."

If Dash had still had his drink, he would've spat it out. "What? Of course you care about it. What was all this for, then?"

"That's what I'm trying to tell you, Dash Howard. I don't care about the Oscar because I realized it's not worth it. Not without you."

Hope sparked in his chest, but he didn't want to fan the flame. Not yet. "Come off it, Joan. All I've ever been to you is a thorn in your side. Maybe if I'm being generous, a warm body."

Joan gasped, clearly shocked at his words, but then he saw a hint of her old fire flickering in her eyes. "I didn't realize we were throwing a pity party at the Grove tonight. Luckily, I booked your favorite booth for it."

Dash chuckled. This was more like it. He didn't know what Joan wanted tonight, but he sure didn't like seeing her look like a lost child. No, if he was going to go toe-to-toe with her, it damn well better be with Joan Davis the movie star.

"You set me up for public humiliation, Joan. And now, what? You regret it?"

"God, yes. But not for the reasons you think. It was the biggest mistake of my life."

"Mine too." Somehow he didn't think they were talking about the same thing. "Believing you loved me, I mean."

She looked him dead in the eye then, holding his gaze as Crosby transitioned into "Once in a Blue Moon." Finally, at least a song that didn't make Dash want to drink until he blacked out. "I did," she whispered. "I do."

His heart ached at the words. Ones he'd waited for. Hoped for. But it still didn't make any sense. "Then why did you do it, Joan? You could've socked me in the jaw and dropped me into the river alongside your wedding ring and it would've hurt less." He was startled to hear the note of sorrow in his voice alongside the rage. No, he had mastered this. He'd spent months alone on a ranch to get this out of his system. "If you wanted to go through with the divorce, if you thought we were moving too fast, why didn't you tell me?" he growled, his voice breaking on the last word.

Joan swallowed and held her head high. He got the feeling they were finally getting somewhere. "I've got two words for you: Leda Price."

Hearing the name of that harpy was like being doused in ice water. But no, she couldn't be behind this. She was the one who exposed his and Joan's accidental marriage in the first place. What would it have served her to tear them apart? "No, you would've told me, would've talked to me if it was just Leda," Dash insisted.

"We'd been through this once before. You spent years believing I'd set you up, was in cahoots with her. I would've understood if it was something that simple. We could've worked it out together, faced down the gorgon of Hollywood as a team."

"A braver woman would have done that," Joan admitted. She paused and seemed to change her mind about something. "Maybe if it had only been Leda, I could've. But once Josephine came into the picture, I got scared. I didn't see any other way."

The name of his first wife crashed into him, like a monstrous tidal wave that'd sprung from calm seas. "Josephine? What has she got to do with this? With us? You couldn't possibly have thought I was still in love with her."

Joan looked sad. Sadder than he'd ever seen her. "No, it wasn't that. I was afraid she'd break you. Afraid she'd make you believe all the terrible things she'd convinced you were true about yourself. The things I'd hoped I'd helped you see were a lie. Dash, the real reason I went through with the divorce and didn't tell you is because Leda Price had a letter from Josephine, offering to tell the world all about how you used her to become a star and then deserted her. For a pretty penny, of course."

"But that's absurd, the opposite is true."

"You know that and I know that. But the public doesn't. You gave everything up for this job. A job you told me was your only source of happiness. How could I be the one responsible for taking it from you?"

Dash put his hands to the back of his head and looked at the ceiling, barely making out its art deco tiles through the paper palm fronds. He wished he was outside right now. Far away from all of this.

"Look at me, Dash." He snapped his head to attention and met her eyes. They took his breath away. He'd committed them to memory, their rich brown color and the flecks of bronze that dotted the center of her eye, turning her iris to liquid gold when she was emotional. He'd thought of them every day for the last seven months. And they still had the power to rob him of speech.

"I was afraid, darling. Afraid of what she would do to you. She'd already taken so much from you. I convinced myself that I'd been right all along. That love cost too much and that I couldn't let that cost be allowing Josephine to cut out another piece of your heart. She'd already taken enough pieces of you. And you'd just come back to yourself, at last. You deserved to be protected from all that. So I took Leda's deal—and broke both our hearts."

He gaped at her as if her words had sucked all the air from the room, looking at her like she was a miracle. "You cared for me that much that you sacrificed your own happiness for my career?"

Dash could barely process this new information. The wheels in his head started turning. Josephine? Joan had gone through with the divorce, broke his heart, all because of Josephine? Because he'd been a coward. He'd been so afraid that someone—his fans, a starlet, Joan—would prove Josephine right, would confirm what she'd made him fear was true. That the real Dash Howard would never be good enough for anyone. Instead, he'd become a self-fulfilling prophecy. And opened the door for that woman to take even more from him. The only thing that maybe ever really mattered. He sat in stunned silence.

Joan reached across the table and took his hand. "I'm so sorry. I should've come to you. I should've believed. In love. In us."

Dash gripped her fingers so tightly they turned white in his fist. "No, Joan, you did what you thought was right. What I had convinced you was the only choice. And you were probably right too. If you'd come to me and told me that about Josephine, I would've run away with my tail between my legs. I would've thought we were licked. Not because I didn't believe in you, but because I didn't believe in myself. I've learned a lot about who I want to be from now on while I've been gone. So maybe you did me a favor." His voice was choked with tears now. Realizing what a fool he'd been. How easily he'd believed the worst of her. And of himself.

"There's something else," she gulped.

He furiously blinked the tears from his eyes. How could there be more? But he owed Joan a promise. One he should've made clear months ago. "Whatever it is, we'll face it together."

She hung her head and became suddenly very interested in the pattern of the table's wood grain. "It wasn't only you Leda wanted to blackmail. I have a secret too."

He could tell it was costing her to admit it, whatever it was. But suddenly, she looked up and jutted out her chin, putting on a brave face as a steely look came into her eye. "I'm not ashamed of it, you understand. But I know what people in this country are like—and what it could mean for my career if it ever got out."

Good God, what had she done? "Tell me, Joan. Tell me and let me carry this secret with you."

She swallowed and spat it all out in one breath. "Imadeastagfilm."

"Come again?" Had he heard her correctly? He could barely make out one word from the next.

She cringed, her face scrunching up and that adorable wrinkle between her eyes appearing. "I made a stag film." This time she overenunciated every word.

"As in?"

"As in I had sex on camera for money, yes."

He was speechless. Joan Davis—the woman he'd once believed was so haughty butter wouldn't melt in her mouth—had taken off her clothes and made love to someone and they'd filmed it. He started laughing.

She threw the napkin she'd been trying to tear to shreds on the table. "What's so funny?"

He recovered himself. God, he was cocking this up. "It's not you, I swear." He caught his breath. "Well, it kind of is. It's hard for me to imagine you doing that."

She smirked. "Why? As I recall, you were never disappointed." There was a hint of the Joan he loved. But he knew that note of confidence in her voice was false. She was trying to recover, to act like it wasn't a big deal.

"I assure you, there are zero complaints in that department," he said. Her shoulders lowered an inch. "But the whole ice queen thing… I didn't think you had it in you. I thought maybe you were only that passionate behind closed doors."

"I needed the money," she explained.

"Joan, look at me." He squeezed her hand. She met his gaze, and he could see the internal war happening behind her eyes. "Nobody needs to know."

She gave him a hard look. "I refuse to be ashamed. Even to you."

"Nor would I want you to be! I'm just trying to figure out what I ever did or said that would make you think I couldn't handle this. That between me, you, and Harry we couldn't work this out. Protect all of us from Leda and her slippery ways. Hell, you could strip naked at this table and run around the club for all I care."

"I've upset you," she whispered.

"Yes, but not for the reasons you think," he continued. "I'm disgusted with myself."

"What? Why?"

"Because I should've known better," he confessed, squeezing her hand ever so slightly and trying to hide the barbed-wire edges in his voice, how much this was costing him. "It wasn't only Josephine, was it? It was this too. This is what Leda threatened you with."

She was so overcome with emotion she couldn't speak. Instead, she nodded her head. She reached her hand out to touch his cheek and he leaned into it. "Leda wanted you to hate me. Said I had to make sure you did or she'd publish everything. She told me I had to be cruel, to make you suffer. She wanted to make me a villain in your eyes. By my own hand."

Joan was straining in her seat, her fury causing her to rise. Dash wrapped his strong hands around her wrists and urged her to sit back down, calming her. "She could've never made me truly hate you. Never make me stop wanting you."

"You still want me? Even after what I did? Even now, knowing I kept all of this from you?"

"Of course I still want you. I never stopped wanting you. I hated myself for it, but your fire, your passion, your…everything—I knew I would never love anyone the way I love you. But Joan, you should've told me."

There was so much regret in her eyes. "I should've been braver. Should've trusted we could find our way through together, instead of thinking I was just like my sister, my mother, like all the people I've watched love turn into shells of themselves."

"No," he gritted out. "No. You were protecting me. Both of us. I should've been smarter. I felt all along that something wasn't right. I wasted so much time thinking it was me. Feeling sorry for myself, feeling like once again I'd come up short."

"I know, I know," she whispered, tears welling in her eyes. "I'm so sorry, Dash. I hate myself for making you feel that way. You are enough, you have always been enough."

He nuzzled her hand before tangling her fingers in his. "I've been such a fool."

"No, I was the fool. For not standing up to Leda. For feeling like letting you go was the only way, for believing that loving someone was as dangerous and as reckless as I'd always feared it would be."

He lifted her hand to his mouth, kissing her knuckles. "All right, it's settled then. We were both fools. Prize idiots, really."

She caressed his face, and he leaned his cheek into her touch. God, how he'd missed the feel of her skin against his. "I missed you, Dash. I wish I'd had the courage to tell you that first night in Reno and every day since that I love you."

He placed his hand over hers and turned his mouth to kiss the inside of her palm ever so tenderly. Joan loved him. Him. Dash Howard. He wanted to say he couldn't believe it. But that's what had ruined everything in the first place, wasn't it? He did believe it. He cherished it. And her.

"I could kill Leda for the time she's stolen from us," he growled.

"Yes, but then you'd go to jail and I'd lose you all over again." Joan gave him a watery grin, and they both laughed.

"Look at us, the King and Queen of Hollywood brought down by love." He tangled his fingers with hers, wanting to forget where his hand ended and hers began.

"Not brought down by, no. Triumphing in it." She flashed him a thousand-watt grin, one that still had a hint of something shy about it, and if he hadn't already been sitting down, it would've brought him to his knees.

She looked like she wanted to say more, a heavy weight settling onto her shoulders for a moment. But just as quickly it was gone and she was absentmindedly stroking her thumb against the inside of his palm.

"Do you want to get out of here?" he asked. Those nights in Reno were running through his memory now faster than light. He'd decided she was wearing entirely too many clothes.

"No."

"No?"

She chuckled. "I mean, I do, but maybe we should start a little slower this time. Besides, there's one more surprise I have for you tonight. Will you dance with me?"

"Here? Where everyone can see? What about Monty? The engagement?"

"I'm sick of doing things because of how they'll look to other people. I want to dance with the man I love."

Dash would never tire of hearing her say those words. He took her hand and wordlessly led her out onto the dance floor. He needn't have worried. Everyone was too wrapped up in each other to care that two of Hollywood's biggest stars had stepped onto the floor. He took her in his arms and waited for the music to start.

He recognized the song before Crosby even started warbling the words. It was "Cheek to Cheek." The song they'd been playing the night he'd danced with Joan at the ranch. The night he'd first realized he was falling for her, even if he didn't want to. "You remembered." He met her eyes and found them dancing with tears.

"How could I forget? I was so mad at Monty for insisting I dance with you that night." She chuckled. "Little did he know what he was starting."

Dash followed the instructions of the music and pressed his cheek to hers, pulling her closer to him. "Oh, I think he knew perfectly well."

Joan giggled, a trilling little laugh that he loved more than the sound of his favorite song. Which, he decided, would be this one from now on. He palmed her lower back and twirled them both across the floor, as Joan let out a breathy sigh of delight. There was still so much to discuss. What to do about Jerry and Monty. The engagement. Leda. Josephine! But it could wait. Everything could wait. All that mattered for now was that Joan was in his arms again.

CHAPTER 29

JOAN ARRIVED AT THE TOP OF THE STAIRS AT THE ENTRANCE to the ballroom and took a deep breath. The brisk early March air had chilled her in the short walk from the valet to the inside of the Biltmore, and she absentmindedly rubbed at the gooseflesh on her bare arms, trying to warm herself.

She fluffed the red, black-tipped feathers lining the neckline of her black velvet gown and began to descend into the room. She scanned the crowd, looking for Dash. And, if she was honest, for Leda Price. There were no secrets between Joan and Dash now. They'd tried to be discreet. Harry was still working out how to keep Leda quiet.

A bubble of dread rose in Joan's throat. Seemingly, Leda still bought the pretense of her and Monty's engagement, but they'd been drawing it out for ages. What if Leda was tired of waiting and decided to blow everything to pieces? Tonight would be the night for it, if there ever was one. She hated that Leda Price still held so much power over them, but she was hard pressed to see any other way than continuing to play her game until Harry devised a solution. Likely in the form of an egregiously large check. And even then, how long would that hold her? How long before she blew through the money and decided their secrets were worth more?

She'd said she wanted to destroy Joan, to make Dash hate her.

What if she published the story or, hell, showed up and grabbed the mic during the ceremony and told the whole world? What then? Maybe she wasn't holding out for a payout, but the optimum moment to humiliate Joan. Her stomach churned at the thought. She needed to get ahold of herself.

The Academy had outdone themselves this year. The annual banquet was always an elegant affair, but this was truly extravagant. Lush, velvet burgundy curtains lined the wide archways surrounding the ballroom. At its center were the bandstand and the acceptance podium. The bandstand was backed by the same velvet curtains and topped with a proscenium arch displaying ornate, gold-gilt seashell patterns. There were tables all around the room festooned with arrangements of orchids and freesia spilling over onto the fine china and crystal they'd used for the place settings.

The bandstand had a full orchestra, already playing a twinkling version of "Puttin' On the Ritz." A grand piano stood behind the banquet table at the front of the stage, and the table was lined with the Oscars on pedestals. Joan's breath caught in her throat as the light hit their gold surface and they glistened and sparkled in the warm light of the ballroom. They were like a siren beckoning her forward, and she found herself walking down the stairs as if in a trance. There it was—the symbol of what she'd almost given everything for, the mark of approval and success she'd nearly chosen over Dash.

As if she'd summoned Dash with her thoughts, he appeared before her, looking stunning in a tuxedo, a black satin bow-tie at his throat. He'd pomaded his hair back in the current style, and she mourned the loss of his untamed curls. He offered her his arm. She gladly took it and chuckled when he followed her gaze to the table of statuettes. "Still mean what you said about not caring if you win?"

She looked up at him and smiled. "Would you believe me if I said yes?"

"Ha, no, not really."

This was nice. Being able to tease each other. "It would mean a lot to me, I can't lie. But it would mean more because it's yours too. I wouldn't be here if it weren't for your sensitive, thoughtful performance. And for the support you gave me on set. You made tonight possible."

"It was easy. I believed in you."

She swallowed and fought back the urge to cry. It meant so much to hear him say those words. After everything. She squeezed his arm in thanks, and he ushered her to their table. The Academy had placed them nearest to the stage, and she hoped that boded well for success. Harry was already there, with some blowsy new starlet hanging on his arm as his guest. Joan looked at him, raised her eyebrows, and he shrugged as if to say, "What's it to you?"

Dash released her arm, and she immediately missed his warmth and his strength beneath her hand. A rush of nerves flooded her stomach and her whole body tingled, anxiety overwhelming her. He'd been a pillar of support as they'd walked through the ballroom in ways she hadn't realized until the solidity of his arm was gone.

But that was the case with Dash, wasn't it? She hadn't realized how much she'd had, how much she needed him, until he was gone. It was a lesson she never wanted to have to learn again. It was why she was still terrified of Leda. Because she couldn't bear the idea of what could happen if Leda really did expose them. She didn't know if they could weather that—or whether she was brave enough to find out.

Arlene arrived at the table breathless, the exhilaration of attending her first Academy Awards pink on her face. She was dressed smartly in an expertly tailored emerald women's suit, an adorable flouncy pale-green bow at her neck. “Hello, everyone,” she chirped, trying to look at all of them and marvel at the finery surrounding them at the same time.

“Welcome,” Harry bellowed. “To Evets’ Studio’s budding star scribe.”

“And director, Harry,” Joan added.

“What?” he sputtered.

“It has always been my dream,” Arlene admitted.

“Well, you win tonight and we’ll talk about it,” Harry grumbled.

“She doesn’t need to win to prove herself,” Joan protested. “She could run circles around half the men on the studio payroll.”

Arlene blushed deeply, and Joan swore she could see it extend straight to her toes. This could be a big night for them both. A night that could change everything.

Dash leaned over and kissed Arlene on the cheek, welcoming her. Then he reached for another chair at the table, pulling it out for Joan, resting his hand on the top of the chair. She brushed her manicured hand, painted with deep burgundy polish to match the feathers on her gown, over his as she swept past him to sit down. His fingers quivered under hers, the slightest movement, reaching to meet her. She briefly stroked his hand, reminding him that they were in this together. Regardless of who won or lost.

She reached for the glass of champagne at her place setting. The bubbles floating to the top matched her insides. The persistent trill of anxiety making her feel as if she were a bottle of champagne someone had shaken.

Joan looked distracted. Tonight should be her greatest triumph. She should look like Arlene, rosy-cheeked and flushed with joy, soaking in every moment. Instead, Dash was dismayed to find her like a drooping hothouse flower, the extravagant feathers lining the neckline of her gown like wilted petals.

He wanted this for her so much. And he wanted her to enjoy it, to revel in it. He leaned over and whispered in her ear, "Relax. They'd be crazy not to give it to you." This didn't seem to help. Instead, her shoulders crept even closer to her ears.

The evening passed in a blur of champagne and awards speeches, punctuated by jokes from the host, George Jessel, and the odd one-liner from the presenters. The first half of the evening had been dedicated to the technical awards, categories like editing and art direction, as well as scoring and song. Harry was pleased, as the studio had already taken home three trophies, one for their picture's editing and two others for projects Dash and Joan had nothing to do with.

They all held their breath when it got to Arlene's category, and Dash watched as Joan reached for her former assistant's hand and grasped it tightly. Their entire table erupted into thunderous applause when the presenter called Arlene's name. Arlene sat in her stair, stunned, tears rising in her eyes. Joan gripped her in a rapturous embrace, pulled her from her seat, and prompted her toward the stage. Arlene gave one last look over her shoulder at them both and shot them a grateful, watery smile.

"I can't believe it," she murmured into the microphone as she was handed the trophy. "Um, I'd like to thank the Academy, of course. Harry Evets, for taking a chance on me and this story. Dash Howard, for being brave enough to give the performance of his life."

Dash swelled with pride at Arlene's acknowledgment. Her words were a gift. They'd not only given him the best material of his career, but they'd helped him realize how essential acting was to his happiness. How he could be so much more outside of the corner the studio had painted him into.

"And to Joan Davis, for trusting me, for fighting for me, for rescuing me from a studio bathroom one day and changing my life. You're my best friend, Joan, and you taught me what it means to be a fighter in this town. To make the world acknowledge you and give you what you deserve. Thank you."

Arlene gave a little curtsy, losing her balance for a moment, and then rushed back down the steps to their table. Joan engulfed her in a hug, showering her with praise as the band started playing strains of the best-song nominees.

Suddenly, they were at Dash's category, Best Actor in a Motion Picture. When they called his name, listed alongside the other impressive names, he smiled and then looked at Joan. She raised her glass in salute to him and whispered, "Good luck." In this moment, on the precipice of the first potential back-to-back acting wins in the brief history of the Oscars' existence, he felt like a fraud.

Here he was. Doing what he'd always done. Pretending to be the King of Hollywood. Keeping his distance from Joan to keep Leda quiet until Harry fixed the problem. Well, to hell with that. It was high time he honor his pledge to himself. Stop pretending. Be as brave, as fierce, as forthright as Joan.

Then it happened. Carmen del Rio, an actress known for her string of pictures as the Mexican Spitfire, inserted her perfectly manicured thumb under the seal of the envelope, cracked it open, and called out his name. Suddenly, Harry was clapping him on the back. Arlene knocked over a glass of champagne, she jumped up so quickly to applaud.

The blond on Harry's arm—Billie, Dash thought he'd heard her say her name was—was applauding wildly and yelling at him over the din about how she'd seen the picture ten times and knew he was going to win. He could barely make out Joan's face through the crowd of people swarming him, but she was smiling, a bright, genuine toothy grin. He wished he could kiss her. He never wanted to spend another night where he couldn't kiss her anytime he wanted.

He rose from his seat, too stunned to do anything but what he knew he was supposed to, and started for the bandstand to accept the award. He had only to cross a ten-foot expanse of a parquet dance floor, having been seated nearest the stage. He took the statue from Carmen, and she offered him a light peck on the cheek and turned to face the crowd. He'd been up here last year. In this exact spot. Only a few months before the world learned he and Joan were married and this entire crazy thing had started.

Yet, standing up here, it seemed like both everything and nothing had changed. Because he was still the same SOB pretending to be someone he was not. It was long past time that he punctured the illusion and was honest with everyone. If he'd been able to be himself, to not hide behind the allure of the studio's version of Dash Howard, maybe Joan wouldn't have broken his heart. Because she would've known that he was strong enough to face whatever came their way together. Instead of being reminded, yet again, that the only way to handle things was on her own. Didn't she deserve to know that he was the kind of man who could face anything? That he was sure enough in himself and who he was that he didn't need to apologize for it.

The cameras flashed and the applause quieted as the bandleader shushed the guests. All Dash could hear was the soft hiss and crackle of the wires attached to the microphone signaling that the world was listening. But all he could see was Joan. Sitting at their table, a look of pride in her eyes and tears streaming down her face. It was time to stop playing Harry's games, stop kowtowing to people like Leda Price, and be Dashiell Howard, a farm boy who happened to like to make movies. If not for himself, then for Joan.

"I'd like to thank the Academy," he began. He looked at Joan again. She gave him a wistful smile and his heart twisted in his chest. "But most of all, I'd like to thank my costar, Joan Davis. This is really her picture. To be frank, every picture we've ever made together was hers. I made some good window dressing to pair with the lady, that's all."

The crowd chuckled. "I wouldn't be up here tonight if it weren't for the wonderfully talented pen of one Miss Arlene Morgan, who you've already honored this evening, and the performance of Joan Davis, which I hope the Academy will be recognizing very shortly."

The bandleader looked at Dash, clearly hoping for a nod that he was finished and could be played off, back to his table. But he wasn't done yet. "It's an incredible honor to be the first person in Hollywood history to win this award two years running. It's a vote of confidence in me and my abilities I never expected. But you see, I came to Hollywood to prove something to myself." He took a breath. "And all I ended up proving was that I'm very good at pretending to be something I'm not. How can I ever prove anything if the measuring stick is being held up to something that doesn't really exist? I need to be enough. Just me." He dared to glance over at Joan and she was clutching her hands to her chest, nodding at him as if to urge him on.

"Enough for myself, for the studio, for the fans listening at home," he continued, suppressing a laugh as the bandleader gave him a strained look. "Acting makes me happy. Knowing that I bring a little levity or joy or escape to your lives makes me happy.

Being a movie star does not. It never has. I realize now it never will. I like performing, being a character, but everything else has always been an act. You all believe me to be a self-made man, a bachelor with not a care in the world. Nothing could be further from the truth. I'm a twice-divorced man. You all know my second wife. She's sitting right over there."

He gestured at Joan, and she smiled, tears welling in her eyes. The audience laughed, and it gave him the confidence he needed to go on. "But I've never told you all about Josephine Alvarado, the woman who made me. And my first wife. We met in Houston, before I was the Dash Howard you know and love. When I was still myself. I'd like to say it was love at first sight. It was for me. But in me, she saw something she could mold. I guess, if I'm being honest, she never really loved me. She saw me as a project, something to be fixed. And once she'd accomplished that, she didn't want anything to do with me anymore."

All the gaiety in the room had evaporated, replaced with a solemnity that indicated the entire room was hanging on his every word. There was nothing for it but to finish it now. "I haven't heard from her since she left me in Houston with signed annulment papers and a note that read, 'My work here is done.' But tonight, if you'll indulge me, I'd like to give her a message. Josephine, if you're out there somewhere, know that I forgive you. I don't know why you left, but sometimes you gotta go, I guess. It's taken me a long time to make my peace with that. But someone I know taught me that I'm worth a whole lot more than you or I have given me credit for." He looked up then and caught Joan's eyes, delivering the rest of his speech straight to her.

"They showed me that being myself is the only way to get by in this business—and that if people don't like it, well, I shouldn't give a damn. From now on, I'm going to try to be the truest, most honest version of myself. Not the version I think people want me to be. I've spent too long now pretending to be, maybe even becoming, something I'm not because I thought that was the only way people would like me. But I've realized now that anyone who doesn't like the real me can go to hell."

The room gasped at the curse word and the now miserable-looking bandleader buried his face in his hands. Well, Dash did say he was only going to be himself from now on. Cursing on the radio was one way to start. "The work is the only thing that matters. To me, anyway. I hope you'll still be with me for the journey. Thank you."

He nodded at the bandleader, who broke into the love theme from *Reno Rendezvous,* as Dash put his head down and walked off the stage, clutching the Oscar to his chest. A handler waved him down the stairs.

"Congratulations, Mr. Howard. Now, if you'll follow me to the back of the ballroom, we'll take your picture for the press."

Dash almost followed him. Almost went along with it, doing what was expected of him. But he thought about the flashing lights, the press pool yelling questions at him, and it made him want to heave. No, this was what he'd been talking about. He'd do this on his terms or not at all. "Sorry, I appreciate you're just doing your job." He smiled wanly. "But I'm going back to my table." And to Joan.

CHAPTER 30

JOAN SCARCELY HAD TIME TO REGISTER THAT DASH HAD returned to their table instead of going to pose for photographs, when they were moving on to her category. She was reeling from his speech. He'd been so honest, blowing up any hold Josephine would ever have on him. She was so proud of him she could burst. There was a ball of emotion in her throat, and no matter how much she tried to clear it, it would not dissolve. But it wasn't only pride. It was shame too.

She'd always told him she couldn't live by anyone's terms but her own. But right now, she felt like a fraud. Because he'd just told the world everything. And she was still keeping a secret from the world. Still letting Leda and fear rule her choices. She'd told Dash she loved him, and she'd won him back. But was it a true victory if they had to sneak around? If she couldn't openly give him every part of herself? If she hadn't risked it all? But she didn't have time to think about it now. Because she was about to find out if her dream of the last nine years was going to come true.

Joan twisted her hands in her lap and moved to the edge of her seat, as comedic favorite Henry Powell read out the names of the women in her category. She thought she might throw up. Arlene laid an encouraging hand on her shoulder and squeezed. Joan's knuckles were white, clenched in the skirt of her gown.

Would it have all been enough? Losing Dash, playing Leda's game, embroiling Monty in the whole blasted mess. Had the price she paid to be here in this moment earned her the adulation she once believed mattered most?

Time stopped for a moment as Henry Powell opened the envelope. The dim murmur of tableside chatter hushed, the gentle sway of the centerpieces as people jostled the tables utterly still. "And the winner is..." he began. Joan squeezed her eyes shut, not certain she wanted to hear the next words. "Joan Davis for *Reno Rendezvous*."

A roar of sound whooshed toward her as the room erupted into applause. Arlene practically screamed in her ear, and then looked abashed. "Sorry, I'm just really, really happy for you."

Harry reached for her, capturing her in a side embrace. But she only had eyes for one man—Dash. She looked over Harry's shoulder and met Dash's gaze. He smiled at her. "Congratulations," he called out to her. "You got what you wanted."

She was already on her way to the stage and didn't hear him continue the second part, as he called after her, "What you deserve."

Because it had finally happened. She had reached the pinnacle. She'd won. But this moment that she had always believed would mean so much, that should be the utmost reflection of her success as an actress and the world's love for her as a movie star, was hollow.

Hearing Dash say those words, "You got what you wanted," she knew with absolute certainty it wasn't what she wanted at all. She wanted her career, yes. She wanted this recognition, this success. But she wanted Dash too. Having him was one thing, but keeping him, keeping him meant being honest the way he had been. She wanted those stolen moments in the bungalow, that sense that someone had seen to her very soul and loved her for what they found there. But she also wanted to love him openly. To free them both from Leda Price forever and tell the world what he meant to her. Tonight, and all the rest of the days of her life.

Because Dash had taught her a lesson. Miraculously and through no intention of his own, he'd taught her that loving someone and being loved wasn't foolish or reckless or the road to ruin. It was the only thing worth risking everything for.

It was time to do just that. Dash had shown her how. She climbed the few steps to the podium, clutching her velvet gown in her hand and trying not to trip. Her shoulders were back, her head held high, but her palms were so sweaty with nerves, she thought the dress might simply slip from her fingers and bring her careening to her knees. But miraculously, somehow she made it to the podium, offered her cheek to Henry, and took the Oscar from him. She looked out at the crowd, who grinned back at her expectantly.

"Um, I… Well, I don't know what to say." *What a start. Come on, pull yourself together, Joan.* "Thank you to the Academy. I have been dreaming of this moment for nine years, and it's not at all what I imagined. This business is tough on women. You have to be as hard as nails to end up standing where I am, and still people will try to take it away from you. Label you 'box-office poison' because you were saddled with a string of bad scripts. Deny you the roles you know you can play because you have a pretty face. Value you only for your body and not the things in your head. Being here right now is the proof I've always wanted that you love me, you respect me. The way I always imagined you would."

Joan took a breath. This was it. Now or never. Only she had the power to end Leda's hold over her. Over them both. And let Dash see her, and love her, in front of the entire world. "But there's a part of my story none of you know. A part of my story some people think I should be ashamed of. But I'm done with shame, and I'm done with hiding."

The bandleader, sensing another long speech, snapped his conductor's baton in half in a fit of pique and frustration. If her knees weren't shaking under her gown, Joan might've laughed.

"Before I became Joan Davis, back when my name was still Mildred Shalk, I made a film many of you might call indecent. I laid my body bare for a camera, and I made love for money, for the entertainment of others."

She heard gasps from the crowd and more than a few judgmental scoffs. She looked out and found Arlene. Her hands were clutched beneath her chin and her eyes were pooling with tears. "Proud of you," Arlene mouthed from the table.

Joan looked down at the microphone, the one she knew was broadcasting her words around the world at this very minute. The hiss and crack of the microphone was enough to stop her, to make her words stick in her throat. But then she imagined her words going out to women listening, reaching those who'd done what they'd had to in order to survive in a world not built for them. She hoped Leda was listening too. That perhaps even she found solace or inspiration in the words. Because at the end of the day, they were both women doing what they had to do. She inhaled and imagined speaking to any woman who had been made to feel less than. And she went on.

"I'm not ashamed of this. I would do it again. The work paid my rent for months, and it provided my ticket to catching the attention of the people who would give me my shot in Hollywood." She resisted the urge to glance at Harry. Not that he would face any backlash for having watched such a film. The pleasure was mutual, but the cost was not. Only women had to pay for admitting they had urges and desires just like men.

"I sell my body to all of you on a daily basis. I have been public property since the day I arrived in this town. It was a price I was willing and still am content to pay. The film for which you have given me this award asked me to be more naked on-screen than I had ever been before by exposing the most vulnerable parts of myself. It is only hypocrites who will distinguish between flesh and feeling. Who see my body for their taking, but only if it's in a way they deem proper. Who expect me to bare my soul, but condemn me if I choose to bare my body. I'm done living my life by other people's terms."

The room was silent now, and Joan had no idea if she'd guaranteed she'd never work again. But she had to keep going, had to finish it. "Keeping this secret has cost me a great deal. It's made me feel like I have something to be ashamed of when I have nothing to apologize for."

She looked at Dash now, who looked stricken in his seat. Rather like a gaping codfish who'd been boiled in arsenic. Oh God, had she miscalculated? She remembered his words in the Cocoanut Grove only a few weeks ago. *Nobody needs to know.* He'd sworn he wasn't ashamed of her or disgusted with what she'd done, but did that change if she told the world? Well, it was too late now.

She held his gaze and continued. "I thought keeping this film hidden would protect me. I was certain it would protect someone I love. My fear gave others power over me, and in the end, it made me weak. Unable to be the woman I know I'm capable of being and that the people I love deserve to have in their corner."

She turned to face the crowd once again, imagining all the women listening tonight, the ones at home in their aprons, the ones pouring coffee at a diner, and the ones on a ramshackle farm, dreaming of a night like this one.

"Tonight, I release myself from shame." She exhaled as she said it and felt something inside of her unfurl, as if she'd undone a knot she'd never even known she'd tied. "I thank you for this honor, for helping me to realize that I will always be Joan Davis, the movie star, because this woman up here is who I really am. And no one, no reporter or fickle fan, can take that away. Joan Davis is who I've always known I was meant to be. And who I will continue to be. But I've also learned that Joan Davis is nothing without the people she loves. That it's fear, not love, that makes us weak. I hope you will all learn from my mistakes, and that you won't let guilt or others' judgment force your hand into losing the one thing that matters most."

Joan exhaled one last time. She had done it; she'd freed herself from Leda, from shame, from any barriers that still existed between her and Dash.

She clutched her Oscar to her chest as the stillness of the room erupted into shouts, flashes of light, and a barrage of questions from the press pool at the back of the room. Poor Henry Powell struggled to shush everyone so they could move on to the directing category.

Joan held her head high as she climbed down the few steps. She swept past the handler, ignoring his hurried suggestion that she make a beeline for the press line at the back of the ballroom. She knew she'd have to answer to them eventually. But right this minute she didn't much feel like it. She wanted to enjoy this victory and the choice she'd made to set herself free.

But the press weren't willing to wait. As she descended from the stage, she found herself in a mob of photographers and reporters. They'd practically rushed the stage and were popping flashbulbs and bellowing questions at her so loudly she could barely distinguish what anyone was saying. "I've said everything I have to say on the matter tonight," she called out, pasting a serene smile on her face and trying to push through them.

In the distance, she could make out their table. Arlene looked both proud and worried, trying to reach her, but Joan called to her, "Arlene, it's okay." There was Harry. He didn't look nearly as angry as she'd expected him to. In fact, he looked rather amused. And was that… My God, he was winking at her. Well, that was something anyway. If Harry Evets was still on her side, she hadn't completely blown up her career. But the man she really wanted to see was nowhere to be found. His chair at the table was empty, and a quick glance at the room suggested he'd made a hurried exit in the madness that had followed her speech. Dash Howard had apparently been so humiliated by what she'd done that he'd left.

The knowledge of this was as bracing as the Pacific in January. Had she divulged her secret for Dash? Not entirely. She'd done it to release them both from the clutches of Leda Price. To choose love and courage over fear for once in her life. But had she hoped that he would love her all the more for her honesty? For following the example he'd set only moments before? Yes.

She needed to get out of here, away from the vultures clawing at her and safely home where she could think, with the help of a stiff drink. Finally, she managed to break free from the mob surrounding her and made a break for the stairs. She hiked her skirt up in one hand and held her Oscar in the other, climbing the steps at a breakneck pace. She had to get to the door before they caught up to her, had to get away.

She could see the light of the Biltmore's hallway through the crack in the red velvet curtains hanging in the archway at the top of the stairs. *Almost there,* she told herself. *Just a few more steps.*

And then it happened. The heel of her shoe caught in her skirt, and she was falling backwards. It seemed like an eternity as she waited to collide with the stairs and cause her second scene in the ballroom within minutes. But it didn't come. Instead, she hit something solid and warm, something alive.

A deep, masculine chuckle she'd know anywhere rasped above her, and suddenly in her ear she heard his voice whispering, "Well, I've heard of falling for your leading man before, but I didn't realize it was literal."

She blushed deeply, looking down to find his strong hands wrapped around her, holding her back from a potential tumble down the ballroom steps. "Dash, what are you… I thought you'd left."

"Let's get you upright, then I'll answer questions." He helped prop her back up onto her feet, holding her steady until she found her footing in her pumps. Her Oscar had fallen down a few stairs in the tumble, and he turned around to fetch it, like Cinderella's prince reaching for her glass slipper. Only this time it was plated in gold.

Over the bulk of his broad shoulders, she spotted the crush of reporters. They'd been corralled by Harry Evets and Arlene, and the two of them were fielding their questions, looking tickled by the entire turn of events. Buying her time. Bless them. In the meantime, the ceremony had started back up at the bandstand. No one in the crowd cared that she and Dash were enacting some upside-down fairy tale on the steps at the back of the room.

He returned the Oscar to her and offered her his arm, whisking her up the last few steps and into the relative quiet of the hotel hallway. "Stop for a minute, catch your breath. Harry and Arlene will hold them off," he told her. "Now, what were you asking me on the stairs?"

She marveled at him. His face had never looked lovelier to her. His five-o'clock shadow was starting to shade his strong jawline, despite the fact that she knew he must've shaved right before coming here. His tuxedo was tailored perfectly to his body, as if he had been the model for the gold-encased man she held in her hand. His hair was mussed from their mad dash up the stairs, the stray curl she adored springing onto his forehead. But it was his smile that did it, a crooked, wicked grin that was brighter than any flashbulb or searchlight Hollywood could muster.

"I thought you'd left," she said. "I looked for you after my speech and you weren't there."

That golden smile fell, and it was as if someone had extinguished a flame. He reached for her and pulled her to his arms, tucking her to him and resting his head above hers. "Joan, I went to get the car."

She lifted her chin to look up at him. It took every ounce of her self-control not to reach her hand to his jaw and caress it. "Why?"

"Because I had a feeling you weren't going to want to stick around to answer questions after that."

"There they are," a voice called from behind the curtain. "Joan, what is the name of the stag film—?"

Dash didn't wait for the man to get closer or to finish his questions. He grabbed Joan's hand and yanked her to the brass double doors. She giggled as he pulled her outside onto the red carpet, sprinting to the valet. The early March air was cold, but Joan didn't feel it at all, warmed with desire and the breathless escape they were making.

The valet already had the door to her Packard open and waiting for them. Dash dove into the back seat and then pulled her in after him, practically yanking her into his arms. The car pulled away from the curb as the photographer and reporter that had spotted them burst through the doors, looking wildly around for their prey.

Joan burst out laughing, tossing her head back against Dash's shoulder. Dash followed suit, a loud, infectious laugh filling the back seat, until they were both doubled over. "Did you see the looks on their faces?" she wheezed out.

"They looked like a golden retriever who didn't know where the stick his master threw went." He laughed. They collapsed into another string of giggles, gasping for air. Joan swiped at her eyes, wiping away the moisture that had gathered there with the force of her laughter. Only then did she realize that she was sitting in Dash's lap. He noticed it at the same time, the back seat going silent as if they'd sucked all the air from the vehicle.

She slowly raised her eyes from the sight of her dress splayed across the tops of his thighs to meet his gaze, and she was thrilled to find a hunger there. "Joan," he growled, making the single syllable of her name a prayer for a starving man.

He wrapped his arms around her, pressing her to him, and brought his lips down on hers. She kissed him back, a bruising kiss powered by the confusion and loss of the last several months. She teased at his bottom lip with her teeth and tugged at it until he moaned and opened for her. She would never get enough of this impossible sense of feeling safe and desired at the same time. He was warm and hungry for her, and she knit her hands in his hair until she could no longer tell where her body ended and his began. She lost herself in him, falling into the easy way their bodies fit together like the broken shards of a mirror made whole again.

But all too soon it was over. He pulled away and pressed his forehead to hers, his breathing ragged. "Why did you think I'd left you?"

She climbed out of his lap, slipping into the space beside him on the bench seat. "Your face during my speech," she whispered, struggling to get the words out. "You looked stricken. I thought what I was admitting upset you. That I—" The next word caught in her throat, and she had to push it out, fight against how raw it made her feel, how heavy her tongue felt in her mouth saying it. "That I disgusted you. By telling the world."

"Your speech did upset me." And there it was. Confirmation of what she'd feared. She pulled away from him, edging her body closer to the door and pressing her face to the cool glass of the window. She was feverish with need, pulsing with adrenaline after making that speech and then running for the exit. She couldn't be here with him like this. She wanted him too much.

He leaned down and brushed the softest kiss to the exposed curve of her shoulder. "It upset me for not thinking of this sooner. For not suggesting we both free ourselves from Leda's clutches until you felt so cornered that you had to do it tonight. In front of the whole world."

"No!" She sat straight upright, making the driver jump. "Sorry, Will," she called. He didn't reply but simply waved his hand as if to say it was all right. "It needed to be my decision. And you showed me the way."

He answered her with a bruising kiss before breaking away and muttering, "I'd like to throttle Leda Price. The nerve of that woman."

Joan smiled into his neck, enjoying the clean, fresh smell of soap and aftershave that lingered there. "I think I've given her quite the fright tonight. She desperately wanted to punish me for refusing to kowtow to her, to make you see me as the terrible, selfish person she believes I am. Perhaps that I was, once. But I've robbed her of all her fuel for revenge now."

Dash pulled her to him, sprinkling kisses across the top of her head, through her hair, over her brow, her cheeks, and finally coming to her lips. "You were so brave tonight, my darling."

She traced the corner of his mouth with her fingertip before placing her mouth in the space she'd outlined and murmured against his lips, "Only because you were first. You had the courage to show the world who you really are. How could I want you and hold myself to anything less than that level of honesty? I've spent months, years really, being a coward."

He grabbed her wrists, wrapping his hands tightly around them. "Joan, look at me." She did as she was told and was amazed to find fire and ice in his gaze, desire and something harder, more ferocious. "You have never been a coward a day in your life. You've always done what you had to. I understand that now."

She swallowed hard. Because no one had ever seen her, all of her, Joan Davis the movie star, and Mildred Shalk the frightened little girl, the way he had. And he was doing it again. Understanding her, accepting her, loving her. "Then you know that I did what I did tonight because I had to."

He closed his eyes and a smile danced across his face, lither and more intoxicating than Fred Astaire in a top hat and tails. "And why was it that you had to?" he murmured, his voice barely above a whisper.

She could say it was because she was tired of living under the weight of this secret, tired of being in thrall to Leda Price, tired of being judged for knowing the power and the pleasure of her own body, tired of trading even an ounce of herself for the fame and success she thought was the only thing she'd ever need. But there was only one true answer to his question. "Because I love you."

He brought his mouth down on hers, crushing her with the intensity of his embrace. Her arms went around his neck, and she was lost in him again. One hand in his hair, the other unknotting the satin bow tie around his neck. She kissed him and in between kisses, she told him all the things she had been yearning to tell him. "I love you, and I cannot live without you." She kissed his brow. "All the fame, all the Oscars in the world, they don't mean anything without you in my life."

She moved to his eyelashes. God, she even loved his eyelashes, kissing them gently as his eyes fluttered closed and the lashes dusted the tops of his cheeks. "I realized that almost the minute I lost you. And I feared you'd never want me back. But I had to try. And even then, this was hanging over us. Because I was afraid of losing you again. Of letting Leda destroy us. I should've known all along that for us to truly love each other, there could be no more secrets. Not between us or between us and our public. Only then could you truly see—and want—all of me."

"Let me show you how much I want all of you." She whimpered as he kissed the side of her mouth, teasing the edge of her lips with his tongue. Then he moved to her neck, pushing the abundant feathers of her gown aside to suck at a place behind her ear. "These damn feathers," he muttered.

She couldn't suppress a giggle, but then he nipped at her neck and a shiver of desire ran down her spine. "We're almost home," she whispered.

"I like the sound of that," he growled, still continuing to apply his ministrations to her neck. "Home. With you."

"Mmmm," she hummed, turning to jelly in his arms. "Me too."

She lost herself in him, and before she knew it, they had turned onto her quiet street. Will rolled to a slow stop in front of her driveway and cleared his throat, studiously loath to interrupt the clinch happening in his back seat. The sound had her breaking away from Dash only enough to lean her cheek against his. Her eyes were still closed, but she could feel him smile, a goofy, dazed grin that matched the fireworks show currently happening in her chest.

At last, she opened her eyes and reached for the door handle, fumbling with it in her nervousness and excitement. She practically tumbled out of the car, drunk on Dash and desire, but she managed to catch herself and find her balance by clinging to the heavy car door.

"Thank you, Will," she squeaked, avoiding his gaze. They would never speak of this again. And that was why she paid her people well.

Dash growled from his post in the back seat, but her back was toward him as she looked up at her big, gaudy mansion, feeling for the first time in her life that she'd come home. It had nothing to do with the location and everything to do with the handsome man in the back seat of her car.

"I've missed this view." He chuckled, gently patting her ass and climbing out beside her, snaking his arm around her waist and nuzzling her neck.

She swatted at him half-heartedly. "You're incorrigible."

He grazed her neck with his teeth, running them along the skin, lightly enough to send goose bumps prickling up her arms. "I think you mean *encouraging*."

She wrapped her arms around the barrel of his chest, feeling his heat and his strength beneath the fabric of his jacket. She looked up at him, and all the stars of the Nevada sky were in her eyes at the sight of him. They stumbled up the drive, drunk solely on each other, and she fumbled with the front door.

It swung open, revealing the tiled entryway which led to Spanish-style steps with a wrought-iron railing across the way. There was still so much uncertainty, so much she didn't know about her future and what it would hold. But for the first time in her life, that didn't feel scary. It felt like an adventure, one she was ready to take with this man by her side cheering her on, holding her hand when it got hard, and always seeing how much she had to give—her ambition, her talent, and her capacity for love. She'd dreamed of Hollywood, of adulation, of riches and respect. She'd never known she could dream of this.

Before she crossed the threshold, she turned to face Dash, grabbing at the hanging ends of his unknotted bow tie. She used the satin fabric to pull him down to her, kissing him hard and fast, before breaking away and pulling him to the stairs. "Baby…" She smiled, loving the sound of the word on her lips. "Let's make up for lost time."

CHAPTER 31

DASH AWOKE TO SEE THE DAWN BREAKING THROUGH THE white smocked curtains in Joan's bedroom. He was tangled up in her, their legs and arms a joyous jumble in her bed. One arm was curled up beneath her, one hand resting gently on her heart. Its strong, steady beat beneath his fingertips sent an ease rippling through him unlike he'd ever felt before. He gently slid his arm out from under her and pressed the lightest kiss to her hip bone before pulling the sheet over her and rising from the bed.

He glanced at the pair of Oscars they'd propped on the mantel across the way. They looked like they were kissing. Copycats, he thought, chuckling at the idea that even their awards couldn't keep their nonexistent hands off each other.

He picked his way through the shreds of clothing on the floor, the evening wear they'd discarded the night before in a hurried rush to get closer to each other. His boxers were buried under the heavy morass of Joan's gown. As he pawed through the black velvet fabric, a stray feather from the elaborate neckline floated into the air, and he suppressed something halfway between a sneeze and a giggle. Once he retrieved his shorts, he pulled them on and walked to the window, pulling the blinds aside only enough to see out, but taking care not to spill too much light into the room to wake Joan.

He turned his head to look at her, the slivers of dawn that eked through the window kissing her shoulder and the tip of her nose with their purple glow, as he'd done only hours earlier. She was more beautiful than he'd ever seen—completely at peace, her mouth hanging slightly open, and her body so still and vulnerable. It was the side of her she'd shared with him in Reno, that he'd feared had all been a mirage. His heart swelled to see it again, to know he could wake up seeing this every morning if he wanted to.

The light shifted and he peered through the curtains to look out at the quiet street. Rexford Drive was still at five thirty in the morning, a line of cars parked along the curbs and in manicured driveways like wealthy sentinels standing watch. The perfectly trimmed lawns and beautiful houses looked like a movie set in the early morning light, waiting for the stars inside to wake up and give them life. It was one of those glorious sunrises that made waking up early feel like going to church. The sky was a deep, dusky purple and glimmers of pink and orange were streaking across groupings of feathery clouds.

It reminded him of a moment in reverse, the night he'd sat on the back steps of their Nevada bungalow looking at the stars. In those moments before Joan had come to him, he'd been so uncertain about everything. Last night, he'd made a bid for himself, for living his life on his terms. But this morning, in the mists of dawn, he was realizing that meant nothing if it didn't include Joan. He'd spent long enough doubting himself, doubting her, instead of trying to find the truth. They'd found each other again last night inside these four walls, rediscovering each other's bodies and souls.

She—oh God, glorious Joan—had risked it all. For him. For herself. He moved to the armchair with the chenille slipcover next to the window and sat back in the chair, watching the light grow warmer and more orange. Snatches of her speech came back to him, the look of determination on her face, the fierce pride and ownership in her voice, and the way she looked at him when she'd admitted that she'd lost the one thing she'd loved most. He'd wanted to be her knight in shining armor in that moment.

But silly him, he should've known better. Joan Davis did not need to be rescued. She was no damsel in distress. She slayed dragons all by herself. And loving her was enough. He didn't need to be the playboy King of Hollywood, the hardened masculine image he projected on-screen—he just needed to love her. And let her love him. It was really that simple.

She stirred under the plain white sheet, a slight, nearly inaudible moan sending a flicker of white-hot desire through him. She turned and propped herself up on her elbow, her mass of curly brown hair hanging over her eyes in a peekaboo, come-hither style that her makeup team couldn't have manufactured if they'd tried.

His eyes fell to her chest, the swell of her curves making him hungry with need. She noticed the direction of his gaze and blushed, pulling the sheet up to cover herself.

"I don't believe it. Joan Davis, are you feeling shy?" he drawled, forcing himself to stay in the chair.

She grinned sheepishly. "I'm still not used to this… You here, wanting me. Things being the way they were in Reno. I was afraid—"

He leaned forward on the seat. "Afraid of what? Joan, I don't want you to ever be afraid again. You are fearless, and I never want to give you reason to be otherwise."

She sat up, letting the sheet fall and not caring. "I was afraid maybe that was a stolen season. That maybe there was something about the mountains and the picture that we couldn't replicate here. It's why I didn't want you to come home with me after I explained everything at the Cocoanut Grove. I was worried it wouldn't be the same."

He stood, came over to the side of the bed, and leaned down to kiss her. It was a gentle kiss, long and languid, full of yearning. "It's not the same," he admitted.

A flicker of doubt flashed through her eyes before he added, "It's better."

She reached for him, pulling him to her in the bed, kissing him until he was seeing the stars that had faded from the morning sky. He lay down next to her, brushing aside the fan of her hair to nestle his cheek next to hers. He stroked her bare skin, exploring the hills and valleys of her body with a languid touch. "I thought I made it pretty clear last night that Reno was just the beginning." He moved his hips so she could feel the hardness of him press into her. "But I can show you again now. As often as it takes until it sinks in. And longer still, so that you'll never forget it. Forever, if you want."

She turned to face him so that their noses were touching, looking deeply into his eyes and tracing the line of his jaw with her finger. "I do have a bad memory," she whispered on a rush of laughter that made him think of larks greeting the morning.

He huffed, something between a laugh and a puff of desire, and placed his hand on her upper thigh, pulling her leg over his and pressing the top of his leg to the spot that made her moan. "That ringing any bells?" he growled.

She didn't answer, only closed her eyes and threw her head back in ecstasy, so he moved his mouth to the rosy peak of her nipple, sucking at her until she was breathless. Her hand was in his hair, holding him to her, when she stilled.

He forced himself to stop and lifted his face from worshipping her body to catch her gaze. "What's wrong?"

"You said forever."

He rolled onto his back and pulled her across him so they were lying cheek to cheek, her arm sprawled across his chest and her fingers lightly teasing as they stroked up and down. He reached for her fingers and pulled them to his mouth, kissing her knuckles. "Only if that's what you want, Joan. We don't have to rush into anything."

She pushed herself up to look at him, squinting as if trying to assess him. "You're all I want." A sad look came into her eyes. "But I could be a liability for you now."

He reached up to cup her face, and she leaned into the strength of his palm. "Things are changing for both of us, and I'll probably have an easier time of it because people are absurd, but neither of us is perfect. I made it clear last night. From now on, I'm doing this my way. Besides, I think Harry's on both our sides."

"But the Legion of Decency and the blasted Production Code office… They'll blackball me. Leda Price might try to tar you with that same brush. Especially now that Josephine's threats are no good to her."

"That's Harry's problem. And I expect he'll give them hell, if last night was any indication." Dash sat up and pulled her to him, stroking her hair as he held her in an embrace. "Darling, last night, we both made choices to free ourselves from Leda's web. But wasn't there a part of you that did it for me? For us? That hoped the truth would bring me here, back to your bed, with absolutely nothing between us any longer?"

She balled up her fists against his chest and shook her head as if chastising herself. "Will you think I'm pathetic if I say yes?"

He gripped her by the shoulders and pulled her back so he could look in her eyes. "God, Joan, no, I could never think you're pathetic. You're the bravest woman…hell, the bravest human being I've ever known. I wasted so much time being angry because I thought you'd decided I wasn't enough for you. Well, the truth is I will never be enough for you. Because you're too good for me—too strong, too brave, too beautiful, too miraculous. But if you'll let me, I'd like to spend the rest of my life trying to be the man you deserve."

She reached for him, stroking his cheek with her thumb. "You are so much more than I deserve, and if you're all I have every day for the rest of my life, that would be enough. It'd be more than I ever thought I could have any right to."

"You deserve your career. You're a damned good actress, and you should have the work and the respect you've earned. Let Harry deal with the morality police."

"Of course I want that. Of course I hope Harry will be able to protect me. But I need you to know that if I had it to do over again, I would choose you. I would choose us every time. The rest of the world be damned. I need you to know that if I were asked, you would always, always be enough for me."

He kissed her once, hard. Then he pulled her hands back from his chest and gently placed them on her knees, backing away and untangling himself from the sheets. He placed his hands on the edge of the bed and knelt, his bare knees pressing into the soft, plush, gray carpet. She looked at him, a quizzical smile on her face.

"What?" he grinned.

"It's just that you really do look like the King of Hollywood right now. Half-naked, the sun rising over your shoulders, your hair burnished with the dawn."

"You know, Joan, if we can't save your acting career, you really have a future as a writer. Maybe Arlene can give you some tips," he teased her. He looked down. He did look rather ridiculous, kneeling next to her bed in nothing but his underwear with the sun painting them both in its mellow orange light, making her entire bedroom feel like they were inside a scoop of sherbet. But it didn't matter. He needed to ask her a question.

"Joan, I choose you too. I'd be lying if I said I haven't always wanted you. Haven't hoped since that very first picture that somehow, someday, we might end up here. But this time, this, us, will be on both our terms. This time it will be for real and it will be for keeps. Because you make me a better man, you make me believe I can be enough, you make me believe I deserve to be loved for the person I truly am. You make me believe that as a team, anything is possible. I love you, and I will never stop loving you. Never stop choosing you."

She was crying now, pressing the butt of her hands to her face to try to stop the tears. "Joan Davis, will you marry me? Again?"

She crawled to the edge of the bed, leaning over to kiss him. It was unlike any kiss they'd shared before, full of passion and promise, a thousand yeses in her lips. It was an answer without words. The one he'd been waiting for his whole life. And how was that for a Hollywood ending?

EPILOGUE

HONEYMOON IN RENO?

The divorce capital of the country hardly seems like the place for a romantic getaway, but Hollywood's most unexpected lovebirds were spotted leaving the courthouse today with a freshly minted marriage license in tow. It's only been a week since that disastrous Oscar night, but that eventful ceremony is hardly the freshest gossip when it comes to Dash and Davis. Though rest assured we are still working on getting to the bottom of Miss Davis's shocking revelations.

After the Academy Awards, the two were nowhere to be seen until news of their elopement reached this trusty reporter. The two flew the coop, with Joan Davis breaking her engagement to Monty Smyth in a sudden change of heart. My loyal readers will, of course, remember that Miss Davis was previously married to Dash Howard through what was deemed a clerical error, which was only discovered as a result of her engagement to marry Monty Smyth. But it seems her marriage with Dash was so nice, they had to do it twice.

Our favorite matinee idol Mr. Smith is taking the blow quite hard. "I'm over the moon for Dash and Joan," he told an unnamed source before slugging a photographer. Maybe we can find him a new starlet with whom to drown his sorrows? Who do you think is the right girl for the dashing Monty Smyth?

For now, we wish Dash and Davis many happy returns at this felicitous news of their matrimony. Perhaps the second time will be the charm?

This writer will be taking a holiday to get some much-needed R&R, but never fear, *What Price Hollywood?* will return to get to the bottom of Hollywood's secrets once more.

—xoxo, Leda

AUTHOR'S NOTE

The Golden Age of Hollywood has always felt both impossibly glamorous and shockingly close to me. It was an era where the movie business was just finding its legs and discovering its potential as an art form and a commodity. Though the characters of this novel are entirely fictional (except for Neal Dodd who was, in fact, a real minister who played men of the cloth in studio films, including *Merrily We Go to Hell*), they are inspired by the real men and women of this era who created the celluloid of our cultural past.

Joan Davis is, as you might have guessed, a mash-up of two of the era's greatest stars (and rivals)—Joan Crawford and Bette Davis. Whether or not the infamously feuding women would've loved or hated this, I can't say. But Joan is more broadly a reflection of the incredible women of the era (like Crawford, Davis, Barbara Stanwyck, and more) who offered up brassy, nuanced dames to audiences.

Joan's backstory hews closest to Crawford's. She was dubbed "box-office poison" in the late 1930s and found herself struggling to escape the sexist label. Additionally, she did purportedly make a stag film early in her career, the negatives of which MGM studio head Louis B. Mayer is said to have sought out and destroyed. For more on her life specifically, I'd recommend *Not the Girl Next Door* by Charlotte Chandler.

Dash Howard is based on one of Crawford's most indelible leading men and the real King of Hollywood, Clark Gable. Gable did marry his older acting teacher before coming to Hollywood—and she helped transform him into a man who could be a movie star. *Clark Gable: A Biography* by Warren G. Harris was my main source for background on his life.

But nearly every setting, character, and film referenced in these pages is my take or wink to a real piece of this bygone era. I hope it will inspire you to seek out more of the films and history of this fascinating time. If you find yourself thinking this book feels entirely too modern, I urge you to watch some of the films of this era, particularly pre-Code films, which deal with subjects and jokes that defy the neutered version of society that groups like the Legion of Decency preferred be put on screen. If you're not sure where to start, there's a helpful list of some of the titles that inspired this novel contained here.

We like to place the figures of our past, particularly gods and goddesses like movie stars, behind glass, imagining that they were somehow not as capricious, scandalous, and complicated as we are today. But the reality couldn't be further from the truth. They were, after all, people just like us. People who just happened to be significantly more glamorous than the rest of us. I hope you've enjoyed this journey into the silver-screen past—and that you'll come back for more.

—xoxo, Maureen

FILMS THAT INSPIRED *IT HAPPENED ONE FIGHT*

***It Happened One Night* (1934)**—This classic not only lent this book its title but some major plot points, including the sheet strung across the bungalow dividing Joan and Dash's beds. Clark Gable won an Oscar for his portrayal of Peter Warne, a newspaper reporter who sees a surefire story when he bumps into runaway heiress Ellie Andrews (Claudette Colbert) on a bus. But things go awry when they start to fall for each other.

***The Women* (1939)**—This ensemble piece starring some of Hollywood's biggest female stars (no men appear on screen ever) also marked a comeback for Joan Crawford as homewrecker Crystal Allen. The film contains a sequence in which Norma Shearer's Mary travels to Reno to secure a divorce, which along with copious research on the real Reno of the 1930s inspired those parts of the book.

***Love on the Run* (1936)**—One of ten films Clark Gable and Joan Crawford made together, this is MGM's blatant attempt to cash in on the popularity of *It Happened One Night*. Crawford is runaway bride Sally Parker and Gable is undercover reporter Michael Anthony, who find themselves stumbling upon an espionage ring while on the run.

***Possessed* (1931)**—This is more typical of the Gable and Crawford pairings, a melodrama about a factory worker,

Marian Martin (Crawford), who climbs her way to the top of society by becoming the mistress of attorney Mark Whitney (Gable).

***Merrily We Go To Hell* (1932)**—This scorching commentary on marriage was emblematic of the possibilities of pre-Code moviemaking (and it boasts a female director, the legendary Dorothy Arzner, to boot). Fredric March is drunken reporter Jerry Corbett, who is seemingly rescued by the love of heiress Joan Prentice (Sylvia Sidney) until he relapses. And don't miss real minister Neal Dodd officiating the wedding ceremony!

***Dark Victory* (1939)**—When Joan speaks of Arlene writing a true women's picture, this is the type of project she means. Bette Davis stars as socialite Judith Traherne who falls in love with the doctor (George Brent) who diagnoses her inoperable brain tumor.

***Mildred Pierce* (1945)**—Though this was made several years later, this domestic noir that finally earned Joan Crawford her Oscar was a major inspiration for the type of projects my Joan is hungry for. Crawford stars as the titular waitress and mother who must contend with romance, divorce, and her scheming daughter's deeds.

ACKNOWLEDGEMENTS

They say writing is a lonely process, and I suppose the actual act itself is, but in my experience, it takes a village. I absolutely could not have got this book into the world without the help and support of so many—and that includes you, dear reader. Thank you for taking Joan and Dash and this glamorous world into your hearts. There's a lot to read out there, and it means the world to me that you chose to spend some time with my book.

Taylor Haggerty—I said for years that you were my dream agent, and now I don't know what to say because you've fulfilled that dream and then exceeded it exponentially. Having you on my team is the greatest gift. Thank you for believing in this book (and a historical romance not set in the 19th-century)—Joan and Dash wouldn't exist without you. And to the rest of Root Literary, especially Jasmine Brown and Holly Root, for their kindness, advice, and epic cheerleading.

My editor, Christa Désir, is absolute magic. Christa, your edits are not only perfection, they feel like they came from within a part of my brain that I just didn't know how to find. It's uncanny how much we're on the same wavelength. Thank you for loving this book—and Joan and Dash—as much as I do, and making it an infinitely improved read. To the rest of the Sourcebooks team, every author should be so lucky to have people like you behind them—Pam Jaffee, who I started this romancelandia journey with as a critic, Katie Stutz, Heather Hall, Shannon Barr, Letty Mundt, you are all romance heroes! Jenifer Prince, you created the cover of my dreams and plucked Joan and Dash right out of my head as I'd always seen them, thank you.

I had some really lovely beta readers, namely Jenny Nordbak, Lindsay Grossman, and Liz Locke. Thank you all for seeing ways to make this book better! Liz, I am so grateful to be sharing a debut year with you and can't wait for more author adventures together (with lots of movie-themed cocktails). Also, Jenny Holiday and Kate Clayborn, who beta read my first book that caught Taylor's eye. You ladies are amazing.

Jeanne De Vita, you are such a FORCE for good in the romance world. Thank you for being an incredible editor and an essential part of my querying and agenting process; my query letter would've been terrible without your guidance. I wish you all the joy and support you give others—you are one of the most generous people I've ever met.

The number of friends I need to thank here would probably take up ten pages if I named them all, but there are a few people I have to shout-out. To Jenny Nordbak and Kristin Dwyer, thank you for being my romance gurus and sounding boards. I truly could not have got here without you both and all our book (and other!) chat these last few years. You are my romance rocks.

Laura Rensing and Lauren Gorski, words can never capture what you both mean to me. You've been the most amazing support system throughout my publishing journey and some weeks the only thing keeping me sane is our ongoing message thread. All the milestones along the way would not have been as sweet without you. Laura, thank you also for my absolutely stunning website. It's beautiful and perfectly pink and glam!

Oriana Nudo, your old movie love has made me into a better cinephile—and I'm so lucky to call you my Old Hollywood pal. The world on these pages is the classic Hollywood of my dreams, but I hope you find some of the glamour and magic we both love here too.

Kristin Avila, the O.G. romance reader in my life. You are an epically great friend and the best hype woman—thank you for just being you. Your unbridled energy and enthusiasm make any accomplishment that much sweeter.

I've had so many mentors along the way that I can't possibly thank them all. But to Deborah Harkness, my undergraduate thesis advisor, you told me over lunch nearly seven years ago that you were so glad I was writing a book. That's kept me going more times than I'd like to admit. Don Frazier, you made history so incredibly fun. I hope anything I write captures that feeling and the joy you convey to your students. Regina Ortiz, Jill Verenkoff and Lara Patterson, I wouldn't be a writer without all of your teaching. Rick Jewell and Drew Casper, you made me fall in love with the movies more deeply than I ever thought possible. Each of you made me the storyteller I am today.

Thank you to my coworkers at EW for throwing your support behind this book. Devan Coggan, thank you so much for revealing my cover. Dan Snierson, your genuine excitement makes every win feel more meaningful and your advice is always cherished.

To Romancelandia as a whole—you are my true home. I wish I could thank every author and publicist and bookseller here who has inspired me along the way and encouraged me in my own journey. They are innumerable, and my gratitude is immense for always being so lovingly welcomed in this space. I'm so thrilled to be crossing over into author territory as we continue on this journey.

On a sillier note, thank you to Keanu and Winona for the inspiration (and helping me break the internet inadvertently). And thank you to Turner Classic Movies for the never-ending film education—this book is a love letter to every classic movie lover out there.

To Joan and Dash, I love you so much, you are the characters of my heart. Thank you for giving me the courage to start my own love story. The day I signed the contract for this book, I finally got the gumption to reach out to someone that I felt had potential to be an important part of my life. This book has taken shape alongside that relationship. John, I love you. Thank you for always being proud of me and championing me in all that I do.

And last but certainly not least, to my family. I cannot express how much I love you, how much I am lucky to call you mine. People make a lot of the family you are given versus the one you choose, but I would choose you every time. To the number one readers in the family, my Grandma Alpha and my Teta Liza, I'm ecstatic to be able to share a book of my own with you. You are my favorite bookworms. To my sister, Margaret, you are the absolute best cheerleader anyone could ever ask for—I am so lucky you're my sibling. You never fail to make me feel special. Uncle Lee, you will always be the coolest, best person on this planet in my eyes. Dad and Mary, thanks for always cheering me on.

And to my mom—I would be so lost without your love and support. You made me into the bibliophile I am today with every summer trip to the library, every story hour at Bookstar, every beach reading session, every bedtime story. Thank you for not being too upset by the obscenely large piles of books on my floor that you rightfully worried would be a hazard in an earthquake. Sorry about all the money you spent on football tickets only for me to read in the stands (and an extra apology for the numerous complaints from teachers about my reading under my desk in science and math class—I still can't add or subtract to save my life, but hey, I wrote a book). We've come a long way from "Marbley and the Missing Sanddollar," but you never stopped believing I could write and hold a book of my own in my hands one day. This one, and every one after it, will always be for you. I'll end this with the inscription I scrawled in crayon in the front of every picture book you bought me—"Maureen. I love Mommy."

ABOUT THE AUTHOR

Maureen Lee Lenker is an award-winning journalist who has written for Turner Classic Movies, *The Hollywood Reporter*, *Ms.* magazine, and more. She is a senior writer for *Entertainment Weekly*, where she maintains a quarterly romance review column, Hot Stuff, in addition to covering film, TV, and theater. She is a proud graduate of both the University of Southern California and the University of Oxford. Maureen calls Los Angeles home, where you'll either find her at the beach or in a repertory movie-house if she's not writing. Visit her online at maureenleelenker.com, on Twitter and Instagram @themaureenlee, and on Facebook.com/molenker.